# M. A. MADDOCK

# The MOON Chasers

## Book Two
### *The Sixth Amulet Series*

# Acclaims by authors

"An impressive read, delivering a world of intrigue, treachery and magic.
Fans of epic historical fantasy will love this series."

Julie Embleton –
Author of *The Turning Moon & Coveted Power series.*

"A film-worthy, rich and riveting novel."

B. K. Sweeting –
Author of *Pearlized & Bubbly by the Sea.*

"A tapestry of familiar mythology – and wholly original creations –
weaved through a world you'll happily get lost in.
A story that truly sings."

Gavin Gardiner –
Author of *For Rye, The Last Testament of Crighton Smythe &
Rücken Ridge.*

"Weaved together with strands of traditional folklore and real Scottish
locations, I found myself catapulted into this exciting series."

Graeme Johncock –
Writer, Storyteller & Author of *Scotland's Stories.*

*Dedicated to all struggling artists.*
*Never give up!*
*Anything is possible.*

*For Shez & Coops*
*Always in our hearts*

# Molyneaux-Shaw

# FORWARD

By

Eilidh Stiùbhar

Seanchaidh à Peairt –

Scottish Artist, Storyteller & Author of Ossian Warrior Poet

This book is for you, dear friend.

For you to read and dream of another time and place.

A place where the Old Gods sink their feet into the peat, spread their fingers into the rock of the mountain and fill their hair with stars.

Their breath sends the dawn hare across the grass and their sighs release the moths from the heather tops, to dance in the cool glow of the moon.

This is the world of stories I grew up in. The Scotland of myth, wherein each loch there swirls a spirit, and in each wood there creeps a beast.

You are welcome here, but tread lightly, for the dead are easily woken…

)

# prologue

*From within the bowels of Elboru, it has reawakened—the immense force once locked inside its sacred stone. It now waits, to give its bearer the power to be a formidable Ruler. It belongs to him—the Magus—Lord of all Warlocks—and he belongs to it. But two worlds now lie under the evil threat that wants to dominate them. And yet, all is still not lost; from within this precious stone, an ember of hope has also been reignited, instilling courage into the hearts of those who are about to unite and risk everything, to see it placed in the hands of the chosen one—to see him quench the darkness.*

# Chapter One

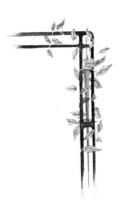

*The Realm of Meddian – (middle Europe) – Late Spring: 1630*

'They have gone, my lady!'

L'Ordana spun on hearing the urgency in the voice, and yet the words had not registered.

'What?' she said, her brows knitting in a moment of confusion.

The small, agitated figure stood dwarfed in the great, oak doorway frame, staring at her mistress, reluctant to enter.

'They—have gone!' she repeated, her voice now low and edged with fear.

L'Ordana moved towards Wareeshta—the look of confusion still etched on her face as she approached the Dhampir.

'They? Who?'

Wareeshta swallowed, took a deep breath and then released it … along with their names; 'Reece, Asai and—'

'What?!' she yelled. The mere mention of Reece's name was all it took for the Sorceress to grasp her servant's meaning. As the expression on her face gradually changed to one of realisation, her eyes widening, woken to it, she lifted her head. Wareeshta braced herself. She knew what to expect.

L'Ordana battled against her composure as Wareeshta's words now bellowed inside her mind. *"They have gone!"* The tension inside her mounted, ready to give way. Intoxicated by burning rage, she finally erupted, unleashing it on the nervous Dhampir.

'Gone?!' she echoed, her eyes now wild with anger.

Wareeshta jumped at the ferocity of her mistress's voice, believing the whole citadel had also been subjected to it. Perhaps she could have worded it differently, broken the news to her in a gentler manner. Then again … What difference would it make? They had escaped …

'Impossible!' L'Ordana persisted.

'But—my lady … we have searched the grounds, and—'

'How could they possibly escape—when they are bonded to *me?!*' she roared.

Wareeshta flinched then, trying to hold her stance, replied, 'I assure you … my lady … they *are* gone.'

L'Ordana glowered at the Dhampir for her insolent tone, and yet seeing her look of determination—eyes set, lips pressed hard—made her wonder … She lifted her head, eyes momentarily drifting from her servant, thinking …

'*If* what you say is true,' L'Ordana pressed further, now scowling at Wareeshta from across the chamber, 'then *how* did they go undetected?' When silence stared back at her, she snapped. 'Answer me!'

The Dhampir jolted from the outburst, shaking her head, unable to respond.

L'Ordana glared at Wareeshta—the turquoise in her eyes intensifying as they bored into the Dhampir.

Tempted to run from her mistress's fury, Wareeshta knew it was far better to face her wrath than flee from it; to avoid any form of conflict was considered a sign of weakness.

The young Dhampir swallowed, desperately calling on her inner voice to justify the prisoners' disappearance. She also wondered *how* they broke free from their bonds; it had not been part of the "plan." A thought struck her, but she was unwilling to voice it.

As Wareeshta contemplated her next move, her mind racing, searching for something to say—*perhaps I should tell her*—she flinched when the Sorceress turned her head sharply.

L'Ordana's eyes darted about the chamber, surveying its entire contents.

*Something is not right*, she thought.

Deciding to speak up, Wareeshta dared to step forward. 'My lady, there is—'

'Do - Not - Move!' the Sorceress growled, turning her attention back to the *Boy with the Flowers* painting. She was sure she had detected something in his stare before Wareeshta's untimely interruption. Curious, she approached it, tilting her head until she came within inches of its canvas and stared up at him, hoping he would "tell" her something. But the boy, with the enigmatic eyes, persisted in his blank stare, reluctant to share what he may have seen. She stretched her neck and leaned closer, whispering, 'Traitor!'

Turning her back on the painting, she scrutinised her quarters until her eyes fell on the heavy, burgundy drapes hanging to the ground. She rushed towards them, then stopped, aware something was not in order. She drew back.

'Someone has touched you!' she hissed, noting the slight ruffle in the material; she always made sure they would hang perfectly straight— especially after each "visit."

Wareeshta, wary of her mistress's growing anger, kept her silence *and* her distance, just inside the doorway. Uneased, she looked over her shoulder, agitated, wondering where Kara was; she would not take the sole blame for the prisoners' escape. No, the Valkyrie also had a part to play in their negligence; she, too, had been idle in keeping a watchful eye on them.

'What if it's gone?' L'Ordana muttered to herself as her eyes ran over the drapes. She hesitated. 'No—impossible! They could not have—' She threw out her hand. 'Part!' she commanded. The drapes drew back. 'Unlock!' she then ordered the ebony, panelled doors concealed behind them.

The doors swung open.

She stalled, holding her breath, fearing someone had entered her secret domain. With mounting dread, she barged into the sanctity of her hidden chamber.

L'Ordana froze on seeing the orb; although it remained on its red, lacquered perch, the light that once glowed from its centre had now dimmed, greatly, as if drained of its energy.

Eyes fixed, she edged towards it, expecting to see Oran—the Warlock either bored in his luxurious prison or smiling to himself—as he often did—which irritated her. And yet, the closer she got, her heart pounded, her dread persistent.

She stopped, her eyes widening as she stared into the orb's void. She shook her head, her mouth opening and closing in silent fear. Then it came …

'No!'

Oran was gone.

So, Wareeshta was right about the others—and it was clear who had helped them escape. 'Damn you, Oran!' she seethed. Without thought—too caught up in her fury—she threw her hands forward. Before her eyes registered what her hands had done, the sound of glass shattering told the Sorceress all she needed to know.

L'Ordana stared down in disbelief, her mouth gaping at the remnants of the orb. The lengths she had gone to acquire it: the long and treacherous journey to the caves of Alucard, high in the Red Mountains, where the eccentric little old man had created it to her requirements. It had become her eyes, to spy on the Warlock. And now, the perfect sphere was reduced to useless fragments of glass—beyond repair.

Outraged by her carelessness, she turned to leave, pausing, when her eyes were immediately drawn to the strong, shard of light reaching out to her between the two black wooden panels. *It is still here*, she realised, sighing with some relief. She rushed towards them, then hesitated before opening the panels, her curiosity beckoning. *But why did you not take it?*

Pulling back the little doors, she drew a sharp breath as the intense light stretched out, dominating the chamber. It was evident, while the orb's light had shone, it had shrouded the item's true strength … until now.

The amulet, she had stolen from Magia Nera, had now lifted itself from the hook where she had left it. Now suspended in front of her startled eyes, its inner light radiated brighter than before; new energy surged inside the weight of its spectacular centred stone—the diamond, now a deep shade of yellow, resembling the lowering of a setting sun.

She reached out to touch it and recoiled from its penetrating heat.

'Is *that* the reason why Oran?' she muttered. She regarded the amulet with intrigue. Something had changed, driving her interest. She then gasped, suddenly aware of its force drawing her in. 'Can it be possible?' She considered its purpose, surmising it was now an object of *greater* importance; she could feel it. She leaned towards it. 'Can *you* show me the way?'

Spurred by the possibility, it could now lead her to the Shenn, she knew she would have to find a way to remove the amulet; she needed to have it with her when they left—sooner rather than later.

Encouraged by the prospect, she smirked to herself. 'You haven't won yet, Oran,' she said, turning on her heel. She then stopped, feeling the smugness being wrenched from her; while the amulet and the Warlock had dominated her thoughts, she had briefly forgotten …

Wareeshta remained rigid, inwardly cursing the Valkyrie as she waited with apprehension for her mistress' return. The seconds passed in wary silence until she heard the muffled sound of L'Ordana's voice. *Whom is she talking to?* she wondered, wanting to look inside the hidden chamber, then thought better of it, on hearing the return of her hasty footsteps. Tempted to retreat, the Dhampir cautiously inched back towards the door, bracing herself when the Sorceress stormed back into her presence.

L'Ordana swiftly returned to the bedchamber and, ignoring the nervous individual lingering in the doorway, rushed to her most cherished item. Eyes narrowed, she looked over the large, circular bronze mirror with suspicion, carefully studying the precious antique; something was out of place. Raising her finger, she let it follow the faint outline of the long, hidden panel—on the mirror's reverse—until it found the tiny indent: the *secret* only she was privy to … or so she had thought. She let the tip of her finger hover over it. Holding her breath, she hesitated, her suspicions mounting, heightening her concern.

*What if …?*

She pressed the groove.

The long panel—no more than a foot in length, and the width of her slender hand—snatched itself away from her. Her mouth fell as she drew back, staring at the space where the weapon had once rested in secret.

Her precious dagger was gone.

She then noticed the single, strand of black hair, caught in a crack below the groove. *How careless!* she thought, leaning closer to inspect it. She paused, noting something else that had not been there before. L'Ordana knew this was no error, on their part; in the bottom, left-hand corner of the panel, she recognised the symbols where the perpetrator had purposely named himself:

## 浅井長政

'Asai!'

Inside, L'Ordana reeled from the theft of the dagger. In a moment of weakness, she lifted her hand to her face, letting her fingers touch her skin, guiding them over the contours of her features: it felt different. As fear seeped in, she promptly consulted the mirror, recoiling from her reflection, sensing the subtle change, it threatening to expose her vulnerability.

Her eyes flashed about the chamber, returning to the painting. The *Boy's* eyes continued to stare at her, but now in a different way, as though they were mocking her.

'Stop it!' she growled, confronting the canvas. 'Do not look at me like that!'

'My La—' Wareeshta stopped abruptly when L'Ordana spun round; she recoiled, seeing her mistress' demented stare. Had she gone mad?

The Sorceress hesitated. Her eyes then slid to the little piece of furniture nestled beneath the window. She tilted her head, eyes wide, scrutinising it. Had that, also, been tampered with? She then shook her head, mumbling to herself; 'No. No, you wouldn't—you couldn't have—not that, too!'

As panic took hold again, she rushed to the ebonised, wooden table. At first, it had appeared untouched, but as the dread persisted, spreading its shadow of doubt, she slowly lowered her eyes, seeing it—the small drag of dust on the floor; the inlaid, spindle legs, supporting the Moorish table, had *moved!* The same *thief* had neglected to check the small, ornate piece of furniture before his hasty departure—the error now marking her fear.

She drew back, her chest heaving, afraid to look … But she had to know.

'Open!'

# Chapter Two

othing, but the space where she had left it, stared up at her now; the little table had been relieved of the sinister burden it had kept hidden, inside its sealed drawer.

'Damn you, Asai!' she whispered, trying to contain her anger. But her inner demon was battling against her composure. 'Damn you!' Her voice grew louder, unleashing her fury again. 'You will pay for this!' she yelled, wrenching the drawer from the table before casting it away in disgust.

'What—what are you looking for?' Wareeshta nervously asked, having observed the frenzied attack on the invaluable piece of furniture.

Wrapped inside her frantic world of rage and uncertainty, L'Ordana failed to hear her servant. She had kept the other item hidden there since "unburdening" Magia Nera of its possession—before their untimely parting, in Triora—almost sixty years previously; it had felt, to L'Ordana, much longer. Yet, despite its constant presence, she had barely scratched the surface of its sinister knowledge—knowledge the dark Warlock had refused to share with her.

Only *she* had had the power to open the drawer, the panel on the back of the mirror, and the drapes. *How could Asai have*— She stopped on her train of thought when it occurred to her: *Of course!* It was evident the Warlock had outsmarted her, by teaching the Samurai a *trick or two,* in exchange for getting him to do his dirty work. *And why not?* She surmised. Had he not taught her everything he knew? 'Not quite, Oran,' she uttered, through gritted teeth. *How could I have been so imprudent?* She reeled over her misjudgement, believing he had been unable to sever the bond that held her warriors. *More fool I.* Too self-indulged in her arrogance, to notice his misconduct, she thought she had had the upper hand, assuming her plan to outsmart him had worked.

Having acquired the relevant information from the Valkyrie, with the help of the unsuspecting Tam—Kara's liaisons with him proved quite informative—she considered the situation … After countless bribes, to draw the secret of the Shenn amulet from him, she soon realised Oran would remain loyal to his Magus, by keeping his silence. Therefore, she made a point of taunting him, boasting that she still possessed Magia Nera's amulet—in the hope he would weaken—while making a point of revealing her "meetings" with the dark Warlock; she wanted Oran to believe Magia would side with her. She recalled the glint in his eye when she told him of their rendezvous.

Convinced she had won Oran's jealousy, she had then decided to take a bold risk: she would allow him—under pretence—to escape, by discreetly removing the invisible barrier from his *prison;* she was certain he would be tempted by its absence, regardless of any suspicions. He would then escape—alone—leaving behind his three conspirators; they would be unable to venture beyond the barrier of their bonds, causing her no concern. Then, she would secretly follow the Warlock, presuming he would lead her to the Shenn—and the Magus. However, after observing him for a while, through the orb, she grew frustrated and bored when he failed to "take the bait!". Certain he had not noticed the barriers' absence, she eventually restored it, discreetly, during one of her "visits."

Yes, he had outsmarted her. *He knew all along.* He had been biding his time until it was safe to break the Dhampir's bonds, releasing them. He had played her, knowing too well she would tire of him and divert her attention to Magia, in a bid to prize the information she needed from *him.*

'What have I done?' It had all been unexpected and swift—not what she had planned. And, to make matters worse, they had taken with them her precious items: the book and the dagger. The question now was … who had them? The Warlock or his allies?

The *Dagger*—once dominated by the *Order of the Dragon*—was recognisable by the unique symbols engraved below its black, onyx handle: an unorthodox, heretical cross; and along the centre of the blade, a winged dragon, displaying its malevolent strength, its tail touching the tip of the cross, uniting them in power. The long, steel dagger partnered the book. Jointly, they were potent, giving her what she required: eternal youth and power. Together—and guided by the Shenn—she could reign supreme, possessing the ultimate dominance and revenge. Everything she craved. But, with both items now missing, dread ripped through her.

Without the book, she would lose her power, and without the dagger—the weapon she had used on her victims—her beauty and youth would fade. Time was now her true enemy.

Her thoughts momentarily drifted back. She had forgotten the other young women, except for one: her first—Oran never forgave her for the slaughter of their servant. The dagger had taken the girl's beauty and youth—as with the other victims—and by transferring those attributes to her, she knew she would never age. The thought of the weapon's absence horrified her, along with its missing accessory: the book.

The *Book*, Magia had claimed from another—centuries before—had been the *Master* of all his teachings in the *Black Arts*, bestowing its unique powers on those who let it.

She had been ignorant of its knowledge when she first looked upon it, discovering later, what it was truly capable of. Bound by the *Devil* himself—according to myth—the hard, outer cover was made of thick, leather and dyed in oxblood. Shaped to fit its length perfectly, its spine was lined in black onyx while its paged edges were, not of gold but, deep scarlet—said to be the blood of Vlad Tepés.

Seared into the hard-worn leather, the two symbols, matching those on the dagger, were vivid in detail, despite its age. The workmanship had been so precise, it was thought—if the eye beheld it for long enough—the dragon moved. She had tried staring at it once, but when

Magia Nera mocked her, she quickly dismissed it as a "myth" conjured up by those who had once briefly owned it, to send fear into the souls of anyone willing to challenge the evil of its pages. However, the malevolence attached to its antiquity was far from folklore. Having witnessed this, she had eventually persuaded the dark Warlock to share with her its "secrets"—some, at least. She recalled how he eventually bowed to her "persuasion"—as long as she did not abuse its power. Naturally, she gave him her word.

But, as time wore on, it soon corrupted her, its powers enticing her to steal it.

How could she resist?

But what *she* had purloined, had now been stolen from her. She might have laughed at the irony of it, had it not been for its necessity; without it—without both—she would fall victim to the plague of time. All her defences would gradually weaken, leaving her vulnerable to every source who would willingly prey on her. The Valkyrie came to mind; nothing would satisfy Kara more than to overthrow her mistress. *Not if I can help it*, she thought, discarding all foreboding thoughts. *I must have them back!*

L'Ordana stalled, now sensing the other presence lingering at the chambers' entrance. She could feel their eyes burning into her as the smell of their heady scent attacked her nostrils.

'I see Kara has not left you to deal with the consequences, this time, Wareeshta,' she stated, turning.

In the doorway, towering over the Dhampir, stood the Valkyrie. Kara eyed her mistress, her manner smug and daring.

Inside, L'Ordana was seething. 'Where have you—'

'Searching for their trail,' Kara casually interrupted, adding fuel to L'Ordana's frustration.

'And did you find it?'

The Valkyrie sauntered over the threshold, followed by a nervous Wareeshta—who was prepared for the onslaught of abuse the Sorceress usually hurled at them when antagonised; to her surprise, it did not come.

Kara rolled her eyes. 'Of course,' she sneered, irked by the question. '*They* will be easy to track. However, I was unable to pursue the Warlock, after their footprints parted.'

L'Ordana cast a suspicious eye on her servants when Wareeshta's eyes darted towards Kara, throwing her a cautious glance. L'Ordana glared into the dubious face of the Dhampir.

'You knew the Warlock had escaped?!' she cried.

Wareeshta side-glanced Kara, who was now smirking at her. L'Ordana then looked to the Valkyrie, who shrugged in return as if passing the blame on Wareeshta.

'Well?!'

'I tried to tell you, Sorceress,' the Dhampir pleaded, 'but …' Her words drifted into nervous silence.

'The small detail you neglected to mention,' L'Ordana stated, casting her a scathing look before dragging her eyes back to Kara. Something then came to mind—something the Valkyrie had said. She recalled her words:

'Their footprints … *parted!*' she echoed, turning to the Valkyrie with intent. 'What did you mean by it?'

'They had grouped,' said Kara. 'Before …' She paused.

'Before what?'

'Before going their separate ways.'

L'Ordana drew her head back, frowning. 'Are you certain?'

'Almost.'

The Sorceress tilted her head forward. 'Think before you speak again,' she warned. 'And, this time, I would suggest you be more … *specific!*'

Wareeshta looked at Kara, with unease; the Valkyrie appeared unperturbed as she casually replied, 'We discovered four sets of footprints,' she continued, '… at first.'

'At first?' said L'Ordana, concealing her mounting fear. 'Do you mean—*more* have escaped—to join them?'

Kara shook her head.

'Reece, Tam and the *Strange One* parted ways with the Warlock; they went north—not that they will get far, by the time we—'

'North?' L'Ordana cut in, lifting a brow with interest. She paused, momentarily musing over it. Her eyes then slid towards Wareeshta, regarding her with another intimidating look.

The Dhampir, withering under L'Ordana's penetrating stare, slowly nodded, confirming Kara's words.

'What takes them north?'

'Tam did not say when I—'

'Then we must assume he did not know,' she broke in, aware that the Valkyrie's sordid—and regular—rendezvous with the Highlander was no secret, therefore, adding to her suspicions. 'I suspect Oran kept some vital information from Tam'—she glared at Kara—'for obvious reasons. As for the others who escaped …? Why separate, leaving my old adversary to his defences? How curious?' She then nodded. 'This may be to our advantage.'

'It is unlikely,' Wareeshta bravely joined in.

The Sorceress now turned her attention to the Dhampir yet remained silent, holding her with a rugged stare as she waited impatiently for her to proceed.

The Dhampir cleared her throat, then swallowed. 'Three sets of footsteps parted from the Warlock,' she went on. 'The fourth, however, was …' She stalled.

'Well?'

'… "replaced" … by an animal,' said Kara.

Turning away, L'Ordana resisted the urge to laugh. *Oh, how clever of you, Oran,* she thought, aware the Warlock had now reclaimed his powers. *So … you left this citadel as you entered it, allowing you to travel, undetected. But of course! To travel on foot would only waste time,* she deduced, taking a turn about her chamber, paying no heed to the mirror or the little table; they were of no use to her, now. *A clever move, yet again, Oran. I almost admire you for it.* She paused by the window and looked out, staring at the wall of trees, looking like giant vigilant soldiers, masking what lay beyond them: the sheer drop to the rocks beneath the citadel—and *death* to the uninformed intruder.

'It appears we have all taken our eye off the mark,' she stated, turning to face her servants. 'Oran has … fooled us.'

Kara narrowed her pale eyes at her mistress' hidden refusal to admit her negligence—for letting the Warlock slip through her fingers. Still, she should have seen the signs herself: Reece's ability to distract her, by tempting her with Turloch—the new addition; he was, after all, a willing contender—too good to ignore. And Reece knew it. Then there was the *Strange One*—Asai; he had been more obliging in letting her occasionally train *his* warriors, knowing this little weakness of hers would distract her, while he discreetly slipped away. Yes, she could see it now. But now was too late …

In a sense, she knew she was partially to blame, for letting them indulge her ego, though she would never admit to the untimely distraction.

Kara glanced at Wareeshta with suspicion. *And where were you, all this time?* she wondered; she was sure the Dhampir was up to something. In the meantime, as far as she was concerned, the blame would fall on their mistress; after all, it had been *her* plan. *Some plan*, she thought. The Sorceress had completely underestimated the Warlock. It was clear he knew her better than she knew herself.

Turning to the Valkyrie, L'Ordana clasped her hands in front of her, in forced composure; Kara noticed the whites of her knuckles almost protruding as the skin stretched over the bone—a sure sign of her hidden aggravation. However, the Sorceress would not give her servants the satisfaction of revealing her inner esteem for the Warlock—or her misjudgement of him.

'Two objects have been stolen from me …' she blurted. 'A book and a dagger. I want them back. I can only assume Oran has them …' She paused for thought. 'But there is only one way to find out … Also, it is clear his journey is urgent!'

'But we cannot track the Warlock,' insisted Kara.

'We may not know what direction he has gone, as of yet,' said L'Ordana. 'But—'

'Yet?' Wareeshta interrupted, with new interest.

'I assure you … we *will* find out,' she said. 'And I know who will tell us,' she added, with certainty.

'His conspirators?' said Wareeshta.

L'Ordana's eyes met Kara's. The Valkyrie's mouth curled into a knowing grin.

'The Warlock may have released them from their bonds, but I have no doubt *you* will find them,' she said, confident of the Valkyrie's ability to track the absconders, while at the same time, distracting her from her blunder. 'Use the wings you were given, Kara. Find them!'

Kara's eyes widened; the idea of having her way with Reece and his two companions stimulated her senses and stirred her blood.

'Perhaps he—the Warlock—sent them?' Wareeshta suggested.

L'Ordana and Kara slowly turned to Wareeshta, who had clearly been making her own deductions over the escape. The Dhampir shrugged. 'Who knows?'

'Now there's a thought!' said L'Ordana, contemplating it. She looked sharp. 'Time to leave!' she blurted. Kara and Wareeshta glanced at one another. 'Aside from the fact that I cannot bear another day in this forsaken place,' she went on, 'we have outstayed our welcome here.' She looked at Kara. 'Yes, it is time to go.'

The Valkyrie displayed her approval with a sneering grin, and as it sprawled across her face, she said, 'North?'

'Of course,' L'Ordana replied, with a wry smile. 'North to—'

*"Urquille!"*

L'Ordana flinched, hearing the voice in her head as the word unexpectedly slipped into her mind. What made her think of it? *Urquille?* She lingered on the name, querying the familiarity it suggested when a murky image abruptly entered her head: her body was floating; she sensed its dead weight; the desperate urge to breathe; the struggle to escape from its suffocating effect. But the moment was short-lived when a sharp intake of breath filled her with life again, releasing her from its drowning influence.

'And the other one …?' Kara prompted, regarding her mistress.

Ignoring the Valkyrie, the Sorceress hesitated, drawing on the unexpected images in her head, trying to make sense of them. *Urquille*, she thought, now conscious of its lure pulling her north.

Inside, Kara was seething, having been shunned by her mistress. Mindful of the sword on her back, pressing against her silver bodice of armour, she fantasised about thrusting it through L'Ordana's heart. She then thought of her lance—the *Obsidian*—but had been forced to leave it outside the chamber.

"Never bring *that* into my presence!" the Sorceress had warned her before, having witnessed the weapon's capability: driven effortlessly into its victim's torso, its silver tip would ignite in a spectacular display, lighting up the Obsidian's deep-emerald glass in all its glory, before consuming its victim in flames.

But it was nothing more than that: a *fantasy*. Despite L'Ordana's insistence, Kara knew she could no more inflict a scratch on her mistress let alone kill her; although, perhaps, one day … It had been an alluring thought, nonetheless, but nothing more.

Still reeling from the sting of the insult, Kara boldly stepped forward. 'I said, what about the—'

'I heard you the first time!' L'Ordana snapped, dismissing the disturbing images from her mind. Settling into a poise of self-composure, she eventually turned to face her servants—Wareeshta staring at her with her eager expression, while Kara remained frustrated by her mistress's secretive behaviour.

L'Ordana paused, as though in a moment of reflection. Her eyes then glided to the oriental rug beneath their feet. 'I had almost forgotten *him*,' she replied, arching her brows. Lifting her head, she then regarded her servants' curious gaze and held it, keeping them in suspense. Slowly, the vindictive smirk crawled across her face. 'Magia Nera will accompany us,' she announced. 'I should imagine *he* will be of great use to me, now.'

At the mention of the dark Warlock's name, Kara threw a sinister look at Wareeshta. *I am watching you*, she silently threatened, her deadpan stare unnerving the Dhampir; intimidated, Wareeshta diverted her gaze.

The Sorceress swiftly turned to make her way back to her secret chamber, her mind on releasing the one object they had neglected to steal from her: Magia Nera's amulet, her only hope of finding the Shenn.

Before taking her leave, L'Ordana paused and glanced over her shoulder, her eyes resting on the mirror she had once held sacred; it appeared different, now that its beauty was "tainted."

Unable to dismiss—or forgive—its new flaw, she turned to the Valkyrie.

'Destroy *that!*' she commanded, pointing to it, then turned away, leaving it for the last time. 'And when you are done, Kara … come with me.'

As the great, panelled doors closed behind her, they drowned out the sound of shattering glass …

# Chapter Three

*One month earlier*

The citadel's bleak walls stood dark and unusually silent within its gloom as he kept within their shadows, creeping so eloquently that his footsteps went undetected. He hesitated, hearing the distant sound of clashing blades resume in their training. He looked up, following their regimented sound with his dark, almond-shaped eyes, knowing they would persist as they ceaselessly strived for perfection, in the hands of their unskilled masters.

"Masters of their swords," *she* had called them. He grunted at her idealism of the warriors she had abducted into her domination. Despite her convictions, he knew no other matched *his* skill; he was more than the *Master* of his "Daisho"—the two blades he always carried: the large katana and the small wakizashi. No, he was their *Emperor*. Only the best wore the *Masamune* sword with esteem—he being one of the exceptions.

Ever his constant companions, there was no need to check their purpose; both weapons were always by his side. And if fate allowed it, he knew he could slice her warriors down with a single sweep. *She*, however, was a different matter entirely—untouchable—while her two servants lurked in the wings, under her protection.

The possibility of being free from their clutches—from her bond— urged him on, renewing his hope in the Warlock's ability to convince him of his integrity. *He* was convinced, unlike his two colleagues; he had seen certainty in the Warlock's eyes and, after some persuasion, he eventually convinced Reece and Tam of his honesty. Yes—Oran could be trusted.

Asai then dared to indulge himself, by imagining his revenge: to dispatch the Valkyrie. By doing so, it would help him to lay to rest the tortured souls of his past.

The risk would be great. But should the opportunity offer itself, he would gladly take it, leaving the Sorceress and Wareeshta to his colleagues; Reece and Tam were welcome to them. *His* sights were set on the Valkyrie.

But to linger on his task was not an option. *Not now*, he thought. *There is little time.* The Warlock had chosen his moment—sooner than expected—so as not to arouse suspicion.

Oran had instructed him to follow the Sorceress, discreetly. Her meetings with Magia Nera had become more frequent—an indication of her growing desperation. He mused over the possibility that Oran knew something—the Warlock choosing to keep it to himself … for the time being.

Asai kept the inferior noise of the Dhampir's blades fixed in his mind; if they continued to ring their ugly sound above him, he then knew the citadel's core would remain empty. And, while the Valkyrie liked to take precedence over their training—he smirked—he also knew he would not be disturbed.

He had slipped away without Kara knowing; she was preoccupied with her new distraction, Turloch—the new addition to the hoard, and a willing contender who vied for her attention. From a distance, he had observed her as she stroked the newcomer's long, white hair while admiring his amber skin—a sure sign of her infatuation with the recruit. This, he knew, would be a great advantage to their escape.

The timing of Kara's "distraction" had been carefully scrutinised, with some cleverly-applied encouragement from Reece; he knew, from experience, how to feed her ego. However, Turloch had proved to be unusually advanced and cunning, making him a potential threat to their plans; one sceptical meeting with the Warlock confirmed this, prompting their premature escape.

Shrugging off any notion of interference, Asai proceeded down the passageways he had familiarised himself with, taking heed to stay hidden along their deep shadows.

On several occasions, he had noticed the Sorceress stealing herself away to the quiet part of the citadel. Driven by curiosity, he had risked following her, aware of keeping his distance; to venture too close would betray his presence. By doing so, he soon discovered her secret. During his observations of her, she appeared to vanish between the walls of a deep alcove—the "illusion" deepening his suspicions. Induced by his determination, he had taken it upon himself to investigate, leading him to unravel her mystery: a hidden stairway. With further observation of her infrequent behaviour, a pattern gradually emerged, allowing him the ability to pursue his task.

Asai calmly waited in his carefully chosen place: a darkened stairwell, leading to a stone maze of complex passages, beneath the citadel's deep foundations. And, should the need arise, he could simply lose himself within its enigma, away from any pursuit. He recalled the occasion when Tam lost his direction among their winding ways; it was he who finally fished his colleague out. That was when his inquisitive nature called on him to venture into the maze, challenging him to master its complicated puzzle.

A means of distraction from the ruthlessness of their insufferable lives, Asai took himself into the mazes' passages—when time allowed—persisting until he solved it, unaware of its true purpose. And Just when he thought he knew every turn and curve, the maze gave up its secret, as though rewarding him for conquering its obscure design.

Hidden at its far reaches, he had discovered another of the mazes' mysteries: the ancient, bronze door.

Despite his great strength, he had been unable to open it; the task would eventually require the help of his two colleagues. But it was what lay on the other side of its thick shield that willed them into believing—one day—they could be free.

No wall or boundary had prevented their escape … except for one—the Sorceress. There were times she had taunted them into leaving, but in their attempts to do so, the crushing pain inflicted on them by her had almost led to their demise. Mocked and shamed for their failure, they quickly learned to abandon all hope until the Warlock shared his intentions: the promise of freedom, in return for their help. After much encouragement, a bargain was then made, allowing the three Dhampir to believe all their hopes would soon be realised.

It was through good fortune the maze had gone unnoticed; no one outside their group was privy to its existence. Because of the Samurai's knowledge of the labyrinth—not to mention his calm demeanour—Oran chose Asai for the task. The Warlock was more than aware—had Reece volunteered—it was most likely his ability to maintain his restraint would have been short-lived, endangering their lives. As for Tam? The risk had been greater—and for one obvious reason: his prior connection to the Valkyrie.

Asai suddenly turned his head at the sound of advancing footsteps, recognising them instantly, having familiarised himself with her hasty footfall.

He held himself in complete silence, eavesdropping on her every movement as he envisaged her lithe figure passing quickly by him. The timing was crucial, warning him to be mindful of his distance; she could pre-empt his move, should he make any errors.

"That is a mistake you will never make again," she had once threatened.

"I do not make mistakes!" he had staunchly replied, after leaving the scar below her left ear, on their first meeting. Since then, he had made a point of glancing at it while in conversation with her, as a simple reminder—while she, aware of it, would tilt her head away.

He stepped forward, listening to her fading steps until they stopped; he knew she had reached the place. He closed his eyes, visualising her next move, knowing when it was safe to follow. Satisfied, he took a cautious glance over his shoulder before moving silently into the alcove's shadowy secret.

Asai paused, staring at the blankness of the alcove's damp wall, listening intently to the faint echoes above; below them—where he now stood—all remained silent.

Stepping into the niche, he turned his back against the wall, looking out into the dimness of the passage. He waited for the familiar, subtle draught to catch his eye; when it touched, he moved towards it, letting his hands search for the crevice in the wall until his fingers slipped through the gap, his eyes searching through the dark as he edged closer to the concealed corner. As he did so, the gap grew wider with each step, allowing him to move easily beyond its hidden threshold—the clever illusion masterfully crafted by ancient hands.

As he moved discreetly behind the alcove's wall, his foot collided with a step—the first of which would take him onto the granite, spiral staircase. He knew precisely where it would lead: to her chambers.

He lingered on the first step, staring at the ascending darkness, aware the narrow staircase only allowed one individual at a time. He would then have to count the steps, taking care not to stumble on the *eleventh*; it had been designed differently from the others. Narrower in width, and deeper in height, it maintained one purpose: to trip the intruder, making their presence known. Once, he had almost fallen victim to its trap.

Almost.

The staircase was bleak and dank, lacking air, its narrowness proving difficult for his broad frame; it irked him to reposition his weapons, in order to climb them swiftly. As he made his ascent, the cold, rough-edged stone cut into his bare arms, making them bleed. Asai ignored it, knowing they would heal by the time he achieved his task. Unperturbed by the gloom, and dismissing its awkwardness, he focused on the eerie silence, confident her chamber would now be vacant.

Asai attacked the final steps, conscious of his weapons; should they collide with the walls, their echoes may attract unwanted attention.

*An inconvenience*, he thought.

As he reached the stairways' peak, he was met by a blank, solid wall. He had not been aware of its existence, having never ventured to the top. He quickly checked its sealed edges. There were no gaps. Stepping back, he tilted his head from side to side, surveying its structure. He felt its domineering presence almost mocking him, provoking him to advance. Un-swayed by its hindrance, a thought entered his mind: something the Warlock had shared with him—something vital.

*Could the same apply, here?* he asked himself, toying with his curiosity. *I wonder …*

In the foolishness of his own company, Asai closed his eyes and stepped forward …

His senses were met by the unexpected aroma of sweet, amber oil. The Samurai's eyes flickered open. Once more, he found himself in the luxurious surroundings of L'Ordana's boudoir. It had not changed since his last intrusion—when Reece was with him during her heated encounter with Magia Nera—when the dark Warlock came looking for his amulet.

Asai glanced back to where he had just made his entrance. A Baroque-style painting of a boy holding an elaborate basket of fruit stared at him. He could not help but admire the masterpiece; it was a prime example of the finest quality demanded by the Sorceress when it came to her possessions. He stole a few more seconds, taking in its strange beauty. There was something pleading in the image's eyes. Intrigued, Asai reached out to touch its canvas, flinching when his hand passed through it.

*Another illusion*, he realised, raising a brow. And yet, it looked so real.

Retrieving his hand, he turned away from it; there was no time to dwell on the symbolic work of art.

Asai then eyed the heavy drapes, perceiving what he would find behind them, praying the Warlock was right. He promptly moved towards them, pausing, when his eyes suddenly caught his reflection. He slowly turned, eyeing himself in the highly-polished glass of the exquisite bronze mirror the Sorceress had stolen from his ancestry. He stepped closer, imagining how she would admire herself, constantly searching for the cruelty of time.

Unable to recall when he last looked upon his features, he slowly approached it with added interest. He inched closer, narrowing his eyes. He had barely aged.

*So, you are her dictator of time!* he thought, admiring the pilfered piece of his legacy.

Lowering his chin, he regarded the priceless artefact, then scowled; it had altered since his eyes last admired its grandeur. The fact it had remained in her presence—and under her influence—for so long, suggested to him that it had been tainted by her beauty; it appeared to be losing its lustre.

'It was never yours to keep,' he whispered, shaking his head with disapproval.

Removing the wakizashi dagger, he stood back. Raising the weapon, he prepared to strike the glass with the heavy, ironwood handle, denying her the ability to look upon it again. Within an inch of striking its ancient glass, Asai stopped himself, unable to obliterate the sacred piece of his heritage. With a sense of failure, he dropped his hand to his side, staring at it, then quickly discarded the feeling, shamed for having thought it.

He then moved to the mirror's reverse, pondering on its beauty for the last time, and grinned. 'If I cannot bring myself to destroy you,' he told it, 'then I shall reclaim you … in the name of my ancestors.'

With a single bow, and still clutching his dagger, Asai Nagamasa carefully etched his name:

浅井長政

Reflecting on what he had done, Asai, at first, felt an element of guilt, sensing he had defaced the precious object and offended his ancestors. Leaning back, he regarded his name with pride, then bowed, casting his blame aside. *The damage had already been done*, he thought, justifying his actions.

As Asai moved to turn away from the mirror, he was distracted by the faint outline of a long panel. He noticed a small indentation—visible at the base—its groove a perfect circle. He regarded it carefully, having never seen it before. Instinct urged him to touch it.

The panel sprung back, revealing a sinister-looking dagger; he sensed something evil about its unique design. Initially, he did not recognise its engravings, surmising—by the Warlock's description—it was the one the Sorceress used for her "personal use," and, without it, she would be vulnerable to the ravages of time. The mere idea of it prompted the Samurai to snatch it from its hiding place.

The moment the weapon came into his contact, the panel slammed shut. He stared at the ominous dagger, sensing its bloody past. He was now reluctant to take it. Then, reminded of the young lives she had needlessly taken, for her vanity, he changed his mind and tied it alongside his wakizashi. But as he placed it next to the other of his prized possessions, he felt repulsed for doing so.

*Not for long*, he thought, knowing he would soon hand it over to the Warlock.

Wary of its disturbing presence, he moved swiftly, eager to finish his task, then noticed the ebonized table beneath the square, leaded window. He hesitated, letting his eyes rest on the piece of furniture and its little drawer.

'I will return for *you*,' he told it, as though it were privy to his movements.

Making his way towards the drapes, his eyes glided over the large, oriental rug beneath his feet—aware of who still resided below. 'Be sure to extend your conversation tonight, Sorceress,' he muttered, treading lightly over it.

With great care, Asai gently pulled back the heavy curtains, turning his nose from their musty smell.

As informed by the Warlock, a huge, triple-lancet window greeted him, displaying a view he imagined he would never see again. He stepped back, unable to comprehend the familiarity of the beautiful sight, beyond the window's leaded glass.

The small, ornate garden—reminiscent of one he had frequented with his wife, Ayumi, during their courtship—held his gaze, leaving him astonished. The grass was rich and lush, constantly watered to keep it damp and green; he could smell its herbaceous scent. Cherry blossom trees were coming into their full bloom—a sign of late Spring; it had been their favourite time of year. He recognised the familiar little path and could still hear the crunch of the small, white pebbles beneath their feet, as they made their way to the entrance of her favourite tea house. Along its route, a *Waiting Bench*—for guests—sat patiently alone. He recalled the times he had watched her approach, admiring the beauty of her porcelain skin and jet-black hair, tied up perfectly away from her small features, in the traditional *Shimada* style—the light catching the *Mokume Gane* silver and gold butterfly, it standing out; he had had the piece of jewellery commissioned for her, for their engagement, it adorning her hair each time they visited the tea house. For a moment he closed his eyes, listening for the faint rustle of her silk kimono; it never came. In his mind, he saw them wash their hands and mouths in the stone, water basin near the tea house before entering through the little, square door—she mocking him for hitting his head upon his entry.

His eyes flickered open, catching the movement of a figure in the distance, silently calling for his attention. He leaned forward, narrowing his eyes as they made their approach, over the small, red wooden bridge; he could hear the faint trickling sound of the water running beneath it. He recognised the ornate structure—the one they had crossed over on their engagement before sharing a feast at their prenuptial table.

The figure continued to move gracefully towards the tea house, distorting with each advancing step. He strained to see as they paused to wash their hands, observing the familiar way they took care of drying them; it haunted his thoughts. As the fading figure made to enter the small structure, they lingered before slowly turning their head to look at him.

He caught his breath, glimpsing her for a fleeting moment. 'Ayumi!' he whispered.

"Remember, it is simply a mirage, to play on the intruder's intimate thoughts—nothing more."

Asai jolted from the cruelty of the illusion Oran had warned him about. Closing his eyes, he blocked the image from his mind, scolding himself for having been taken in by it. Well, almost. The Warlock was right; it had been nothing more than a delusion, created by the Sorceress as a deterrent. But as he slowly opened his eyes, the figment of his imagination persisted; he chose to ignore its falseness.

"You will simply pass through it."

The Warlock's words continued to echo, willing him on. Determined, Asai leapt forward—eyes wide open.

Within moments, he passed through the fading image, then left it behind … along with the figment of his past.

A large, ebony door now faced him, commanding his presence. He glanced behind, checking the drapes; they had drawn together, concealing him.

Asai regarded the door's iron latch, noting its key was still attached. *Why is that?* he asked himself. Perhaps the confidence in her presumption, that no other would discover her hidden gem. *How wrong you are, Sorceress,* he thought, and yet something was not quite right. On a niggling instinct, Asai quickened his pace.

"One word of command is all it requires," Oran had said. "Just one—use it wisely."

'Unlock!' Asai ordered it.

A few seconds passed before the key eventually turned itself.

He waited.

Nothing.

Placing his hands on the great door, he pushed; it refused to budge. He stood back, staring at it, contemplating his next move.

"Sometimes, it is the simplest of methods that are the most effective," the Warlock had told him.

*Simple yet effective*, he thought, then smiled. 'Open!'

The great door finally swung wide, inviting him into her innermost, secretive chamber. There, before his eyes, the crystalline orb rested peacefully on its red, lacquered pillar, bathed in its bright light, dominating its surroundings.

Mindful of his limited time, Asai moved rapidly towards the orb and peered into its perfect sphere. From within its core, he saw the image of the Warlock, who appeared to be looking back at him.

Oran grinned at the Dhampir, nodding with satisfaction; it was evident he was privy to the Samurai's presence in L'Ordana's hidden chamber. He now waited eagerly for Asai to complete the task.

Asai looked around him, observing the unknown figures carved into the black, wooden panels on the walls. He had no interest in their past—only that of the item hidden behind two, which were cleverly designed as doors, their outlines now visible, by the narrow beam of light escaping from them, it guiding him towards them.

Asai worked his fingers, feeling along the edges of the little "doors" until he found a tiny groove; when he pressed it, they clicked open. As he drew them apart, he turned his head, closing his eyes from the brightness emanating from inside.

Still holding the "doors", Asai cautiously opened one eye. The light had dimmed a little, allowing him to look back inside. He lifted his brows when he saw the amulet; it was suspended by its energy, and its precious stone was shining like the sun. He stared at its beauty for a moment before observing the thick, gold chain hanging loosely beneath it.

"The power is not in its chain, which is why you must handle the amulet itself," the Warlock had also informed him.

Almost identical to Oran's—save for its markings—Asai knew to whom it belonged: Magia Nera. However, its master was still held deep below the citadel, where the Sorceress continued to pursue him for its source of power—the *true* amulet: The Shenn.

'Let us hope your master keeps his silence—for now, at least,' Asai stated to the item, his only interest, it being the key to the Warlock's freedom … and his own. Without it, he and his two colleagues would remain prisoners.

Asai lifted his hand, then hesitated, alerted to the amulet's immense heat, as though warning him of its threat.

*What of it?!* he thought. He would happily withstand the pain it inflicted if it meant his imminent freedom. He reached out, wincing as he touched it, feeling it burn into his skin.

Blocking out the influence of its searing heat, he promptly returned to the orb, raising the amulet high. Asai watched as Oran mimicked his movement, by lifting his.

Each amulet now sensed the other's state of presence. United by power, they appeared to acknowledge one another in a glowing display of pulsating light, as though lost in conversation. He felt the vibration of their unity as the heat intensified with each passing second.

Forced to turn away from the extremity of their combined powers, Asai struggled against the magnitude of their force and the severe pain he had to endure—something the Warlock had failed to mention. *Now I know why,* he thought, grimacing.

Asai fought to the point where he could no longer tolerate its infliction. His hand shook as his pain heightened; it was becoming unbearable. Unable to withstand its stabbing heat, he knew he would have to release the amulet, hindering their planned escape. With this dread in mind, he tried desperately to hold on, but the stench of his burning flesh forced his hand open, making him lose his grip on the precious jewel.

As he watched the amulet slip from his blistering hand, Asai saw all their hopes go with it.

# Chapter four

Time held its breath as the chamber's brilliant light subsided, throwing it into complete darkness.

Asai remained still, clutching his scalded and swollen hand, but as the seconds rolled by, the searing pain receded as his skin began to heal itself. He opened his eyes slowly, unable, at first, to see his surroundings.

*I feel no different,* he thought, save for his heavy heart.

Lingering within the chambers' darkness, and convinced he had failed in his task, Asai then considered his next move when the absence of silence was marked by a sudden glow of dim-blue light.

As his eyes adjusted, the crystalline orb gradually came into view; he was reluctant to approach it again. And yet, despite his presumptions, he had to satisfy his desperate need to know if they were free of their bonds.

He edged towards it, pausing when something caught his eye. Looking down, he observed an object hovering below him. He leaned down to inspect it. It was the amulet, suspended in its own protective space, its inner light now altered to a pale, yellow glow.

'The orb!' he whispered. Asai quickly rose and stared into its sphere. The Warlock's cell was empty! Oran had disappeared! Now that freedom truly beckoned, Asai knew he had to act quickly. Then the Warlock's words came back to him:

"Take it! We will be long gone before its absence is noted."

Asai rolled his eyes and sighed; he did not relish the thought of having to endure the amulet's burning influence again. But with freedom beckoning …

Reaching down, he braced himself for its impact, but the amulet and its chain were cold. Unwilling to make any further assumptions, he seized it. But within seconds of touching it, he began to feel the effect of the amulet's heat returning—tenfold—to protect itself from his thieving hand. 'Forgive me, Oran-san,' he muttered, then quickly returned it to its hiding place; besides, he was certain Oran only wanted it to spite his nemesis. As he closed the little, panelled doors, concealing it, once again, he jolted when the light shot out at him through the narrow gaps.

A sudden sense of urgency washed over the Samurai, his instincts warning him to leave. Promptly, he returned to L'Ordana's bed chamber, moving cautiously over the ornate rug, then paused. Tilting his head sideways, he listened for her recurring footsteps.

Silence.

Asai grew suspicious, questioning her lengthy visit with the dark Warlock as the niggling feeling returned. *It is too quiet*, he thought.

His thoughts were then distracted by the ebonized table. He moved towards it, looking down at its exquisite workmanship, but the beauty of its exterior was no reflection of the evil it housed inside its drawer. As he opened his mouth to command it, his attention was seized by the view beyond the window. He observed the beauty of the new dusk as it quietly fell, arriving later by the day—Spring passing itself to the waiting embrace of Summer—the trees now feeling the weight of their new foliage as their branches were renewed with life. His slow-beating heart ached, longing to walk among them and feel the softness of their rebirth.

With hope in his heart and a sense that freedom was within reach, Asai returned to his task.

'Open!' he calmly ordered the drawer.

He regarded it intensely as it slid towards him, revealing what was hidden inside: the other item Oran wanted …

The *Book*.

The book's hard leather was rough and worn from centuries of provocation, its colour alone—oxblood—symbolising its evil.

Everything about it was immoral and sinister—marked by the corrupt hands that had mauled it, over the ages.

Reluctant to touch it, he surveyed its devilish cover, noting the unusual cross and— Asai flinched and drew his brows together, certain the dragon's tail had moved. *Another illusion?* he thought, then drew back when the tip of its tail curled into a nefarious grin. It reeked of corruption.

Hesitant, he stepped away from the sinister piece.

"Without it, her powers are vulnerable."

Oran's words taunted him again. Asai then knew he had no choice. He *had* to take the book; he had vowed to do so. Like the dagger, he would persevere with its company until both items were placed in the Warlock's eager hands.

A distant—but familiar—sound forced him to stop. He looked sharp, over his shoulder. This time, he was sure; *she* was returning.

In a swift move, he hid the book inside his kimono, then slid the drawer back into its place, by its gold handle. His eyes darted about the chamber; all appeared to be in place. With both items now on his person, he ran towards the painting, then stalled. The *Boy's* enigmatic eyes continued to stare at him as if to warn him. He held their gaze, then raised a curious brow, convinced the *Boy* had just winked at him.

Asai smiled. 'Say nothing!' he whispered to the "painting," as though the *Boy* understood.

With a sharp bow of gratitude, the Samurai then composed himself before passing through the *illusion* again—confident he had deceived her.

Oran stared at the open door to his place of holding, regarding the two anxious figures, who stood on its threshold as they waited, eager to get moving. Although the void between them was now rid of its obstacle, he remained hesitant, hiding his concern for Asai. He had sensed the disconnection of the two amulets, believing the Samurai had dropped it. Oran felt a pang of guilt; perhaps he should have warned Asai and told him not to take the amulet. But, on the other hand …

'Well, Warlock?' Reece began, glancing back over his shoulder. 'Why do you hesitate? Do you doubt your capabilities? For I am inclined to do so.'

Oran cast a wary look at the two Dhampir, detecting the hint of doubt in Reece's piercing green eyes. It seemed he would have to reassure them; there was no room for errors, or complacency, on his part. They had to leave the citadel … *Now!*

Oran stepped forward and then wavered. Glancing at the little table—laden with the Playwright's works he had read, on numerous occasions—he swiftly returned to it. Having developed a certain sentiment towards the "Tale of the Tragic Prince" he snatched the little book and placed it inside a brown, buckskin satchel.

Turning to face the impatient Dhampir, he was ready to abandon his "prison" and leave behind the comforts she had provided him with. Despite her endless bribes—though tempting as they were in his darkest moments—she had failed to obtain what she needed: the secret of the Shenn.

Placing one determined foot in front of the next, Oran kept going without looking back.

Tam grinned as he approached them, noting the Warlock's eyes firmly fixed on Reece.

'Freedom is waiting,' Oran stated, reaching for one of the torches that had kept him company during the lonely nights.

Mindful that "liberty" had not opened its door to them, just yet, they moved with caution towards the lower reaches of the citadel's tunnels—the only sound, the shuffling of their hasty footsteps, Tam's being the most prominent, given his size. It was evident no one else had passed through them for an age; the ground beneath their feet had remained relatively undisturbed, save for their own footprints, marking the Dhampirs' previous visits.

One entrance gave access to and from the citadel: through the great, iron gates—and in full view of their captors. Any suggestion of absconding had been out of the question until Asai discovered their only means of escape …

Through the maze.

Oran, however, had had his concerns about Asai's discovery—when it had been agreed to meet the Samurai at the centre of the maze. What waited beyond, he did not know, leaving him to rely on Asai's word, to guide him to the bronze door he had spoken of. Fragments of doubt began to pick at him.

'I have *seen* it,' Reece assured him, sensing the Warlock's reservations.

Released from the confines of his cell, Oran felt susceptible in the Dhampirs' company. With no invisible barrier dividing them now, he felt an underlying threat in their strength—no doubt acquired from years of brutality, during their captivity. Still, he had to trust them.

*What choice do I have?* he realised. *There's no going back!* Oran knew he was right. His only solace, though, was knowing they had kept Tam in the dark, regarding their plans; the less the Highlander knew—for the time being—the better.

They hurried along the wide-arched tunnel in silence, carefully following the route. Oran then had a sense of going deeper into the bowels of the citadel. Eventually, the passageway rose sharply, forcing them onto a steep incline, it gradually narrowing on their ascent.

Lifting his flaming torch, Oran looked over the shoulders of Tam and Reece. In the distance, ahead of them, he observed what looked like a dead end. He glanced behind, on a feeling, then dismissed it, casting away any notion that they were being followed. And yet …

The two Dhampir stopped.

'Have we taken a wrong turn?' asked Oran, his concern growing.

'You need to be more trusting of us,' said Reece. He paused, listening. A heavy silence crowded the narrow passage. Satisfied, he stepped forward, then disappeared—followed swiftly by Tam. Oran drew his head back, bemused; it was as if they had vanished into thin air. He edged forward. Without warning, the blackness reached out, hauling the Warlock into its presence.

Blinded by darkness, Oran reached out. There was no trace of the Dhampirs' movements. As he groped the void for guidance, he jolted, feeling the firm grip of a large hand leading him through a side gap.

'This way!' Tam whispered, urging the Warlock to hurry. 'Trust me when I say … you do *not* want to lose yourself in this place.'

As Oran emerged to the opposite side of the darkness, his expectations began to wane until he came face to face with the Samurai's discovery …

The *Maze*.

It was immense—its labyrinth of complex passages extending to every crevice of what resembled a huge hall. Eight entrances invited those who were willing—and brave—to "step inside" and challenge its baffling puzzle.

'Asai claims to know every inch of it,' Tam remarked, staring at its complexity.

'Do not doubt his abilities, my friend,' Reece reminded him. 'Did he not find you wandering about between its lofty walls, once?'

Disgruntled, Tam frowned, recalling their mockery of him:

"A wrong turn indeed!" they had teased after Asai had fished him out.

Despite shrugging off his past "miscalculation," Tam remained close to his colleague, passing him a warning glance. Reece grinned, shaking his head at his associate's false threat.

'I assume you know which one?' Oran enquired, pointing to the entrances with his chin.

Confident, Reece quickened his pace, heading directly towards the one the Samurai had shown him, with Tam and Oran close at his heels. Oran surmised—had Reece hesitated—he might have doubted the Dhampir; but Reece pursued it as though he walked its web, daily. It reassured him.

Made of solid granite, the labyrinth's dark and gloomy walls rose high on each side of them, touching the stone ceiling above. There was no escape. Oran felt intimidated by its confinement; its tortuous passages were so narrow, those who were willing to walk through could only do so in single file … and at their own risk.

Oran stared into the labyrinth's vastness as it waited to lure them into its domain, as though daring them to challenge its complex passages. A feeling of dread came over him.

*I hope, for all our sakes, you do know the way*, he thought, as he stood behind Reece, regarding him anxiously.

As if reading his mind, the Dhampir turned his head and looked at him. A suspicious, faint curl then appeared at the corner of his mouth.

'Are you ready?' he said.

Apprehensive, Oran slowly nodded. Despite his reluctance, he knew they had to take the intimidating route if it meant their escape. There was only one way out—through the bronze door—and *that* was on the other side of the maze. Beside him, Tam's anxiousness was obvious as the young Dhampir continuously checked his weapons, his clear, blue eyes focusing hard on the task ahead. Oran narrowed his eyes, musing over the Highlander's change of mood. He could relate to it.

The instant they stepped inside the labyrinth's charge, Oran sensed they were about to enter the *Lion's Lair*, its sinister presence fastening its grip. He cast the feeling aside, along with his doubts, as they made their way into its territory.

This was it. There was no going back.

As they ventured farther into its reach, the passages became treacherous and uneven, forcing the Warlock to watch his footing. Dust and grime rose to meet them as their footsteps tread the ancient soil. Oran covered his mouth, preventing its dirt from filling his lungs.

The maze appeared to take on a life of its own, breathing light and darkness of its own accord, at intervals. Oran thought it a trick of the light, and yet he could feel it watching him.

Quietly and swiftly, they moved on, staying close to one another until Oran hesitated, perceiving they *were* being followed. He looked behind him but saw nothing. Still, the feeling persisted. As he turned to join his colleagues, a subtle movement stole his attention.

Narrowing his eyes, Oran stared back towards the way they had come, observing a dark misted image; it seemed to envelop the passage, giving an illusion of drifting lazily as if contemplating its journey. It then moved, meandering like a snake, gradually creeping nearer. His eyes widened, awakened to the reality that it was no illusion. No, it was something else—something sinister—and it was coming towards them.

Oran recoiled as it loomed closer. 'What the hell is—' He quickly reached for the item hanging around his neck, then felt the grip of a determined, cold hand.

'No!' Reece snapped.

The Warlock wrenched the Dhampir's arm away. 'I can stop it!' he insisted.

'Then try'—the Dhampir leaned closer, lowering his voice—'if you dare!'

Oran glared at Reece then turned his attention back to the menacing dark cloud, having detected the warning in the Dhampir's voice. He paused, watching it creep closer by the second.

'To even attempt it is pointless,' said Reece. 'Your amulet's power is contained while we are here. *That*—he pointed—'rules this labyrinth. Nothing can overthrow or escape it … except for a cunning mind.'

'But—what is—'

'Quiet!' whispered Tam. ''Tis almost here.'

Heeding their warning, Oran promptly concealed his amulet as the mist crept closer, growing darker on its menacing approach.

'Close your eyes!' added Tam. 'And—Do - Not - Move!'

Anticipating its coming, Oran shut his eyes tightly and braced himself. He swallowed, not knowing what was about to happen. He cursed the Dhampir. *Damn you, Reece! You should have*— He flinched, feeling its unexpected cold, damp breath on his face as it finally made its impact. He felt the gold metal against his skin turn icy-cold as if his amulet had been drained of its energy; he panicked, fearing the unknown menace had removed its power.

It crawled over his skin like a sickness, enveloping him in its deathly cloud, mauling and groping him as though making its mark, within its potent silence. The sensation of its mere existence made him shudder. His eyes stung in his effort to keep them closed, and yet a part of him wanted—*needed*—to open them. Unable to hear it, he felt compelled to see the *thing* keeping them temporarily trapped within its hold. *I must know!* he told himself, about to open his eyes. And then it was gone, releasing them from its grip—Oran feeling its drag as it left.

'Keep moving!'

The Warlock's eyes flew wide open, hearing Reece's eager voice. He glanced down, feeling the warmth of his amulet's energy return to him, then looked up, seething at the two Dhampir.

'What the hell was that?!' he insisted, pointing at the menace as he observed it fading from view, continuing in its predatory-like search of the passages.

Reece remained silent as he proceeded.

'Well?!' Oran persisted, following behind.

'The *Black Shroud*,' Tam answered, wanting to avoid any conflict; his only concern was to reach the other side ... *Alive!*

'Something you clearly neglected to warn me about,' snapped Oran.

Reece paused and turned to the Warlock, tilting his head. 'Now you know!' he retorted, 'and what is more ... it will come back ... which is why I urge you to keep moving. Do not be swayed by its attempts to distract us.'

Oran raised a brow, taken aback by the Dhampir's casual remark. 'You mean ... it *knows* we are here?'

'The closer we get to our goal, the more it will try to confuse us,' said Reece, 'which is why we must remain quiet and still, while inside its grip.'

'What will happen if ...?' Oran's words drifted, unsure if he wanted to know.

'It will suffocate us, leaving us here to rot.'

'How do you know that?'

'Asai found the remains of others who tried to challenge its riddle, foolishly thinking they could outsmart it.'

'Outsmart it? How?'

'By running from it.'

'It chased them?' Oran snorted at the unthinkable.

'No,' answered Tam. Oran looked up at the Highlander, confused. 'It *hunted* them,' he then added.

The Warlock's face dropped. He then looked behind him, his eyes lowering, moving over the ground, searching. 'But—I saw nothing to indicate that there are—'

'Nor will you,' Reece interrupted. 'Asai—being the noblest among us—felt it his duty to … *bury* the victims.'

Oran glanced around and then back at the Dhampir. 'Where?'

Reece and Tam shared a brief exchange before looking down; the Warlock followed their knowing look as their eyes rested on the ground.

'Why do you think it is uneven?' said Reece. He looked at Oran. 'Beneath each mound of earth, we walk on, lie the remains of those who failed to outsmart the black shroud.'

Oran remained speechless, his concerns mounting, knowing his amulet was powerless within the shroud's hold and feared they, too, would succumb to the maze's sinister threat.

'However, the labyrinth did not bargain on Asai being its challenger,' said Reece. 'As long as you stay close, and remain focused, we will reach the centre in no time. Trust me.' He grinned, his tone now brightening. 'I *do* know the way.'

In silence, they moved through what seemed like endless corridors of weaving passages, hesitating at intervals when the black shroud crept over them, its eerie cloud continuing to haunt its domain, forcing them to stop until it passed. They counted the seconds, timing its unwanted presence.

'*Thirteen!*' whispered Tam, after each departure.

They had no way of knowing when it would return, throwing its sinister veil over them—one wrong turn threatening to separate the intruders.

When Reece suddenly heightened his pace, Oran perceived they were nearing the core, where he hoped Asai would be waiting; it was now clear to him Reece knew where he was going. It gave him some reassurance.

Pre-empting the shroud's return, Reece hesitated again, and raised a hand, silently motioning them to stop. Together, they remained still, holding their breaths as the next surge of darkness poured over them, flooding them in its bleakness. Quietly they lingered within its hold, counting ...

*Fourteen ... Fifteen ... Sixteen ... Seventeen ...*

The seconds dragged on—longer than they anticipated.

*It knows we are here*, Oran thought, wanting to run—escape—from its disturbing effect. Nervous, he carefully reached out, searching for Reece and Tam in the darkness. *Where the hell are you?!* He winced when his hand unexpectedly collided with the wall. He cursed it, then paused in the temporary blackness, listening ...

Ensnared inside the shroud's threat, Oran became aware of the victims buried beneath his feet; he imagined their hands of death breaking through, grabbing him, pulling him down. For the first time in his life, the Warlock felt the fear of being utterly alone and vulnerable.

'Reece?' he dared to call, keeping his voice low.

'Wait!' Reece's voice answered back. 'It will pass and—' He stopped, hearing a shuffling sound, assuming it was the Warlock. 'Do not move!' he warned.

As the darkness passed, with the welcome return of shallow light, Reece quickly turned to see only one face peering back at him.

Thinking instinct had guided him, Tam felt his way through the darkness. He slowed as uncertainty soaked in, then lingered, waiting for the black shroud to pass over again. But as he watched its ominous departure, an underlying sense of fear took hold of him. He looked up and down the passage; there was no sign of the others. It was as if they had been plucked from existence. He looked again, unsure, his sense of direction thrown by the shroud's influence. *Damhnadh! Which way?* He opened his mouth to call out but stopped himself; he could not risk being heard, should the cloud react to his voice.

Lost and alone within the silence—save for the sound of his slow-beating heart—Tam quickly realised his dilemma.

Again, he glanced up and down the long passage, contemplating which direction to take. He paused when movement snatched his attention. He narrowed his eyes in the dimness and craned his neck forward. Whatever it was, it was inching towards him, from the far end of the passage. He moved to take a step towards it then drew back, alerted to the low, grating sound.

The wall was moving towards him, and closing in, fast.

*I'll be crushed!* he told himself. If he did not make a run for it … Panic gripped and he spun, looking to the opposite end for a way out. All appeared still. But for how long?

There was only one thing to do …

As he made his assault down the passage, not knowing where it would lead, Tam felt the passage vibrate as the wall gained momentum. He kept running, its grinding sound getting louder as it pursued him. But as he heightened his speed, he was suddenly forced to stop again when the thick cloud returned, meeting him head-on, swiftly enveloping him in its black veil.

He stopped dead and held his breath, then counted. *One … Two … Three …*

With all sense of direction gone, and aware of the crushing sound gradually drawing nearer and louder, all Tam could do was wait. But desperation got the better of him; he reached out into the darkness, feeling the cold, bare walls on each side of him, hoping they would guide him somewhere—anywhere! Another sound made him jolt; this time from above. He looked up, his eyes widening. The ceiling was moving down towards him.

Now trapped within the shroud and the shrinking passage, Tam felt the mass of its presence tighten his lungs as it began to suck the life out of him. It was not the way he had planned to die—and so close to freedom, too. Alone, dejected and struggling to breathe, the Highlander slumped against the wall, knowing his great strength could not save him now. Despite the darkness, he closed his eyes, and as he prepared to face his end, he felt the hand of death clutch him from behind.

# Chapter five

'Lost again, my friend?'

Tam flinched and opened his eyes. He turned, having recognised the calm, melodic voice, and sighed with relief. And as the pale light made its welcome return, he looked above and behind him, releasing a long-winded sigh as he caught the tail end of the black cloud, creeping round a bend before disappearing into another passage, persistent in its "hunt."

'What is the matter?' said Asai, staring at him with curiosity.

The young Dhampir slowly shook his head.

'My mind … 'Tis playing tricks on me.'

The Samurai stepped up to him, his face serious. 'It is not your mind that plays tricks on you,' he warned. 'It is the maze. Do not let it sway your thoughts; it will only deceive you with its illusions, should you allow it.'

Tam drew back. 'Illusions?!'

Asai nodded sharply.

'And the black shroud? 'Is it also a—'

Asai stepped closer. '*That*, however, is real. So, if you must concentrate on something, let it be that, otherwise you will lose yourself—and your mind—within the labyrinth, with no way out. Stay with me,' he urged, turning away. 'Oran and Reece are waiting for us, at the core.'

'I was so sure …' said Tam, scratching his deformed ear as he followed the Samurai. 'But *had* I lost my way …' His voice trailed, trying not to visualise what may—or may not—have happened had he … He shuddered at the thought of it then grunted.

Asai paused and turned to his colleague, regarding him with care. 'I would not have left you, my friend,' he assured the young Dhampir. 'I would have found you—like before. Now, we must go!'

Tam cast a warning glance at Reece as they emerged into the labyrinth's core. His colleague smirked, tempted to mock him, then decided against it; now was not the time.

'Have you got it?' Oran asked the Samurai, extending a hand as he approached him.

Asai removed the book from inside his kimono and handed it to the Warlock. Reece and Tam stepped closer, scrutinising its foreboding cover.

'What is it?' Reece asked.

'Something that should never have been tampered with,' said Oran, swiftly concealing it inside the buckskin satchel tied about his waist. Oran turned to address Asai again when he noticed the obvious scar on the palm of his hand, prompting him to ask;

'Did you take it—the amulet she kept hidden?'

'No!' Asai replied, scratching his palm. 'I was unable to—' He stopped, detecting a look of guilt in Oran's eyes. 'But you already know that,' he then stated, holding the Warlock with an accusing eye.

A look of awkwardness appeared on Oran's face. 'Forgive me,' he returned, with a faint smile of apology. 'I had hoped *you* would have been able to retrieve what I could not.'

Asai bowed.

'My apologies, Oran-san. I hope it does not hamper our task.'

*"We need all five!"*

In his mind, Oran could still hear the grating sound of Tuan's voice and see his deep-set brooding eyes boring into him. But the Great Warlock's orders had been clear:

"Stop this threat … no matter what!"

Inside, Oran was relieved the Samurai had failed to take the amulet. However, had *he* been faced with the task … He now began to doubt his ability to destroy the Sorceress; his sentiments were manipulating his duty, threatening everything. *No, I cannot let that happen*, he silently vowed. Oran looked at Asai. 'What's done is done!' he said. 'You tried. And … accept my apology; I should have been honest and warned you.'

'It would not have influenced my decision,' said Asai, glancing down at the scar. 'Even if I had known it was beyond my reach, I still would have attempted to take it. Regardless of your warning.'

'What warning?' Reece enquired.

'A minor inconvenience,' the Samurai replied, shrugging off the pain he had to endure to steal their freedom. He turned to Oran. 'I think you will also want *this*,' he added, removing the dagger from his sash. As with the book, he had felt the weight of its evil burden for long enough and was glad to be rid of both. 'You are welcome to it, also.'

Oran's eyes widened. 'How did you …?' He paused, meeting the Samurai's dark, almond-shaped eyes. A curl appeared at the side of Asai's mouth. Oran nodded, smiling at the warrior's shrewdness—and pleased he had made the right choice. 'And no one saw you?'

Asai hesitated before answering. 'No.'

Oran tilted his head. 'You seem doubtful.'

'Despite my uneasiness, on entering her chamber,' he said, 'it was almost … too easy.'

Reece approached his friend. 'Are you sure no one—'

'*Hai!*' the Samurai snapped, irked by the suggestion that he was incapable of "watching his back." 'I am certain! It was merely an observation—based on intuition.'

'You succeeded,' said Oran, cutting in on a potential difference of opinion between the two Dhampir. 'And *this*'—he held up the dagger— 'will be to our advantage.'

'And our disadvantage,' commented Reece, turning away from the Samurai's frustration.

'True,' Oran admitted. 'When she discovers its absence, along with the book, L'Ordana will come looking for us. She needs them and will do everything in her power to have them back; she will overthrow any threat made upon her, by anyone who tries to stop her from stealing the

Shenn amulet. However, the advantage *we* have is that, while L'Ordana can no longer inflict the dagger's fatal influence on another young, innocent woman, she will be vulnerable. Time will catch up and weaken her powers.'

'And it is for those reasons … she may persuade Magia Nera to side with her,' Reece suggested.

Oran shook his head.

'Even *he* is not that foolish.'

'She still possesses his amulet,' Reece stated.

Oran frowned, considering the Dhampir's words.

'Surely, he will want it back,' Reece went on. 'I would imagine it is more than … *subject to the requirement.*'

Tam stretched his large face, nodding.

'Aye, Reece has a point.'

Oran suddenly became conscious of the three Dhampir scrutinising him with intrigue. *Surely not!* he thought. *Magia would never side with her… Then again …*

As if reading his mind, Reece turned to Oran—the ominous tone in his voice instilling the Warlock with a feeling of dread. 'Then let us hope, in her weakening state, Magia Nera does not influence her vulnerability.'

Putting the dagger into his satchel, Oran faced the three Dhampir. 'Gentlemen! Time is pressing on us.'

Eight narrow open arches marked the labyrinth's midway point—each identical and perfectly aligned beside one another; the four escapees studied them, their entrances dark and foreboding.

'To lose one's bearings in these tunnels is not an option,' warned Asai.

'And you know which one to take?' Tam foolishly remarked.

Asai declined to answer, stabbing the Highlander with a steely glance—the look of insult on the Samurai's face answering the question. Tam lowered his eyes in silent apology.

'As you have discovered,' Asai continued, 'the maze is complex'—he moved towards the second exit, on their left—'which is why I did … *this!*'

The others looked up as the Samurai pointed to the arch—above its curve, at its centre. He had cleverly marked it with two tiny symbols:

## 自由

Oran narrowed his eyes, focusing on their subtle presence. 'What do they mean?' he asked.

"'*Liberty!*'"

Inspired by what they represented, Asai had, intermittently, used the symbols as his guide, to mark his way through the maze when he explored it on his own. He exchanged a knowing glance with Reece, who returned with a smirk and slight nod; it was obvious the Samurai had shared his secret with his colleague.

*So that's how he found his way,* Oran realised.

As they moved to step through the marked entrance, Asai halted and looked up. The black shroud was making its return.

'Quick! Back to the core's centre,' he urged. 'And keep still!'

Once again, they watched as the shroud's malevolent presence crept towards them, casting its black shadow again.

It slowed and then stopped, hovering above the core and its four intruders.

'Wait!' Asai whispered to them in the dark, imagining it could hear him. It seemed to be "thinking" as it pulled itself back and forth, as though at odds with itself.

Oran was sure it had sensed the challenge of their unwanted company as it searched for them in its game of *Hide and Seek*. Then the unexpected happened; the black shroud moved on—as if it had given up the chase.

'Luck favours us, it seems,' said Asai, turning to the three anxious faces behind him. He nodded. 'We have been given a reprieve. Come with me!' he urged.

Without hesitation, they sprinted as quietly as they could back towards the marked arch and away from the maze and its ongoing threat, Oran finding it difficult to keep pace as he chased the three Dhampir through the tunnel's winding passage. Keeping them in his sights, he glanced behind, at intervals, for any sign of the cloud's unwanted return; it did not come.

As Asai guided them safely through the tunnel, the sight of a faint light came as some relief. The small exit appeared—the sight of it spurring them on. As they emerged, leaving the maze behind, there was a sense of victory about it, having beaten the labyrinth. But they were not done yet. There, waiting to greet the victors, stood their next challenge:

The great bronze door.

# Chapter Six

The three Dhampir stared at the Warlock as he contemplated their next obstacle. The bronze door's thick, bolted rivets armoured its great façade, adding strength to its exterior. He searched for a lock; there was none.

'No *mortal* could ever penetrate this defence,' Oran perceived, placing his hands on the barrier that stood between them *and* their freedom.

'Then how fortunate that *we* are not … at present,' Reece sneered, motioning his two colleagues towards the door.

'No!' said Oran, blocking their way.

Confused, the three Dhampir eyed one another.

'Let me!' A broad smile appeared on the Warlock's face. 'I insist!'

Curious, they stepped back.

Closing his eyes, Oran raised his hands to his amulet, relieved when he felt the warmth of its energy return, it pressing against him as he bonded with its inner power again, welcoming back his ability to use it; too long had it remained dormant under L'Ordana's influence.

Cautiously, he placed his hands on the door, feeling the sharpness of its cold, uneven surface. Oran soon felt the rising heat from his amulet emanate through his body, then into his hands as its energy began to take hold. Asai rubbed his palm, sensing its effect as he, along with his two friends, witnessed the forcefulness of the Warlock's influence. Reece slowly nodded, impressed, while Tam's eyes widened at its potency as the door's metal began to glow.

Oran edged away from its surging heat as it gradually intensified to that of a fiery, red-hot furnace, illuminating the walls surrounding them. Forced to recede from its impact, the Dhampir promptly followed suit, keeping their gaze on the Warlock as he maintained his deep concentration. The door began to heave and swell as the rivets melted into droplets of liquid metal, turning to ash as they hit the ground. In a matter of seconds, the great bronze door disintegrated before their eyes, leaving nothing of its past dominance behind, save for its residual energy.

'Time to take back what was stolen from us,' Oran stated, stepping over the threshold, and into the arms of freedom. He paused, then closed his eyes, inhaling the freshness of the night air. Spring's soft breeze carried nature's scent from its foliage; it was new and inviting, coaxing the Warlock to step into its embrace.

Lingering in the precious moment, Oran immersed himself in his taste of freedom. His eyes suddenly sprung open, alert to their reality: they were not out of the woods yet.

He looked over his shoulder at the three unlikely individuals he had taken into his confidence—the ones who had helped him escape. They stared out at him, unsure and motionless.

*Why are they just staring at me?* he thought. *Why don't they—* Troubled, he quickly approached them, observing their reluctance to leave.

Oran looked at Tam scratching his left ear—or what remained of it—as the Highlander looked to his two colleagues, hesitant. Asai stood staunch and proud as freedom beckoned, his hands resting on his precious weapons; it was clear he was more than ready to leave his prison behind. Oran then turned his attention to Reece; it was written all over the Dhampir's face, his apprehension to step forward. He sympathised with his hesitance to do so.

'You have come this far,' Oran reminded them. 'You even placed your trust in me, knowing the risks. What are you afraid of? Freedom is waiting … Right here!' he added, pointing to where he stood. 'You must take that step.'

Spurred by the Warlock's influence, Asai, determined to take his place beside Oran, inhaled deeply before taking the first, brave step forward. But as his foot passed over the threshold, he froze, seized by unimaginable pain. Reece and Tam rushed to help their friend but found themselves caught in the path of the force that refused to let them go. Oran stared in disbelief as the sting of L'Ordana's bond made itself known, displaying its torturous effect on the three Dhampir, in their bid to escape.

*Their bonds are not broken!* Oran realised. 'Step back!' he called out, panic growing in his voice.

Together, the three Dhampir tried desperately to break free from their bonds. But in their efforts to do so, they felt L'Ordana's dominance as it thrust deeper and deeper, slowly weakening, and restricting their movements. Like insects, caught in a *Black Widow's* web, they would soon lose strength, knowing she would come for them. Tam, the strongest of the three, struggled hardest against her might; he was the first to suffer its impact.

As desperation took hold, Oran called on the power of his amulet to help, with ill effect.

'What type of sorcery is this?!' he said, struggling to recognise it. He ran his hand over his head, letting his mind search deep into its core, hoping to find a solution. In a moment of weakness, he glanced back into the darkness of the open space beyond the citadel, where freedom silently called to him; he took a hesitant step towards it, then swiftly recoiled from its temptation.

Through the anguish of his suffering, Reece caught sight of the Warlock, sensing a moment of betrayal. But as his pain intensified, he threw his head back in agony trying, against all his might, not to cry out. In a hopeless fight to contain their suffering, the Dhampir soon felt their bodies failing them. As the effects began to take their toll, Asai suddenly fell to his knees.

'Fight it!' Oran called out. 'You must—' He stopped, his instincts bringing his attention to his satchel. *The book!* he realised.

Oran snatched it from its hiding place. With limited knowledge of its power, he surmised it to be the foundation of L'Ordana's black sorcery, merged with everything he had taught her, stained by the evil of his antagonist—Magia Nera. And, because of that, he knew he *had* to try something, to help his fellow escapees.

Staring at the book's sinister cover, he let his hand glide over it, flinching when the dragon unexpectedly sprung to life! Its tail curled and writhed, having been disturbed by the stranger's hands as it protested against him, refusing to give up its secrets.

But Oran ignored the sinister illusion.

*The key to their freedom must be inside!* his inner voice hinted.

Determined it would not dominate him, Oran persisted against its disapproval. Incantations poured from his mouth, demanding the book's attention. As his rage spewed onto the ancient cover, Oran disregarded its objection. Finally—and against its will—the cover flew back.

Oran glanced up at the three Dhampir; they were writhing in agony, gradually losing all sense of control as their pain mounted. His eyes fell on the book again as his mind worked at a frantic pace to battle against its evil. Its fine pages fanned back and forth before his face; he felt the effect of their erratic movement, in their attempt to confuse its intruder. Ignoring its protest, the Warlock persisted.

A sudden movement grasped his attention. He glanced up again, his eyes widening as he now witnessed Tam drop to his hands and knees in excruciating pain.

*Find it!* he urged himself, trusting his mind to guide him. As his eyes continued to dart between the book and the Dhampir, the pages heightened their speed. Time was now forcing its hand against him— against them all.

Oran felt his anger escalate. 'Show me!' he snarled, gritting his teeth.

But the pages refused to stop as chaos ensued.

Without thought, a name from his past flickered in his mind, jolting his memory. Desperate, Oran closed his eyes and seized it. *It is worth a try!* he thought.

'In the name of your master, Lord Tepés, and by the *Order of the Dragon,* I command you to *cease!*'

The pages stopped abruptly, falling wide open. Oran drew his head back, stunned, convinced it would not work.

'No time to dwell on it!' he muttered, glaring down at the puzzling script.

Its strange letters surrounded a symbol which dominated the centre of the faded, yellow page—*The Devil's Trap*: a circle with a five-pointed star inside its boundary. Despite its familiarity, Oran could not decipher the disorder of its words.

He glanced up, seeing Reece; the Dhampir was now struggling to keep his balance while, beneath him, Asai lay motionless at his feet.

*No! No, they cannot die!* Oran felt the tip of his frustrations begin to cloud his judgement, fearing he was failing them.

He looked down. 'Reveal your words!' he demanded, his eyes now burning with hate. Throwing his wide-opened hand on the page, he vowed: 'Or I will destroy you—here and now!'

On his threatening command, the ancient words began to move freely about the page, their letters gradually taking shape, forming the vital text he so desperately needed. Oran's eyes narrowed as they began to unravel their meaning; they were finally making sense.

With time running out, he moved closer to the threshold and stared down at his colleagues, horrified; all three now lay unconscious—and there was no way of knowing if they were dead or alive.

Frantic, he held the book forward, feeling its rage as the dragon continuously thrashed out in its defence; he continued to ignore its objection. Taking a deep breath, the Warlock took command of the words on its page. With precision and clarity, he began to recite them:

*I call these words, here in my rage*
*And pluck them from its cursed page.*
*Lift away and do your will*
*Lift away this darkened spell.*
*Be gone all foul energy*
*By the light of the waning moon*

*Let the bond be undone.*
*No longer shall their binding*
*Keep them in this place*
*I send to them this pivotal curse*
*Let this evil spell reverse.*

Silence rained down on the Warlock as he stood, in disbelief, seeing the three lifeless individuals, who had almost been within his reach. His heart sank, along with the eerie heaviness that followed the quietude, as though all life itself had stopped. Racked with guilt, he shook his head, in despair of his fallen colleagues.

'Please, forgive me!' he whispered, closing his eyes with a feeling of desolation, unaware the book had slipped from his hand. Oran clenched his fists, inflicting the pain of their loss upon himself when something suddenly occurred to him: he did not hear it fall to the ground. His eyes flew open. He looked down at his empty hands, then caught a movement beneath them; it was the book. He watched as it hovered between him and the three Dhampir, its pages still spread wide.

Gradually, Oran felt the stillness dissolve as a resurgence of energy began to take its place, its power exuding a propelling force, driving him back from the threshold. As it grew stronger, dispersing itself, he struggled to hold his ground as it pushed him further away. Fearing defeat, Oran battled against its might.

'Is this your revenge?' he growled at it.

Without warning, its force clutched him, wrenching him off the ground. For a moment it held the Warlock in its powerful grip as though it were studying him, then simply hurdled him away like a piece of rancid flesh.

What had seemed like an age passed in seconds as Oran roused himself from the blow he had received. Dazed, he groped at the hard ground, struggling to find his way. He felt the lump on his temple and winced from its throbbing pain. He slowly opened his eyes, trying to focus in the dark, envisaging curious, shadowy silhouettes crowding in on him. He wavered, assuming the blow to his head was toying with his mind. Turning his thoughts to the book, he crawled on his hands and knees, desperately rummaging for the item. He then hesitated, sensing he was not alone. Slowly, he lifted his head, listening intently. He then heard it: the sound of encroaching footsteps, making their way towards him.

Abruptly, they stopped.

'Is *this* what you seek, Warlock?'

# Chapter Seven

Oran looked sharp, blinking through the haze of his blurred vision. As his eyes focused, he slowly looked up at the three faces peering down at him. He reached out to take the book, his fingers barely touching its cover when it was snatched away from him.

He looked up sharply, then slowly rose. 'How is it possible?' he asked, subconsciously shaking his head. 'I was certain you—'

'Were dead?' came the flat response.

Oran's eyes darted to the item in Reece's hand, but as he motioned for its return, he was met with the Dhampir's judgemental, piercing green eyes.

'Never!' the Warlock retorted. 'I would never have betrayed you!' he insisted, snatching the book from Reece's grip before hastily slipping it back into his satchel, reuniting it with the dagger the Samurai had willingly returned to him.

Tam shared a wary look of confusion with Asai, sensing the tension between Reece and the Warlock; it was not a good time for disputes.

'Look!' Asai interrupted, distracting them. His tone was calm and rational.

Their eyes followed the Samurai's extended hand as he pointed to the citadel's towering wall; its huge, granite façade stretched as far as the eye could see—an indication of its intimidating and immense size and width. Its menacing presence stared down at the four absconders, as though it were spying on them.

The wall protected the whole citadel, widening out as far as the edge of the escarpment's peak, where the fortress had been constructed, to deter the enemy. Rows of beech trees, innumerable in size and height, also marked its surrounding border, adding to its concealment. Beyond their coverage, a sheer drop into a deep, crevice of sharp boulders waited—for the doomed traveller who had the misfortune of losing their way. It was evident, whoever had built the fortress centuries before, had guaranteed its impenetrable stronghold.

Oran stared above the outer walls as the waning moon made its presence known, it gradually rising, showering its eerie glow on the citadel beneath it. There, in the distance, he could distinguish the outline of the *Keep*—her inner domain—it reigning in silence over the "little city", now devoid of mortal life; he feared L'Ordana had rid it of its once innocent occupants. But by what means? The mere notion of her performing such atrocities disturbed him deeply.

With a sense of urgency, Oran turned to address the three Dhampir then hesitated; they were standing, transfixed, unable to grasp the reality of what had just happened to them; in those desperate moments, as the hand of death prepared to make its final grasp, they had been plucked from its harrowing grip—and, ironically, by a book stained with a history of perversity.

Oran then realised, Reece, Asai and Tam simply did not know *how* to react. *How different life in the outside world will be for them, from now on,* he thought as he observed the Dhampir. The possibilities that awaited them: the chance to live their lives again; the chance to walk among mortals freely; and the chance to love. He imagined it would be a daunting prospect for each, in his own way—after years in bondage—but was confident they would readjust, in time.

He then felt a pang of guilt, knowing he would have to disturb them as they tried to absorb their new freedom, while briefly forgetting the dangers facing them—and the repercussions that would soon follow.

'It will have to wait!' he informed them as if reading their thoughts.

Assuming Reece had turned a blind eye—forgiving him for his slight misdemeanour—Oran brushed it aside, but when the Dhampir slid his eyes towards him, it was clear his assumptions were wrong.

'We agreed, Reece,' he reminded him, observing the Dhampir's intimidating approach. 'I have delivered my side of the bargain, now you—'

'Not quite!' Reece retorted.

Oran stood his ground. 'Have I not released you from L'Ordana's bond?'

'Perhaps,' said Reece. 'However, we'—he nodded, indicating towards Asai and Tam—'still carry this cursed affliction.' He regarded the satchel the Warlock now clung to. 'Release us from it!' he demanded. 'With *that!*' he then added, pointing with his chin.

Wise to his meaning, Oran shook his head in protest.

'You know I can't! You must destroy Wareeshta. Only by her death, will you be free. Then—and only then—can you truly *live!*'

Frustrated, Reece lunged forward, grasping Oran's shirt collar.

'Then I insist you *try*,' he snarled.

'No, Reece-san!'

Reece felt the Samurai's sudden firm grip on his shoulder, luring him away. Forced to release the Warlock, he turned to protest when Tam stepped in, ready to assist.

'This is something Oran cannot do,' Asai insisted. 'You know he is right, my friend.'

Oran cautiously moved towards Reece; the Dhampir refused to withdraw his stabbing look, his face a determined display of anger and frustration. They both knew the reason behind it.

'It was not my intention to leave you,' Oran began, feeling the need to justify his faults.

'I *saw* you!' Reece snarled, shrugging away Asai's hold. 'Tell me you were not tempted!'

Oran sighed. 'What you saw … was a moment of weakness—a momentary lapse in our long lives. It passed as swiftly as it entered my mind. It was a foolish error on my part—one I will not repeat. You have my word, Reece. This journey has only begun for all of us. And the outcome?' He shrugged. 'Truly, I do not know. But I believe you will have your reward. And when the opportunity arises, grab it! Destroy Wareeshta! Take back your lives! But, for now, I need the strength that comes with your "affliction"—and, despite your loathing of it, you will also need it for the duration—when L'Ordana, along with her warriors, come looking for us. And they will. The mere suggestion of being deceived will drive her fury … and without mercy.'

Reece pondered over Oran's words; they had strength and power attached to them. But he knew, deep inside, the Warlock was still a man with hidden weaknesses. His face softened, slightly. Oran smiled, relieved; if it had been the Dhampir's silent display of an apology, then he was content with that.

'And you have *our* word, Oran-san,' Asai vowed, lowering his head. 'We will keep to our side of the agreement.'

Satisfied, Oran turned and glanced up at the citadel. All was silent and still, and yet he was wary of it. 'You remember everything I told you?' he asked anxiously.

Asai and Reece nodded; however, Tam glanced from one to the other, his brow furrowing.

'Where are we going?' he enquired, scratching his deformed ear. All eyes turned to the Highlander as he stared back at them, eyes darting, and frowning, somewhat bewildered. He shrugged. 'I seem to have forgotten …'

Oran, Reece and Asai shared equally confused glances at Tam's untimely loss of memory.

'We are going north?' said Asai, trying to jog the Highlander's memory.

Tam stared at the Samurai, his blank expression telling them he was non-the-wiser.

Reece rolled his eyes. 'North?' he snapped. 'Beyond these borders?' But the Highlander slowly lifted his shoulders, still unsure.

'… into Urquille?'

'Ah, Urquille!' Tam quietly echoed, slowly nodding, suddenly recalling the name, though remained a little perplexed.

'And on to Scotland,' Oran prompted.

'Then north-west, to Elboru,' Reece added.

Tam's brows shot up. 'Aye, right!' he said, nodding with enthusiasm. '*Scotland!*'

Satisfied, Oran nodded, then continued, with a cautious reminder.

'And remember—stay east of the Ardmanoth range, until you reach the Glen, before going west. And be mindful of your journey,' he warned. 'When possible, travel during daylight; we must now assume Magia Nera is her willing companion. If so, then he will hamper her journey, as he can only travel by night—a slight advantage, in our favour. But do not underestimate L'Ordana. She may send the Valkyrie to track you.'

'Then we will watch the skies,' said Asai, assuring him.


As Oran concluded their plans, Tam lifted his nose, distracted by the sudden arrival of a soft breeze as it climbed over the citadel's wall, carrying with it a familiar scent.

'The night watch is scouring the grounds,' he stated, warning his colleagues.

Reece and Asai looked sharp, detecting another scent. They promptly followed it until they heard the sound of Nakia's large wings; it was not unusual to see Kara's black, hawk glide overhead, hunting for prey, in the dead of night.

'Aye! Time to go!' Tam urged, '… before the wind changes.'

A silent acknowledgement to each other marked their departure, along with a sense of apprehension.

The three Dhampir turned to begin their descent from the escarpment when Oran unexpectedly seized Reece.

'If … *when* you meet my wife,' he began, with optimism, 'tell her … all this time … *they* have been watching us. I had no choice. I had to return to the Elliyan.'

Reece drew his head back and frowned.

'*If* … we should meet her,' he replied.

Sensing his scepticism, Oran held the Dhampir's gaze. 'If you don't … then we have failed,' he said. 'For where you find her, you will also find my son—Gill.'

Reece hesitated, then turned on his heel, leaving Oran with growing doubts. But as he walked away, the Warlock heard the Dhampir's parting words.

'Then we will *not* fail.'

Oran silently moved through the columns of trees lining the cliff-edge, after watching the three colleagues—his only hope—drop from sight and into the cauldron of night. He glanced up at the sky, noting the moon's absence; thick, black clouds now weighed down on the citadel, throwing a pale hue over its brow. He then felt the spill of their heavy droplets and thanked them for their timely arrival; the wet ground would temporarily mask the Dhampir's fleeing footprints and scent. Time, it seemed, was on their side. For now.

Throwing his concerns aside, Oran turned his nose south, knowing, should he travel by foot, it would take him a week to reach the portal of Meddian. *Out of the question!* No, he would leave the citadel in the same guise as he had entered it: as the unsuspecting young stag; only this time, without Wareeshta's "assistance."

Though conscious of their sinister presence, Oran double-checked the book and dagger, making sure they were secure inside the satchel, then threw it over his head and across his body. As he prepared to alter his shape, he stopped dead.

'You fool, Oran!' he uttered through gritted teeth, cursing his negligence, before turning the blame on Reece; the Dhampir's unexpected outburst and accusation had completely distracted him.

He had forgotten to tell them—warn them.

He glanced back in the direction the three colleagues went.

It was too late. They were gone.

# Chapter Eight

*Balloch: Scotland (Realm of Urquille) - 1630*

*Five months later …*

Asai stole himself into the night, away from the chaos that had erupted inside the household; Gill had blamed Reece and his two colleagues for their negligence, after discovering the Sorceress had *let* them escape, in order to follow them, to find out where Oran had gone. For the Samurai, though, the only voice he longed to hear again was Eleanor's, but the sound of disruptive voices inside the abode had drowned out hers. He thought he had been mistaken, at first. But no—he had, without doubt, heard Eleanor's familiar voice cry out to him.

Hearing her call his name, from her imprisonment, had prompted him to leave the company of her argumentative family, to seek out the privacy he required.

He moved swiftly into the thicket of trees, leaving the raised voices behind until they had faded completely.

Asai's thoughts instinctively brought him to the place where he and Eleanor had spoken intimately, but the image of the Valkyrie carrying her unconscious body away from them—away from *him*—still haunted his mind; he tried to block it out.

*Kara will pay for this,* he quietly vowed, imagining her under the threat of his blades, struggling in her last moments. *No mercy.* He would take great pleasure in "dispatching" the Valkyrie—as she so brazenly described her infliction of death. With much reluctance, he shook the mental picture from his mind. There was a time and place for everyone to have their revenge … *His* would have to wait.

The great Samurai looked around the secluded place where they had all initially stood, in the aftermath of Eleanor's abduction. It seemed so tranquil now in comparison to the mayhem the Valkyrie had spawned. Above him, two owls emerged, engrossed in their unique conversation, giving him a sense of calm. He could hear the distant rustling of a badger going about its business as it foraged for food—the sow scurrying about with her cubs in tow. But he would have to ignore the nocturnes and block all traces of life if he were to take himself into his innermost world.

His dark, melancholy eyes fell on the place where they had sat; where she had watched him display the skill and beauty of his weapons; where she had listened to his story; where they had touched; and where they had finally "discovered" one another …

Asai sat on the stray piece of wood where Eleanor had. Sensing her energy, he then placed his hand where her brother, Gill, had thrust his sister's dagger—into his heart. It had ached, since then; not from pain, but from something else—something he had not felt for an age. He stirred, suddenly feeling her presence; it was stronger, reaching out to him.

*This is the place*, he told himself.

Asai closed his eyes and took a long, deep breath before releasing it again into the universe. He now knew he would have to delve further into the sanctity of his innermost thoughts to find her. It was the place he had always gone—deep inside his mind—to temporarily escape the turmoil of his imprisonment. He had only ever reached one point—the place of *serenity*—where he could see his loved ones, knowing they were at peace. To go there had kept him sane throughout his incarceration, allowing him to believe he would—one day—be reunited with them. But everything had changed since meeting Eleanor. He had been given something precious—something he thought he would never have again: *hope*; however, just when he had been handed the prospect of a life with someone new, it was brutally snatched from him. But now he was willing to go beyond that point—to delve into the realm of his soul, to find Eleanor.

Asai focused on the sound of his breathing, letting its profound rhythm merge with that of his slow-beating heart. Each long, drawn-out breath followed the other, gradually becoming slower and slower until it seemed all life around him had come to a standstill. He no longer noticed the distinct sounds of the woods gradually cease, or the gentle, cool breeze brush over him on its unknown journey as he opened his mind.

The Samurai immersed himself, letting his conscience explore his inner thoughts as he began his familiar journey—the welcoming soft, yellow light guiding him, bringing him away from his surroundings.

*"Go to her!"* the gentle, compassionate voice whispered in his mind. He recognised it instantly, as that of his deceased wife, Ayumi. He saw the faint outline of her image and longed to stay with her a while.

*"No, Asai! Not this day,"* she urged, spurring him on in his search. *"You must find her!"*

Asai delved deeper, leaving the smeared and misted image of his wife behind, resting on his thoughts.

A sense of the unknown came over him as he slipped into his subconscious. The comforting light that had been his beacon, steering him through his mind, began to diminish as it merged with darkness; he felt its unsettling impact when it lay its heavy blanket over him. He was determined not to yield to its menace.

Asai then pushed his mind to a deeper level—a level he had never explored—then felt its immense pressure taking hold of him. His heart ached as he moved further into it—the feeling growing stronger as he drew closer to his goal. Sensing he was near, he waited in his repressed state for a moment, then called out to her.

'*Eleanor!*' His voice was sturdy and calm.

He listened. Nothing. Un-swayed by the unknown, he called out again.

'*Eleanor!*'

Asai lingered in his reverie, then stirred when a pale, grey light appeared. It seemed to expand as he drew nearer, but his vision was still blurred. He called on all the strength that his great mind would allow, remaining steadfast yet cautious.

Asai stopped when the silhouette of a figure suddenly crossed his train of thought, almost throwing him back to consciousness. But the Samurai proved superior, holding his own against his mind's intruder. He pressed on. The figure crossed his path again, lending him a sense of recognition as it took the form of a woman.

'*Eleanor?*' He had to be sure.

She stopped.

He called to her again, his voice now strong and determined. '*Eleanor!*'

She turned.

He sensed her breathing; it was rapid and uncontrolled. He was sure he heard her voice, then. She was sobbing.

'*No!*' she wept. '*I can't be here!*'

'*This way!*' he urged, desperately trying to communicate with her. He called out—again. '*It is Asai. Tell me—where are you?*' he pleaded.

He now sensed her fear and felt her pain. He felt everything she did but knew he had to stay calm, for her sake. Shapes of her surroundings began to appear; he narrowed his eyes in a bid to see them, all the while aware of her searching for him, from inside her prison. But panic gripped him when he saw her clasp her hand to her chest; he felt it, too. No, he could not allow it to dominate her.

'*Fight it!*' he urged, his voice calm and controlled. '*Fight it, Eleanor!*'

'*Asai!*'

The sound of his name, falling from her lips, ignited hope.

'*I will come for you!*' he assured her. '*I swear it! listen to my voice, Eleanor. Where are you?*'

*'I … I went to the window,'* she began, in her confused state, struggling to speak. *'Tis impossible! Why would she bring me here—to this place?!'*

*'We have little time, Eleanor!'* he persisted, fearing her state of mind. *'Think! Where are—'*

Without warning, a second—and larger—figure came into view, crossing their path. Asai jolted—the unexpected presence disrupting his thoughts. All he could hear now were Eleanor's faint and desperate cries, carrying strained words before he was plunged into undisclosed darkness, endangering his life.

The suddenness of Eleanor being torn from Asai's mind threw the Samurai's body into disarray, causing it to spasm violently. He fell to his knees, feeling the impact of the hard ground, but without a sense of attachment. His head throbbed with disturbing images of the Valkyrie inflicting pain on her victim. In his awareness, he could hear Kara's harsh voice and smell her sickly scent of lemon oil. Also, vivid pictures of her icy, grey eyes mocking him, toyed with his emotions. No—he could not let her influence his mind.

Asai's entire body began to shake uncontrollably as he strained to master his thoughts. He sensed he was losing battle as the seizure began to take its toll, forcing him into submission.

'Asai!' a voice called.

The Samurai wrestled with his conscience, struggling to recognise them.

The voice gave strength as it echoed his name: *'Asai!'*

Asai reached for the surface of his mind as the voice persisted, guiding him back. He gladly followed it until he finally felt the hands of friendship wrench him from his tormented mind.

The tranquillity of the night comforted him as he searched for a sense of reality again. With a deep intake of breath, Asai gradually returned to life, as he knew it.

A rare sense of weariness came over him as he dragged himself to his feet, struggling to focus, mindful he was no longer alone. As he slowly turned, four anxious faces peered back at him, in the dead of night. One of the figures approached him, with care. He stepped back sharply from their advance, then paused and looked down when he felt the gentle touch of a small hand on his.

'Where is she, Asai?'

His eyes glazed over.

When he failed to answer, they were impelled to question him again: 'Where is Eleanor?'

The Samurai's weary eyes flew open. Rosalyn jumped back, releasing her hand. His eyes looked heavy and distant, and yet he seemed attached to those around him. Undeterred, she promptly returned, searching for clues behind their darkness.

'Please, say something!' she begged, wanting to reach out and touch him again, reassure him.

'Give him a moment,' Reece advised, moving to his daughter's side.

'Aye! It takes time for him to come back to us,' Tam added, cautiously stepping into the fold. The Highlander narrowed his blue eyes as he circled his unwavering comrade, his hands clutching the thick belt about his waist, where two daggers were concealed within their sheaths, attached to it. *Better to be safe, than sorry!* He felt the precaution was necessary, after the Samurai's unexpected attack on him when the Valkyrie abducted Eleanor. Since then, Asai had appeared unpredictable—and Tam had no way of knowing how he would react when he came around.

'"*Come back to us?*"' Gill echoed, following Tam's inspection of the Samurai.

'Aye, lad! 'Tis his state of *meditation*. It's where he goes … in *here*,' he added, tapping his finger on his head, 'when he—'

'Wait!' Reece interrupted.

The impatient four edged closer to the Samurai as they were forced to wait in eager silence, watching as the flickering signs of life returned to his eyes. Reece shared Tam's relief with a simple nod. Their friend was unharmed.

Asai surveyed them individually before speaking:

'I found her!'

Rosalyn covered the look of shock on her face with her shaking hands as her daughter's location was finally revealed. Her distinguished eyes battled against the tears, in disbelief, in her recognition of it.

'No! Impossible!' she cried, shaking her head in denial as she subconsciously sat where Eleanor had, earlier that night. 'How could you possibly know that?'

'Though faint, Eleanor's words were clear,' said Asai.

'Are you certain, my friend?' Reece asked, glancing around as though they were about to be attacked by their enemy, at any moment.

The Samurai nodded, assured by what he had seen and heard.

Sensing his colleague's tension, Tam checked over his right shoulder for his sword; the claymore was firmly intact, and he was prepared for any potential assault on the group. He, too, longed for his chance to destroy the Valkyrie, should the honour pass to him.

'No—you must be mistaken,' Rosalyn insisted, shaking her head again, still doubting it.

The great warrior stared down at her. "*Why would she bring me here? To this place?*".'

Rosalyn dropped her hands and, holding his gaze, frowned, unable, at first, to decipher his meaning. She then gasped, her brows shooting up when it dawned on her: Asai was relaying Eleanor's exact words to them. And yet, she was confused. As she turned to her son, she saw Gill's expression change from that of shock to one of recognition. He slowly nodded as his sister's words resonated with him. It was now clear to everyone present that the young man understood.

'You know this place?' Reece pressed on him.

'Unfortunately,' Gill admitted, his tone filled with dread and foreboding. 'We had often played near it—as young children. Heckie used to taunt Eleanor with ghost stories about it.'

Rosalyn pressed down on her lips, displaying the line of disapproval.

'Heckie said that spirits, from a different age'—he tried to avoid eye contact with his mother—'crept through its foundations. While *I* found his stories amusing and exciting, Eleanor hated them. The very day *you* arrived,' he went on, nodding at the three Dhampir, 'we passed near the castle. She said she had noticed something, from behind a window'— Gill lowered his head, releasing a heavy sigh of guilt—'and I mocked her for it.'

'You were not to know *who* was there,' Reece assured him. 'None of us knew.' The Dhampir's tone was warm as he did his best to sympathise with his grandson—despite his restrained emotions.

Gill's eyes narrowed as he shot an irritable glance at Reece. 'All this time,' he sneered, through his teeth, 'they were here—in *Balloch!*—right under our noses!'

Reece leaned towards him, feeling his aggravation. 'And there lies the arrogance of her ways,' he retorted. 'It is evident the Sorceress stole the castle beneath the closed eye of society.'

'But there was nothing to take,' Gill replied. 'Balloch Castle has been empty for decades.'

'Which made it convenient for her,' Tam remarked.

'It is what she does,' Asai broke in; the Samurai was now fully restored and had resumed his place among them. His welcoming voice borrowed Rosalyn and Gill's attention as he continued to explain: 'She chooses a place—preferably a fortress, or citadel—while she gathers her small army of warriors. Sometimes … these places are inhabited.'

'Though not for long, to the misfortune of anyone who should reside there,' Reece added, thinking back on the sieges they had been forced to take part in. His eyes found Asai's, recalling the Samurai's harrowing story, and was thankful not to have been part of the blameful death of his family, back then.

'Her *warriors?!*' Rosalyn blurted, her eyes searching as she nervously rose from her seat, feeling exposed and vulnerable, regardless of those in her company.

'He means … more Dhampir,' Gill informed his mother.

'*Her* Dhampir,' Reece disclosed: 'Young, innocent men, who were simply plucked from their normal lives, without warning.'

'Just as ye were,' Rosalyn stated, glancing at the three comrades. A shiver of dread touched her spine when her eyes slid towards her son again, her look of fear evident as they widened.

The three Dhampir watched as Rosalyn contemplated her son; her look of dread was clearly preying on her mind. They watched as she then paced the small clearing in circles, wringing her hands, struggling with her thoughts. She gradually slowed as it suddenly registered with her: her conversation with Heckie's wife—Blair—earlier that day, at the Faire.

'Maw?' Gill asked, tilting his head.

She cast a worrying glance at her son.

'What is it?' he said.

'How could I have forgotten?' she muttered. They drew closer as she looked to the night sky, cursing herself for not paying heed to what she had been told by her neighbour. But the events of the day—not to mention all the unexpected revelations—had distracted her. And for good reason, too.

'Rosalyn?' The touch of her father's hand on her shoulder called for her to openly share her concern.

'Blair informed me that four young men have recently disappeared,' she began. Reece recalled the buxom woman waving frantically at Rosalyn, from The Ferry Inn. It was now clear that she had been seeking her friends' immediate attention, in a bid to relay the sinister rumours. 'At first, it was thought they had chosen to take themselves into hiding,' Rosalyn continued, '… to avoid being called to "duty". But their disappearance gave rise to suspicion when none of the four took their personal belongings with them. It was hoped the young men would return for them … But they never did. I had completely forgotten!' She shook her head. 'How could I forget that?!'

'And how could *I* have missed it!' Gill replied.

Rosalyn felt a hint of shame when she looked at her son; he was not aware of *whom* had gone missing. Two they knew—Athol Keir and Marcas Logan. How could she tell him that two of his friends were missing? She turned to the three pale faces staring at her. 'Is it possible they are …?' Her voice trailed, fearing the worst.

'Aye, lass,' Tam confirmed, to her dismay, nodding. 'Ye can be sure of it. And there is no distinction of class in her choosing, either, especially Kara's; although, the Valkyrie favours them'—his eyes moved to Gill—'*young!*'

Rosalyn stared at her son, her eyes filled with alarm when the shudder of doom crept down her spine.

'L'Ordana has no regard for life,' Asai stated, recalling the bloodshed caused by her influence.

'She always enters and leaves her place of abode, in the dead of night, unnoticed,' said Reece. 'And once she has achieved her "requirements" she simply departs, without a mere glance at the trail of destruction she has left behind.'

Rosalyn folded her arms, now feeling a sudden chill reach into the marrow of her bones. She turned her head and stared bleakly in the direction of the Castle of Balloch, then shuddered at the thought of what could be going on behind its sinister walls. The reality of it gripped her, raising her fear, knowing who—and what—resided there; it turned her stomach. She imagined the depressed state of the conditions Eleanor was most likely being kept in. She closed her eyes tight, desperately trying to chase away images of her tormented daughter. How would Eleanor survive? *She'll never cope*, she thought. If there was a time she longed for her husband, it was now. But Oran was in Elboru, waiting for their son. A new dread wrenched at her heart, instilling more fear in her ever-growing concern; it was knowing—without a shred of doubt—that Gill was now in mortal danger.

The others observed the look of horror slowly emerge on Rosalyn's face as her eyes and mouth widened. They expected to hear her fear; it did not come.

Rosalyn quickly turned and marched towards her father, her hands clenched tight, ready to stand against the forces that were willing to destroy everything she loved.

'You must go, now!' she insisted, peering into his green eyes, then nodded. It was at that moment she recognised their true likeness. And Reece, looking through his daughter's distress, saw their shared determination staring back at him.

'That *Witch* took my daughter!' Rosalyn seethed. 'She will not have my son, too!'

'We will not let that happen,' Reece promised his daughter.

'Remember, L'Ordana is unaware of Gill's true identity,' said Asai, adding his piece of encouragement.

'Perhaps!' she replied, turning to acknowledge the Samurai. 'But the longer he stays here, the more he is at risk.'

'And don't forget,' said Tam, calling for their attention, 'the Valkyrie is now aware that Eleanor has a brother. Did ye see how she looked at the lad?' he added.

Reece nodded, his brows drawn together in thought.

'Indeed. And, in knowing this … we can be sure that Kara will long for the "sibling" too.'

'Nor will she be alone in her wanting,' Asai warned. 'The Sorceress will have the Valkyrie return here.'

'What?!' Rosalyn blurted, aware he was referring to her home.

'Although she is unaware that Gill is to be *Magus*, she will see his potential as a new warrior,' Asai revealed. 'Regardless of who he is.'

All eyes fell on Gill. The young man stared back while they scrutinised him.

'That cannot—and will not—happen,' Reece added. 'It would be catastrophic!'

In his silence, Gill tried to comprehend everything that had happened in the space of one night. He felt useless and alone as they discussed his fate. And still, there was no attempt to save his sister. He had ignored his inner frustrations for as long as he could bear. He felt the presence of Eleanor's dagger press against him, as though she were calling out, urging him to find her; he did not need her weapon to remind him of her plight—of *their* plight. Gill was more than aware of his sister's anxiety when outside the comfort of her familiar surroundings. He felt his anger rise, his breathing now heavy and tense. *They don't even notice!* he thought as he glared into their faces while they conversed in low voices, his mother wrought with concern, while the three Dhampir remained stagnant in their thoughts as they searched for a solution.

Gill could no longer endure it. Disheartened, he peered in the direction of the house, where Onóir and Kai had remained. Eleanor's abduction had affected his grandmother's deteriorating health—more than she would admit. He wondered if Reece had any knowledge of the seriousness of his wife's illness.

'If you are going to do nothing,' he cried out, preparing to hurl his promise of vengeance, 'then I will!' He turned swiftly on his heel. '*I* will bring Eleanor back!' he vowed, stomping away.

'Wait, Gill!' Rosalyn yelled, following him. But her son was too quick.

'Stop him!' Rosalyn shouted as Gill made for the house.

The three Dhampir acted instinctively. But as they were about to stop the young man in his tracks, Gill, having pre-empted their pursuit of him, turned and stepped back, drawing his sister's dirk; the Dhampir stopped at his sudden retaliation and looked at one another, undecided.

Asai sighed and rolled his eyes, then, disregarding the previous altercation with Gill—where the young man had stabbed him in the heart with the same weapon—took a step towards him, extending his hand. As he reached out, the blade glowed pale crimson—the Samurai feeling the pressure of its influence tugging at his heart.

'Someone has to do *something!*' Gill cried, with disgust, as he tightened his grip on the dirk. 'And if it means dying to save Eleanor, then I will!'

'As shall I,' Asai returned.

Gill met the three Dhampir with a challenge he knew he could not win yet kept his eyes rigidly fixed on them. Asai drew his head back, tilting it with new interest; the young man had grown in stature since their first meeting—a few days earlier—and was now staring back at him, at eye level. A curious glance towards Reece confirmed his colleague had noticed it, too. The Shenn amulet was already influencing its master.

'This is not the way, son,' Rosalyn begged, catching her breath when she caught up with them. Through his adult eyes, she saw the little boy she once knew, playing out his frustrations for all to see. Rosalyn's heart sank as she empathised with her son; she could not begin to understand the enormous pressure he was being held prisoner to. Her mouth quivered, feeling the sadness about to descend on them when Reece stepped forward. He looked down at the blade gripped firmly in Gill's hand, surveying the distinguished engravings on its steel. Its most recent addition, "E.M.S"—Eleanor, Molyneaux, Shaw—was now being highlighted; no longer by Asai's nearness, but by the waning moon as it dipped in and out between the passing clouds. He moved to offer some words of support, then hesitated, sensing another presence.

'Eleanor would be proud of your loyalty to her, Gill,' said the unexpected voice emerging from the trees. No one had heard the Servitor's approach.

Gill and Rosalyn threw a second glance at Kai's ghostly appearance, its eeriness more prevalent in the moonlight. The notion that he was not quite a "living being"—and was a servant to the Elliyan—had yet to sink in; after all, they had only been subjected to his revelation, that same day. It would take some getting used to, after being accustomed to his earthly form for so long.

Kai's tall, ethereal figure seemed to glide towards them. Reece's eyes darted to the house when he realised the Servitor was alone.

'She is well,' Kai assured him, bowing.

The Dhampir narrowed his eyes in a threatening manner.

'I would not lie to you, Reece. Onóir sleeps, with Rave by her side.'

The Servitor's luminescent skin glowed beneath the blanket of night. He shared a smile with Rosalyn, sensing her comfort by his welcoming presence; it made him feel "accepted" by her.

'Your mother is right, Gill,' he began, in his softly-spoken voice. 'This is not the way. Should you set out on this path of destruction, the Sorceress will kill Eleanor … and then *you!* —leaving the Shenn amulet there for the taking. If we fail in our duty, I assure you … L'Ordana will find it, and claim it. Then she will have won.'

Kai lingered a moment, staring into the gloom of the young man's dark, hazel eyes, racked by insecurity and indecision. However, behind the frustrations, the Servitor had already noticed the visible changes in Gill: his strength, his spirit, and his staunchness—the makings of a true leader.

'You are far too precious!' Kai stated, giving him a sense of priority. 'And you are not alone in your task.' He lowered his head towards Gill. 'Do not forget that.'

'Kai is right!'

The Servitor slowly turned his gaze to Reece. Despite being aware of the Dhampir's reluctance—and dislike—for him, Kai was somewhat impressed that Reece restrained from his disapproval of his company. For this, he offered his gratitude with a single nod, then turned back to Gill.

'You simply cannot go!'

# Chapter Nine

*Balloch Castle.*

'Who were you speaking to?'

Eleanor looked sharp; the intrusion had been unexpected. No warning.

Kara loomed over her with intent and determination. Eleanor recoiled, turning her face away from the Valkyrie's sickly, heady scent. The terrified young woman stepped back, then flinched, feeling the jagged wall behind her; the Valkyrie sneered, leaning closer, forcing her prisoner against it, making her look her in the eye.

Eleanor tried hard not to rise to the intimidation, but the Valkyrie's strong physique was over-bearing; clad in her bodice of silver armour, Kara made her presence weigh more heavily on her prey as her icy, grey eyes leered down her crooked nose at Eleanor, inhaling her fear. She then reached down, grasping the young woman's soft, round face, forcing her attention.

'I asked you a question!' she demanded, tightening her grip. Her voice was raspy and strong and blackened by manipulation.

'No one,' Eleanor mumbled, her eyes narrowing from the force of Kara's hand as her thick, grubby fingers pressed harder. 'I—spoke to no—'

Slighted by the response, Kara stopped her short and slowly nodded.

'One insult is enough to warrant your death. Do not play me for a fool! I heard you speak to *someone!*'

Hand still clamped on Eleanor's jaw, the Valkyrie smirked as the girl's steely-blue eyes widened. The scent of the young woman's fear excited her. She pressed harder; so hard Eleanor thought her jaw was going to crack. Eleanor's face tightened—the veins in her temples bulging from the pain of Kara's unyielding grip as she slipped her large, coarse hand over her mouth; she now struggled to breathe, frantically shaking her head, unable to speak.

Finally, Kara loosened her hold and pushed the young woman to the ground.

As Eleanor saw the hard surface rise to meet her, she reached out for something to break her fall, her head almost colliding with the great fireplace. As her hands slid on its cold stone, she grunted from the impact, then winced, feeling the pain as the skin tore, gathering remnants of solidified ash—the tiny particles embedding in her soft skin.

Nursing her hands, now stinging and throbbing, Eleanor's watering eyes followed the frustrated movements of the Valkyrie. She watched the creature pace back and forth across the stone floor of her imprisoned chamber. Then, as Kara turned away, musing over her next move, Eleanor caught sight of the bulk of the Valkyrie's great wings; they were tucked away and partially concealed by her thick, golden plaits, hanging heavily down her long torso.

Without fair warning, the Valkyrie swiftly removed a sword from her back. Eleanor braced herself when Kara rushed her and held the thick, sharp blade against her throat; she felt the coldness of the weapon's steel as the creature slowly influenced its ominous presence with her trained hand. One sharp movement and Eleanor knew it would slice into her slender neck.

'If it were my choice,' Kara sneered, 'I would cut it off and let Nakia pick out those pretty blue eyes.'

'Enough!' a female voice called out, from behind.

Eleanor lifted her eyes, trying to look over Kara's shoulder, but the Valkyrie's stature was obstructing her view.

Reluctant to withdraw her sword, Kara kept her stance. She could not help herself. Ignoring her mistress's order, she leaned towards

Eleanor and whispered; 'I heard you speak to him,' she hissed. 'The *Strange One*. Your lover!'

Overcome by the heat of the Valkyrie's foul breath in her ear, Eleanor felt the sudden urge to heave.

'Leave her!'

The demand was so threatening and final, Eleanor almost flinched, her instincts stopping her, conscious of the blade still pressed against her throat.

'Now, Kara!'

The Valkyrie held Eleanor's gaze, for a few seconds more. Then, with a silent—and deathly—warning, she stepped aside, slowly removing the sword, but maintaining the contemptuous smirk on her face before turning to face her mistress.

As Eleanor looked up in a bid to view the woman, she noticed the silhouette of another, beside her. Both lingered in the shadow of the doorway, withholding their identities.

As the Valkyrie approached them, with malice, L'Ordana slid her pale, brown eyes from her servant's derisive stare, as though repelled by the sight of her. Wareeshta tilted her head, listening, as Kara mumbled menacing words under her breath before taking her leave. The Dhampir cast her eyes upwards and shook her head; she had heard it all before. The Valkyrie's snide remarks simply washed over her now—a far cry from the days when she would shrink from her presence.

Eleanor saw how the Valkyrie towered above the two figures as she strode by them, without acknowledgement. Or perhaps they *had* exchanged a look; if so, she failed to see it. She strained to look beyond the dim of her strange abode, watching the Valkyrie fade from view, relieved when her heavy footsteps finally dissolved into the shadows beyond.

Eleanor's eyes then moved to the two figures, who continued to linger in the doorway. She swallowed, aware of their probing eyes on her within the silence. Anxious, she looked around as if searching for her escape; it was hopeless. The silence mounted, along with the tension—the strain of their notable and unavoidable presence adding to her vulnerability.

*Get up, Eleanor!* she told herself. *Stand your ground!*

Keeping her eyes fixed on them, she slowly clambered to her feet, refusing to display any pain that had been inflicted on her. Suddenly, the smaller of the two stepped into her company, her small, lithe figure moving with the grace and agility of a small deer. Eleanor hesitated, swallowing her fear. She regarded the young woman as she drew nearer: she looked lean and strong; her pale skin exaggerated her deep-set, brown eyes and long chestnut hair, which fell thick and straight and exuded youth. She suspected they shared the same age—give or take a year. Although she carried no weapon, her attire had the look of a hunter. There was no flaw in her outward semblance—not a trace of a blemish. From the outside, she looked … *perfect!* However, what lurked beneath her exterior remained to be seen … But it was the other individual, who chose to waver from view, that kept her attention.

Even without seeing her face, Eleanor knew who it was …

The Sorceress made to enter the chamber, then stopped, as if something blocked her path. She shuddered as a sense of deep loneliness crept over her, it leaning on her cold heart. She had not ventured to this part of the castle before. But when she stepped over the threshold for the first time, into the soft, warm light, the feeling diminished. She lingered a moment as if expecting its unwelcome return; it stayed away.

From the moment they had entered Balloch Castle, un-noticed, the Sorceress had sensed the melancholy attached to its fortification; it seemed to cling to her. She assumed it to be remnants of its past, refusing to give up its ghosts. How long it had remained unoccupied, she did not know—nor did she care. It had been convenient, its location proving its worth more than she realised, at the time. Nonetheless, its feeling of desolation occasionally plagued her, distracting her from her task. She hated it—hated everything about it. The sooner they left the better.

There had been no room for distractions of any kind. That is until Kara brought her the girl. "A prized possession!" the Valkyrie had told her. Therefore, she had to come and see for herself.

)

L'Ordana sauntered by Wareeshta, without a glance, completely ignoring her. Her eyes flickered momentarily at the young woman, who followed her every move. She would give the captive her attention when *she* chose, silently letting her know who the dictator was, here.

Within moments, L'Ordana was alerted to the chamber's oppressive environment. Its peculiar, angled walls seemed to close in on her. She took herself to the tall, narrow lancet window and lifted her head to peer out. In the far reaches—beyond the distinct tree line—she could see the faint outline of the Highlands, their ragged summits marking the backdrop of the charcoal sky, where rain threatened. Beyond their sprawled vastness, she detected the pale hue of dawn, where it struggled to rise through the darkness. If they were to leave, it would have to be soon. But should the light of day fail to shine its rays down, then luck would be on her side; Magia would then be permitted to travel in comfort, under nature's grey and dismal sky. Besides, she did not relish the thought of wasting another day inside the castle.

'No doubt you are here to finish what your creature started!'

L'Ordana spun round to meet Eleanor's striking blue eyes and raised a curious brow at her brashness. Wareeshta looked from one to the other, musing over what her mistress would do and say. Intrigued, she moved—unseen—to a corner of the chamber, where she could quietly observe them. *This will be interesting,* she thought.

The Sorceress, her keen eyes on Eleanor, strolled towards her under the high, crisscrossed beams of red-painted wood. As she passed the small, plain oak table, where the young woman now stood, her fingers glided over its scratched surface; she quickly snatched her hand away from its attachment, fearing a rogue splinter. Pausing by the fireplace, she looked at the faded tapestry loosely clinging to its crumbling wall. She admired the intricacy of the work the unknown skilled hands had created, contemplating how it would have looked, in its former glory— *magnificent!* —and then turned away from it, sighing over the loss of its true beauty.

Eleanor eyed her captor as she moved closer: her long, silk gown reminded her of the colour of pine—like the forest—and it flowed in perfect harmony with its mistress as she moved about—the bodice and sleeves caressing her shapely form. Eleanor then drew her eyes up—the light in the chamber emphasising the woman's deep, auburn hair, which hung in soft locks and nestled to one side of her slender neck; when she tilted her head slightly, Eleanor noticed a small, raised scar, beneath her left ear—the woman promptly fixing her hair to cover it.

L'Ordana studied Eleanor, with ardour: the girl's face was washed from its natural colour, and black circles under her eyes marked her lack of sleep. And yet, it did not seem to deter her. The young woman's stomach rumbled for the want of food; she might feed her later. But that would depend … She surveyed her attire, noting the dark stain of blood that had drained from the small wound on her neck, and tutted, cursing the Valkyrie for tainting its beauty. Her brown bodice matched that of her skirt; L'Ordana noticed how they hugged her narrow waist, accentuating her youthful frame. She envied it—envied everything about the girl's youth.

The Sorceress drew even closer, lured by Eleanor's blue eyes. 'Their colour may not be the same …' she mused, her tone filled with intrigue. 'But there *he* is! I see him now. There is no mistaking your lineage, child.'

Eleanor tilted her head and frowned. She thought it strange—the irony of being called "child"—when the woman encroaching on her person was perhaps no more than five years her senior. And yet, there was an air of maturity in her conduct.

'I had intended to use you for …' She trailed off, eventually pulling away. 'But I shall spare you … for now.'

'What do you—'

'Quite the family reunion,' she interrupted, turning abruptly from Eleanor's attempt to question her, '… from what I have been informed.'

Eleanor chewed on her lip, keeping her silence.

The Sorceress faced her again, persistent. 'I would like to meet her,' she said. The statement was sudden and unusual. 'I had wondered what became of their child—*your* mother. And now I know; for here stands *her* offspring.'

Eleanor drew her brows together, slowly shaking her head, confused.

'I suppose you should be … *thanking* me, really.'

'And why would I do that?!' Eleanor retorted, through gritted teeth, her fists clenching.

'When Reece …' L'Ordana paused, lingering on the idea of him being the girl's *grandfather*. She had never expected such an outcome; it fascinated her. 'When Reece came to us …'

Eleanor snorted. 'You mean when you took him and stole his life.'

L'Ordana's eyes slid towards the insolent outburst. She would have to do something about *that*. 'His wife was with child, at the time,' she informed her. 'Though, he had no idea. Such a pity. I was tempted to tell him but'—she slowly raised her shoulders—'where was the point in that?'

'How could you be so heartless?!'

'I am not completely heartless!' L'Ordana snapped. 'It was for *that* reason I let her live. I allowed it to happen. *I* am responsible. And you "child" would not be here, had it not been for my—'

'Perhaps you should have let her die,' Eleanor cut in, without any thought for the words she had spat back.

The Sorceress lunged at her. 'I would *never* harm a child!' she cried in defiance.

L'Ordana suddenly drew back, startled by the words that had spurted from her mouth; they were not hers.

She drew a breath when another child slipped into her thoughts: *child? He would now be a man—almost "of age." He will soon be their Ruler.* She regretted that she had failed to find him, then. *Too many wasted years, searching for a child I would have willingly killed.* How easy it all would have come to her, then. But the years had disintegrated, and now the time was edging closer. She now regretted not having done away with the two Warlocks. She had been naïve, thinking they would reveal his location. *It is time!* she told herself. *Time to leave—or die!* The latter was out of the question.

L'Ordana's attention was suddenly drawn to another part of the chamber. Wareeshta and Eleanor's presence seemed to fade into the background as her mind became distracted by a sinister influence. She peered into the far shadows of the solar room, where the lingering presence of a small object seemed to call out to her. Detached from everything around her, she took a step closer. She could make out its shape as her eyes focused on it. She approached it cautiously, thinking she had heard the haunting sound of a child's cry. Unsure, she hesitated. It stopped. She edged forward. It cried out to her again, only now it was clearer and relentless as if the child were in distress. She then saw the object that beckoned her: a cot—and it was empty. But still, the cries persisted, pounding in her head, to a point where she felt compelled to scream.

*Stop! Stop!* she pleaded to the child inside her mind.

Then it ceased.

The child cried no more. Inside, she sighed with relief. But her release was short-lived when its cries were replaced by the faint sound of a woman's devastating voice, relentlessly wailing, her mournful cry unnerving.

Aware that something was wrong, Wareeshta stepped out from the shadow she had taken herself into; L'Ordana glanced around and then flinched, to find herself staring into the face of the Dhampir. As Wareeshta side-glanced her mistress with curiosity, Eleanor saw something in the Dhampir's expression—something she could not determine.

Aware of their eyes on her, the Sorceress composed herself as though nothing had happened, and advanced towards Eleanor, with purpose.

'Tell me, child ... where is your father in all this?'

Eleanor's eyes widened at the unexpected enquiry. She swallowed through the tightness in her throat. *Is it possible?* she thought. *Could she know?*

'He's dead!' she blurted, trying hard not to divert from L'Ordana's unnerving gaze.

The Sorceress raised her brows. 'Dead?'

Eleanor nodded.

'Aye!' she promptly returned. 'The war took him from me—when I was a bairn, and—' Eleanor stopped dead, tearing her look away, realising her error.

Wareeshta slipped back into her corner, remaining quiet in her reverie. She cast the occasional sidelong glance between her mistress and the compelling, young woman, pondering over the outcome. Things had just become more interesting.

'How sad for you,' the Sorceress returned, without a shred of emotion. It then registered—what the girl had said.

'And what of the young man? Your ... "little" brother, I believe?'

Eleanor bit down on her lip, cursing herself inside. *What possessed you, you fool?*

'What of *his* father?'

*Think Eleanor!* Her inner voice screamed in desperation. *Think!* She cleared her throat. 'He went to Eddin,' she lied, '... to trade. But when he returns ...'

'He will find you gone ...' The Sorceress threw her head back in laughter '... along with your brother.'

Eleanor's mouth fell. *Oh, no! She knows about Gill!* As her head swirled with thoughts and notions, her mouth slowly opened and closed, trying to get the words out as she shook her head, fearing the worst.

'No!' she then cried out. 'Leave him alone! Do what you want with me, but don't harm my brother. I beg you!'

L'Ordana observed Eleanor's display of loyalty to her sibling. The girl was staring into her face, eyes brimming with tears as she cradled her hands on her breast. *Quite the performance*, she thought; it was almost touching—had she cared.

'He has a sweetheart—Meghan,' Eleanor added, hoping the Sorceress would see—react to—the humanity in her pleas.'

But L'Ordana continued to stare at her, stone-faced.

'And—they plan to marry.'

L'Ordana pulled a sombre smile, mocking her.

'Would you deny my brother *that?*'

As they regarded one another, Eleanor held her breath; for one flittering moment, she imagined the Sorceress had faltered to her appeal. But L'Ordana's false display of sadness and pity fell to the depths of hell when a sinister grin crawled across her unwavering face.

'But of course!' she sneered. 'And why not? He is young and strong and will make a fine addition to my force.'

Eleanor glanced towards the arch, where she knew Wareeshta was watching and listening in its shadow and visualised her brother under the Dhampir's vicious hold. She now knew exactly what the Sorceress had meant; Gill would be cursed—bonded to her—just like the others. He would never be Magus, as was intended from the day of his birth. The Sorceress would then find the Shenn and take it for herself, and then … And then it would all end. She would rule—control everything! *I can't let this happen!* Eleanor told herself. *I just can't!* She looked sharp, ready to challenge the Sorceress.

'However, I am willing to barter with you,' L'Ordana continued, disrupting Eleanor's thoughts.

Eleanor threw her captor a sidelong look, surveying her with scepticism. It was at that moment she caught the Dhampir moving promptly from the arch again, to join her mistress.

'I will tell Wareeshta to leave your brother alone,' she began. 'He can then live his sorry little life …' L'Ordana paused, almost tempted to say, "for what it is worth," then changed her mind; she preferred the element of surprise. They would all eventually end up living out their pathetic lives under her rule—as soon as the Shenn was hers.

'If …?' Eleanor prompted, lowering her head, her eyes set, wary.

'Reece—and his two colleagues.'

Eleanor's eyes flickered at the mention of her grandfather and his friends. She swallowed, hard, sensing doom in the imminent proposal; she knew only one person would benefit—and it would not be her.

Although aware of the girl's hidden concern, L'Ordana detected it was mixed with an underlying current of secrecy. *She is hiding something,* she thought.

'I believe your … shall we say … "reunion" was no … "coincidence!"'

'I assure you,' Eleanor quickly returned, desperate to hide her thoughts. 'We had no knowledge of Reece's existence until recently.'

'And already you are quite taken with the *Strange One*—Asai,' the Sorceress replied, subconsciously rubbing the scar beneath her left ear.

Eleanor diverted her eyes, her mind racing, searching for inner guidance—but was unable to find it.

Through the paleness of Eleanor's tired and worn features, the Sorceress noticed a faint flush on the young woman's cheeks as she diverted her embarrassment. A lazy, smirk then appeared across L'Ordana's face. *So, it is true!* She persisted. 'They know something I wish to know,' she said.

Eleanor gnawed on her lower lip; she had no idea what was to be asked—or demanded—of her.

'Someone helped them to escape,' the Sorceress then stated. Her stare intensified, intimidating the young woman. Eleanor's eyes darted to Wareeshta—the Dhampir's narrowing, seeing the pleas ingrained in the girl's eyes. 'And I want to know where *he* is gone,' she went on. 'Reece claims to know nothing of their whereabouts.' She rolled her eyes and sighed. 'But I know your grandfather is lying.'

Eleanor shook her head, frantic. She would deny all knowledge.

'I don't know whom you refer to,' she blurted, maintaining her lie.

L'Ordana dared to move closer to Eleanor. The girl should have been her *next*—her last. But without the dagger—and the book—she knew her youth would soon diminish. The ravages of time would begin to gnaw away at her beauty. Already, she could feel the subtle signs of ageing seeping in. No one had noticed; at least, not yet. But for the sake of a few days, she would risk it if it meant possessing the Shenn. Then she would have eternal youth. She would have it all. There was no question of it. No—she could not fail. The mere idea of defeat terrified her, and to display her fears, publicly, would only compromise her existence. She would lose everything to the pendulum of time. And then the signs would be there for all to see, through her vulnerabilities. And then there was Kara; she would wallow in self-satisfaction. Yes, the Valkyrie was only too willing to step into the fold. She could never let *that* happen. For now, she had no choice but to spare the girl. As she peered into Eleanor's eyes, she could not help but agree with Kara: the girl was, indeed, "a prized possession." Nevertheless, she was flawed; her loyalties to her family were stained with lies.

L'Ordana recoiled from Eleanor with a sense of urgency, her energy filling the chamber as she swiftly turned away from the terrified young woman, who now stood, open-mouthed and confused, with no understanding of what was to come.

As her mistress made for the door, Warreshta moved to follow but was then forced to stop.

'She knows something,' L'Ordana informed the Dhampir. 'And I want you to find out.'

She then turned to face Eleanor and paused, regarding her, one more time, then nodded with certitude. *Most definitely,* she thought. 'Therefore, "child" I suggest you think hard—and not too long—about my inquiries. I will leave you in the capable—and less threatening—hands of Wareeshta until you decide to indulge me.'

'I have nothing to tell,' Eleanor retorted, now lifting her head in defiance, her chest heaving, her loyalty admirable as she remained staunch in her lies. 'They'll come for me, you know!' she insisted.

L'Ordana smiled sweetly at her captive. 'Do not count on it,' she returned. 'They risk death, should they attempt it. Did you consider *that?* And what is more … did you consider your brother?'

Eleanor drew a sharp breath at the mention of him. *Oh, Gill!* Her heart sank, feeling her world about to crash down. Her face slowly fell in anguish.

'I thought not,' L'Ordana sneered, then turned to Wareeshta, to clarify her final demand. 'Should she continue in her deception …' She hesitated, pondering her next decision before muttering, 'Then give her to Kara.'

Wareeshta waited until the Sorceress left the solar chamber. She moved to the door and wavered. Eleanor observed the Dhampir's nimble movements with interest; she appeared to be listening. Wareeshta then slowly closed the heavy, blackened oak door on her mistress's fading footsteps, keeping her ear to its thickness. Satisfied she would not return, she spun round to face the unsuspecting girl. Eleanor stepped back and swallowed, suddenly aware of the Dhampir's hostile presence; her poise and demeanour had now taken on a new façade, changing the atmosphere in the chamber.

Eleanor blinked.

It was all it took.

Wareeshta leapt forward ….

# Chapter Ten

*Balloch*

Silence reached in, temporarily removing all their differences as they prepared for the task ahead.

Rosalyn preoccupied herself by organising the provisions they would need for their journey, while Onóir looked on from the comfort of her chair. Kai remained by her side, his subdued presence relieving some of her pain, when in her company. Also, the Servitor silently refused to leave her, ignoring the occasional look of resentment from Reece. Kai was relieved, knowing Rosalyn, despite her stubbornness, was staying for the sake of her ailing mother. Still, Onóir tried to remain sprightly by insisting on helping her daughter. Also, she was aware of Reece's suspicions of her. She smiled brightly at him and then rose, making him believe she was recuperating; despite his doubts, it pleased Reece to see his wife on her feet as she made her way around the lounge. Somewhat satisfied, he discreetly left the house to talk with Tam and Asai; his colleagues had chosen to remain outside, away from the tense atmosphere still lingering in the overcrowded house.

Rave kept to Onóir's heels, scooping up the smell of food being packed away. Her sensitive nose lifted above the edge of the table, sniffing at the cured meat and dried biscuits—mere inches from her—the temptation making her drool. Occasionally—and when she thought no one was looking—Onóir slipped the hound the odd morsel, followed by a discreet pat on the head.

Gill sat at the table in deep thought, his mind a whirlpool of perceptions—occasionally interrupted by nostalgic images of his sibling.

He glanced at the dish of broth in front of him and pushed it away, unable to eat; besides, it would be cold by now. He looked away, catching his grandmother resume in her sluggish, methodical movements as soon as Reece had left. *When did she suddenly become so old?* he thought, able to see beyond the front of her valiant efforts, in her bid to prove she was better, while in reality ... But in a way, he understood, however, was not fooled; she was clearly putting on a show of *bravado!* for them all—particularly for her husband.

But Gill knew the reason for his grandmother's insistence on helping her daughter; it was a feigned attempt to keep occupied, her way—*their* way—of masking the thoughts and mental pictures of Eleanor's abduction.

He hung his head and stared at the item still clutched in his hand: Eleanor's precious heirloom—her dagger. He turned it over, staring at the engraved initials of its past descendants: the female line, on his mother's side. The gold and silver fittings—down its centre—gleamed from his constant cleaning of it, in her absence; he knew his sister would chastise him, should he return it marked with his grubby fingerprints. He ran his thumb over the deep-blue sapphires embedded in its pommel, realising he did not know their origin. It then occurred to him, he had never asked. Then again, perhaps it was not for him—or any man, for that matter—to ever know.

His eyes fell on the initials "E.M.S". The dirk was Eleanor's—and did not belong in his hand. He was determined she would have it back; after all, it was what had bonded her and Asai together—another secret behind its mystery. He closed his eyes tight and pursed his lips, still feeling the guilt of stabbing the Samurai with it.

*"You simply cannot go!"* Kai's words churned in his head. The Servitor was right—they all were—and yet he so desperately wanted to help in his sisters' rescue. But he was denied the right, it making him feel utterly useless.

The sound of his grandmother's soft, voice distracted his wandering thoughts. He looked up to respond but she appeared to be in private conversation with Kai. Their close bond made sense to him, now, as he observed them. Another pang of guilt hit him: his mistreatment of their family friend when they discovered his true identity. *A natural reaction*, he thought, trying to justify his verbal assault on the Servitor.

As a child, he had been naïve—oblivious to his grandmother's protection of him. And all that time, his family had been unaware that she was the *Watcher*. Surely, the signs had been there all along; if they had, they had failed to see them—whereas now … It was obvious.

He recalled elements of their past and the times they had shared. There were so many. They had always been close, however, when he let his mind ramble through those early years, he quickly realised, his grandmother had spent more of her time with *him*, than with his sister. Despite Eleanor's taunts at him for being "Gran-maw's favourite", it all made sense to him, now. There were times he had felt over-protected by his grandmother—not to mention a little embarrassed—while being unaware of her motives. He remembered the time when she had taken the brunt of a fall for him, when he tripped, almost falling into the loch: the old woman had slipped on a boulder as she wrenched her grandson by the arm, to save him.

His mother scolded him for taking such "bold risks" on the treacherous rocks. "Beware of the kelpies!" she had warned, through her scowl, as she placed the poultice on his grandmother's grazed shin. Gill smiled to himself, remembering the envious look on Will's face as he sported the large bruise on his arm, which, at that point, had turned every shade of grey, black and green, while relaying to his best friend an exaggerated version of the incident: that it was he who had been the one to save his grand-maw from the perilous loch as she clung to him for dear life!

"Oh! 'Tis a wee scratch," Onóir had disputed, dismissing the incident as being nothing more than the "adventurous mind of a young boy."

*Oh, to have those times again!* he thought, pining inside. But they were gone now—for good—and it was something he had to accept. But wherever his impending journey was taking him, he would carry with him those cherished memories and lock them away in his thoughts, where no one could steal them.

He then recalled when Kai first settled in the village—soon after taking over *The Ferry Inn* from Ned McGregor, as its new Landlord. It was not long after that when his grandmother and the newcomer became great friends; they were almost inseparable and had remained so, ever since. Now he knew why. The unique friendship was one to be admired, and not envied by others … unlike Reece. He snorted; the Dhampir truly had nothing to be jealous of.

Gill felt the tug on his heart, knowing he would be leaving his grandmother, soon—then felt the real heartache when he realised, he would probably never see her again. Nor would she be the only one; it was unlikely he would get the opportunity to say goodbye to Heckie and Blair Grant. The heartbroken couple had taken him into their affections after the tragic death of their son, Will. He missed his childhood friend and, secretly, still mourned his untimely death—the putrid splinter from his father's axe having claimed his short life. There were times he was sure he felt Will's presence, or perhaps he just liked the idea of it. Whether it was true—or not—he felt great comfort in it, hoping the feeling would always stay with him.

The image of Meghan Downy's young face then interrupted his thoughts. He sighed, feeling the weight of her despair on his aching heart. He had rehearsed it countless times—how he would tell her: "I must leave. I am to be an Overlord—a Magus to the—" He quickly dismissed the absurdity of it, knowing precisely how she would react; he would have to witness her quivering lip, and then her pale blue eyes bulging with tears as she tried to compose her devastation while hiding her anger as she wrung her hands in the folds of her skirt. He recalled how her face had flushed with beauty and wild excitement at the notion of their planned elopement. But it had been nothing but a doomed fantasy, conjured up in the heads of two young adults in love.

His mother was right—and annoyingly so; what life *would* they have had, when faced with the stark reality of it all? The odds of their survival had been stacked against them from the start. No—he could not face Meghan. He felt like a coward. *I am one!* he realised, with shame. Also, he could never destroy the bond she had with her father. *At least she has him,* he thought, trying to reassure himself. The old man had needed her ever since her mother died. No—she would have to get on with her life and live it, and it was up to him to make sure she would have one. She deserved better. She deserved a chance, like everyone else. She would meet another, get wed, have bairns, and then die. That was how it should be. *Isn't it?* he imagined. But then the thought of her being with someone else ...

He closed his eyes as the memory of their "first time" slipped into his mind, infiltrating his thoughts, refusing to let him forget. It had been awkward, at first, fumbling over one another in the dark, unsure what to do, in their desperate need to discover one another. But nature's *natural progression* intervened, finally showing them the way and filling them with emotions never before experienced. But what was the point of holding on to the memory when there would no longer be any physical attachment to it? He would have to forget—have to face the life chosen for him, without her—without his Meghan. He wondered if he would ever feel like that again. It was unlikely; she had left a scar on his broken heart.

Regardless of his feelings, he now knew it was a hopeless situation; he would outlive her, anyway—and her children. Not theirs. Frustrated, Gill looked down at the fist he had made in his hand and closed his eyes, envisaging striking his father with it. *This is all your fault, Oran!*

He flinched at the sudden touch of a cold, wet nose, nudging the hand still holding Eleanor's dagger, it taking him from his torture. He looked down at the beckoning face of his beloved dog and smiled. Placing the weapon on the table, he stared into his loyal companion's large, brooding eyes, wondering if she was aware of it—that he would be leaving her, too. He had always believed dogs possessed a sixth sense. He looked deeper, searching for it, but Rave simply sat, facing her master, waiting for his hand to feed her.

'Do you *ever* think of anything else but your stomach?' He grinned, reaching out to scratch behind her oversized droopy ears. The hound closed her eyes and leaned in, languishing in his tender touch. He ran his hand along her spine, noticing how her black-and-tanned coat was already fading with age; and she was only three! Her life would be short—*a mere flicker of time,* he thought—compared to his, however long it would be. It saddened him to know he would not be there with her, in her final moments, and, in a way, was thankful to be spared the devastation of her passing, too. Gill lowered his head to meet hers and sighed. He then held her, never wanting to let go, his heart breaking, knowing he had to. For a few precious moments, Gill could feel their hearts beating in time together, their unique bond silent and unspoken.

'I am going to miss you so much,' he mumbled in her ear; it twitched in response to his voice. 'But I rely on you to stay here,' he added, feeling the lump in his throat. He coughed, to clear it, then drew back, looking at her. 'You must guard the house, Rave.'

She looked up at him, titling her head from side to side at his familiar tone, her eyes wide and bright as though in complete understanding of his expectations of her.

Rosalyn, quietly observing her son, knew he was plagued inside with confusion. She had watched the benevolent moment between him and Rave; it broke her heart. The two had been inseparable since he found her—half-dead, beneath the wheels of a disused wagon—in the village. Rave had only been a pup, then—unloved and tossed away like a soiled rag. But he had begged her to keep the poor thing and, after much persuasion, along with certain rules, she allowed him. And after he nursed her back to health, the dog remained by his side, ever since. And now they were to be parted … for good.

Rosalyn cleared her throat. 'Gather your things, Gill,' she urged, hating herself for separating them. 'You must be ready to leave when they are,' she added, throwing a nod towards the door.

Gill raised his head, releasing his hold on Rave. Hearing Rosalyn's voice, the hound turned sharply, her bright eyes scouring for more food.

Reluctant, Gill dragged himself up from his seat. As he passed the door, the tail end of a wandering breeze outside caught it, and it gently swung open. He stalled when he noticed the Dhampir; the three of them were standing around the fire, in the yard, engrossed in conversation. He scowled. *Why aren't they doing anything?* he thought, clenching his fists, irritated by their lack of response.

'They know what they are doing,' the calming voice behind him said.

Gill glanced over his shoulder and saw Kai; he had failed to hear the Servitor's approach. 'Do they?' he sneered, looking out at the Dhampir again.

'Do not let your doubts eat away at you, Gill—or they will be your downfall, should you let them. Rely on your growing instincts, for they are stronger than you realise, and will continue to guide you with clarity.'

'At this moment, my instincts tell me—I would be happier if *you* were coming with us.'

'They, too, share our concerns,' Kai assured him, eyeing the three colleagues. 'Even though, at times, they fail to display their emotions. Do not blame them for that. Be thankful for their presence; it was by fate—not luck—that Reece is your grandfather. And, it is because of that, he now has something to truly fight for. He has a reason to live again.'

Gill turned to face him. Kai's big, wide friendly smile beamed back at him, his warm, brown eyes displaying compassion—despite Reece's ill-treatment of him. It was then Gill noted the features of his human form: Kai's well-groomed beard still matched the colour of his dark hair, which he still wore neatly tied back; however, it had not grown an inch, nor was there a trace of a single grey hair—not one! He had simply … not aged. Nor would he. Though conscious of Gill's scrutiny of him, the Servitor said nothing.

Gill's curious eyes then rested on the scar lining Kai's throat, where his self-appointed condemners *had*—to the family's horror—hanged him. Gill recalled Eleanor's story of how Kai had finally found his vengeance when his path crossed again with his "assassins." The perpetrators—or what remained of them, after Kai had had his way—never returned to the village, having seen the "ghost" of the man they had "murdered."

Since the revelation of his true identity—shortly after the Dhampirs' unexpected arrival—Kai no longer hid the *mark of death* which had been placed upon him. Such was his comfort, now, within the family unit, the Servitor had finally removed the interwoven thread of gold he had worn, to conceal the scar on his throat. Nor did he hide the reason for his fatal punishment; there was no sin in loving someone of the same sex—and no one in Balloch judged him for it.

'You know I cannot go with you,' Kai replied, placing his hand on Gill's shoulder.

Gill, releasing a long-winded sigh, nodded.

'Now,' Kai continued, 'you remember the way—which I instructed?'

Gill nodded and tapped the crown of his head with a finger.

'Good. And remember, Reece will be there to guide you.'

'I know, but—but what if we get lost …' he said, feeling the edge of doubt picking away at him. 'I have never travelled so far north, beyond the Aber Hills.'

Kai leaned in and whispered; 'Trust the power of your instincts, for they, too, will guide you—more than you know.'

He drew back then smiled at the young man with a sense of pride—as a father would his son. He had watched Gill thrive, during the three years of their acquaintance, and felt it his duty to continue what Oran had begun: to take him under his wing, without conviction. Despite his father's absence, the boy's training had been vital—the importance of it unknown to Gill, at the time.

Kai had expected changes in Gill; though, not as rapidly. And now, as their hopeful Magus stood on the threshold of adulthood, he noticed the diminishing signs of youth; they were almost gone. The dark, beard—Gill had so desired—had now grown in strength on his maturing face. Lost was the innocence, now replaced by prowess and resolve—although he did not know it yet. Gill's eyes bore the same intensity as his parents, in spite of the difference in his mother's—Rosalyn having the uniqueness of one blue and one green. Gill, however, inherited his father's dark-hazel eyes. But even they were changing; the Servitor noticed tiny speckles of gold glinting back at him in the candlelight. His frame had broadened, too, in every sense, and it was clear to see in the tightness of his clothing—Gill had cast his mother a doubtful look when she suggested he wear some of his father's attire, heaving a sigh of relief when she did not refer to his "undergarments."

'And you, Kai?' asked Gill.

'I have my orders,' said Kai. 'I must return to the Elliyan—and soon.'

Gill looked sharp at the mention of their name. 'You'll see my father, then?' he asked, with an eagerness that roused Rosalyn's suspicions; she stopped what she was doing—the loaf of bread in her wavering hand tempting Rave, who was drooling as she eyed it.

Kai slowly nodded in anticipation of the young man's next enquiry.

Gill wrung his hands together, letting his mind gallop in thought. His eyes blinked uncontrollably, glancing around as if searching for something that was not there.

'Tell him …' He paused, returning to Kai's fixed stare, thinking of something to say. He glanced out at the three Dhampir again as they stood over Rosalyn's night fire. What were they discussing? It gnawed at him. Then, knowing the Servitor could not lie, Gill turned to challenge him. 'Will they bring her back, Kai?' he asked in a flat tone, glancing at the door, it still ajar.

Rosalyn moved to intervene but was discreetly prevented by Onóir. 'Leave him be!' she whispered. Her daughter had to accept that her son was changing; it was part of the process.

Rosalyn, a little reluctant, stood back, masking her concern. But for whom?

'Well?!' Gill leaned towards the Servitor. 'Will they, Kai? *Will* they bring Eleanor back?!'

The Servitor lingered, contemplating his reply. Gill could see his eyes thinking. But when Kai failed to respond—in the way he had hoped—

Gill plucked his sister's dagger from the table. Consumed with anger, he marched towards the door, pausing, before taking his bold step over the threshold. He looked back at the Servitor.

'Tell him ... tell my father ... I'm coming! But not without my sister.'

Reece stared up at the sky, seeing the pale, light of dawn in the distance as night handed itself over to another unpredictable day. He then marked the outline of heavy dark clouds; they were gathering fast and looming closer as if preparing to battle against the rising sun. He hoped they would lose. But it was the nights to follow that held his concern ... He hoped they would also stay clear and bright; they needed the moon to guide them. Its waning light was desperately needed, and its unusual intensity a welcome advantage—provided the clouds did not smother it from view. And should *Mother Nature* be on their side ... then time would be their ally. He had calculated their journey and was fully aware of the difficulties that lay ahead.

He glanced at the house; the door was closed. All seemed quiet and peaceful now, behind its exterior. No doubt Onóir would be in deep conversation with *him*. He shook the image from his mind, frustrated by his envy of his wife's friendship with the "creature." Still and all, she appeared in good health whenever he was near her. And, if his presence benefited her, then he would have to put aside his disapproval.

The flames danced on command with each passing breeze, throwing warm, red light on the pale faces staring into it—each oblivious to the influence of its comfort. Reece narrowed his eyes from its healthy glow; it was irritating.

'Forgive me, Reece-san,' Asai continued, in their conversation. 'It was my presumption Eleanor knew about Elboru—when we spoke.'

'There is nothing to forgive, my friend. I also assumed it. It will, however, change our plans.' Reece then turned to his friend, on a notion. 'Do you think you can find her again?' he asked, trying to ignore the flame's nagging effect.

'I have tried, Reece-san … to no avail,' Asai returned. There was a hint of frustration in the Samurai's soft-spoken voice. 'I fear she is not alone; I cannot find her in my thoughts unless she is so, and even then …' He shrugged.

'Then let us hope the wee lass can find her way back to ye,' Tam added.

'And if she cannot …?' Reece paused, blocking it from his mind; he refused to let thoughts of his granddaughter's imprisonment hamper any decision. 'Who was your *intruder?* Who kept her company?'

'I cannot be certain,' said Asai. Something then registered in his formidable mind. 'My instincts, though, tell me it was the Valkyrie.'

Tam and Asai watched their colleague return his gaze to the night fire as he lost himself in its annoying and aggravating distraction. Its wavering light cast its shadows on him, distorting his features; his face appeared to take on a false evil. They sensed his rising frustrations fuel his anger, knowing how he abhorred the Valkyrie. They all did.

They flinched when their colleague began to douse the fire with his foot, pounding it repeatedly as he released his rage on its diminishing flames.

'Stop!' a voice called out.

But Reece persisted in his anger; he would not be satisfied until the fire was completely out, his fury throwing the melting embers up into the fading night.

Gill lunged towards his grandfather but was then stopped by Tam— the Highlander side-glancing him as a warning. The young man shook his head, staring in disbelief at the remnants of the symbol he associated with his mother and their home.

'Why did you do that?' he asked in a sombre voice, as though Reece had stamped out humanity with his foot. 'Maw has always lit it as a beacon—a guiding light—for when myself and Eleanor are away from the house.'

'Do not fool yourself into thinking it will guide her home, this time,' Reece snapped.

Gill's mouth dropped at his grandfather's bluntness.

'Oh, pay no heed, lad,' Tam started, throwing a vexed look at Reece. 'He means no—'

'He is no "lad" or "boy" for that matter,' Reece retorted.

Tam raised a brow as his comrade turned on Gill, with grit and determination.

'You are almost a man, Gill!' Reece persisted. 'You need to leave your youth behind in this place and face what lies ahead. From today, there will be no light to guide you home to your mother.'

Gill craned his head forward, grinding his teeth as he met with the Dhampir's intense eyes, their whites red with anger. 'Do you not think I'm aware of *that?!*' he hit back, lifting his clenched fist, tempted to strike his grandfather.

'Eleanor knows about Elboru!' Reece blurted, releasing the cause of his aggravation.

Gill dropped his hand and drew back sharply. 'She what?! How could she—'

'I am to blame,' said Asai, swiftly stepping in to defend his innocence, sensing it was his duty to admit his fault. '*I* assumed she knew—when we spoke—just before she was …' He hesitated, trying not to dwell on Eleanor's abduction. 'It was her reaction—one of *surprise*—that struck me, at the time. I immediately regretted it.'

'What else does my sister know?!' Gill demanded.

The three Dhampir eyed one another as Gill waited impatiently for an explanation.

'I assure you, Gill-chan,' said Asai, bowing. 'That is all she knows. It was an error, on *my* part.'

'More of a weakness, I should think,' Gill sneered, mocking him.

For once, the Samurai felt as though he had been cut down to size; he knew Gill was right to blame him, and, therefore, would accept it, willingly.

'Enough of this!' Reece hit out. He would not have his colleague humiliated, especially by someone of Gill's inexperienced youth—no matter *who* he was. And Gill was not yet Magus. Until then, the young man—as long as he was in their company—would have to abide by his rules, if they were to reach Elboru … *Alive!*

'Our plans have changed,' Reece informed him. His tone was defined and flat.

Gill drew his brows together, tightly, displaying the lines of vexation. 'What do you mean, they have *changed?*' he insisted.

'We are leaving, shortly,' he announced, to the confused face staring back at him. 'Dawn is almost upon us. So, I suggest we prepare our goodbyes.'

Gill's heart sank as his mouth fell, completely at a loss as he struggled to understand the cold-heartedness attached to Reece's abrupt decision. It seemed as if they were abandoning his sister. Inside he was seething, his sudden distaste for his grandfather discarding any sympathy for the Dhampir's affliction; it was not his concern. And if *they* had changed their plans, then he had no option but to ride to Balloch Castle himself—with or without them. He was going nowhere without his sister. *To hell with the outcome!* he screamed inside.

Gill turned on his heel, checking his sister's dirk; he was going nowhere without it. He would also need his bow. He then thought of his father's sword—the Albrecht. His mother was unaware Eleanor had seen her with it that day—when Farrow returned without his master, their father. His sister had told him about the sword, and so, they agreed to keep it as their "little secret." The problem, however, was that he had no idea where his mother had hidden it, though he had an inclination, she might have moved it, since—even if he had known of its whereabouts.

'Your valour is to be admired, Gill!' Reece called after him, with an element of guilt for his outburst. 'But your efforts to save her will be pointless now.'

Gill stopped dead. *Pointless?* he thought, looking in the direction the Valkyrie had taken Eleanor. The image of his sister's limp body, being carried away by the *creature*, would be ingrained in his memory until she was safely returned to him. But until such time, it remained vivid, haunting him, spurring him on. He turned to challenge his grandfather.

'If Eleanor knows of the Elliyan's location, while they wait for their Magus,' said Reece, 'I can assure you, the Sorceress will soon be privy to it—if not already.'

'Eleanor will not talk!' Gill retorted, intent on carrying out his pursuit of his sister. 'I know her. She will remain loyal and will never utter the word *Elboru*.'

'It is my hope, she does,' Asai interrupted, his tone solemn and foreboding.

'Aye,' Tam added, nodding in agreement. ''Tis for her sake.'

Gill shook his head, stumped, doubting the Dhampir's loyalty again. *Have they gone mad?!*

Sensing Gill's reservations, Asai signalled to his friends to remain, as he moved with majestic poise towards the brave, young man.

'I speak the truth when I tell you this, Gill-chan.' His voice was low, and Gill detected his honesty when he spoke. 'The Sorceress will force it from her … regardless! When Eleanor reveals it—and she will, without choice—let us hope she utters it to *her*.'

'Why the Sorceress?' asked Gill, drawing his head back.

'Should L'Ordana fail to steal the name from Eleanor, she will gladly hand her prisoner over to the Valkyrie.'

'Life is meaningless to Kara,' Reece reminded Gill. 'I am also convinced the Valkyrie has her own agenda.'

Gill turned to his grandfather and slowly leaned his head sideways. 'Meaning …?'

'That she, too, has her sights on the Shenn amulet. I suspect she may want it for herself or, perhaps, to merge with the Sorceress.'

'Therefore, she will do anything to locate it,' Asai resumed. 'If Kara is unleashed on Eleanor, she …' His voice trailed, reluctant to divulge the truth.

'Tell me!' Gill urged, through gritted teeth. His unswerving eyes peered at the Samurai, silently waiting for an answer. Asai held his gaze.

If the young man standing before him was to be a great Overlord, he would have to accept some harsh truths—and this was one he did not relish delivering.

'The Valkyrie will "dispatch" her.'

Gill's eyes widened as he swallowed the brutal reality of Asai's words. 'All the more reason to save her!' he cried. 'And I am willing, should it mean sacrificing my life for hers.'

'As would I,' Asai stated, bowing to Gill out of respect for his courage. 'But it is unlikely the Sorceress will turn Eleanor over to Kara.'

'What makes you think that?' Gill returned.

'Because of *who* she is,' said Reece, assuring him. 'No doubt L'Ordana has been well-informed, by now. She will see the benefits of keeping Eleanor alive. Ease your mind, Gill. I am confident your sister is safe.'

'For now,' Gill muttered, beneath his breath.

They ignored his remark.

Gill looked sharp. 'Then—it is possible the Sorceress knows who *I* am,' he suddenly realised. '*She* saw me—the Valkyrie.'

'Auch! Aye!' said Tam, slowly nodding. 'And liked what she saw, too. Aye! Kara would gladly have you, la—' The Highlander almost said "lad" but stopped himself. '—as another warrior.'

Reece shook his head.

'No. I am certain L'Ordana does not know your true identity, Gill.'

'How *certain* are you?' Gill replied, expressing his doubts again.

'There have been no attacks,' Reece stated. 'Had the Sorceress known, her small army would have descended on us, by now. Need I remind you, Gill ...' Reece paused. 'She intends to kill the *one* for whom the Shenn is intended: *You*. Be thankful for your sister, for she may have just saved your life.'

'Do you think so?'

'I stake my long life on it.'

The four held their silence as Reece's words resonated.

Gill glanced around, peering into the surrounding woods. The trees began to take on a new life as the early dawn spread its eerie, pale light over them. A faint mist meandered its way through their widened gaps. For an instant, he imagined the ghostly assault of an unknown army of creatures. He caught a shadowy movement in the distance and narrowed his eyes, seeing a young buck. He was acquainted with its familiar movements. It then darted, disturbing the lazy movements of a large, black grouse that had been foraging for insects. The gamebird called out to its mate as if to warn it, before taking flight. Nature had woken to a new morning.

'I believe … L'Ordana has begun her journey to Elboru, with Eleanor in tow, knowing we will pursue her,' Reece surmised. 'She will have a head start …' He hesitated, raising his head to the brightening sky, and smiled. They followed his gaze. Shards of yellow light reached up, stretching their long, lazy beams above the diminishing clouds. 'But then again …'

'It seems *time* may be our ally, after all,' Asai remarked, welcoming the clarity of the morning.

'And let us hope the sun is its companion,' Reece added.

Gill looked at him and frowned, confused.

A smirk appeared on the Dhampir's mouth. 'For while it shines, Gill, Magia Nera is limited in his movements.'

'Perhaps,' said Gill. 'But do not become complacent, where our northerly weather is concerned; it has a habit of changing its moods, without warning.'


Tam and Asai parted company to prepare the horses Reece had purchased at the Faire, the day before. Gill lingered a moment, resisting the urge to look towards the castle. He stared down at the fading embers of the homely night fire—the beacon he would never see again. *It's just a fire*, he realised, shrugging off the sentiment. He mused over the Dhampir's words, clinging to their belief; after all, they *were* acquainted with the Sorceress and her habits. He had to take their word for it. *What do I know?* he admitted to himself. Within the hour, he knew they would be departing, starting a journey to an unknown world—a strange world his friends and neighbours had been unaware of all their lives; and—if destroyed by the menacing threat looming over them—a world that could not protect their innocence. And should L'Ordana purloin the Shenn, those deathly powers—hers—would also see the demise of those he had known all his life. He could not let that happen. *He* had been chosen to save them all. They had to reach Elboru before the Sorceress did. *No!* he realised: *The Shenn belongs to me—and no other.*

In the first light of his new dawning, Gillis Shaw finally accepted his fate. He flinched when a hand rested on his shoulder, removing him from his thoughts, and turned.

'Time to leave, Gill.'

'I'm ready, Reece,' he returned, forcing a smile; it was a convincing one.

As they made their way across the small yard back towards the cottage, Gill stopped when it suddenly occurred to him: the great hazard he knew they would soon have to face. With everything happening so quickly, he had forgotten.

'Oh, no!' he groaned, not wanting to think about it, let alone … 'There's no avoiding it!'

Reece, hearing the dilemma in his grandson's voice, paused and turned. 'No avoiding what?'

'The Cordhu Pass?' Gill prompted, assuming he knew.

Reece, somewhat perplexed, tilted his head and frowned as he looked into his grandson's anxious eyes; it was clear he was oblivious to the infamous *Pass*—and the history behind it.

Gill released a long, drawn-out sigh, then shook his head, inwardly frustrated with his father.

'He never *warned* you.'

# Chapter Eleven

*Balloch Castle*

The girl's scent was strong and enticing. Had it been another time and place, Wareeshta knew she would have been tempted by it. Luckily, for the mortal, she had learned to control her wants and needs, and no longer craved them; in fact, the mere idea of it disgusted her now.

The two regarded one another intensely, bringing about another unsettling change within the chamber. Eleanor waited as Wareeshta peered into her blue eyes as though she were searching for her soul; she refused to divert her steely gaze from the Dhampir's deep-brown eyes, noticing the faint hue of red in their whites. She thought the creature's beauty unique: her pale, flawless skin enhanced her rich, auburn hair, its strands of gold standing out in the warm light of the solar chamber, matching her smouldering eyes—unlike the Valkyrie's, whose deep-rooted evil oozed from behind their deadness.

Eleanor perceived a softness behind the young hunter's intelligent face. She opened her mouth to speak, stalling, when the Dhampir suddenly inched closer, taking her in, contemplating her. Eleanor, however, sensed no malice in her scrutiny—just an inquisitiveness—which she found equally intriguing.

Apart from what Asai had told her, she knew little about *Dhampir*. She sensed an aura in this one's closeness; it was overwhelming—the closer she drew—forcing her to recede from its influence. In doing so, Eleanor felt a hardened surface behind her before hearing the small, oak table screech as it slid across the stone floor. She almost stumbled;

Wareestha—in slight of error—quickly moved forward. When she did, Eleanor swore she had seen the discreet movement of the Dhampir's hand. Had she intended to catch her?

Now, as she stood within a breath of her face, Wareeshta regarded Eleanor's suspicious eyes. 'So, it is true,' she stated, in her soft, foreign voice.

Eleanor frowned at the declaration, somewhat perturbed by their obsession with her eyes. *What of it!* she thought.

'Be thankful for your lineage,' said Wareeshta. 'It is because of it you are still alive.'

Eleanor's face dropped as she stared, wide-eyed, at the Dhampir. 'Wha—what do you mean?' she enquired, failing to hide the tremble in her voice.

'If you had not been related to Reece,' Wareeshta began, while gracefully withdrawing, to Eleanor's relief, 'you would have been tossed on the same pile of all the other young women gone before you.'

Eleanor drew her hand to her mouth, preventing her shock from escaping. *'Dead?!'* she mumbled, from behind her cupped hand, wondering why she had uttered the sinister word when she knew what the Dhampir had meant.

Wareeshta slowly nodded, but nothing was alarming in her admission.

'The Sorceress had plans for you—initially for her own use—but they were then discarded for … other reasons.'

Eleanor's hand slowly slipped from her mouth as she stared back at the Dhampir, confused, her mouth now slightly parted.

'Instead, she will now use you as a trade for …' Wareeshta hesitated. '… for something she needs. You are of little use to her … *mort!*'

*'Mort?'*

*'Dead!'*

Eleanor turned away, trying to conceal her look of fear as she absorbed the word—*dead!*—then spun round to face Wareeshta again. 'What exactly is it she … "needs"?'

Wareeshta diverted her eyes from the girl, reluctant to answer her questions. But the innocence and fear pouring from the prisoner had stirred a tiny feeling of guilt inside her, mixed with an emotion she had not experienced for a long time. She reached inside her thoughts, searching until the found it: *sympathy*, she realised. She actually felt an element of sympathy for the girl. Her face unexpectedly softened. 'You may not wish to hear this ...' she said, giving Eleanor fair warning.

Eleanor dropped her hands to her side, then, lifting her head, stood staunch, and waited; however, beneath her brave front, she knew she was unprepared for what she was about to be told.

'Then again'—the Dhampir, impressed by the girl's bravado, acknowledged her to take a seat—'it appears you might be.'

Eleanor retrieved the small, decorative chair she had sat on, earlier, paying no mind to its faded paintwork of elaborate English roses attached to their long, thorny stems; save for their outline, they were barely visible now, giving way to the influence of time.

'The Sorceress sees beauty in youth,' Wareeshta began. 'However, she also sees weakness in strength, and preys on that vulnerability. It makes her victims easy to distinguish. Then, when she has made her choice, she draws the life from the young woman, taking it for herself. This is how she maintains her youth.'

'And *I* was to be her next!' Eleanor stated, placing her hand where her heart was beating wildly as if she instinctively knew.

'Your connection to Reece has bought you time,' Wareeshta informed her. 'Though, there is still no guarantee your life will be spared.'

Hearing this, Eleanor's heart sank as she slumped back in her seat, burying her head in her hands. Her mind raced with thoughts of her demise—thoughts of never seeing her loved ones again—thoughts of never seeing ...

She shook her head.

'What am I to do if—' She stopped herself, for fear of giving up her secrets.

Wareeshta looked down at the young woman, contemplating her for a moment; she imagined they shared the same age—the difference being, the girl may not live to enjoy the prospects of a full and happy life—a life she herself could never have. Inside, she craved the normality of it, envying the girls' mortality. Touched by the same pang of guilt, she felt it urging her to show some remorse towards Eleanor. But Wareeshta knew if she were seen to display any sympathy for a prisoner, her own life would be rendered pointless—more than it already was. She pondered on it, for a moment, when something inside compelled her to *warn* the young woman.

Wareeshta's eyes flashed towards the door, then back to Eleanor. She stepped closer and, dropping her voice, said, 'Make sure you survive!'

Eleanor looked up, sharply.

*"Make sure you survive!"*

She gasped when it echoed in her mind. But had she imagined it— what the Dhampir had just said to her? Her eyes then widened with recognition.

*No! I did not!*

Her heart now renewed with hope, Eleanor needed to know more. But when she saw Wareeshta suddenly reach for the door, she panicked. *Oh, no! I can't let her leave!*

Eleanor jumped up, ignoring the tumbling chair behind her.

'Wait, Wareeshta!'

The Dhampir hesitated when she heard Eleanor speak her name for the first time.

'Please, Wareeshta?'

There—she had said it again; only now there was something melodic in her tone. No one had ever spoken her name so beautifully. It enticed her to stay. She turned to meet Eleanor's eyes; they were now smiling at her, through her anxiousness.

'Stay—and talk with me a while,' Eleanor beckoned, extending the hand of friendship, but with caution.

Wareeshta looked down at Eleanor's open palm—the subtle shaking of her hand exposing her nervousness—and saw the graze caused by her fall; the grimy dust was still embedded beneath the bruising skin.

'Courtesy of your colleague,' Eleanor remarked, shrugging. 'It hardly hurts, now,' she added, subconsciously wiping her hand on her skirt.

The flame from the lantern, hanging on the wall behind the door, quivered as Wareeshta closed it. Eleanor smiled with gratitude yet remained wary of the Dhampir's unpredictable movements as she faced her again.

The two young women stared at one another in complete silence, alert and aware, their deep scrutiny of each other holding court within the chamber; Wareeshta, a stranger to human conversation, stood silent and perfectly still, while Eleanor chewed on her lip, feeling the awkwardness of her presence as she scrambled for something to say.

'How—how long have you …?' Her voice trailed, still struggling for the words.

'Been this way?' came the blunt reply.

Eleanor's eyes flickered at the Dhampir's abrupt response. *It's a start,* she thought, but knew she would have to approach her with caution if she were to draw any information from her unassuming guest. Perhaps play on her weakness? After all, she was half-human.

As Eleanor fished inside her mind for something else to say, Wareeshta unexpectedly took charge of the conversation.

'I was not'—she frowned, then momentarily looked away as if searching for the right word—'*created* this way.'

'Unlike the others,' stated Eleanor.

Wareeshta's brows shot up. '*Da!*' the Dhampir replied, with a cumbersome nod. 'And I would ask, how you were informed …?' She paused, tilting her head. 'But I think I know the answer to that.'

'It—it was … *explained* to me by—' Eleanor stopped and lowered her eyes.

Wareeshta smirked, seeing the flush in her cheeks. So, she *was* enamoured by the Samurai; it was plain to see, by her embarrassment.

However, she knew she was not alone in her thinking; she had heard Kara whisper it to the girl.

'By your … *lover?*'

Shocked, Eleanor slowly lifted her head and stared at the Dhampir, speechless. The look on the girl's face reminded Wareeshta of her mistress; L'Ordana had displayed the same expression when she discovered her precious book and dagger had been stolen—by the Samurai, no less—the theft of the items sparing the girl the horror of the daggers' immoral influence. Wareeshta smirked to herself, savouring the moment.

'I know it was you!'

The Dhampir's eyes flicked at Eleanor's outburst. She drew back, curious.

'Me?'

Eleanor nodded.

'Aye, it was you who inflicted your *curse* on them!' she hit back. 'And you who—'

'I had my orders!' Wareeshta retaliated, her expression now hard as she edged towards Eleanor, in defence of the appalling acts she had been forced to commit upon innocent victims.

Eleanor recoiled, seeing the threatening hue of anger in the Dhampir's eyes—the visible taint of red intimidating her. Aware of it, Wareeshta promptly drew away, avoiding her gaze.

As the conflicting quietness divided them, once again, Eleanor pressed down on her lips, her thoughts racing while Wareeshta remained motionless by the door as if guarding it.

*Say something!* Eleanor prompted herself, while, at the same time, wanting to avoid any potentially damaging questions related to her family or Asai.

'You—you said you were not … *created!*' Eleanor then blurted, hoping to sway the conversation. She held her breath.

Wareeshta nodded once.

'I was *born* this way.'

'Born?' said Eleanor, slowly taking her seat again, and ignoring the stinging in her grazed hands. She purposely held the Dhampir's gaze with a look of sympathy, hoping it would encourage her to talk.

Drawn by the young woman's interest in her, Wareeshta could no longer divert her eyes from Eleanor, though still regarded her with suspicion, searching for the ulterior motive in her appeal. But when she saw none, she believed it to be nothing more than a distraction or, simply, a need for company.

Wareeshta looked back at the closed door, her senses heightened, working, listening for the signs of a threat, or any interference; she heard nothing in the passages, beyond.

Returning her attention to Eleanor, she noted the look of patience on the girl's face as she waited to hear her story; there was something "calming" in her demeanour that made her want to talk. *Why not!* she thought; besides, it would be a welcome distraction from the Valkyrie's constant suspicions.

'My father,' Wareeshta began, 'was once like you—*human*. He was a Prince of Wallachia. It is a place far from here—in Romania—in the Eastern Realm of …' She paused, realising she had almost said "Saó," preferring to call it by its true name: 'Eastern Europe,' she continued. 'He was a soldier and great ruler—two hundred years ago.'

Eleanor tilted her head. 'You say he was once … *human?*'

Wareeshta nodded.

'*Da!* He gave up his mortality, in vengeance, for the death of his wife.'

'Your mother?'

Wareeshta shook her head.

'While he was away, gathering support for his battles, his enemy advanced on his castle—where his wife waited for him. Thinking he was there, a former—but loyal—servant shot an arrow into my father's quarters, to warn him of the threat. But his wife, having read the warning—and with no news of her husband—threw herself into the river.'

'She thought he was dead!' Eleanor deduced.

'That was her thinking. She was loyal to my father, vowing that she would rather have her body rot and be eaten by the fish—than be taken into captivity by their enemy. My father was so devastated by her loss, he renounced all that had been good and holy in his life. His grief turned to anger and resentment for all mankind. He lost his way, his path leading him to make a pact with the *Devil*: he gave up his soul, in exchange for immortality. He became a creature of the *Underworld*, living an endless life of tyranny, under the shadow of night, imposing cruel punishments on those he felt deserving of it. But love eventually re-entered his life, in the form of my mother. It was from *that* union I was born.'

'She was mortal,' Eleanor assumed.

'And a kind soul … from what I was told. She died within a year of my birth.'

Eleanor tilted her chin slightly and frowned at the Dhampir's lack of emotion, about the death of her mother. Nevertheless, she could not help but feel some empathy towards her.

'How sad—that you never knew her.'

Wareeshta leaned her head to the side, drawing her brows together.

'Do not feel pity for me!' she said, somewhat confused by Eleanor's response. 'How can I feel something for someone I never knew?'

'And yet, it's clear you retain her human qualities,' said Eleanor. 'Or at least *some* of them.'

Wareeshta's eyes drifted as she gave thought to it; she was unable to recall the last time she was reminded of her *human* side. Denied the company of mortals for so long, she had subconsciously stored it deep within the crevice of her mind, where it had remained dormant for more years than she could remember. As the realisation of her human side was brought to the fore, Wareeshta's eyes returned to Eleanor, who silently encouraged her more, with a smile and subtle nod. It was then the Dhampir knew, that those unspoken qualities had just been reawakened and released, because of her—because of this compelling young woman.

Observing the Dhampir's moment of contemplation and realisation, Eleanor decided to strike while the iron was hot and pursue her with her enquiries.

'Did your father raise you?'

Lured from her thoughts, Wareeshta's eyes darted towards Eleanor as if she had been woken suddenly from a dream. 'He did—with the help of three servants.'

'Mortals?'

Wareeshta nodded.

'Although they were aware of my father's true form, they were loyal to him and protected me from his acts of violence—on his orders. But, with the passing of time, my protectors grew old; I watched them die, while I still retained my youth ...' She paused on a memory, remembering one in particular—Seneslav. He had been more of a father to her than her own. But he, too, was gone. She released a subtle sigh, then continued. 'And so, without their protection and guidance, I became more inquisitive. But through that inquisitiveness, I discovered horror; I witnessed the appalling acts of torture my father was inflicting on innocent people, earning him the undesirable name: "*Vlad the Impaler.*" While he took pride in his new "title", I, however, could no longer stand back and watch his atrocities, knowing he took pleasure in them. Thousands were tortured, while he sat and feasted, enjoying the spectacle as their bodies were mounted on stakes—as a display of his power. There were times he used them to entertain his guests, but even *they* were subject to his scrutiny—should they disapprove of his *crimes.*' Warreshta hesitated, watching the look of horror emerge on Eleanor's face as she went on to describe her father's methods, and how he inflicted death on those who objected to his ruling.

'Such was the fear he instilled in his people,' she went on, 'he would test them—for his amusement. Once—to assess their loyalty—he filled a gold chalice with precious gems and left it in the centre of the street, knowing their hungry eyes were watching. When he returned the following day, to retrieve it, it had not been touched.'

'How can someone—*anyone!*—inflict such control and terror on others?' said Eleanor, unable to grasp the reality of the monster the Dhampir had called, "Father."

'Everyone, including myself, feared him. He was capable of anything. Images of his repulsive deeds have stayed with me, since. And those who were like him—those he "created"—stayed loyal to his madness.'

'Created? You mean—like—Reece and—'

'No! Not like *them!*' Wareeshta interrupted. 'My father had to ... *feed!*'

'Feed?'

'On human blood.'

Eleanor's eyes widened.

'It was part of his "pact" with the *Devil*,' Wareeshta explained as if to justify her father's affliction. 'And, by doing so, he discovered his victims could be like him—should he choose it. In a matter of months, my village gradually became a pit of mounting "corpses" who could rise from the dead, leaving those who remained "alive" fearing they would be next. It was then I realised, my father had to be stopped.'

'But how?' asked Eleanor. 'How can something already dead be ...' Her voice trailed when she was reminded of Kai; he had been brutally murdered, and yet ... he *lived!* But that was different; he had been taken from Purgatory by the Elliyan, and allowed to walk among mortals as a "human" to disguise his ghostly form. No—it was not the same. Kai was a good soul.

'You mean ... be *killed?*' said Wareeshta.

Eleanor nodded.

'There is still *life*—so to speak—within them. And as long as there is a flicker of that ... well ... all living things eventually die—no matter what. Therefore, I secretly chose to be the one to stop him.'

'You—*killed* your father?' Eleanor whispered aloud as she leaned forward, to engage herself more with the Dhampir.

'To kill him, was only to maim him,' Wareeshta returned. 'No—my father had to be *destroyed!*'

'Did you succeed?'

'While the betrayal was difficult—the task was harder. I was naïve, thinking I could end his reign of terror—and I tried—but, my attempt was in vain; I failed to deliver the final blow.'

Eleanor shook her head, unable to make sense of the Dhampir's statement. Wareeshta paused and looked down at the young woman who was clinging to her every word and toiled over whether to divulge the reason behind her failed attempt to execute her own father. But, despite the look of disbelief on the girl's face, it was evident she was curious to know; she sensed Eleanor's eagerness, saw it in her body language when she leaned a little closer to her, intrigued. Yes, the girl wanted to know.

*Then you shall,* she thought. 'I neglected to remove his head.'

Eleanor gasped and recoiled in her seat as she raised her hands to her face, horrified. Wareeshta almost smiled, thinking it amusing, but knew there was nothing humorous in the devastation her father had left behind.

'What happened? What did you do, then?'

'Because of my ... error of judgement, I had no choice but to flee. It was only a matter of time though, before his loyal followers would come looking for me. So, I left my home—Wallachia—for the last time, with a new life beckoning.'

'Then ... is he—your father—still alive?'

Wareeshta shook her head.

'*Nu!* He fell victim to another.'

'Who?'

Suddenly aware of dawn's lazy ascent, Wareeshta hesitated and looked up at the window, leaving Eleanor eagerly waiting for her reply; her brief contemplation of the coming day was interrupted, by the sound of the young woman's beating heart, vying for her attention.

'Justice was done,' she then resumed, looking back at Eleanor. 'That is all that mattered. And though the "deed" was carried out, it made no difference to my situation; I could never return home.'

'Where did you go?'

'For years, I travelled from village to village, and, to protect my identity, I changed my name …' She paused, in a moment of reflection.

Curious, Eleanor leaned forward again, another question hanging from her tongue …

'I tried to keep to myself,' Wareeshta then jumped in, avoiding it; she did not want anyone to know her real name. 'But I was cast out by the arrogance of those who judged me for *what*—and not *who*—I was.'

'How did they find out?'

'I, also, needed to *feed*,' she revealed in a flat tone. 'It was all I knew. I had to survive.'

Eleanor peered at the Dhampir, stumped. *Feed?* she thought, swallowing, then squirmed, now feeling extremely uncomfortable in her chair. Her eyes darted about the chamber as if searching for a way out. When their eyes met, the Dhampir grinned, adding to her mounting concern.

'You have nothing to fear,' said Wareeshta, conscious of Eleanor's distress. 'I was taught to control my urges, a long time ago.'

Eleanor released a short sigh of relief, along with the tension that had built up inside her, then asked; 'Taught? By whom?'

'The Sorceress,' she replied. 'She came upon me, by chance. I had become careless and weak—I barely knew my mind. And, because of my "sickness," I was eventually sought out—by the residents of a village, where I had taken shelter—and hunted, like a wild animal. Had it not been for the Sorceress, they would have succeeded. L'Ordana took me under her wing, and, in time, I learned to favour human food. It is now my preference. I was—' She stopped short, to correct herself. '*Am* indebted to her—for saving my life.'

Eleanor narrowed her eyes, detecting an element of doubt in the Dhampir, then bravely said, 'And she intended on having that debt re-paid. In other words—the Sorceress had plans for you.'

Wareeshta hesitated, hearing the irony in Eleanor's words. *"The Sorceress had plans for you."* She shared a knowing glance with the girl, suddenly woken to how clever she was—and admired her for it. But when something reminded her of her loyalty to her mistress, Wareeshta turned away, shaking her head, knowing precisely what it was: retribution.

'The Sorceress protects me from those who would have me destroyed,' she retorted, feeling the need to justify her loyalty.'

'While she uses you to create warriors for her benefit,' Eleanor argued. 'Look at the innocent lives that have been destroyed: my grandfather was denied the right to see his daughter grow, and then to see *her* become a mother—*my* mother! And Tam, who was simply in the wrong place at the wrong time. And then—and then there is Asai—'

'I was not responsible for the death of the *Strange One's* family!' Wareeshta swiftly retorted, her nostrils flaring at the accusation. '*They* destroyed themselves!'

Eleanor abruptly rose from her seat to confront Wareeshta. 'Perhaps—but they were driven to it!'

The Dhampir drew back, impressed by the girl's valour as she stood her ground.

'And his wife was murdered by that—that vile creature,' she added, pointing at the door as if the Valkyrie were standing there.

'I am aware of the perpetrator!' Wareeshta hit back. 'While Kara takes pleasure in the misery of others, I—' She stopped herself. 'None of it was *my* choice, I tell you!'

Eleanor withdrew her vocal attack on the Dhampir, in response to her defiance—the hint of regret in Wareeshta's defence confirming her suspicions as it dawned on her: 'You mean—you were *forced?*'

'At first, I refused,' said Wareeshta. 'But, in time, my human side began to wane; my lack of contact with mortals eventually brought to the surface my other side—my father's influence. It proved quite challenging—trying to hide it. But the Sorceress knew and I quickly became her obsession. She then plagued me to use my "gift", as she calls it. However, I stood my ground and ignored her requests. But as time wore on, those "requests" became urgent and demanding, making it difficult for me to refuse. So, I planned to escape. That is when Kara intervened. She had had her suspicions and threatened to inform the Sorceress of my plans. I denied it. But Kara persisted and tormented me with her demands, insisting I "change her," or else …'

'Change her—into a Dhampir?'

Wareeshta nodded.

'In exchange for her silence. Kara knew it would make her powerful—and a great threat to the mistress. I refused, of course—making matters worse, which infuriated her. And, because of it, she betrayed me; with no shred of loyalty in her bones, she took great pleasure in divulging my plans to the Sorceress—for which I was punished.'

'But why did you not betray Kara, by divulging *her* intentions to the Sorceress?'

Wareeshta grunted. 'You have no idea what the Valkyrie is capable of,' she stated. 'Kara was clever. She bided her time, slowly planting the seed until she finally convinced L'Ordana—not only of my betrayal—but of a plot to kill her. Despite my denial and pleas of innocence, I knew it was pointless. Therefore, I had no choice; I had to bow to L'Ordana's demands, then. Any refusal, on my part, and she would have had Kara "dispatch" me. That threat still holds—which would please the Valkyrie.'

Eleanor's mouth gaped as she listened with intense interest, finally grasping the Dhampir's situation. 'So, you are also *bound* to her,' she stated.

'Because I have been denied human contact,' said Wareeshta, '—save for the brief encounter with any *mortal* I am forced to change—I am more Dhampir now than ever,' she admitted.

'Surely, there must be a way out for you?' Eleanor suggested, with an edge of sympathy. Wareeshta considered the young woman she had been ordered to interrogate—even torture, should the need arise; she was showing her kindness—another human trait she had misplaced, along the way. In her short acquaintance with Eleanor, she had come to recognise some of the attributes she herself had simply … *forgotten!*

'There … could be a way out,' she said.

Eleanor's brows shot up. If that were true, then perhaps … Dare she even hope?

'There is … *someone,*' Wareeshta revealed. 'But—I do not know if I can trust him,' she added, returning to the window. Time was pressing, and at odds with her now; if she failed to act quickly, there was a risk Kara would soon show her face and take matters into her own hands. She then caught sight of the sun's rays doing their best to burn through the early morning mist. She contemplated them, deciding they would soon be lost to the darkening clouds, already creeping in like a sinister plaque.

'*Him?*' Eleanor quizzed, watching her closely. 'Whom do you speak of?'

'A Warlock,' she replied.

Eleanor froze.

# Chapter Twelve

*Balloch*

The first light of dawn barely pushed its way through the thick, grey clouds that had formed, bringing with it a heaviness—the weight of its arrival bearing down on the six figures beneath it. Reece raised his head sharply to the distant rumbling of nature's warning, telling them it was about to deliver its wrath on all it coveted. With no allies or enemies, every living thing was at its mercy.

Asai and Tam followed his gaze.

'I hear it,' the Samurai remarked.

'Aye!' added Tam. ''Tis coming from the north.'

'What is coming from the north?' Rosalyn asked, followed by curious looks from Onóir and Gill, who shared confused glances as they searched the morning sky.

'Nothing to concern you, here,' Reece assured them, forcing a smile. 'There is a storm building, but I doubt it will come this way.'

'But that is where they're taking her,' said Rosalyn, fearing the worst as she strained to listen for the sound of thunder. 'Eleanor is terrified of storms!'

Reece felt helpless as an awkward silence fell between them—each not knowing what to say to the other. *A storm is the least of our worries*, he thought, refraining from sharing his real concerns with his daughter; she was upset enough, as it was. He glanced at Asai.

The Samurai discreetly shook his head. He still sensed nothing of Eleanor. Perhaps that had been a good thing. He would *know* if Eleanor was dead; he would feel it inside—the emptiness. His eyes then rested on Rosalyn, knowing her pain.

'She is well, Rosalyn-dono,' he lied, in his attempt to ease her dread.

Although she doubted Asai's words, Rosalyn forced a smile, thankful for his ongoing efforts to convince her. Still and all … a mother's instinct …

'We will bring her back,' he added, sensing her reservations. 'That much I promise.' *Dead or alive.*

A quick subtle nod from Tam begged the Samurai to follow him as he made his way to the outhouse, where the horses waited by the small stable. Asai, misreading the Highlander's signal, at first, lingered; when Tam prompted him, again, eyeballing him, the Samurai gave him a brief nod, and they both discreetly left, leaving husband and wife, mother and son, to say their last farewells.


Reece and Onóir held one other's parting gaze. He slowly moved towards his wife and peered into her blue eyes; they reminded him of Eleanor. As he opened his mouth to speak, Onóir gently placed her small hand on his full lips. Rosalyn and Gill looked on, feeling awkward.

'I may never see you again, my love,' Onóir began, insisting on his silence, 'or look into those enticing green eyes. You stole my heart with them the first time … every time!' Holding on to her husband, Onóir then raised herself onto her toes and, tilting her head, placed her lips against his, languishing in their softness, never wanting to part from them.

Reece drew back and, holding her at arm's length, looked down into the face of the woman he had never stopped loving, knowing she was right; the possibility that they may never see each other again …

'It was providence that brought us here,' she continued, disrupting his thoughts. 'At least, this time, we have been given the chance denied us, all those years ago. The time, so cruelly snatched away, has been given back—to make right the wrong that was done to us. Now we can say goodbye, as goodbyes should be said.'

'Listen to me, Onóir,' he said, with intent, refusing to believe that this was the end for them. 'We will fulfil our vow to Oran, then *I* will finish this. I will take back my life from the one who took it and end my days with you. Just a few more, and then we can live in peace, together. For this time, I will return. Will you do that? Will you wait for me?'

As Onóir held her tears under his grip of determination, she finally nodded; it was all she could do. And when she smiled, the years seemed to slip from her face. For a brief moment, time was handed back to the couple; the young, vivacious woman Reece married had briefly returned. He could not help himself. He pressed his lips firmly on hers, returning what was given, with the purity of a love no one could divide.

Onóir peered into her husband's eyes for the last time, savouring every precious moment. Before they parted, a single tear trickled from his right eye; she caught it as it fell, clenching her fist so as not to let it escape. Closing her eyes, she opened her hand and kissed it, tasting the sweetness of his sadness. And, when nothing more was to be said between them, she simply turned and made for the cottage. She never looked back.

Caught in their moment, Reece watched the young woman leave him, with her head held high as she walked away with the familiar air of confidence, he had always admired in her. But when he blinked, reality delivered its brutal blow; he now saw her, bent over with age as she fumbled at the door. He stirred, wanting to go to her when she paused, holding her chest, where the pain had returned. But he remained, knowing there was nothing he could do. And yet, there was one thing he could do … and that was to return to her, to be with her for as long as she had left, and to keep telling her— His heart suddenly skipped a precious beat when she closed the door, disappearing behind it, leaving him once again—the empty feeling telling him he was fooling himself.

Rosalyn observed her parents with poignancy as the two parted with a sense of mutual understanding. She envied their strength and bravery. She knew her mother was in acceptance of their fate, however, was uncertain of her father's feelings. It broke her heart to see him as he kept his eyes fixed on his wife until she left his sight. Rosalyn heard him take a deep breath before letting it go, in a slow release of longing. She doubted his awareness of it.

Whatever his feelings, one thing was clear to Rosalyn: Reece was a man of his word. She now believed he would follow through with his vow to Oran—but most of all, to his wife. There was no doubting the purpose of his pledges.

'She will not be alone … Reece,' she told him, still unable to bring herself to call him "Father." 'I will not leave her. We will be here—waiting—until …' She paused and then swallowed. '… you return.'

Reece remained motionless before slowly turning his head to acknowledge his daughter. He hesitated. 'Let us hope so,' he replied, then turned away to join his two colleagues, still carrying with him the emptiness inside his slow-beating heart.

Rosalyn closed her eyes as he walked away, plagued by the terrible guilt of having to lie to him, again, about the true extent of Onóir's illness, and yet, deep inside, she had an inkling he already knew.

She then became aware of her son's lingering presence, it dragging her from her inner torment—and the overwhelming sense of dread that was waiting to pounce. There was no avoiding it; it had finally come, in all its glory.

It was now *her* turn to say goodbye.

Rosalyn delved deep into her heart and mind, hoping to find the same strength as her parents—to have the courage to let her only son go. Taking a deep breath, she turned and smiled, gradually releasing her nerves. Gill smiled—an unconvincing smile—back at his mother, from the side of his mouth, dreading the inevitable.

A sudden, awful quietness crowded the air around them. It was the first stillness of the morning—a stillness Gill had not noticed before. *So why now?* he thought. An unexpected, cool breeze swept by, brushing the nape of his neck, and disturbing the calmness; he shuddered as it crept by.

Staring at his mother, Gill sensed the anguish building inside her; it was etched on her face as she tried to fight the tears. But he understood her sadness was divided—between him and her parents. He stepped closer.

Rosalyn looked up at her son and narrowed her eyes; he had grown taller—leaner, too—and even looked … "mature". *How is that possible?* she thought. *And in such a short time!* It was then she was quickly woken to the realisation, that the "boy" was gone forever. And now, in his place, stood the key to their future—and their fate: her son—the *man.*

'Look at you!' she grinned with pride, acknowledging his new physique. 'You are turning into a fine man, Gillis Shaw.'

Gill raised a curious brow. She had called him "Gillis". Now he knew she was being serious; she only called him by his full name when he was being scolded for some wrong-doing. Despite occasionally passing the blame to his sister, his mother could always see through him—and his grandmother was not always there to protect him from her chastising. But that was when he was younger. Again, he longed for those days.

Gill was now more than aware of the unknown journey he faced, and it preyed on his inner dread. Kai had been right about the Dhampir, and he was now grateful for their company, secretly admitting he would not have been able to face the arduous task alone. Yet, beneath the dread, an edge of excitement picked away at his inquisitive side but was then quickly diminished the moment he met with the desolation in his mother's heartbroken eyes. He did not want to leave her, knowing Eleanor was still out there … *somewhere!* His reluctance began to show as he battled between his head and his heart. The farewell to his grandmother was heart-wrenching enough. "You will never be alone," she had promised him, with a sly wink. He had thought nothing of it, at first; she had always shared a wink with him, out of fondness. But there had been a defined look in her eye that rang through—just before they parted—a look that would never leave him. He sighed.

'Listen to me, Gillis Shaw!' Rosalyn began, taking him from his torment. She engaged with his hazel eyes, blinking when she noticed unusual tiny flecks of gold in them; they seemed to glint at her. She had never noticed them before. But how could she? They were never there … until now. 'Place your trust in the three who will accompany you on this journey. Do not forget who they are. Beneath their affliction lie the hearts of *men!*'

'Men?' he echoed, raising his brows. It was a failed attempt to lighten the mood.

'You do as they say,' she told him, spurning his remark. Her voice was stern and urgent. 'They have a duty to protect you—as you will them—when the time arrives. You need to stay safe—to stay *alive!*—for all our sakes.'

Gill's face dropped into the gloom and dismal reality of his mother's insistence. She glanced over at the stable, where the three Dhampir were making their final preparations. The time was approaching.

'They are who they are—through no fault of their own,' she reminded him, sensing the need. 'We are all given choices to make throughout our short lives. Some choose well, while others do not. Reece and the others had no choice. Remember that.'

Rosalyn stared up at the sombre face of her son, longing for the "boy" to return, reminding herself he was now a man—and it was only right she treated him with the integrity of one.

'Your path has been waiting for you to tread, beckoning since your birth, and will lead you to your destination. And I am thankful you will not be alone. Although I have my misgivings, regarding the Elliyan, your fate is also their great concern. I see that now. You cannot change the course of your path, Gillis. As with *them,'* she added, pointing to the Dhampir, *'you* also have no choice.'

Her blunt statement rang through, to the core of his heart. Her words had been simple, honest … and powerful. She was right, and he knew it.

Gill's foolishness and immaturity melted away with every word his mother had just spoken. He stood tall, inhaling the morning dampness, feeling his growing strength guide him—along with her honesty.

'I will not fail you, Rosalyn,' he stated, with pride.

She threw him a sideward glance; it was the first time he had called her by her name. Tempted to scold him, she thought better of it, and let it go—along with the "boy."

'And I vow to return—with Eleanor,' he persisted.

'And your father?'

Gill stopped and frowned. *'That* remains to be seen.'

Rosalyn pressed her lips together, seething through her nose. She opened her mouth to dispute his comment.

'Gill!' the voice called, distracting mother and son.

A sense of relief came over Rosalyn, hearing Reece call out; she was grateful for his intervention. The notion of herself and Gill parting on harsh words would have been too much to bear. She then prompted her son to join them, avoiding the dispute, but most notably the prolonged farewell.

*Some things are for the best!* she dubiously told herself.

As Gill turned to leave, he paused when a sudden rush of exhilaration came over him. It urged him to throw his strong arms around his mother, enveloping her in the same way he used to, when he was a child, with repeated promises of their return—"no matter what!"—before releasing her. She forced him away with words of encouragement, watching as he checked to make sure his sister's precious dagger was firmly attached to his hip. As he strode away from her, wearing the luxurious damask cloak that belonged to his father, she took a sharp intake of breath; he looked so much like Oran, from behind.

The longbow Gill had mastered—thanks to Kai—with its leather barrel filled with new arrows, clung to his back. Rosalyn prayed he would never have to use it, but knew, deep down, she was fooling no one but herself. She had contemplated giving him the Albrecht sword—the one that returned with Farrow—when she was reminded of a remark once made by Oran, regarding the weapon: "It must be given by *me*, come the time." He had never explained why, like so many other things, and so, she decided to hold on to it, hoping it was the right decision. She assumed Gill had been privy to its presence yet was confident he and his sister had never *seen* it. Oran had always kept his prized weapons hidden from the eyes of their curious children. *No!* she decided, avoiding temptation. *The Albrecht stays with me … come the time.* Besides, he had the Dhampirs' protection; Reece and his companions would see to that.

Rosalyn clasped her hands together, watching the four as they rode away. Regardless of the simple nods from Asai and Tam, as they bade their farewell, something was comforting in their brief goodbyes—like a guarantee of their return. Her thoughts then briefly turned to Meghan—Gill's young beau. She would think of something to dissuade the girl. It was only right *she* broke the news to her; had it been left to Gill …

Rosalyn felt the lure of their departure battle against her duty to stay with her mother. Inside, she felt the want—the desperate need—to saddle Farrow and follow them. She swallowed the rising lump in her throat, urging them to look back. Now she knew how Onóir had felt, all those years ago. The parting was intolerable. But the need to go was short-lived, by the distraction of Rave pounding by her, howling as she longed to join her master.

'No, Rave! Wait!'

Rosalyn spun, on hearing her mother, as Onóir beckoned the hound to return. However, the dog had failed to hear the old woman's timid voice, on her slow approach, prompting Rosalyn to call out; 'Come, Rave!'

The hound stopped, indecisive as to which way to go. Rosalyn called her again. This time, Rave obediently retreated, with her tail tucked between her legs.

As the dog sat between them, looking up from one to the other, itching to go, she whimpered and whined, sensing the loss of her companion. Onóir and Rosalyn felt for her as their eyes filled with tears. But the fight to restrain them was now no longer necessary, as the last few days of overwhelming mixed emotions finally gave way, in the privacy of their own company.

Mother and daughter held one another in the quietness of their humble surroundings. A defined chill filled the damp air; late autumn had finally arrived, and with it the feeling that winter was ready to sneak up, at any given moment, should they become complacent. A feeling of loneliness suddenly washed over Rosalyn. It was then she realised its meaning when Onóir's weakened body fell limp against her, bringing her to her knees.

'Maw?!' she whispered, exasperated.

Rosalyn's heart pounded, feeling the rush of fear through her body as she held her mother in her arms. Rave scurried around them, sniffing and whining at Onóir's side. Rosalyn looked sharp along the path where the four had ridden away. She wanted to call out—force them back. But when Onóir slowly moved her head from side to side, urging her daughter to resist, Rosalyn understood why.

Then something struck her. She glanced towards the house.

'Kai! He will help us. He will know what to—' Feeling the grip of her mother's hand, Rosalyn stopped and looked down.

'He is gone!' Onóir whispered.

Rosalyn's eyes flinched with panic as she shook her head in denial.

'Oh, no, Maw, not now!' she pleaded, staring into the old woman's serene face. A single drop of rain fell, bringing Rosalyn's gaze up to meet the grey sky as it bore its heavy blanket down on them, its unwanted, sombre presence, adding to the foreboding atmosphere that had taken grip. One by one, the droplets followed in perfect rhythm, *Splat! Splat! Splat!* persisting, growing louder as they hit the dry ground.

Rosalyn could now see the weakness in Onóir's heartbroken eyes as her tears merged with the rain; life was fading from their vividness. Then, in what seemed like an admission of defeat, they slowly closed …

# Chapter Thirteen

*Balloch Castle*

*Warlock!*

Eleanor felt the rush of life flush through her exhausted body, reigniting her energy, and alerting her.

*Surely not!* she thought. She stared at the Dhampir as the word "Warlock" echoed in her mind, asking herself; *Could it be Oran?* Eleanor's mind raced, fearing Wareeshta's motive was one of trickery and tomfoolery. Had it been a ploy on the Dhampir's part, suggesting they *knew* who her father was? *How could they possibly know?* she thought, chewing on the side of her lower lip. The Sorceress would have hinted at it and, if not, then Kara, for sure; the Valkyrie had made no secret, letting her thoughts be known. No. They could not know. *They can never know!* she told herself, determined. *Stay calm!*

Eleanor held her silence while, inside, her mind screamed with thoughts of dread. She stared at Wareeshta's slight frame as the Dhampir continued to look out the window. *What is she staring at?* she wondered.

In the distance, Wareeshta caught sight of Nakia—Kara's pet. There was no mistaking the hawk's black, plumage as it circled, searching for food. She loathed it, as much as she did its vile mistress.

Lured from her wandering thoughts, by Eleanor's agitated silence, Wareeshta spun, catching the girl off-guard. Eleanor jolted. As the Dhampir approached her, she swallowed, seeing the curious look in her deepening gaze. Wareeshta then tilted her head, her eyes slowly narrowing, filled with inquiry. She could hear—*feel*—the pulsating beat of Eleanor's heart; it seemed to pound in her ears, within the quietude of the chamber. Something was making their prisoner anxious. Wareeshta then paused within inches of Eleanor's face—the girl's rapid breathing a sure giveaway.

*She does know something!* 'Would you like to share it with me?' she asked, her voice slow and steady.

Eleanor lowered her eyes, intimidated by the Dhampir's intriguing presence.

'I heard Kara whisper it to you,' she pressed.

Eleanor's mouth slowly opened as she lifted her eyes, her breath quivering from nervousness.

'"Your lover!"' the Dhampir then prompted.

Eleanor's eyes widened; she thought she had swayed the Dhampir's suspicions.

'I know you have spoken to him—to Asai—through his thoughts. I used to observe his moments of solitude, in his private world of *rumination*. I envied his ability to do so.'

Eleanor edged away, her eyes fixed, challenging the Dhampir's suspicious stare as she fumbled through her thoughts, searching for something to say—*anything!*—to prevent her from mentioning Oran. She could not even begin to imagine the implications, should they discover the connection between herself and the Warlock, and the pleasure it would give them, knowing Oran was her father.

'What did Asai tell you?' Wareeshta persisted.

Eleanor, defiant in her loyalty, remained silent.

'I would strongly suggest you tell me, or'—Wareeshta paused, throwing a glance at the door—'it will be forced from you … by Kara.'

The mere mention of the Valkyrie's name made Eleanor shudder. 'It is my belief …' she began, then hesitated, trying to dismiss the horror of Kara's malevolent influence, '… that they plan to save me.'

Wareeshta drew back. '*They?*'

Eleanor swallowed, her words then stuttering as she tried to speak; 'My—my grand—Reece, Asai and T—'

'The fools!' Warreshta whispered to herself before returning her attention to the girl. 'I urge you to tell me what you know,' she insisted.

'Why should I?' snapped Eleanor, finding her strength again. 'It seems I have nothing to gain by telling you *anything!* Why should I trust you?'

Wareeshta, clenching her fists, glared back at Eleanor with her deep-set eyes, trying, with great difficulty, to maintain composure against her rising anger; no, the girl did not want to witness her wrath.

'Because … it may save your *life!*' she revealed, gritting her teeth. 'And *theirs!*' Still frustrated, she turned away from Eleanor, pacing the stone floor to find some inner calm.

'*Theirs?*' Eleanor blurted, following the Dhampir's movements. 'I—I don't understand.'

Wareeshta halted, struck by an absurd notion. Her eyes flashed to Eleanor. For several moments she stared at the girl, with uncertainty, and wondered … It could mean the end for both of them if … No—it was out of the question. But as she witnessed the look of alarm on the girl's face and the growing fear in her pale, blue eyes as she stood there helpless in her silent plea, it was clear how much she cared for the fools, who were willing to risk their lives to save her.

*No one has ever done that for me,* she thought. Suddenly, Wareeshta felt compelled to act—to make a bold move—then stopped to ask herself; *Why should I?* She was more than aware of the consequences, should she interfere, however, knew the reason for doing so, her human side influencing her. She glanced at the door and listened; all appeared quiet, beyond it. *Good.* Acting on impulse, she rushed to Eleanor's side—the girl flinching from her advance.

'Listen to me!' she said, her voice low and full of purpose. 'If your friends come within sight of this place, the Sorceress will know it. They will be captured and lured into her bondage again—and this time, she will show them no mercy. Nothing would please her more. *You*, child, are simply *bait!* She wants to know—in exchange for your life—the location of the one who freed them from their bonds. He was also her prisoner. It was he who conjured the plan to escape, along with the help of your grandfather and his two companions, who helped to release him. In return, he deceived the Sorceress, by breaking their bonds. For that, she is out for revenge. Should your—Asai, and his colleagues—fall into her lair, they will be without their liberator's help.'

As Wareeshta delivered the harsh reality of Eleanor's situation—should the others make any attempt to rescue her—she found herself scrutinising the girl's reaction: she was chewing on her lip—a clear sign of nervousness; and her eyes … they were now diverted in thought, and constantly blinking—a sign of apprehension. But she could smell it—the young woman's mounting fear. And yet, she was asking no questions, still choosing to keep her silence.

*Now, why is that?* she thought, narrowing her eyes as Eleanor continued to avoid her suspicions. Wareeshta's eyes shot up, with realisation.

*She knows!*

'L'Ordana will find out where their "liberator" has gone, one way or another,' Wareeshta persisted. 'And when she does, I assure you … she will have Kara "dispatch" him; in fact, she will have the Valkyrie "dispatch" them all. And who will save you, then? Your brother?'

Eleanor looked sharp, momentarily frozen, her mouth gaping from the shock of what she had just heard.

'*Nu!*' Wareeshta continued, shaking her head. 'She will enslave *him,* and then I will be forced to inflict on your brother that which I have done to all the others … against my will. This is why I urge you to tell me. Already, I have risked enough, by speaking with you in this unspoken manner.'

Eleanor hesitated, alerted to the sudden conflict between her head and her heart. What was she to do …?

'Have I not shared my story with you?' the Dhampir pressed further. 'And in confidence?'

Despite it, Eleanor was still unsure, and at a loss. *Oh, Asai, where are you?!* she inwardly cried out.

Wareeshta, her frustrations gnawing at her again, by the girl's stubbornness to stay quiet, sighed. 'I can help you,' she then admitted, as though hearing her inner cry for help.

Eleanor drew back, thrown by the statement.

'But you are still bonded to the Sorceress.'

'To my misfortune,' said Wareeshta.

'Then how could you possibly help me?' she returned, frowning. 'And *why* would you?' What's in it for you?'

Wareeshta lifted her head and raised a brow, taken aback by the girl's unexpected retaliation; she did not expect it. Nevertheless, she still had to admire her courage as she stood there, staunch, determined, and with her innocent eyes firmly fixed on hers, waiting for her response.

'*Something* that is rightfully mine,' she retorted. 'However, it is no longer your—' She stopped abruptly, her eyes darting, distracted by something.

'What is it?' Eleanor whispered, dropping her brave front, then edging closer to the Dhampir.

Wareeshta leapt to the door and listened.

'Footsteps!'

Eleanor recoiled, holding her breath … then felt it: the sudden, uncontrollable rise and fall of her breathing, it returning to feed on her fears.

Sensing her anguish, Wareeshta promptly turned to her.

'I believe—you know of whom I speak,' she said—the urgency in her tone, preying on Eleanor's anxiousness. 'The *one* who released your grandfather and his colleagues.'

Eleanor drew a frantic breath and shook her head.

'I know nothing of the Warlock,' she blurted, her eyes now watching the door—unaware of her fatal error.

Wareeshta tilted her head again. 'I did not say he was a "Warlock."'

As the colour drained from Eleanor's features, and with fear now visible in her startled eyes, the truth became clear. Wareeshta knew the girl could no longer hide it.

Eleanor's body shook as she raised her trembling hands to her face, unsure what the Dhampir might do. She then gasped when Wareeshta moved closer. Too close. *Think! Think, Eleanor!*

The Dhampir hesitated and glanced at the door again. Irritated, she looked back at Eleanor, her face set, committed.

'It is your choice,' she warned, glancing back and forth, between the door and the young woman—the perseverance in her voice driving Eleanor's fear. 'Tell me'—she pointed at the door—'or you will have to answer to *her!*'

Eleanor stared at the door, her chest heaving as she shook her head, in denial. Her mouth opened, her silent fear now filling the chamber. She tried to swallow it, but the tightness and dryness in her throat would not let her.

'Then say goodbye to everything you knew. By the time Kara is finished with you, you will have no recollection of it—or *them*—should you live.'

Eleanor clamped her hand over her mouth, trying desperately to prevent the words from escaping. She shrunk back, battling with her thoughts as panic took hold. *Tell her! Say it! No! No! Say it!* Where was the voice of reason, now, when she so desperately needed it? And Asai? Where was he? Her head throbbed.

Wareeshta's eyes continued to dart between Eleanor and the door. Back and forth, back and forth, intimidating her further.

*I can't do it!* she screamed inside. But the looming threat of everything she loved eventually forced its disturbing hand on her. '*Elboru!*' she blurted, then drew a sharp breath, eyes wide, shocked by her revelation.

As the seconds went by, they both stared at one another, carefully gathering their thoughts within the charged silence, waiting for it to settle.

Having put the girl through the rigour of her questioning, Wareeshta felt an element of guilt, after witnessing her reaction. But she had to do it. She needed to know—for their sakes. She then tilted her head towards Eleanor and nodded.

'Go on,' she said, her voice now soft, encouraging, wanting to reassure the girl.

'He—the *Warlock*—is gone to Elboru,' said Eleanor, her voice sombre, almost mournful. 'It's north of here.'

Wareeshta's mouth curved into a brief smile. 'You have done the right thing, Eleanor,' she said. But then, in a cruel—and unexpected—move, the Dhampir, casting off all evidence of emotion, simply turned and left, locking the door behind her.

Confused and distressed, Eleanor ran after her, on hearing the lock being turned. She tried the handle—*Oh, no!*—then placed her ear to the door's thick, barrier. Holding her breath, she listened to the sedated silence, on the other side … No footsteps—coming or going.

Nothing.

In a moment of intimidated madness, Eleanor convinced herself that she had betrayed her world with the utterance of one word:

*Elboru!*

Stepping back from the barrier that prevented her freedom, she closed her eyes and hung her head, feeling the shame of her betrayal. She then looked at her hands, where the blood and dust had dried, now feeling the stinging pain. And yet, it failed to mar her shame.

'Oh, Asai … what have I just done?'

# Chapter Fourteen

Magia Nera stood alone in the confines of his holding, taking in the so-called comforts *she* had purposely provided for him. Although time had picked away at its contents, the effect of its toll had hardly blemished the furnishings. He admired the quality the former occupants had lovingly applied to it, it adding to the grandeur of what had once been their home. His new "abode" had initially been a most welcome consolation—a far cry from the loathsome, rotting cell he had been thrown into—*like a common thief!*—in the citadel. He recalled the smug look on her face when he realised, he had been housed inside the castle's private chapel—a deceitful display of humour on her part. However, despite his initial discomfort within its virtuous walls, it had little or no effect on him now; all traces of righteousness had been stripped away, after the condemnation of the poor soul who had once stood trial at its altar.

*Oh, the irony of it!* he thought.

But he would always resent her favouritism towards the other Warlock, she lavishing Oran with the finer things they had once known and shared, in their previous lives together. But Oran was gone now and, with no one else to bribe, he knew she was desperate—regardless of her attempts to hide it. Yes, he could see right through her.

He glanced sideways, smirking to himself, now aware of her lingering presence behind him—not to mention her growing anger.

'Well?!' she snapped, staring at his long, sable hair as he stood before the white-marbled altar.

Magia remained with his back to her, musing over her words of bargaining, even though, in truth, they were stained with betrayal. As he considered his options, his eyes lowered and glided over the altar. He then ran his long fingers over its cold surface, gathering the thick dust that had settled from years of neglect, and raised his hand to inspect it. Repelled by its smell and touch, he flicked it away.

Finally, he turned to acknowledge her.

As he did so, he saw Wareeshta slip from her shadowy corner, and caught her eyes; they glowed amber with warmth and calm. He smiled at her before diverting his gaze back to L'Ordana.

Magia drew his head back slightly, scrutinising the Sorceress as she sauntered up the aisle towards him. His pale lips parted, tempted to remark, "What a stunning bride you would have made!" But as she moved into the chapels' candlelight, he paused …

*How different she looks!* he thought, regarding her altering appearance, thinking it a trick of the light. He inclined his head slightly. *Oh, but I think not!* The subtle signs of time were beginning to make their mark: her pale skin had lost some of its glow and the lines across her forehead—though faint—were visible. *Interesting,* he mused, concluding she had not been "renewed."

'What have you decided, Magia?' she inquired further, attempting to meddle with his thoughts while struggling to maintain her composure against his arrogance.

'I have grown quite fond of this humble place,' he sneered, lifting his hands as though in admiration of it. 'It has a familiar … *ambience* attached to it. Would you agree?'

L'Ordana glared at him, bemused by his unusual remark. 'If that is how you feel,' she snapped, 'then stay, where you can rot within its reverent walls, for all I—'

'Ah! But it would be a great shame to be parted from my *Bella,*' he teased, in his seductive tone. 'Our reacquaintance has stirred up memories—despite *this* separation,' he added, indicating the constant, invisible barrier she insisted on having between them. Wareeshta, standing near, pursed her lips at his suggestion.

'Is this your choice, then?' L'Ordana persisted.

The Warlock slowly tossed his head from side to side, pondering his decision. 'Perhaps!' He shrugged. 'I have not yet decided.'

'Then I insist you make up your mind … and promptly! We are leaving—with or without you.'

'So soon?' he queried, glancing up. The early morning shone brightly, stretching its way through the small, stain-glass windows above, deftly evoking an enduring sense of radiance and colourful light. As alluring as it was, he was thankful for their raised position. 'Is this place not to your liking, or …?'

'The castle was not my choice,' she snarled, casting a wary look at Wareeshta. The abruptness of her manner was evidence of her discomfort within its depressing walls.

Magia pulled a long, sombre face. 'Painful memories, perhaps?' he suggested, preying on her thoughts.

Wareeshta's twisted face of confusion peered at her mistress when she disregarded the dark Warlock's remark, refusing to entertain his games. But as L'Ordana stared at him with a forced façade of no emotion, he, however, saw doubt and fear seeping from the pores of her ageing skin.

Fragments of a tortured past suddenly picked at her, in muddled images of daunting memories—memories she had no recollection of, and yet they were there: faint, outpouring cries of devastation, similar to those she had experienced in the girl's chamber, echoing in the back of her mind. The feeling it provoked in her was confining. Subtly, she diverted her eyes, not wanting him to see her discomfort.

Inside, L'Ordana tried making sense of the images, with no clear understanding or connection. Then, aware of Magia's disdainful scrutiny of her, she forced herself to look up. She glared at the dark Warlock with animosity, despising him for his attempt to expose her hidden vulnerabilities. *How dare you!* she seethed inside. *And in the presence of my servant.*

But Magia could not help himself. 'I tried to save her, you know,' he stated, maintaining the false sense of sympathy in his tone.

She looked at him, her brows knitting together, perplexed by his statement. '"Save her?"' she echoed. 'What do you mean? Whom do you speak of?'

'*Sarah*,' he hinted, returning his fixed stare. His refusal to sway from her ignorance was palpable as she noted the intimation in his eyes and tone.

'I know no one of this name,' she flatly replied.

Magia slowly shook his head in feigned disappointment, tutting, '*Vergognoso!*'

'Shameful?!' she retorted. 'For what?!'

'That you should forget her name,' he said, still toying with her emotions. He grinned, sensing the rage building inside her. Wareeshta stepped back, sensing it, too; she did not want to be part of their conflicting games yet was finding it difficult to avoid his occasional glances.

'Whose name?!' L'Ordana yelled, unable to contain her anger and frustration.

'Why … your mother's!' he stated, pleased by his ability to antagonise her.

L'Ordana jolted as the name returned, briefly haunting her thoughts. *Sarah … Sarah … Sar*— It then vanished, taking with it any possible reminiscence of her past. Irritated by his constant taunts, she returned her attention to him.

'I have no recollection of my mother,' she insisted, staring at him, bewildered. 'I never knew her.'

Magia regarded her reaction; it had seemed plausible, making him believe she had lost all memory of her mother, and yet she was haunted by something. *Fascinating!* he thought. 'Forgive me, *Bella*,' he mocked, bowing gracefully while pulling another sombre face. 'I did not mean to cause you pain.'

She rolled her eyes. 'I assure you—no "pain" was inflicted.'

A niggling doubt then entered her thoughts when he slowly raised his head to her eye level, holding his poise as he regarded her with the intensity of his warm eyes. For an instant, she feared he had placed the disturbing images in her mind, in a bid to weaken her, then disregarded the notion.

'Do not toy with me, Magia, or I will gladly leave you here with the ghosts of this place until your *thirst* runs dry. And, by then, we shall have moved on to—'

Wareeshta stepped forward, abruptly, stopping her mistress from revealing something she would later regret.

'To?' Magia asked, tipping his head slightly, with genuine interest.

She caught his curious glance, and grinned, it reminding her of the hold she maintained over him.

'I detest unfinished sentences,' he said, joining his hands. '*Per favour!* Do finish what you began.'

She sighed, playfully. 'If you insist!'

'*Grazie!*' he returned, with another graceful bow.

'I have recently become acquainted with someone of interest,' she boasted, relishing the idea of returning his taunts.

'Has Oran crawled back to you?' he said, raising a brow.

While his display of surprise amused her, she detected an underlying hint of jealousy in his tone.

'No. But I do know where he is.'

'How?' he asked, inching dangerously closer to her.

She smirked, grasping the upper hand. *A little more teasing, perhaps,* she thought, before rendering him to submission.

'At present …' she said, eyeing him, 'I have, in my residence, a relative of one of my escapees.'

He stepped back, somewhat perplexed.'

'Apparently, she is Reece's granddaughter.' Magia's eyes flickered, telling her he was musing over the revelation. 'Oh, it is a mere coincidence,' she sighed, shrugging off the monotony of having to explain it. 'But one that came as an unexpected *prize*—and, also, a great advantage to me.'

'Reece has a granddaughter?'

L'Ordana sighed again. 'It appears his wife went on to live a fruitful life. But she is dead now,' she added, dismissing Onóir's existence with the flick of a hand.

'And her offspring?'

'My interest lies with the young girl in our … "care." A pretty thing at that.'

'And does she have pretty eyes?' he sneered, wiping the smug look from her face.

As L'Ordana's face dropped at his insinuating remark, it was clear he had noticed her countenance.

'She must be special if you have not—'

'The girl has been extremely helpful in … "sharing" the location of your rival with me,' she retorted, exchanging a glance with Wareeshta.

He grunted. 'I do not doubt it,' he said, aware of their methods of forcing vital information from unwilling victims. 'But—I fail to understand something: why would Reece tell the girl where Oran has gone? Where is the connection?'

L'Ordana stopped short at his enquiries. 'There is none!' she replied, growing impatient. 'I would know it! No! She is the *fly in my ointment,* should her loving grandfather come searching for her.'

'And you think he will?'

'Reece is no fool. He knows I will not harm her … for the present. I am confident of it. They will know where we are going and will follow us—to save the girl.'

'They?'

'He is not alone. I'm afraid, Reece, Tam and Asai will have to put their new-found lives on hold, while they play the role of *Knights in Shining Armour*—unless, of course, they make an error of judgement and find themselves within their bonds again. This would be more favourable—making my task easier. Therefore, Magia,' she continued, turning to leave, 'I suggest you be swift in deciding your fate.'

He smirked. No, he was not letting her go that easily.

'And the *Book?*'

She hesitated, then glanced at Wareeshta—the two sharing a brief, knowing look before diverting their eyes from each other. L'Ordana composed herself, so as not to betray her uneasiness; she had hoped he had forgotten. 'The book is quite safe,' she lied, convincingly. 'Let it be of no concern to you.'

Sensing suspicion in her forced composure, he silently urged her to turn. *Let me see your face!*

Aware of his cynical eyes on her, L'Ordana held fast, her mind racing. If he decided to stay, so be it; she would then find the Shenn amulet, alone. Saying that … She waited a few moments while he brooded over his decision.

'Let us no longer be divided, Sorceress!' he cried, in dramatic fashion. 'I accept your terms. Willingly!'

Now more curious, Magia waited in her reverie, hoping she would face him; it vexed him not to see her face. But, to his disappointment, she did not turn; instead, she chose to remain steadfast, with her back to him as she delivered her threat.

'Then, let us understand one another, Warlock,' she began, keeping her eye on the door. 'Do not taunt me with your idiotic mind games. And should you attempt, in any way, to leave my company, I will have you cast out into the hands of sunlight, and let it do what is beneath me. The earth can then have your ashes.'

Confident she had won him over, L'Ordana moved casually towards the thick-panelled, oak door, which stared back at her from the end of the aisle. It was worn, having been subjected to the worms that had burrowed their way through its grains, over time. And though it still held some of its beauty, she hated it. She hated everything about the castle. The time for them to leave could not come soon enough.

As she neared the door, L'Ordana paused and lingered in a moment of contemplative silence—the seconds passing while Wareeshta hovered by her side with an air of suspicion. Then, like a statue coming to life, the Sorceress commanded the door to open, then drifted from the dark Warlock's company, followed closely by her servant.

Magia contemplated her exit carefully. *Now, why did you do that?* he thought. *Why did you hesitate, Bella?*

'There is no such thing as coincidence!' he snorted to himself, keeping his eyes fixed firmly on the door after she had left. He then took a turn about the chapel, his footsteps blanketed by the rug, covering the stone floor. He glanced down at its faded, worn threads, thinking how magnificent it must have been, in its former days. The castle's owners had certainly been meticulous in their choice of style and decor. But it had all been tainted by tragedy, forcing them to leave it all behind, in haste. It was evident they did not want to carry the painful memories with them. *No reminders!* He knew why.

Magia paced over the large rug, tapping the tips of his fingers together, questioning the conversation he had just had with L'Ordana. Did she have the book? He had a niggling hunch; however, could not—and would not—presume otherwise, not while he was still indisposed. He contemplated "the girl" in her captivity. There had to be a connection—somewhere. *Questions! Questions!*

He scolded himself for letting her turn the table on him, then damned her for owning the upper hand. But he had made his choice: he would go with her. Besides, he wanted the book, and when it was returned to him … He paused for thought. *So… she thinks she will also have the Shenn amulet.* He grunted at her naivety; she had no preconception of what awaited her, while the reality of him knowing what did … simply exhilarated him. He now hoped he would be there to witness it all when the time came. He had not long to wait.

Through all his self-doubt and questioning, he had momentarily failed to notice the diminished atmosphere within his holding. He stalled, letting his darkened eyes travel around the private chapel; it appeared brighter and calmer. Then drawn to the oak door, he paused and surveyed it with suspicion when something registered inside him:

he had not heard the familiar turn and click of the key—the extra precaution she had taken, despite the invisible—

He stopped, on an instinct, then tilted his head forward, narrowing his eyes, contemplating the menacing space between him and the door … and then casually reached out …

)

'Why did you lie about the book?'

L'Ordana hesitated within the dimly lit corridor that led from Magia Nera's "abode" to the solar room. She turned her head and, glancing back at the oak door, knew he would soon discover the barriers' absence and would walk freely again with her.

'He must never be made aware of the book's disappearance—or the dagger's, for that matter. Should he learn that I no longer have it, then he will do his best to escape. No—he must never possess the book. Do you understand, Wareeshta?'

The Dhampir held her mistress's ardent stare.

'Do you?!' she snapped.

Wareeshta slowly nodded; to disagree, at this moment in time, was unwise.

'It is my only hold over him,' L'Ordana continued. 'For now, it is better to have him on my side. His powers will be of great benefit— come the time—when *I* claim the Shenn. And when I have it—along with the book …' She paused, imagining the unthinkable powers she would own. 'I plan to destroy him …' She then grunted matter-of-factly. 'I plan to destroy them all!'

# Chapter Fifteen

*The Aber Hills: far north of Lac Lomond*

The *creature* glided effortlessly through vast woodlands and dense forests, intent on carrying its critical message to those awaiting it. Nothing stirred as it made its ghostly way through nature's wild and crowded abode. The signs were evident by the overgrowth as if groves of different varieties of trees had been condensed into one never-ending forest. It was unlikely no one had walked its territory; if they had, all traces of their existence had been erased by the elements, over time. But the overgrowth would soon diminish, with the sudden and late arrival of autumn. And being so far north, it was a certainty that winter was lurking, waiting to perch itself on every branch. Already, gold and copper leaves, that had dried from the unusually hot summer, were falling from the weight of the recent downpour or were being snatched from their branches by passing winds, carrying them to their resting place, among the wild shrubbery.

The *creature* listened, alert to the scurrying movements of nature's residents, glorifying in their innocence; however, they failed to notice the swift passing of the unearthly presence.

It had been Kai's preference for travel, enabling him to move swiftly when time pressed itself on the urgent requirements of his superiors— the Elliyan. To travel in the form of a man was out of the question. Too slow. Nor could he risk being seen in his ghostly form—hence the reason for his chosen route. No, there could be no more delay in his journey. He was late enough as it was—the unexpected arrival of the three Dhampir, detaining his return to Elboru. But he would have to make his report to the Elliyan brief; he had sensed Onóir's deteriorating health, and he needed to be there with her—should her time come. Fearing it was close, it drove him on.

Despite his lateness, Kai knew the Elliyan would forgive him, on hearing his *news:* the young man was en route, along with his newly-appointed *protectors*. Yes, this would please them. But time was precious, and he assumed the travellers would not be alone on their journey; he had sensed hostility creeping in from the far reaches of Urquille. It was only a matter of time before the Sorceress would be guided by the amulet, which was still in her possession. This concerned him; who was to say it was already leading her to Elboru? Regardless of it, she would eventually feel its lure drawing her to the Shenn. It was also likely the dark Warlock would be in her company. Likely? No. He was sure of it.

Kai still had some distance to cover before reaching Elboru, his journey including the treacherous *Caves of Loyne;* the location—and its route—were known only to the Servitor—a secret to call their own.

"Why should the Elliyan be privy to all our knowledge?" a colleague once said to him. "It is not right that they should have total control over our movements."

As he quickened his pace, he suddenly became aware of an unnatural yet familiar presence following him. Despite its attempt to keep its distance, he had sensed its movements, questioning the unexpected company.

Kai paused; when he did, it, also, hesitated. Then, listening intently, he let his black eyes wander until he found them, lurking among the trees, where they had been watching him.

'Come forward!' he beckoned, in his silk-like voice, calmly enticing them out. 'There is no need to conceal yourself. Not here.'

From behind a young—but sizeable—redwood tree, the form of a boy emerged. Dressed in a grubby shirt, hanging loosely over his worn, dark-brown breeches, he stomped barefoot towards the Servitor. Kai recognised the arrogant expression the child wore on his youthful features; he was rarely without it. His pale, delicate skin was free from dirt, compared to his garb, while his lifeless, grey eyes lacked any sign of friendliness.

This was Lorne.

The young boy—who had lost both his parents to one of the many plagues that had ravished the world—felt he had been deserted, due to the deadly affliction. Such was his grudge against the *Grim Reaper,* he had carried his resentment on his small shoulders until he himself eventually succumbed to the same plight.

Kai had known Lorne in Purgatory—the place where "lost souls" reside, in limbo, waiting to be plucked for others to use, for their own purpose.

Aware of the boy's anger and denial, when he first entered Purgatory, he had urged Lorne to accept his fate, in the hope the Elliyan would choose him as a Servitor. However, when the time came, and the boy had been selected, Kai began to have his doubts, sensing an underlying and disturbing hint of dark mischief in Lorne's character. Concerned, he had voiced his opinion to the Elliyan. But Lothian—the Great Warlock—had shown compassion to the boy, insisting on giving him a chance.

"Oh, he is but a child—and so cruelly struck down before his time," Lothian had pointed out, seeing the good in all things. "Do all children not display an element of mischief? Surely, we can ignore the common traits of the younger ones."

And so, the boy was given the benefit of the doubt … in spite of Kai's misgivings.

He had hoped the Great Warlock was right in his perception. Perhaps; after all, Lorne had only been in Purgatory for ten years—a snippet of time in *their* world—and, as a young Servitor, he still had much to learn.

Kai observed Lorne scratching his head, on his approach, perceiving it to be the residual effect of the invisible scars that had been inflicted on his body from the deadly plaque. His thick, dark locks lacked vitality, except for their natural red strands—occasionally caught by the light of day. Only then, did they provide any warmth to his persona.

Wary, the boy glanced around.

'Aside from nature's residents,' said Kai, catching from the corner of his eye a red squirrel going about its business, 'we are quite alone,' he assured Lorne, meeting him with a low bow—the respective greeting of their kind.

When he rose again, to converse with him, the boy had already transformed himself into the mirror image of his peer, save for his height—Lorne being a little shorter.

Kai, staring down into Lorne's onyx eyes, released a subtle grunt, irked that he had not shared the customary welcome; to neglect any acknowledgement of a fellow Servitor showed a lack of respect. Then again, it came as no surprise to Kai.

Casting aside the misdemeanour, Kai smiled thinly at his young comrade. 'I am sure nature will keep our meeting a guarded secret, within its domain.'

Lorne inhaled his surroundings, relieved to be back in his true form; he, too, preferred it. To walk among the mortals as the *boy*, brought him nothing but ill-treatment. Seen as a lowly beggar and outcast, some shunned his presence, while others called him "The Devil's Child" — because he never smiled, making his cold eyes more lifeless than they already were.

"There is nothing to smile about," he had once remarked to Kai.

Lorne returned a wry smile towards his elder, followed by a peeved silence, prompting Kai to ask; 'Why do you come to greet me, Lorne? I did not—'

'I am not here to "receive" you, Kai,' he interrupted.

Inside, Kai was perturbed by the young Servitor's lack of esteem; it was unheard of to interrupt a conversation. He pondered whether he did it to the Elliyan. It was doubtful; Tuan would have him returned to Purgatory, should he display any signs of contempt.

'I was "sent"—to find you,' he continued. 'You are *late!*'

'I was delayed … due to an unforeseen occurrence,' said Kai, keeping his poise.

Lorne held his gaze, waiting for him to proceed.

Bound by the Elliyan's ruling—to speak the truth—Kai had no choice but to relay all that had happened since the arrival of the three Dhampir: the reunions; the revelations; the abduction of Eleanor; and the Sorceress.

'Then, we can assume Lord Oran's son makes ground to Elboru?' he maintained.

'This is my hope,' said Kai, with a hint of uncertainty.

Lorne sensed his underlying concern. 'Ah!' He paused. 'The "unforeseen occurrence."'

'*She* is coming!' Kai stated.

'The Sorceress?'

Kai nodded.

'Nor is she alone. She has strength in numbers, which, no doubt, will increase. As the Warlocks' amulets grow stronger, I fear the one in her possession is drawing her to Elboru. She is determined to have the Shenn.'

'Do you know where she is?'

Kai slowly shook his head, then looked to the heavy, grey sky.

'But I sense her wickedness being carried on the back of every black cloud that preys on us. I do not doubt her intentions.'

'Then we must make certain she does not find the Magus or the Shenn.' Lorne hesitated. 'I am to assume the young man is aware of the *Cordhu Pass?*'

'He is,' said Kai. 'But he was not privy to the truth behind the "myth" that had been told to him when he was a child.'

'He cannot afford to be complacent,' said Lorne, annoyed by the mortal's arrogance. 'The danger associated with it is quite real.'

'I have spared them the treacherous waters,' Kai assured him.

'It is not the waters they should fear, but what lurks beneath; *She* is unsparing.'

'Which is why I diverted them to our caves.'

Lorne drew his head back. 'You have shared our *secret* with them?!'

'A necessary precaution,' Kai retorted. 'He vows to keep his discretion.'

'Despite who he is?' Lorne replied, his tone forceful and full of disapproval.

'*Despite it!*' said Kai.

'It appears you have been too preoccupied with the mortals … to *notice*.'

Kai lowered his head. 'To notice what?'

'That the caves are no longer accessible,' Lorne casually stated.

Kai looked up in the direction he had yet to travel, then back to Lorne. 'Why was I not informed?' he demanded, looming in on his associate.

'Had you been more dutiful to your superiors, perhaps you would have been—'

'Answer me!' Kai interrupted, disregarding protocol, his black eyes widening, displaying his rare anger.

'A cruel intervention—on nature's part—I regret to say,' said Lorne. 'It appears … a landslide caused the mountain to collapse, completely enveloping the caves' tunnels. Their way of passage no longer exists. Therefore, they have no choice but to take the *Pass*, now.'

On hearing this, Kai promptly turned. Perhaps there was time; he could follow their path, warn Gill and the Dhampir, and— Something inside stopped him.

'If Oran's son is privy to the lake's secret …' Lorne continued, regarding Kai's indecision; it was clear his fellow Servitor was contemplating following his friends, 'then he will know what to do. The task is not entirely impossible. And, from what I hear of the young man, I am confident he will be successful in reaching Elboru.'

Vexed, Kai turned and approached Lorne with menace.

'Hear my words, Lorne,' he threatened. 'Let us hope Gill knows its *true* secret—and that the Sorceress is ignorant to it. And let us hope they reach the lake before the last light of the moon—despite the challenge that awaits them there. And—heed my warning—if they fail, it is almost certain that *we* have sent the future Magus to his death. You know how vital his role is. We need his guidance, to protect us all … even the mortals. And should he die—need I remind you—it will be the beginning of the end for all of us.' Kai leaned closer. 'And *I* should not be the one to tell Lord Oran that his only son is dead—and, not only his son—his daughter, too. She is still L'Ordana's prisoner'—he tilted his head—'or have you already forgotten that?'

'Ah! The other grandchild—of the *one* you protect … Onóir.' Lorne stated.

Kai detected the subtle tone of jealousy in Lorne's voice—the mere mention of Onóir's name igniting a spark of envy in him. But he chose to disregard the young Servitor's pettiness; he had no time for it.

'If Oran discovers the circumstances of his daughter's disappearance, he will surely go against the Elliyan and desert his council, to search for her … and his son.'

'Then, he must not know,' Lorne insisted.

'We do not tell him?' Kai retorted, surprised by the suggestion.

'Why not?' Lorne answered, unruffled by Kai's reaction.

'*That* will prove somewhat difficult,' said Kai. 'You know we cannot lie under the scrutiny of their questions.'

'That depends on what is asked of us. But while Oran remains in Elboru, waiting for his son …'

Kai nodded.

'Then …' Lorne went on, 'I suggest we agree—here and now—to keep these events from him … unless … there is no other alternative, and we are—'

'Avoid all questions?! From Oran Shaw?!' Kai sneered at the notion of it.

'Precisely!' Which is why *you* will relate everything you have told me, to the Elliyan. While we cannot avoid *them*, we can, however, escape Oran's suspicions, by letting the Elliyan answer his enquiries, on our behalf. It is the only way we can avoid it. They have the power to lie, should it be deemed necessary.'

Kai nodded, in complete understanding; regardless of his misgivings towards Lorne, he knew the young Servitor's suggestion made sense. But it would be based on chance and luck—something he hoped was on their side.

'Are we agreed?'

'Agreed,' Kai replied. *For now*, he then told himself. 'However, it is *you* who must recount everything I have told you.'

Lorne stared back at him with distaste; he did not relish the thought of having to face the Elliyan—and alone.

Ignoring his counterpart's silent—and obvious—annoyance, Kai's instincts dictated his decision: he would have to rely on Gill and the Dhampir to use *their* instincts, to guide them through the Pass. *Perhaps I could reach them in time?* he thought, still contemplating it.

Suddenly he looked back, in the direction he had come, distracted by a voice in his mind, convinced he had heard *her*.

'I must return—to Onóir,' he stated.

'You have grown too attached to her,' Lorne disputed.

'How can we not?' Kai replied, realising he had said "we"—nor would he apologise for it; Lorne had no knowledge yet of what it was like to be a *Protector*. 'I was appointed to Onóir, because of her blood bond with the boy. It was—and still is—my duty to watch over her. Even as I stand here, I fear for her safety and health.'

'She is unwell?' Lorne asked, out of curiosity rather than sympathy.

Kai mused over the young Servitor's enquiry. 'Quite unwell,' he was forced to answer. 'I feel the time she has left is short. When I made my vow, it was to remain by her side—until her final breath.'

'Your loyalty is to be commended, Kai.' Lorne's tone was flat, lacking emotion.

Kai, unable to detect any shred of empathy from his associate, felt obliged to justify his close relationship with the old woman.

'When your time comes, Lorne,' he began, 'the Elliyan will make you a *Protector*. And only then shall you understand the meaning of "attachment." It is a unique and precious bond. You would kill—even die—for them. I do not expect you to understand. But I assure you … it will come to you … if you let it. Have trust in your heart, Lorne, and let nothing taint it.'

Lorne looked sharply at Kai, holding his gaze for an intense moment. He mulled over his words, and yet was unable to conjure up an image of any possible bond with a *mortal*; he felt he owed them nothing. But he could see the honesty and, dare he admit, "love" in his associates' regard for his "soul mate".

*So be it!* he thought. 'Then I shall welcome my duty, wholeheartedly,' he lied. With that, he stepped away, preparing to leave. 'Go to her, and I bid you well on your return journey.'

With a simple nod, Lorne turned and left.

Kai watched as the young Servitor approached the abyss of trees; they seemed to embrace him as he disappeared into their hold, concealing him from the world again.

*No*, Kai decided. *You are not to be trusted, Lorne.*

With a sense of apprehension, and maintaining his true form, Kai faced the direction from whence he came, then stalled, hearing the desperate need of his inner voice:

*"Time is now sacred. She waits!"*

He froze, sensing her failing heartbeat. It engulfed him with dread.

*Onóir!*

In an instant, he was gone.

# Chapter Sixteen

*Elboru: Realm of Urquille – (North-West Scotland)*

'Where is the other one?'

All heads turned, hearing Oran's demanding voice as he marched into their presence. His interruption had been unexpected—since taking up the habit of detaching himself from his fellow Warlocks—much to Tuan's annoyance.

'Well?!' he persisted, eyeing Lorne. Oran glared at the young Servitor, detesting him even more since that day—when he walked into his workshop as the arrogant *boy*, summoning him with underlying threats.

Lorne slowly turned to address the High Warlock's inquisitive and demanding stare.

'Whom do you speak of, Lord Oran?' he replied.

Oran rolled his eyes, aware that the Servitor knew precisely to whom he was referring.

'The one who has been keeping a watchful eye on my family?' he snapped.

Lorne hesitated, casting a subtle look of concern towards Tuan; he received no response.

'Kai … felt it his duty to return,' came the Servitor's cautious reply.

'Quite the *noble* one!' Oran snidely remarked.

'Quite!' Lorne retorted in an equally sneering tone.

At that moment, Oran glared into the Servitor's black eyes in a threatening manner, wishing he could drive his fist through him. But realising it would be a pointless effort, he recoiled, avoiding further contempt from the *creature*. He took a deep breath, suppressing his anger.

'What news of my son?'

Lorne now shared a glance with Greer; the High Warlock's sapphire-blue eyes danced, sensing the Servitor's inner agitation, but said nothing, toying with his silence, knowing Lorne would eventually be forced to reply to Oran's questions, should *he* or Tuan fail to intervene. He partially opened his mouth, as if to speak, then smirked at the young Servitor, smoothing his thick, dark beard before turning away.

Lorne, resentful of the High Warlock's silent dismissal of him, seethed inside as Greer turned his back on him, to take his seat of council.


Presiding over the council chamber, adjoining the Great Hall of Eminence, five throne-like seats stood side by side on an impressive granite rostrum.

Carved from a single piece of hard oak, each was recognisable by its owner's *nomen*—their name—elaborately seared into its high-arched back. All five seats sat crescent-shaped, looking down on the Servitor, within the perfect sphere of the chamber. But only one truly stood out, commanding the attention of anyone who would be present. Sat on its own, on a higher rostrum, behind its five counterparts, it was different from the rest.

This, the *Throne of Council,* would seat the Magus.

Made from cedar wood, the Overlord's throne was adorned in pure gold leaf, with thousands of blue inlays of faience, cleverly placed there by the same ancient hands that had created the Shenn.

The throne depicted the status and power of the Magus. And though it was without its master, at present, Lorne could feel the nebulous of its energy fill the chamber. It was seldom any of the Servitor was allowed in its presence; however, in the light of the revelations he had shared with the Elliyan, Lorne had been permitted entry—despite his dislike of its intimidating nature.

Eventually, Lorne caught Greer's probing eye. Servitor and High Warlock shared a mutual dislike—due to their clashing personalities, it seemed. Mindful of Greer's learned mind—and his gift of insight—Lorne knew their dislike of one another ran deeper. He promptly avoided his stare.

'Did you not hear me?' Oran pursued, ignoring the exchange; he had no time for their differences, whatever they were. He had no time for the Servitor.

'Indeed, Lord Oran,' Lorne swiftly replied, casting another glance at Tuan, in the hope the Great Warlock would support him. Feeling Oran's suspicious eyes on him, he looked around, searching for Lothian, who had always sided with him; the Great Warlock was nowhere to be seen. His concern now mounted; should Tuan and Greer maintain their silence he would be compelled to tell Oran the truth. His mind raced, desperate for an intervention.

Then, hearing Oran move closer, ready with his barrage of questions, Lorne braced himself for the repercussions.

'Leave us!' Tuan promptly ordered, finally dismissing the Servitor with a knowing glance.

Diverting his eyes from Oran's dubious look, Lorne made his swift exit.

Bemused, Oran drew back when the *creature* slithered away from their company into the far reaches of the Great Hall; he watched until its lingering shadows cloaked the Servitor from view.

He swung round to face Tuan's long, hard face.

'Why did you dismiss *it?*' he argued. 'I had not finished with my enquiries. Have I not the right to ask after my family, after three years of separation? And now, as the time draws closer, my concern for my son is paramount. So, forgive me when I tell you, Lord Tuan,' he persisted, his voice rising, carrying his anger to the rafters. 'It is wearing on my patience!'

Tuan closed his eyes, hiding their deadness, carefully contemplating his words before his reply.

The Hall of Eminence seemed to close in, imposing its vastness on the *Chamber of Council* as Oran waited for the Great Warlock to speak. Inside, he was reeling at Tuan's irritating habit of biding his time, as though he had something to conceal. Oran grew sceptical at his stalling. He had waited long enough and could no longer withhold his frustrations. He ground his teeth, wishing it were all over. Then, he could return to his family—and the life he had grown accustomed to. But most important—to know his son had safely taken his rightful place as their ruling Magus.

All he wanted now was to be released from the Elliyan and their formalities; he longed, in particular, to destroy the long, grey tunics Tuan insisted they flaunt, to display their authority at the lowly. He loathed the pretentiousness of it all.

Oran's nostrils flared. No. He would not be forced to wait any longer. He turned to challenge his superior.

But Tuan, having pre-empted his move, intervened. 'Your family are quite well, Oran of Urquille,' he finally informed him—the attempted smile towards his cynical colleague appearing out of place and distorted, on his hardened face; it simply did not belong there.

Oran narrowed his eyes of doubt, unconvinced by the falseness in the Great Warlock's tone and façade. *There's something you are not telling me*, he mused.

'It appears the three … *individuals* you chose—to accompany your son—have been successful in locating him,' Tuan resumed, 'and are now making their way to Elboru with him.'

'And Kris—L'Ordana?' Oran enquired, almost forgetting himself. 'Where is the Sorceress?'

'We cannot say,' Greer added, rising from his seat of council, his eyes now fixed on Oran.

'What a great pity you failed to destroy her,' Tuan remarked, in a derisive tone.

'I have taken responsibility for my failings, Lord Tuan, and refuse to continue to justify them to—'

'We cannot undo what has been done,' Greer quickly stepped in. 'We must presume she still has Magia Nera's amulet, which will eventually guide her to this place ...' He then paused, for what seemed like an eternity. 'However, she does not know our location, giving us the advantage. But—should she discover Elboru, it will not be an easy task for her; after all, there is the little matter of the Cordhu Pass and—' Greer stopped short when Oran's eyes suddenly lowered away from his, at the mention of the cursed place.

'I assume you have warned your son's protectors of the dangers associated with it?' Tuan voiced.

Oran remained silent in his guilt, still cursing himself for neglecting to tell the Dhampir before they parted ways after they escaped from L'Ordana's bondage.

'It seems your assumptions are wrong, Lord Tuan,' Greer answered, on Oran's behalf.

Tuan's brooding eyes flared in anger.

'Do you realise the implications of your neglect, Lord Oran? Here, while we wait—while the Sanctuary of Armistice waits,' he added, pointing to where the transformation would take place, inside the sacred chamber concealed behind the seats of council, 'your son does not know the threats awaiting him? You know what inhabits the Cordhu Pass. How could you be so—'

'I am aware of it!' cried Oran. He quickly recoiled yet maintained his composure. 'But I am also confident they will cross it. The moon will still be in its cycle and will show them the way. The Dhampir are no fools. Nor is my son. He is aware of the myth behind—'

'*Myth,* you say?' Tuan stretched his brows in surprise. 'It is no *myth!* Another error in your duty towards your son, Lord Oran. You should have shared with him the truth of this ... *childhood tale*—however grim its reality. He should have been informed!'

'Aye, and he would have been,' snapped Oran. '... had I been given the chance. Your demands on me denied me the right, and because of it, I failed him. But I will *not* take the sole blame for my negligence.'

Tuan stared at Oran, perplexed and unsure of his meaning.

'I speak of the Servitor—Kai,' said Oran. 'Is he not my son's mentor? Surely, *he* must have warned them.' He hesitated, on a niggling doubt. 'I presume the *creature* is with my son?'

Tuan drew his head back, his eyes sliding towards Greer in unspoken agitation.

Oran could not help but notice their exchange, prompting him to ask; 'There is something you wish to share with me, my lords?'

'Kai was unable to accompany them,' said Tuan, devoid of emotion.

Oran's eyes widened. 'I hope he had a good reason.'

'Kai's reasons were justified,' said Greer. 'But he directed them to a safer route.'

Oran cast them a sideward glance—the lines between his brows drawing tightly. 'There is another way?'

'It transpires, there has always been another route,' Tuan added, still perturbed by the discovery. 'But we were not aware of it until this day.'

'Where is it?'

'It is—*was*—a place known only to the Servitor.'

Oran grunted. 'It appears your "servants" are keeping secrets from us,' he sneered.

'Something we will remedy,' said Tuan, conjuring up images in his mind of how he would punish the Servitor for withholding vital information.

'Tell me of this … *other* route,' Oran pressed on him.

'There were caves hidden in the mountains, beyond the loch of Loyne.'

'What caves?!'

A scathing grin appeared on the Great Warlock's mouth. 'Well, now, it seems you, Oran of Urquille, are still unaware of *all* the secrets of your Realm.'

By now, Oran had had enough of Tuan's sniping and turned away. Greer moved to intervene, once more, perceiving the High Warlock's actions; he had sensed Oran's purpose.

'Whatever your intentions, Lord Oran, *you* are going nowhere,' insisted Tuan.

Oran, inhaling deeply, turned and glared at Tuan—the smug look on the Great Warlock's face prominent as he tilted his head back and stared down at him with his challenging eyes. Tempted to throw a clenched fist at his superior, Oran stood his ground, gritting his teeth. 'I need to be with my son, especially—'

'There is no need,' Tuan broke in. 'He is safe. Besides … it will give you time to acquaint yourself with that which you claimed to know nothing about—now that you have returned after your long incarceration,' he added, referring to Oran's initial denial of Elboru.

Inside, Oran was furious; he would never be allowed to forget *that*, or the shameful guilt he had felt after denying his son's existence when he was summoned by the Elliyan, three years previously. Provoked, he growled under his breath.

Still, Tuan persisted, twisting the knife a little more. A contemptuous smirk appeared at the side of his mouth. 'I am quite sure you shall enjoy exploring her … *crevices!*'

Oran bit down on the Great Warlock's scathing comment, his reference to the castle delivering an underlying comparison to his hedonistic past. His thoughts, now fuelled with retaliation, and refusal to be spoken to in such a derisive tone, Oran could no longer stand it. *That's it!*

'Remember your responsibilities, Lord Oran,' Tuan warned, sensing the potential assault. 'This is your Realm. This is *your* "Elboru"!'

But just as Oran contemplated leaving, he stopped dead. *Were?* he inwardly recalled. He scrutinised the two Warlocks before challenging them again. 'You said, "There *were* caves."'

Tuan promptly diverted his look from Oran; Greer hesitated, then rolled his eyes, vexed at the Great Warlock for choosing to stay silent at that awkward moment. There were times he shared Oran's frustrations with their superior.

'The caves … are no more,' he reluctantly divulged.

At first, Oran stared at them, unable to react. Then, in an unexpected twist, he threw back his head and laughed at the irony of it.

'How can it be, that these … *caves*—which we never knew existed—do not actually *exist?*' he queried, mocking them. 'It is, I must admit, amusing,' he added. Then, letting the smile drop from his face, he turned abruptly, muttering, 'I've had enough of this!'

'Perhaps!' Tuan called out after him. 'But at least we can be thankful the Sorceress has no knowledge of the Cordhu Pass.'

Oran stopped at the entrance to the Great Hall, listening to the sound of Tuan's grinding voice, following from behind.

'It is unlikely she and her associates will survive the waters,' he maintained, with an air of confidence. 'So, all is not lost, Lord Oran.'

Oran's scornful laugh echoed throughout the Hall and beyond its pylons.

'You arrogant fool!' he taunted, turning to address Tuan.

The Great Warlock's mouth gaped as he recoiled at the insult.

'Before Magia Nera lured her from me,' Oran began, 'L'Ordana was once an innocent and gifted young woman, known by another name: Kristene.' He recalled the image of her face, from the first moment she had woken, after her near-death ordeal: twisted in fear, of the world that had falsely accused her of "cavorting with the *Devil* himself." The torment in her devastated, hazel eyes had convinced him to "save her soul." He had felt it his duty, having failed her mother, Sarah, who, to his shame, did not escape the *Witches' Death*. He blamed Magia Nera for that.

A moment of regret seeped into his thoughts, and he questioned it. Perhaps he should have let her drown. *How different everything would be*, he thought. But she had lived—and that was the way of it.

'She—the Sorceress—was born here,' he blurted.

'In Urquille?!' said Tuan, taken aback by Oran's disclosure.

'Aye—*here*—in Scotland!' He shrugged. 'Call it what you will. But she knew it well. We spoke of it on our travels. It held both good and tragic memories for her—but more so the latter, which was why she was willing to leave it all behind. Despite it, she had never forgotten her roots. And, like most children, she, too, was well-versed in local poetry and tales of her home. Aye, Lord Tuan, she was more than aware of the "myth" of the Cordhu Pass; she had *seen* it with her own eyes.'

Tuan, left speechless by this new information, feared it would not be the last of it. Where would it end, should more come to light? They could not afford any more delays. Time was pressing on them, and the days were narrowing. If all was not in place, and if the Magus did not take his seat where he belonged …

Oran took a moment to relish in watching the smug look slip from Tuan's face. However, the moment passed when he realised the immense problem facing them, and so felt the need to point out the possible threat—the threat that would affect them all.

'Do not be overconfident that *we* have the upper hand, my lords,' he warned. 'While time and misguidance may have swayed L'Ordana's memories …' Oran paused, his tone now sombre. 'Let us hope *Kristene* does not return to evoke her past youth.'

# Chapter Seventeen

*Balloch*

The Servitor slowed as he approached the familiar clearing facing Rosalyn's cottage. Gone was the early morning rain and, along with it, the heaviness of the air, leaving behind a cool freshness.

An unusual stillness brought Kai to a halt, as though all life had paused. He regarded the small abode, nestled alone and surrounded by the grandeur of nature's shroud. The terracotta plaster, coating its wooden exterior, had been washed dark from the rain. It looked drab, unkept, and devoid of its inhabitants, adding to the sombre atmosphere. It made him uneasy.

He moved forward, with caution, checking his surroundings; it was uncomfortably quiet. Glancing around, he noticed the large wedges of chopped wood—soaked through by the recent downpour—all stocked and ready for a fire that had not been lit.

From behind the cottage, near the outhouse, he heard the thumping of a horse's hoof on the ground and knew it was Farrow—the horse displaying its frustration for being left alone.

His eyes glanced over the wet ground; all traces of footprints had been washed away, and it was clear Gill and the three Dhampir had long gone. The Cordhu Pass slipped into his mind again. He was confident they could survive the loch's might. But he could not think of that now.

The Servitor approached the wooden door, listening for signs of life from behind its closure. Looking down at the ringed, brass handle, he reached out, then hesitated, hearing the soft lament of a dog's whimpering, it almost playing in time with its mistress's breathing.

*Only two lives!* he thought. *Am I too late?*

Overwhelmed by guilt and regret, he closed his eyes and hung his head in reflection before deciding to enter.

Suddenly, his eyes flickered wide open, sensing the *third!*

*She is still alive!*


The mid-day sun broke through the clouds, showering him in light as he opened the door. Rosalyn, raising her head from her slumber, caught her breath, on seeing the illuminated figure as they lingered on the threshold; for a moment, she lost herself in the beauty of the Servitor's presence.

As Kai stepped in, he changed back into the familiar person she knew, Rosalyn sighing with relief at the welcome return of their friend.

He paused, staring at Onóir.

Somehow, Rosalyn had found the inner strength to carry her mother to the house, after Onóir collapsed. She had made her comfortable, by making an open fire from any leftover dry wood, refusing to leave her side. She forced a smile at Kai, glad of his company, relieved for his help; it would now make things easier.

Rave bolted forward to greet Kai; he smiled warmly as the hound vied for his attention.

'I hope you have been protecting Rosalyn and Onóir, in my absence, Rave,' he said, as though expecting her to understand. She cocked her large ears at the familiarity of their names. Kai grinned at her eager reaction, then turned his attention back to Onóir, his smile fading, struck by her declining health; she looked drawn and grey in her appearance since they had last spoken—only a few hours, since.

'How long?' he asked Rosalyn, without diverting his saddened eyes from his soulmate.

'Not long after the others left—late dawn,' she replied, turning her gaze back to her mother. 'I have tried administering her usual tonic, but it appears to have no effect. It has always given her some relief, but …'

Her voice trailed, refusing to accept the inevitable. Then something occurred to her: 'I thought you were gone!'

'I had to return,' he stated, kneeling by Onóir's side as she slept, his warm, brown eyes observing the old woman closely.

Kai watched the slight rise and fall of her chest, hearing the heavy rattling of the deep-rooted infection as it spread through her failing lungs. Placing his hands on her crown, he closed his eyes in search of her thoughts. Her mind remained steady and calm. Deeper he delved into her subconscious as Rosalyn looked on with great bearing, reaching further until glimpses of her past with Reece surfaced.

Blissful times, filled with ardour and ecstasy, enveloped the Servitor but were then interrupted by feelings of heartrending surrender. Kai stopped himself, shying away with embarrassment at the intrusiveness of his closest friend's intimate memories. *I have no right*, he realised.

'Kai?' Rosalyn gently enquired, taking him from his reverie.

'I regret to say,' he began, 'no tonic or potion can return her to us. We must be prepared.'

Rosalyn's lower lip quivered as she tried to hold back the tears, Kai's admission delivering its blow, with finality. He turned to meet her eyes as they filled with tears—tears she did not want to shed.

'It is not only the illness that wrenches the life from Onóir,' he continued. 'It is also her heart. She has accepted—and welcomes—the end of her journey.'

'I know,' Rosalyn sniffled. 'She told me ... when we said our goodbyes.'

She observed how tenderly he cared for her mother, sweeping his hand gently over her fine, grey hair, and letting it caress her face with a calming influence. His gestures were filled with nothing but love. And, as he carefully stroked her cheek, a faint smile appeared on Onóir's mouth; the old woman's face lit up, momentarily glowing with youth again.

'Is this what happens—when someone welcomes death?' Rosalyn whispered to herself.

'It is a comforting thought,' said Kai.

She glanced at him, realising he had heard her. Encouraged by his words, Rosalyn rose from her seat, keeping a fixed eye on her mother. She drew her brows together in quick thought, her mind racing, then turned and made her way to her bed chamber.

Rave jumped at her mistress' abrupt movement, following her with her nose—only to have the door closed on it.

Alone in her chamber, Rosalyn stared at the old, red woollen blanket, covering what lay hidden beneath it. She threw her hands on her hips, contemplating the other *secrets* the plain, oak coffer concealed; she had only seen the top layer of its contents, once.

The piece of furniture was her husband's and had resided in his workshop until he had been forced by the Elliyan to leave his family. He had then moved the coffer to the house before his sudden—and reluctant—departure.

Stored inside were precious items from his past—items she had never seen beneath the fine, black silk concealing them.

Rosalyn quickly approached it, brushed away the woollen blanket, and then hesitated. Apprehensive, she frowned and chewed on her lip as she stared down at the coffer, feeling a little intrusive of Oran's private possessions; they belonged to his past, to a different era, and to those who were long dead. But that was centuries ago—long before they had met.

*What does it matter now?* she thought, still eyeing the lid; after all, they were nothing more than "things" that held distant memories … in her mind, at least.

"Tis a silly notion to be jealous of *ghosts!* she convinced herself, then glanced at the small, oak sideboard Oran had made for her. She went to it and removed the drawer. Reaching in, she groped for the little, ornate brass key, which rested on a small ledge, at the back.

'Ah, there you are!' she whispered, quickly snatching it from its place.

She had not touched the coffer since hiding the Albrecht sword from her children. For three years it had remained there, untouched. Despite her temptation to delve into the coffer's contents, she could not bring herself to do so, having made a vow to her husband not to meddle. But things were different now.

Holding the little key in her hand, she ran her thumb over its smooth surface, frowning, trying to remember the process for opening the lid. She had heard Oran do it several times, him thinking she slept soundly while he revisited his past.

'Was it … to the left, three times or four … or to the right?' She tutted, scolding herself. 'Now is not the time to forget, Rosalyn!'

Cautiously, she inserted the key, turning it to the left, three times.

Nothing.

A moment of panic set in when she was unable to remove it. 'No, no! Do not do this to me!' she snapped, then released a sigh of relief when it finally came away. 'Think, Rosalyn!' she muttered, through gritted teeth, clenching the key, feeling the metal warming in her closed fist. She closed her eyes tight, then, when they flashed open, in a moment of *Eureka!* she promptly re-inserted the key and turned it to the right, four times.

*Click!*

Rosalyn threw back the lid and looked down. The Albrecht sword still rested where she had left it: thrown hastily among a pile of old, blunt weapons. Staring at the fine piece of weaponry, she thought how out-of-place it looked there among its worn counterparts.

She carefully removed it, admiring the workmanship.

"This is a true Warlock's sword," Oran had once boasted, brandishing it playfully before her.

Her hand looked small in the indentation—made by her husband's—worn from centuries of use. However, the black shagreen-covered grip still felt rough. Rosalyn's hand shook as she gently removed the blade from its scabbard; it had retained its sharpness and still shone like new. She surmised it had never seen a blunt day. She narrowed her eyes, staring at the gold-inlaid hieroglyphics engraved along its spine, but could not decipher their meaning. She looked at the pommel, containing the gold inlay of his *nomen*.

"It lets all Warlocks know who its master is," he had told her.

Carefully setting the Albrecht aside, Rosalyn then removed the old weapons that were, no doubt, a lazy decoy for what lay underneath. When her hand touched the black silk, she briefly lavished in its luxuriousness, having never felt material as smooth and sleek before. She held her breath in anticipation when it slid gracefully from her hand, its softness caressing her skin. And as it fell silently back to its resting place, her eye caught a glint of silver peeping out from under it. Brushing the scarf aside, she picked up the item, instantly recognising it; it was Oran's brooch——the one he had made to represent the *Shaw* name— his name—their motto, *Fide et Fortitudine,* "Fidelity and Fortitude," forever embossed at its centre, beneath the Scottish thistle. And in its centre, a dexter arm grasped a dagger, in a display of resilience. She wondered why Oran had left it. 'Of course!' she whispered to herself— the reason dawning on her. 'For Gill.' But then reality struck a blow when another reason hit her, hard: should Oran fail to return home …

Rosalyn grasped the precious heirloom in her hand, vowing to give it to their son. Regardless of his destiny, she would make sure Gill would never forget his ancestry.

Returning to the contents of the coffer, she let her eyes wander, still clutching the brooch, feeling the warmth of its metal in her hand, it temporarily comforting her. She then paused, narrowing her eyes, letting them rest on a small, long ebony box, inlaid with mother-of-pearl. Its delicate design was reminiscent of an item that may have, once, belonged to a woman. Her lips pursed and her fingers twitched. She had to know …

She reached in.

Rosalyn gently held the curious little box in her hands, admiring its exotic and meticulous handwork, its unusual mosaic design unfamiliar to her. She checked it over; there was no lock. Lips pursed again, she frowned, indecisive, when a feeling of apprehension temporarily touched her. But temptation has its way of luring the curious soul, especially that of a mortal.

Casting her doubts aside, Rosalyn shrugged and threw caution to the wind …

Her curious eyes pondered over the personal item inside. With no knowledge of whom it belonged to, she perceived it to be another hidden fragment from her husband's past. Consumed by mixed emotions of anger, sadness and jealousy, she slammed the lid on the delicate contents and tossed it back into the coffer.

'Not now, Rosalyn!' she muttered to herself.

An hour had almost passed before Rosalyn finally emerged, her attire now completely changed. Kai threw her a peculiar glance; it was almost unheard of for a woman to be seen wearing leggings. However, Rosalyn was not deterred by the political correctness of it; it was simply a *necessity*.

Beneath the buckskin jacket that came down to her thighs, she wore a black shirt that once belonged to Gill; the piece of clothing had gone too small for his broadening physique. Gone were her brogues, now replaced with a pair of her mother's old leather boots; Onóir had worn them when she used to ride Reece's horse, Altan, during their early years together, in England. But after his disappearance, she never wore them again but kept them stored safely, regularly maintaining the leather with wool wax. Now, also aware of the deteriorating weather, Rosalyn wore a heavy, dark-green-and-blue tartan shawl—caught at the front with a silver, interlaced brooch, its centrepiece a pale-blue sapphire. Onóir had given it to her daughter, years before. It had been a wedding gift from Reece, specially made for his new bride—the stone carefully chosen by him to match the colour of her eyes.

Rosalyn recalled the day Onóir handed the brooch to her: her mother had kissed it before parting with it. And now *she* would wear the precious item, knowing she was taking a piece of her mother with her. And, should Reece want it back, she would happily return it, as a keepsake.

Almost prepared for her journey, Rosalyn remained hesitant inside. As she stalled, checking herself over, Rave approached her with curiosity, letting her nose take in the new scents worn by her mistress. She smiled as the dog sniffed her noisily.

'That's all you are, Rave ... *"a nose on legs,"*' she said, echoing her mother's fond description of the inquisitive hound. Then, lifting her eyes from the dog, she looked at her mother as she slept with ease—no doubt the effect of Kai's soothing influence on her. Yes, she was grateful—and relieved—for his years of friendship, especially now.

Kai looked up, observing the large, sword clinging to her back, on a leather belt. There was no need for him to query her plans.

'Maw insisted I go,' she stated, feeling the need to justify her sudden actions. 'I refused, at first—but we came to an agreement: I would stay until you returned. She must have known you would.' She then shook her head. 'Do not judge our decision, Kai.'

'And ... here I am,' he said, rising to meet her saddened eyes, sensing her deep pain. 'You do not have to justify your motives to me, Rosalyn. I have known them all along, and admire your bravery,' he added, though was unable to hide his concerns.

'I hope you do not have to use it,' he remarked, acknowledging the Albrecht.

'Likewise!' she said nervously, raising her shoulders in doubt.

'Before you go ...' he began, 'you must make me a promise.'

Rosalyn pressed hard on her lips and nodded. She then listened intently as Kai went on to warn her about the dangers ahead—namely the Cordhu Pass—as well as advising her of the safest route.

Her eyes widened with panic. 'I thought it was a *myth*—the Pass.'

His silence confirmed her fears.

'All the more reason to leave, then—so I can warn the others,' she said.

'You must promise me,' he insisted, 'if—or when—you reach the Cordhu Pass—if they are not there—you must return. Do you hear me, Rosalyn? Do not attempt it. It is dangerous. No man can cross it.'

'And what if I—'

'Do not risk it,' he insisted. 'Also, you must remember, the others are a half-day's journey ahead of you, and Reece and his colleagues are experienced travellers.'

'I am aware of it,' she staunchly replied, eager to make her start, and yet reluctant to leave, her eyes glancing over at her mother.

'There is an Inn—a few leagues before the Pass,' Kai continued. '*The Inn at Ardgore*. They will need to rest their horses there, for a while. With luck, you may reach it in time. By warning them, they can at least plan a way to venture through the Pass and cross the loch.'

A scratching sound brought their attention to the door; Rave was waiting, sensing she was going on an adventure.

'Take her with you,' Kai urged. 'You will be glad of her company.'

The dog stared up at Rosalyn with keen eyes, her tail wagging and twisting with anticipation.

'Do you want to see Gill, Rave?'

The hound stood to attention, for a moment, on hearing her master's name, her body then swaying, dancing with excitement as her paws moved over the floor, eager to go.

'There will be nothing here for you when—' Rosalyn broke off when Onóir stirred, wheezing heavily. But when she moved to go to her mother's side, Kai intervened.

'Do not linger here, Rosalyn,' he advised. 'Go—now—and be on your guard; sinister threats are looming. Stick to the trail, and do not— even if you are tempted—do not veer away from your path.'

Slowly nodding, Rosalyn kept her tearful eyes on her mother, already feeling the heartbreak of their imminent parting.

'Time is not on your side,' Kai warned.

'I promise,' she replied, her voice almost a whisper.

Having made her vow, she went to her mother, for the last time. Kai stepped back, then looked away, leaving her in her private moment, while Rave remained by the door in silence, as though she understood the sensitivity of what was happening.

Leaning over her mother as she slept, Rosalyn placed her hand on Onóir's cheek, then kissed her tenderly on her brow.'

'I love you, Maw,' she said. She then hesitated and leaned closer, whispering in her ear, 'Wait for me!'

Kai looked sharp, catching Rosalyn's eye; he had heard what she said. But as he moved to question it, she turned on her heel.

The door slammed. Then silence.

Kai stared at the door with unease, inwardly questioning what Rosalyn had meant. He contemplated following her; however, within moments of hearing the pounding of Farrow's hooves, as Rosalyn galloped away, with Rave at her tail, barking with excitement, he knew it would be pointless.

Kai took heed of her parting until the veil of silence gently shrouded the house once more.

Rosalyn was gone.

"*Wait for me!*"

As her words played on his mind, his attention was then lured away by the sudden touch of a cold, fragile hand. He turned to find Onóir standing behind him, frail and barely able to hold herself. For a moment, the soulmates stared at one another and, in complete understanding of the bond they shared, Kai simply nodded.

'My duty is here—with you,' he said, '… until the end.'

Content, she then collapsed into his hold.

Rosalyn drew Farrow to a sudden halt and stared down the path the others had taken. Brows knitting tightly, she then looked right, in the direction of Balloch village and pressed her lips together, in a moment of contemplation. Would there be time? Another glance back at where she was heading, then back to the village … There was something she had to do …

'This won't take long, Farrow.'

# Chapter Eighteen

As Kai looked down at the smile of reassurance looking up at him, he returned his, willingly. Onóir looked weaker now. Her time was short. He knew it. They both did.

'Do not … judge Rosalyn,' she said, in her appeal. Her voice was timid, forcing her to pause, to catch her breath at intervals.

Patiently, he waited.

'She was right … to go,' she continued. 'Her family is out there. It was … the right decision. What is left for her … here … when I am gone?'

'As much as I agree with you,' he returned, 'I have my misgivings that she will reach them on time.'

'Have faith in my daughter, Kai.'

At the mention of his name, he returned to his true form; it would be his last time to do so.

*For you*, he thought.

Seeing Kai as he truly was made Onóir feel at peace. She recalled her fears and doubts the first time she had seen his ghostly form—in the basement of The Ferry Inn. It seemed a lifetime ago now.

'As well as being my *Protector*,' she began, 'you have been my true friend in this adventure. I have no regrets for doing what was asked of me. It was made possible by your …' She stopped short, to catch her breath. It was now becoming increasingly difficult—the effort alone causing her great pain in her lungs, but most of all … in her failing heart.

'Try not to speak, my Onóir.'

*"My Onóir."*

She forced a weak smile when he spoke the words.

'I can die happy now, knowing I have seen Reece again. He—he will protect them ...'

Her breath was quick and short as she continued to fight for air. He knew her time was drawing to its close.

Kai rose from her side and lifted her with ease and great care. He now took her seat, cradling her in his arms.

Onóir let her heavy eyes glance around the little house she had returned to all those years ago after Reece had disappeared. Mr Drew, their kind landlord—*My Saviour!* she thought—came to mind. She hoped she would see him again. Had it not been for his kindness—and his wife's—she wondered what kind of life she might have lived. It no longer mattered.

She looked at the table where the family would eat their meals together, where many conversations were held: the latest gossip, a discussion to solve a problem or dispute, or merely to sit in silence and eat—each conversation now ingrained in the wood. She imagined them all seated around it, just one more time, as though they were still with her. She could almost hear them. A faint smile touched her lips, thinking of Gill—the lad always contemplating his food, by closing his eyes and inhaling its wholesome smell before diving in. Or Oran, scolding his son for eating too quickly, while Eleanor smirked at her brothers' reproach. A basket of bread remained, where Rosalyn had left it, the day before. She tried to recapture the aroma of the freshly-baked produce they used to sell at the market, in Balloch.

Her eyes then travelled to the hearth, where the last embers of the previous night's fire had kept their amber glow as if waiting for her.

Kai left her to her thoughts, still holding her until she returned her gaze to his.

'You know what to do?' she whispered.

The Servitor nodded.

'And now,' she finally added, 'I release you from your pledge. It has been my—' Her body suddenly tensed, and she gasped for air.

Seeing the panic in the paleness of her blue eyes, Kai enveloped Onóir as her body slowly began to release its last breath.

'Let it,' he whispered, guiding her with his tranquil voice. 'Let it go, my love!'

*"My love!"*

These were the last words she would hear, taking them with her.

Kai felt the faint movement of her body against his until it could no longer fight the inevitable arrival of death. The heart soon followed the body—each beat growing further apart—gradually reaching its momentum … until it could do no more.

The lonely quietness that usually follows in the aftermath of one's passing, crept its way into the house. Outside, the wind had momentarily ceased. No bird sang. No animal stirred, as if out of respect for the demise of Onóir Molyneaux.

Kai closed his eyes and waited. For a brief time, he felt the enormous emptiness from her loss. He had loved Onóir, but not in the way two lovers were consumed with no other than themselves. No. It had been an unconditional love; one that neither asked—nor expected— anything from it.

Then … *it* came: the void from her loss being slowly filled again, by the warmth of her soul flowing through him.

It was time to fulfil her last wish.

Kai held Onóir's fragile body with the greatest respect and rose. He then paused for several moments, allowing himself to glance over the place he had come to know as "home." Then, as if grateful for its acceptance of him, he bowed and left for the last time, to take his soulmate to her final resting place, beneath the canopy of a yew tree, beyond the outhouse.

Although he knew she was no longer there, Kai buried Onóir's body, as requested by her, in the traditional way chosen by most mortals—should they be fortunate.

The air was still fresh from the early rain, bringing with it the scent of nature's foliage. For a while, he stood over the solitary mound of earth that now marked her grave. In a year or so, it would be overgrown with "life" again. The irony of it.

He lost all notion of time until darkness made itself known, quietly closing in on him. The strong, blue light of the half-moon forced its way through the trees; it seemed to light up everything around him, pointing to the place where he had laid her to rest. He followed its ray upwards, seeing a clear black sky, sparkling with life. A display of shooting stars passed over, catching his eyes before he looked down at her place, once again. It would be *Her Place* from now on.

He then closed his eyes, absorbed in deep concentration, his body still glowing inside from the warmth of her lingering soul. Kai placed his hands on his heart before raising them skywards. Then, inhaling deeply, he held on, still unwilling to let her go. Feeling the tug of her soul on his heavy heart, he finally gave in to her needs. Gradually, he exhaled, releasing her into the universe, to continue her journey to the next life.


The temporary desolation the Servitor felt in the immediate aftermath of it all, consumed him. But he knew it would pass. And it did.

He then returned to the house that had once brimmed with life, just a few days before, and stared at it, tempted to take another look inside. But he did not go in; she was no longer there.

As he turned to leave the eerie silence of what remained of his second home, a soft, familiar voice came back to remind him.

*"You know what to do ..."*

# Chapter Nineteen

*North of Lac Lomond – The Ardgore Inn*

*"Do not look back!"*

Reece's words taunted Gill for hours. The Dhampir had sensed the immensity of the young man's torment, his temptations toying with him after they had left Rosalyn and Onóir behind; the parting had been torturous. He understood his grandson's desperate need, inwardly praising his willpower to resist when the two women stood in the little yard, watching them until they had disappeared.

"Do not look back!" Reece had advised him—the underlying message hinting that he may never see his mother and grandmother again.

Gill quickly discarded the thought from his mind, telling himself, he *would*. It was then he had some notion of how Reece must have felt, all those years ago, when forced to leave Onóir; only Reece imagined he would see his wife again. Life, indeed, had dealt another of its cruel blows.

"Always say goodbye, as though it is your last, Gill-san," Asai had also advised—compelled to add his piece of wisdom.

It was, at least, the one thing he knew he would never regret: that he had said all his goodbyes. Well … almost. *Meghan*, he thought—the one dread his mother had promised to spare him. And then there was Eleanor … The Samurai had been keeping his silence. He wondered did Asai know something. Her whereabouts? Her state of mind? "I will know it, should any harm come to her," he had told him. Therefore, there was nothing he could do but accept the Samurai's word and wait, in the hope they would know something. The sooner the better.

Occasionally, Gill glanced back at Reece and Asai, all the while checking his bow and quiver.

'Aye, they're all still there—since the last time ye looked,' Tam remarked, mocking the young man's anxious behaviour. Gill forced a smile at his foolishness.

He looked above at the early darkening of the evening sky, it bearing the weight of sagging grey clouds; the days were getting shorter now with the lowering of the late autumn sun, and night would soon throw its frigid air over them—along with the promise of more rain.

The Inn, Kai spoke of, then came to mind: *The Ardgore Inn*... He had never heard of it. He shrugged. But why would he? He had never travelled beyond the Aber Hills. It seemed unimaginable that a tavern could exist within the loneliness of the landscape they were journeying through.

He then considered the distance they had travelled; they had come a long way in a short space of time. Once they had gone beyond Lomond Hills, they followed the rough path along the banks of the swollen Tayflu. On their left, the landscape was marked by mountains, while on the right of the river, a huge canopy of trees stretched alongside, marking the thick, impenetrable forest that lay hidden behind its gloomy, natural veil; their imposing presence seemed to watch the travellers on their journey north, bending with the wind as if steering them in the right direction.

The group followed the river's straight course until it could guide them no more. Here, they parted company with its brown, murky waters, leaving the river and the forest behind. In the distance, the Aber Hills rose tall and vast, ready to lure the strangers into their wild terrain. Gill had only once travelled as far as the mouth of the Tayflu, with Rave, after his father had warned him never to venture beyond their own territory.

He would soon discover why …

A faint trail barely marked the path that would guide them through the mountains. Straight and narrow, it led them on, giving them a sense of being closed in by the sheer height of the black peaks lining the sky.

Reece looked up, following their dark silhouettes; they seemed to weave and fold gracefully into each other. As the dreary shades of the damp evening threw down their haunting shadows, he thought them strangely appealing to the eye. But the Aber Hills dwarfed in comparison to the high-ridged mountain peaks of Ardmanoth, in the far reaches. The name itself boasted their immense size, their distinct pale outline dominating the sky, farther north and beyond, where the lochs of Aber and Nessa met. He knew they would not be travelling that way. He stretched his neck in search of the two identical peaks, their glistening crests easier to spot in daylight.

With no warning, Reece drew to a sudden halt, gripping the reigns of his horse tightly, as a sharp-stabbing pain seized him. He drew a deep breath, clasping his hand over his slow-beating heart. For an instant, it stopped, as though the cold hand of death had wrenched it from his body. Only once had he felt something similar: when he thought he would never see Onóir again. This time, the pain was real … and severe.

Sensing his colleague's sudden affliction, Asai swiftly came to Reece's aid and took control of his horse—the steed becoming restless when its rider unexpectedly keeled over.

'What troubles you, my friend?' the Samurai quizzed, unable to comprehend the unexpectedness of his colleague's discomfort. Through his inner suffering, Reece glanced ahead, seeing Tam and Gill still engrossed in conversation; he was thankful they had failed to notice. He tried to compose himself but felt his heart sink when he looked at the Samurai's look of concern. Asai could not help but notice the deep sadness in his friend's eyes, they lacking the lustre he was familiar with. He then realised what troubled him.

'Onóir?' he whispered.

Reece nodded, unable to bring himself to speak the words, and yet, inside, they screamed at him:

*"She is dead!"*

Asai drew back his head and paused. Closing his eyes, the great Samurai bowed, out of respect for his friend's loss. He had no reason to question Reece, having seen the misery displayed on his features. But the private moment of mourning was soon interrupted, by the sound of a horse's hooves; Tam had turned back, leaving Gill behind—and bemused—by the Highlander's sudden departure, while in mid-conversation. Sensing something was wrong, Tam rushed to his colleagues' side—the grave look on Reece's face confirming his thoughts.

'Say nothing of this to Gill,' Reece confided in them.

Tam nodded sharply.

'If you wish it,' Asai returned.

'I do,' he quickly replied, hearing his grandson's approach, from behind. 'The time is not right—'

'For what?' Gill interrupted, drawing alongside them. Oblivious, he stared at the three Dhampir, from one blank face to the next, waiting for a response.

Reece forced a smile. 'Asai suggests we bypass the Inn and continue for the caves,' he lied, convincingly. 'But the horses need rest and food. It has been a long day, and we have another facing us, tomorrow. This is where "The time is not right." We must plan our journey carefully. Besides, I have no doubt you will be wanting food, Gill.'

*Food!* Gill craved inside. The mere mention of the word ... 'If time allows it?' he eagerly returned, feeling the pang again. The thought of a satisfying meal inside him made his stomach rumble. The food his mother had provided for the journey was suitable yet not substantial enough, to satisfy his constant hunger.

Tam laughed out, his bellowing voice carrying through the vastness, disturbing flocks of birds from their place of shelter, forcing them out into the threatening elements. 'Then food it is, lad!' he said, relieving the tension. 'Is it far—the Inn?' he added, keen to quench his thirst—not for *his* means—but for the want of a drab of ale or a dram of whisky.

'There's a valley—beyond the Tayflu—between the hills,' said Gill. 'According to Kai, the Inn is located on the shores of Loyne and, from there, the caves are north—between the twin mountains.'

Dusk finally made its presence known to the four travellers as they entered the valley. Reece felt the heaviness of his broken heart as he tried to block images from his racing mind—of Onóir, in her final moments. He had sensed it all along, her slow descent towards death, despite Rosalyn's assurance. *I should have stayed,* he thought, torturing himself. He then glanced over at Gill, who smiled back at him, nodding, as if to tell him he was grateful for their company. It was clear his grandson relied on them. No. He could never have stayed; he had made a vow—one that had deep meaning.

It was of some comfort to him, though, knowing Onóir had not been alone. There was a time when he could detach himself from death and everything associated with it. Years of captivity and endless battles had rendered him insensitive to it all. But that had changed in a matter of days. The realisation that his past had survived, giving him a new life— and hope—had softened his unsympathetic demeanour. But right now, he wanted to cry out—for the loss of his wife—to let his pain echo throughout the valley and beyond, and to let the world know how he truly felt, for the first time in his long life. But, for the sake of his grandson, he would have to bury his sorrow and anger and maintain his poise.

*"For Gill's sake!"* an inner voice told him.

As they emerged from the confines of the valley, leaving the Aber Hills behind, a soft, misty rain swept over them. Black shadowy trees lurked all around as they ventured on, hoping to find the loch of Loyne. The eeriness attached to its habitat gave them the impression that nothing was willing to reside within its dwelling. The Dhampir detected no sign of wildlife; it seemed nature's residents had sensibly taken shelter from the dismal night.

Onwards they rode, quickening their pace as the mizzle turned to rain and took momentum, its force driven by the rising wind, it now thrashing against everything it touched. Brown sodden leaves flapped as they clung desperately to their branches, refusing to let go of the remnants of autumn; it was a losing battle—the wind eventually triumphant, wrenching any shred of life from nature's foliage.

Tiny speckles of scattered lights flickered in the far distance, indicating the inanity of those who chose a solitary life, in the desolate terrain. It was utterly depressing in its atmosphere, adding to Reece's sombre mood.

'Who would want to live in a place like this?' Gill called out, pulling the hood of his father's cloak over his head. He shuddered, glancing at the cloaked Dhampir, who appeared unperturbed by the wretched conditions.

'It seems we are about to find out!' Tam called back, pointing with his chin towards a dim light, as it winked at them between the sway of thick growth ahead, luring them forward.

As they waded through the woods, they were brought to the attention of a rushing sound, no more than a stone's throw ahead. Eventually, they came to a clearing. Beneath the low, heavy clouds, the river meandered wildly like a ribbon of silver-grey being pounded by the rain, its length stretching far before flowing into the wide loch of Loyne.

'There it is!' Gill cried out, pointing through the downpour. On the other side—just beyond the shoreline—they glimpsed the outline of a dark structure, through a net of widely sparse trees. A cobbled bridge was their only access, and as they trudged over its uneven surface, to the other side, the Inn finally came into view.

Alone and uninviting, The Ardgore Inn possessed an atmosphere of its own, casting an ominous chill, like a warning to all who crossed its threshold. Its forbidding presence blended with the night's miserable aura. The three Dhampir could smell its unpleasantness as they approached it with apprehension, and it had the look of a place where lost souls kept a rendezvous with evil itself.

The Inn, quite abundant in size, had two stories, its upper floor projecting out, dominating the structure. Its timber-framed exterior had been completely tarred, covering all traces of its traditional whiteness. No curious eye could see beyond the small lead windows—the blackened panes preventing the glory of sunlight, should it show its face, from penetrating—while Iron bars crisscrossed their fronts, for protection. Perhaps to keep something out? Who could say?

There was no indication to show how long the decrepit building had stood in its unnatural location; the sign that swung erratically above its porch had been battered by the elements, making it difficult to distinguish the name, let alone the year of the Inn's resurrection. It was evident, by its state of disrepair, the Landlord took no pride in his establishment.

As the pale beacon of light, emanating from the decrepit old lantern above the sign guided them closer, it cast a ghostly hue over the threshold, daring them to enter. No. It was by no means welcoming. Gill drew a picture in his mind, imagining the interior would be just as uninviting.

From the outside, The Ardgore Inn looked deserted; however, the three Dhampir could hear the low babble of voices, from behind its low-arched door. Two black, iron rods crossed its façade, holding its tarred beams in place; it, too, was in a state of disrepair. The handle—a thick, rusted iron ring—clung to a star-shaped iron panel, and beneath it, a distorted lock for a key they surmised would no longer fit. A single, wide heavy beam of blackened hardwood marked the division between the upper and lower floors. Gill noticed the weather-beaten carvings along its length; they were reminiscent of long-stemmed roses, entwined in an elaborate design. He thought they looked out of place on the building's depraved front. And, with the rain now falling wearily on its wood-wormed timbers, it added to the Inn's foreboding and uninviting ethos.

'Perhaps—Asai was right,' Gill remarked, reluctant to enter. He then recalled Kai's warning: "Do not stay the night!"

'We will not stop for long,' Reece stated as if reading his grandson's thoughts.

'Can I take your horses?'

The four travellers turned, then looked down into the pale, eager face of a young boy, his heavy eyelids blinking continuously from the assault of rain on his small, round face. It was all they could see of him, peering out from the hood of the oversized woollen cloak, which failed to protect him from the rain. Tam glanced down at the boy's small feet; his moccasins were wet-through. He noticed him wriggling his toes, in a miserable bid to fight the cold and felt a pang of sympathy for him.

'I'll take great care of them,' he promised, fervently.

Gill smiled at the boy's enthusiasm, it momentarily lifting his mood.

Encouraged by the child's avid smile, the four riders dismounted. Concerned for the welfare of their horses, Tam accompanied the boy to the stables, behind the Inn, it now almost full of restless occupants. He then grew anxious, seeing the horses, thinking that the Inn would most likely be busy with their owners. *Too many mortals ...* He moaned inside.

Tam paid the young boy handsomely for their horses' care—according to *his* standards; he expected nothing but the best. The child's blue eyes brightened at the coinage in his small hand. Tam smiled at him, reminded of his own youth—eager to please, and eager to prove his worth. Inside, he secretly mourned for the children he would probably never have. As he observed the boy stroke the coins in the palm of his little soiled hand, he wondered why the child was working in such a forsaken place. *Scraping a living for a family without their father, most likely,* he thought. If so, then he was glad he passed him a little *extra*. *Then again, he may be the owner's son.* He grunted. *Och! What of it!*

Slowly, the boy lifted his head, his eyes travelling upwards until he met with the *Giant!* He had never seen a man of Tam's stature before. His small mouth then gaped when he saw his deformed left ear. However, it was when he noticed the hilt of the large claymore sword, peeping at him over Tam's broad shoulder, he gasped in amazement.

'Auch! Ye must be as tall as … William Wallace!' he remarked, stretching as far as he could, on his little toes.

'Aye, lad, 'tis been said,' Tam boasted, leaning down towards him. 'Take good care of them, aye?'

The boy nodded with enthusiastic determination. Satisfied, Tam threw him a wink, then turned, to join his colleagues. The boy, still clutching the coins in his wet hand, watched in awe as the "Giant" strode away and, despite his strangeness, he could not help but like the unusual stranger.

As he approached the Inn, Tam saw Asai and Reece lower their heads as they entered the establishment. Gill, on the other hand, stood hesitant, while the rain continued to pour on his apprehension.

'What are ye standing here for, lad?' Tam asked, coaxing him on, with a playful shove. 'In ye go!'

Gill, releasing a deep sigh, entered.

)

Hardly a soul took note when the door opened, allowing the four strangers to cross its threshold, peacefully. Save for the occasional glance, none seemed perturbed by their presence, and those, who did briefly turn their heads, quickly returned to the huddle of their private conversations. Anyone who stopped by the Inn was there for a purpose, and it was clear, from the lack of friendliness, their visits were not sociable. Each, it seemed, had their own agenda: a journey marked with fear. Reece saw it etched in the eyes of the few who chose to look upon them, noticing they paid little attention to the "Strange One" in their company—Asai. But it was Tam who roused his concerns; he was unsure his young colleague would cope, while in the company of so many *mortals* gathered in the enclosed atmosphere. Wary, he cast him a warning glance; the Highlander obediently understood Reece's underlying threat.

The Inn itself was, surprisingly, not quite as drab and dreary as its exterior. Like any other, the heady smell of stale pipes, hanging from the mouths of most of its customers, threw out a permanent cloud of smoke above their heads.

Though simple in its décor, Gill noted there was nothing to mark the Inn's history or character. It was as though it never had one. It was the custom for a Landlord to display any prized possessions or trophies, on his walls: an array of colourful plaques; a coat of arms—or weaponry—was the norm … But there were none to be seen here. Nothing marked its past, except for the sense of detachment, hanging from its bare walls. With no welcoming smiles, Gill soon grasped its grim reality; not a soul in the sombre establishment was a *local*—each just passing through, minding his own business—huddled in his problems. He looked again, his brows furrowing. Something else was amiss …

There were no women.

*A far cry from The Ferry Inn*, he thought, already missing Balloch's friendly—and more homely—establishment.

A peat fire, someone had neglected to stoke, still provided some light. It was the Inn's only saving grace, bringing a tiny ember of friendliness to the unwelcoming abode. On each table, candles sizzled as their wicks gradually burned out, but as soon as one diminished, it was hastily replaced by the boy, to prevent the Inn from being consumed by darkness.

Reece, spotting an empty table, beckoned his colleagues towards it. As they moved across the busy Inn, Gill felt the grime beneath his feet as they walked over its well-trodden boards. But when the Inn fell silent, he suddenly became conscious of every eye watching them. But the scrutiny of their presence was short-lived; when they stopped and removed their cloaks, the hum of cloistered conversations promptly resumed. Asai, discreetly tilting his head, listened intently to their discussions—the unknown voices engrossed in the same topic of conversation:

"*The Pass.*"

He paid no heed; they, themselves, would be travelling through the caves.

Quietly, they moved to a window—blackened by smoke—and slid into the empty seats, beneath a table that rocked back and forth. Frustrated, Tam frowned as he toyed with it, then glanced over the dusty floor, finding the small wooden wedge that had lost its place. He then returned it, checking the table's sturdiness. Satisfied, he smiled and nodded to himself.

Gill felt a sudden draught across the nape of his neck, its damp breath sighing through the narrow gap in the window. He ran his finger across the cold glass, gathering the thick, black soot that had formed from years of neglect, and peered out through the streak.

The rain still poured.

They had only taken their seats when the young boy approached them again, his features more distinguishable now, without the cover of his cloak: he was pale and thin, and no more than ten-years-old. His black hair was soddened, and as he pushed it away from his eyes, his little round face looked drawn and tired from being overworked. He wore a soiled grey shirt over an oversized pair of faded, black breeches that went above his ankles—clearly too short for his stretching legs. He still wore the wet moccasins; they looked tight on his wide feet—ready to split. Tam cast him a sideward glance. The boy smiled nervously; there was something forced in it.

'Aye, sir, they're watered and fed,' he assured him.

The Highlander grinned, content.

'Would ye be wantin' food and drink?' the child then asked.

'Who's for *Moniack?*' Tam blurted.

Gill's eyes brightened at the thought—and taste—of something familiar and welcoming. The mead would, at least, stoke the chill from the unfriendly ambience. Asai's dark eyes darted from one to the other, perplexed.

'Ah! Ye've never tried it, then,' Tam deduced, judging by the Samurai's curious frown.

Reece smiled faintly at his colleague's attempt to brighten their mood before his face slipped back to his thoughts.

'Well, then, 'tis something we must remedy,' Tam went on. 'Aye, there is a first time for everything, my friend,' he added, mocking Asai. 'And I am proud to boast that I have, at last, succeeded you in something.' He turned to the child who waited patiently. 'Four Moniacks, lad! Large ones! And food!'

Gill raised his eyes at the Dhampir's mention of a *mortal's* requirement. Not once had he seen the three put a single morsel to their mouths, since their first meeting.

'Sometimes!' Reece commented. '—only when we require it. We can go without food for days.'

Gill's eyes slid towards Tam. Secretly, he had been aware of the Dhampir's discreet visits into the woods to, "Search for the Sorceress." It had been the excuse for his occasional absence. Although he had grown accustomed to the Highlander's "eating habits" it was never spoken of, sparing his discomfort.

'I know he won't harm me,' Gill whispered to his grandfather. 'And … I am glad of his company, too.'

Promptly the young boy returned, weighed down with four large tankards of Scottish mead—the drink made from fermented honey— with the assurance that food was on its way. They watched as he went about his business, attending to other customers; he appeared to be alone in his work. Tam looked through the dimness of the Inn until his curious eyes found the individual, he presumed to be the Landlord. The proprietor, who held "court" behind a small counter, at the far end of his establishment, kept a keen eye on the boy. Two lanterns hung on the wall behind him, casting a glow over his head. The Landlord was lean and tall; Tam imagined, if he raised his hand, he could easily touch the low beams that held the Inn's roof in place. His hair was thin and greying, barely noticeable behind its receding line. A man of middle years, his haggard face was long and drawn, and his most prominent feature—his long-hooked nose—seemed to add to its length. Occasionally stepping out to check on his punters, Tam noticed he walked with a slight limp and was carrying a cloth over his right shoulder. Tam contemplated the Landlord's relationship with the boy; there was none, as they did not converse, except when taking an order. The child seemed to avoid eye contact with his employer, and Tam saw how the Landlord kept his gaze regularly fixed on the lad. No. There was something not quite right about it; his demeanour towards the boy was troubling, making the Highlander question it.

Tam's attention was then distracted by the sound of Gill's brightening mood as he indulged in his first sup. Asai, staring down at the unusual beverage, inspected its strange, amber colour and sweet scent, deciding it had a pleasant aroma, after detecting the hint of honey wafting through his nostrils, his eyes twitching, then widening at its *strength!*

Food soon arrived, in the form of broth, cured meat and bread, all served up in well-used pewter dishes. Gill immediately tucked in, somewhat surprised that the dismal establishment served food with an edible appeal.

'It's surprisingly good!' he was forced to admit, shovelling another mouthful. His appetite had increased—tenfold—since they left Balloch. He looked up, half-expecting the unknown cook to appear, then resumed eating; he was too ravenous to care. 'There'll be none left if you don't tuck in,' he then mumbled through his full mouth, encouraging the others to eat. With every mouthful, he felt his strength increase. Reece and Asai finally joined him, eating methodically and slowly until they had had their fill, while Tam abstained; though not yet used to mortal food, the Highlander was quite happy with his choice of beverage.

Content, Tam drew the back of his oversized hand across his mouth, then stared down at Reece and Asai's tankards; they were still full. 'Are ye not drinkin'?' he quizzed, frowning at the waste of good mead.

Not wanting to insult the Highlander's pride, Reece and Asai shared a glance and then raised the strong, sweet-smelling beverage to their mouths. Tam and Gill watched with curiosity, waiting for their reaction—like the response of someone who was about to embark on a new and unexpected experience; to their disappointment, it did not come. Together, the four supped, enjoying the only comforting thing the Inn had to offer.

Gill leaned over the worn-wooden table, and eyed its surface; it was heavily marked, by the hands that once rested on it, over time. It seemed as if every stranger who had passed through the Inn's doors, purposely etched their name for prosperity, as though they wished to be remembered—forgotten souls, leaving nothing behind but a mark, scratched into a piece of wood.

'Do you not find it strange?' Gill quietly remarked, glancing around. He then leaned towards his companions, dropping his voice. 'Look at them!' Their eyes darted over the Inn's clients, each huddled in secrecy. 'See how they watch the door ...' he added, nodding towards their anxious faces.

'Waiting to see what fate has in store for them, I should imagine,' Reece suspected. 'It is the look of apprehension that keeps their eyes focused. Their journey has, no doubt, been tolerant to this point, after which ...' He paused, throwing a quick eye about. 'I am at a loss.' He shrugged. 'Who knows what lies ahead for these ignorant souls.'

'Do you think we should tell them?' Gill asked, with an edge of guilt. 'About the—'

'No!' Reece snapped, through gritted teeth. 'They are not our concern. And what is more, we cannot trust anyone. We tell no one,' he then added, leaning forward—the hostile look in his eyes, warning Gill.

Gill recoiled from his grandfather's glare, then noticed something behind his striking green eyes: a bitterness tainted with sadness and dominated by anger. He then caught Tam and Asai exchanging a wary glance—the surge of tension between them evident by their look. Reece clenched his fists so tightly Gill could hear the grinding of his knuckles. It was evident, by his subtle yet determined outburst, something was wrong. Folding his arms, he slid them across the table towards his grandfather, ready to challenge him when the Inn's door was thrust wide open ...

# Chapter Twenty

*The Aber Hills*

The *Guide* walked alone, knowing where the trail would take him—just as it had done, two nights before—his confidence waning, knowing what he would find. Nevertheless, he had to be certain before being forced to take the *other* route. He could now feel the weary effect of the long trek taking its toll on his body; three days in a row he had walked the same route. And, to make matters worse, the weather was not improving, hampering his journey, altogether. If only the sky had been clear, there would have been no disputing his decision: he would have risked the *Pass*. But there was no point in going near it now; the sky was dense and laden with rain, threatening to teem down on everything below it.

*"The lonely tread to one's unknown fate."*

That was how some travellers described it—the ones who were willing to brave the Pass. *The fools!* he thought, almost pitying them. Almost. However, at times there was no avoiding their persistence— and the bribery of their heavy purses. Unfortunately, he would not be feeling the weight of their coinage this night. Only two nights remained before the moon's light would finally disappear, to the far reaches of the earth.

His head throbbed at the thought of two more journeys—there *and* back. Nevertheless, he would do it, and for one reason only: to replenish his finances. For now, it was decided: he would return to the Ardgore Inn, where he would be forced to look into the pitiful faces of those who were adamant to get to the other side of the loch.

'Not tonight, my *friends!*' he muttered.

He looked up at the sharp outline of trees hanging onto the edge of the mountain, like dark drunken giants swaying in the wind, its force pressing down on them as they fought hard against its might. He glanced above their tops; dusk's light was swiftly diminishing as layer upon layer of darkening clouds crept across the sinister sky. As they descended, the twin mountains looked as though they would disappear into its fold. He studied the clouds, waiting. No, there would be no moonlight to penetrate their thickness. Rain was inevitable; he could feel its dampness seeping into his lungs. He groaned, knowing it would now make his downward climb more difficult, forcing him to slow his pace. He longed for the warmer climate he had once known and shivered at the notion of autumn prematurely surrendering itself over to winter. The transition from the unusual late summer had been sudden. In a matter of days, it seemed as though the world had taken a turn, for the worse. He could sense its hostile presence spying on him. He glanced up, again. *How quickly night falls in this forsaken place!* he thought.

Once again, The Ardgore Inn entered his mind; he would indulge in a large glass of whisky when he got back—perhaps more than one— and imagined the gold liquid gliding down his throat, easing his lungs. He thought of his horse, Nahla—the name he had given her when she took her first drink of water from his cupped hands when she was a foal. He hoped she was not spooked; she hated the rain and would be aware of its imminent arrival. He would have to return to her, soon.

He mused over the caves, hoping to find some way of re-entering them.

*Just one more attempt,* he decided.

On his approach, he looked up at the once familiar terrain, searching for them, but could no longer see the natural curve of their outline.

He sighed. 'That's it! No point in returning here,' he told himself. 'They are gone, forever—lost to the outside world!'

Disheartened, he walked away from them for the last time, though was tempted to look back, for one final glimpse. He then paused, looking over the terrain, and thought it strange; nothing beyond the caves had been disturbed by the "landslide". Surely, had *that* been the cause, it would have had a detrimental effect on everything surrounding it. And yet, all seemed as it was. Even the valley between the *Twins* remained untouched.

*Most likely a freak of nature,* he deduced. Either way, there would be no more access. He would be forced to raise his price now—for those brave enough to use the *Pass*. He was not risking life nor limb for a pittance—no matter who they were.

On his final descent from the mountain, he stalled, surveying his surroundings, certain he had returned from whence he came. He glanced around, looking for his horse, her thick white mane and tail distinguishable against her dark, chestnut coat—unusual colourings for a Friesian. But it was what he had loved about her and had had no regrets paying the merchant the over-the-odds price for her. She was different—something to which he could relate.

He hesitated on his approach, listening for the familiar sound of her eager movements whenever she sensed his return. Nothing. He strained his eyes, combing through the angry dusk, expecting to catch her ghostly mane; she was nowhere to be seen. He quickly checked his surroundings again, certain he was on the right track.

*Where is she?* he wondered, frustrated.

The *Guide* went to the place where he had left her tied: to a lone rowan tree, its distinguishable red berries—and superstition attached to it—proving to be the perfect marker. Although autumn had almost diminished, the small fruit still clung to its branches. It was thought the physical characteristics of the tree may have contributed to its protective reputation, including the tiny five-pointed pentagram on each berry, opposite its stalk. Their colour red was said to offer the best protection against enchantment.

*"Rowan tree and red thread make the witches lose their speed."* He recited the old rhyme in his mind, despite his scepticism towards local superstitions.

Looking down, he saw the disturbance of Nahla's hooves, on the damp ground; they were erratic and scattered.

'Damn you, Nahla!' he snarled, realising she had, after all, been distressed by the elements and would no longer wait around for her master with the onslaught of rain.

About to step out into the narrow valley, he lingered, thinking he had heard her tread, somewhere in the distance.

He called out to her.

'*Nahla!*' His echo was flat. He cupped his hands over his mouth and called her again. But the only reply was the sound of trees being thrown back and forth against their will, and he assumed, knowing how clever she was, that she had come looking for him. He then dismissed the idea; the mountainside was steep and rocky and would limit her climb. No— he would have to look for her.

He moaned, then turned, making his way through the woods, dragging his feet back to the mountainside.

Following the tree line, he skirted along the base for a while, continuously calling her name. Still, there was no sight of her distinctive features. It then occurred to him, she may have been stolen by a passer-by, who decided to brave the long and treacherous route around the loch. Vexed by this thought, he growled, concluding that someone had stolen his precious Nahla. It was his only explanation, as she had never deserted him before.

He decided to return to the lonely rowan tree, to check the direction the "thief" might have taken her. If her impressions pointed in the direction of the Loch of Loyne, then it was possible the perpetrator might take shelter at the Inn, should they still be en route.

'Say your prayers, *thief!*' he seethed, returning to the scene of the alleged crime.


The *Guide* quickened his pace, feeling the notable absence of Nahla's company. It was no place to be travelling alone, especially with the quickening approach of a dismal night. On that thought, he was thankful for the weapon, clinging to his back, it giving him comfort and reassurance that he was not completely alone.

Nahla's hooves marked the direction the Friesian had gone—or been "taken"—but when he checked again, it appeared she had come looking for him. He released a long weary sigh and returned to the woods, allowing himself no more than an hour to search for her. And, regardless of how late it was, he would still make his way back to the Inn; he had no intention of bedding down for the night, beneath a sheet of rain.

Tired and frustrated, by his horses' desertion, he trudged on, then slowed when he became conscious of an unpleasant stillness. It uneased him. Shrugging the uncomfortable feeling off, he marched on, his eyes darting from side to side, watching the trees; they seemed to move with him.

At first, he thought them shadows, cast by the moonlight, but the weight of the menacing clouds above quickly reminded him, the moon was hidden above them. He stalled, nervously glancing around.

Nothing.

He then sensed the company of another presence and tried to discard it, but it preyed on his concerns. It was then, at that moment, he realised … he was not alone.

*Time to go back!* he promptly decided, turning on his heel while, at the same time, cursing his horse again. 'You damn … stubborn Friesian! No apples for you—for a week!'

On his return journey, the feeling of being pursued by the "presence" began to wane. He rolled his eyes, shook his head and smiled, blaming his mind—and foolish superstition—for playing tricks on him, along with the coming of night.

*"Loneliness can fool the mind into thinking sinister thoughts, letting it believe you are not alone."*

His father's words came back to him, providing some comfort; despite them, a nagging instinct eventually forced him to stop. He held his breath, listening …

*There is something out there!* he realised.

A distant movement between the trees caught his eye. An animal perhaps? Despite the disapproval of his instincts, he moved towards it.

As he did so, *it* appeared to mimic his steps; when he stopped, it paused. Then, what looked like a pale red light, winked at him. A fox, no doubt, he resolved, before changing his mind. *No*—the nocturne's eyes shone like silver in the cover of darkness—*Not a fox*. He looked again. He now saw two tiny red lights; this time they blinked at him— the warmth of their unusual colour penetrating the darkening woods, like little round beacons. They were obtrusive.

He tilted his head and blinked, to see clearer, thinking they had moved closer. He was unsure. He drew back and blinked again. There was no mistaking it; they had drawn nearer. He drew his breath, unable to close his eyes, for fear of the dark.

Suddenly the wind rose, bringing with it a pirouette of dry leaves, rustling and swirling around his feet, in perfect formation. Distracted by their performance, he looked down. They appeared to take the shape of something—something he could not quite determine. He narrowed his eyes, leaning his head to the side as they began to take form, separating into two familiar shapes.

'Are those …?'

He looked up, sharply.

Two pale red eyes were staring right at him.

'Does she still sleep?'

'She does.'

With her eyes fixed on the slumbering figure, curled in a protective, foetal position, L'Ordana breezed by Kara, unconvinced; she would see for herself, just to be sure.

Narrowing her curious eyes, she leaned over the form, listening to the faint sound of their breathing, their chest rising and falling so slowly and methodically, she imagined it would stop, bringing an end to their life. She would not let *that* happen; they were too precious a commodity.

*So peaceful,* she thought, tempted to reach out, to brush back the strands of fair hair, lying delicately across the girl's face. Staring down at her beauty and youth, L'Ordana was, again, made aware of time; it was not on her side, making her feel different—older. Subtle yet present, it reminded her of its cruel and constant intervention.

She then became conscious of Kara's fathomless, icy-grey eyes, watching her from behind; always watching with *that* derisive stare. *Has she noticed it, too?* she thought, struck by the Valkyrie's hidden agenda: always waiting in the wings, should she weaken. *No!* she told herself, determined. She would not give Kara leeway to suspect it.

'Good!' she said, lifting her voice, hiding her dread.

Leaving her unconscious and unaware, L'Ordana made to move away from her young captive, then flinched when her slender fingers suddenly twitched. She hesitated, convinced, for a moment, the girl had heard her. *Absurd!* she thought, burying the notion.

Abruptly, she turned to face Kara, relieved to see she had failed to notice—the Valkyrie, too preoccupied with polishing her lance. 'Then let us keep her that way!' she stated, turning her back on her again.

L'Ordana, now in deep thought, slowly moved about the confines of the tent, her eyes occasionally darting towards the sleeping figure. With her mind elsewhere, she tried to hide her frustration, while toying with a small object in her hand. *Why is it taking so long?* she thought.

'For how long?'

L'Ordana stopped—the Valkyrie's raspy voice, disrupting her thoughts. They stared at one another in dense silence.

Kara, her patience wearing thin, lifted her eyes. 'How long do you want her—'

'As long as it takes,' she snapped back before composing herself. Then, extending her hand towards the Valkyrie, L'Ordana opened her palm. 'You will need more of *this* if we are to keep her in constant slumber; we cannot risk her conversing with Asai, through their thoughts—if what you told me is true. *They* must not know where we are.'

The Valkyrie took the ornate glass vial, willingly. Raising the delicate item to the level of her eye, she contemplated it; it looked tiny clamped between her thick fingers.

''Tis rather sweet, when you think of it,' said L'Ordana, momentarily musing over the girl and the Samurai. 'But what is the point when there will be no future for—' She looked sharp when Kara suddenly shook the vial, its potent oily liquid coating the inside of the grey, baroque glass. 'Be careful with that!' she snapped.

A subtle grin crept across the Valkyrie's face.

'Three drops, Kara,' she warned. 'No more. Do you hear?'

'What if …?' Kara hesitated. '… my hand should shake, and I administer more than the required amount?' she sneered.

'Then I will cut it off!' L'Ordana retorted, anxiously moving towards the exit of the tent. She ignored the deep-rooted sigh from behind, though was aware of the Valkyrie's eyes now boring into her back.

L'Ordana, drawing back the tent flap slightly, looked out and up; the rain was trying its best to escape the clouds, but they were not ready to part with it, yet. *Nothing but endless trees and mountains*, she thought. *Who would venture into a desolate place like this?* Nonetheless, she was thankful for them—the dense woods—for their protection and for concealing her drove of growing warriors. She regarded the Dhampir carefully; there was much movement—more than usual—around their temporary encampment. They were growing agitated, making her uneasy. She blamed Magia Nera for that. She noticed the way they would watch his every move—not like harbouring a prisoner but—as though in awe of a leader. It concerned her; the last thing she needed was the dark Warlock having any influence over them. *Not while I am around,* she vowed.

Then, from the corner of her eye—through the hub of activity—she imagined she caught the outline of a figure emerging from his tent. She had kept the dark Warlock's "lodgings" a capable distance from her own, so she could watch him discreetly. But the constant agitation of her warriors' movements—back and forth across her view—blotted her vision. It was clear they were waiting for his return; Magia had gone out into the night with his word that he would be back. And to be sure of it, she had sent Wareeshta to spy on him. Besides, it was unlikely he would desert her now. As long as she led him to believe that she still had the book, she knew he would remain in her company.

Just as it entered her thoughts, she was quickly distracted by the constant reminder of the other item she kept concealed on her person—the heat of his amulet, its burning influence ever-present. At times, she felt it was marking the way for her, but was unsure, blaming its master's closeness of presence for manipulating its "mood."

It had been a laborious task, trying to remove it from the place she had kept it—concealed behind the panels of her secret chamber—the amulet, as time wore on, refusing to be handled by no others but its master. Even the Samurai had failed to steal it; not to mention Kara's several attempts—the ugly scar still visible on the Valkyrie's palm when she toyed with the glass vial, in front of her.

But her powers were useless against it. And so, she had casually asked Wareeshta—who willingly obliged—the Dhampir believing her mistress had favoured her over the Valkyrie. She recalled the stench of Wareeshta's burning flesh as she removed it—the skin quickly renewing itself, beautifully. And, disregarding the caustic look on the Dhampir's face, after, she had lied, by telling her; "You have done me a great service, Wareeshta. I will not forget this."

Now she kept its influence at bay, in a thick, black-satin pouch, concealed in a pocket, inside her cloak. But she knew Magia was no fool; he knew it was there. And yet, he had made no attempt to take back what was rightfully his. *Why is that?* she wondered. *Biding his time, no doubt, should I—*

A sound from behind interrupted her wandering thoughts. She tilted her head sideways, hearing Kara shuffling towards her. She had momentarily forgotten the Valkyrie's irritating presence.

'Daylight is fading quickly,' Kara remarked, staring over her shoulder. 'They are getting restless,' she added, pointing with her chin to where she could hear the warriors' agitated movements outside.

L'Ordana moved away from the Valkyrie, her wafting, heady scent of lemon oil overriding her senses. She hated it!

'Remember what I told you, Kara. I want the girl to—' She stopped, hearing the swift, light movement of footsteps approaching. She knew Wareeshta's subtle tread anywhere, and yet barely heard her pause outside her tent, let alone her entrance. She turned, meeting the Dhampir face to face.

'Well?'

'He has found what you are looking for, Mistress!'

'Are you sure?'

Wareeshta nodded, her eyes discreetly darting to Eleanor's coerced state of inertia. She would have to find a way to speak to the girl, again. *There must be a—*

'Well, well,' L'Ordana began. Wareeshta jolted. But the Sorceress had by now turned her attention back to Kara, having noticed the contemptuous smirk on her face. 'It appears the old man was telling the truth, after all,' she added, recalling his last moments, in the Valkyrie's capable, deadly grip. 'It seems Magia Nera has finally found our *Guide.*'

# Chapter Twenty-One

For an instant, the *Guide* felt certain he was peering into the eyes of the "Devil himself". He stepped back, taking in the figure as they lowered their head, a contemptuous grin creeping across their mouth.

*This is no man*, he realised, with horror. He opened his mouth to speak but was silenced by the sudden grip of their forceful hands on his head—the tips of their fingers pressing firmly, applying unbearable pressure. As it mounted, the immense pain he experienced was crushing. He then felt his feet being lifted from the ground and reached up to grab the hands of death; he was not yet ready to die.

Weakened against his attacker's increasing strength, he desperately wanted to cry out for help but was unable. But who would hear him, in the confined space of somewhere as remote as this—the place where he was now fighting for his life?

No one—but the *Grim Reaper*.

'Leave him!' a firm voice demanded as it emerged from the crowded woods. 'Do not kill him!'

Magia Nera barely loosened his hold on his captive as L'Ordana stepped forward. The dark Warlock leaned towards him, his crimson eyes dancing feverishly as they burned into his potential victim with a wanting stare.

The *Guide* could feel the coldness of death on his face as Magia breathed heavily on him; his nostrils flared from the stench of the Warlock's menace. No warning could have prevented the hopeless situation he now found himself in. He did not see it coming. Unable to move, he was rendered utterly helpless while suspended in his firm grip.

And as the dark Warlock's cold breath worked its way down his victim's throat, the *Guide* felt his head being slowly tilted to one side.

'Enough, Magia!' the female's voice cried, with venom, her raised tone suggesting authority.

Relieved from his grasp, but not his hold, the *Guide* diverted his eyes as the apparition of a beautiful woman came into view, her stride defined and assured. Magia Nera stepped aside, but maintained his hold, while L'Ordana edged closer to study the captive.

'Let him go!'

Released abruptly from the "Devil's" grip, the *Guide* felt the welcome return of the ground, beneath his feet. Although his head throbbed, he was transfixed by the woman's appearance: her pale features peered out at him from inside the hood of the full-length cloak she wore, its deep, rich shade of pine, blending with nature's surroundings; the fullness of her dark hair was hidden beneath the hood, save for a few wispy strands that caressed her pale skin. Her eyes widened as she regarded him, with intrigue. He could not distinguish their colour. At first, he thought them pale—hazel, perhaps—or blue? He could not say; nor did he care, at that moment.

The *Guide's* eyes then slowly followed Magia, carefully observing his assailant as he retreated—the dark Warlock's unusual features standing out, in the grey of the night: his skin was pale and flawless and shone like ivory; his perfectly groomed black hair hung down his slender back, and away from his features, outlining the shape and length of his narrow face; his clothes were of an age and finery he had seen before—worn by men of wealth and power. Though aware of his scrutiny of him, Magia continued to stare at the prisoner with his devilish eyes.

Detecting a lingering scent of sweet amber oil, the *Guide's* attention was lured back to the cloaked woman as its aroma emanated from her. There was something about its exotic and pleasant fragrance that reminded him of his travels, and he surmised, by its origins, that she hailed from afar.

'You are the guide—to the loch?' she enquired, her manner now calm and steady.

He was suddenly drawn by the difference in her tone; there was a maturity in it that did not match her demeanour, making it difficult to determine her age—although she had the appearance of youth. He opened his mouth to reply but found he could not speak. It was as if his voice had been *stolen*. He then became conscious of the weight of his sword, as though reminding him of its presence. He was more than aware of it, and yet was unable to reach for its required assistance.

L'Ordana raised her slender hand and drew it across his lips, her touch light and feathery; he felt the tip of her nail glide against his mouth. In an instant, his words found their way out.

'Who are you?!' he blurted.

She ignored him, momentarily distracted, leaving his question unanswered. She turned her head slightly, listening. His eyes followed her; he had heard it, too, and looked over her shoulder.

The shadows, he had imagined moving with him through the woods, slowly began to emerge, drawn to his scent. The *Guide* swallowed as the black shapes edged out into the clearing, and yet he could not see their true forms. He then saw the woman lift her hand.

'Not yet!' she ordered them; still, they persisted. *Why do they not stop?* she thought, displeased by their disobedience. She moved to implement her demand when another voice intervened.

*'Ritiro!'*

The sound of Magia Nera, telling her warriors to "retreat!" vexed her more. The figures promptly returned to the blackness of the woods, watching and waiting.

Maintaining her poise, L'Ordana turned to her captive and leaned towards him.

'Are we too late?' she whispered in his ear.

He drew back, confused, gaping at her.

'Has the *Hour* passed?' she prompted, in answer to his vacant stare.

Aware of her meaning, he shook his head.

'And tell me …' she added. 'Has your path crossed with any other, this night?'

Again, he shook his head.

'I—I've seen no one.'

Narrowing her eyes, she regarded him; something told her he was telling the truth.

A curl appeared at the corner of her mouth. 'Good,' she said, her tone brighter. 'Then you will take us to the loch, and lead us across,' she informed him in a casual matter-of-fact tone. 'And, in return, I shall spare your life. A fair exchange, I should think?'

The *Guide's* mouth fell, in disbelief. He closed his eyes tight, convinced this—whatever *it* was—was a cruel intrusion on a dream he was having, and nothing more than a vivid nightmare. But the pain in his head marked something different. He opened his eyes again. To his misfortune, the "intrusion" was all too real.

'Perhaps—he has forgotten,' Magia remarked, moving closer.

The *Guide* cowered away. The dark Warlock slowly shook his head, as a warning to his captive. There was no mistaking the obvious threat in his belligerent eyes.

*Do not even attempt it, mortal!*

'Perhaps!' L'Ordana mocked.

'My horse!' he then blurted, now convinced *they* had taken her. 'Where is she?'

L'Ordana sighed. 'I have no interest in your … *horse!*' she said, unimpressed at the thought of even discussing the animal.

He pressed his lips hard, seething inside, believing they had slain his beloved Friesian.

L'Ordana tutted. 'You may be assured that I do not know the whereabouts of your horse. If it has disappeared, it is not our doing. Now, I insist you show us the way to the loch or—'

'Who told you about me?' he demanded, interrupting her.

She lifted her head and brows together, at his insistence. *The impertinence of it!* she thought. 'There are those who are easily tempted to talk. If not—then … "persuaded" to,' she stated, recalling the fear in the elderly man's eyes when confronted by the unusual "creatures," as he had called them. He had been most informative of the lochs' history. And while he relayed the tale, through his obvious fear, she had a vague recollection of a memory. There had been something familiar in it, and yet she struggled to remember. She wondered if the old man was still alive. *Unlikely,* she thought, having left him in Kara's capable hands, then recalled his last word as he uttered it into the universe:

"Blair!"

*No matter!* She shrugged. *What's done is done!* Besides, the fewer who knew of their presence the better—for the time being.

'*Si!*' Magia grunted. 'I think he has,' he remarked, rousing her from her thoughts.

L'Ordana threw him a second glance, momentarily lost.

He rolled his eyes. 'Forgotten!'

'I have not!' the *Guide* snapped, his eyes darting from one to the other.

'Then I suggest you talk … quickly,' L'Ordana urged 'You do not want to antagonise my colleagues,' she added, glancing over her shoulder.

The *Guide* drew his brows, then, narrowing his eyes, stared at her. *Colleagues?!*

The crunching of dead leaves, beneath a heavy step, stole his attention from the cloaked woman. His mouth gaped slightly as he observed the female warrior's determined approach, her bodice of armour shining beneath the ominous sky. She was holding an unusual weapon firmly in her right hand; its deep shade of green was darker than that of pine and had the appearance of glass. He followed its impressive length to the tip, where the spear's head glinted silver, like her armour. He then noted the hilt of a sword over her shoulder, its make unknown to him. It was then he saw the shadow following in her steps and realised she was not alone.

The lithe figure of a young woman moved nimbly behind her yet kept her distance. She wore the garb of a hunter, and though unarmed, was alert to her surroundings.

He had seen nothing like their kind before.

The tall, armoured one marched towards him. He tried to retreat from her advance as her icy-grey eyes leered at him. Try as he did, he could not avert from her stare.

'Not yet!' L'Ordana muttered as the Valkyrie edged towards the prisoner. Wareeshta, however, maintained her distance, hoping her "gift" would not be called upon.

L'Ordana then stalled to let the Valkyrie toy with the *Guide*, for a few moments, watching her rise to her full height as she loomed over him, with intent.

'Not one sinew of goodness exists inside her body,' the Sorceress warned him. 'Therefore, if you do not bow to my will, I shall have her sign your death warrant, with your blood, and seal it with …' Her words trailed to silence, observing Kara. She was curious to see how far the Valkyrie would go—how far she would *allow* her.

As Kara stared down her crooked nose at him, he lifted his head, away from her overpowering scent of lemon oil, to see the black onyx stone embedded in the thick gold band on her forehead. No doubt a representation of her black heart—if what the cloaked woman said was true.

Kara leaned in, forcing him to meet her stare. He could feel her warm, heavy breath on his mouth. She moved closer. The heady aroma of her scent made him light-headed as she placed her hardened lips on his. It was unexpected. Repulsed, he quickly recoiled, feeling the sharp pain. She stepped back, smirking at him. He ran his tongue across his mouth, conscious of the warm metallic liquid gliding down his throat as his lip swelled. He then sensed a growing agitation around him, his eyes watching, wary when the atmosphere suddenly became increasingly threatening and menacing. His eyes moved to the trees, hearing the restless movements behind their curtain; and though he could not see—

nor did he wish to—he now felt the eyes of hunger constant, and fixed on him.

'They are thirsty,' L'Ordana stated, observing him as he watched the trees, his eyes wide and set.

*Thirsty?* he thought, unable to grasp her meaning. He stared in their direction, now seeing their pale-red eyes blink uncontrollably as they gradually came into view, their waxen faces leering at him, with a craving that alerted him to their physical existence.

'No! Impossible!'

She smiled, hearing him quietly speak his thoughts.

He pressed down on his mouth, sealing his lips, in a desperate bid to stop the flow of blood; but it was a useless attempt to sway them. He could hear the low sneering of the one who bit his lip. His eyes darted frantically, searching for a way to escape the terror of what would happen to him. *Is this it? Is this my end?*

Closer they drew, steady and alert, lowering their fixed gaze on him. The seconds dragged as he held his breath. He was in no doubt of their intentions. It was there, plain to see, in their craving eyes; they were preparing to pounce.

As he braced himself for their attack, they froze. Reluctant, at first, to look away from his aggressors, his eyes were diverted from their impassive stare to the cloaked woman. Her right hand was raised high, determined in her command to control the *creatures*.

'I will also let *them* have their way, should you fail to tell me what I wish to know,' she warned him. 'I think you have seen enough to "persuade" you.'

The *Guide* blinked, in agreement. He then heard their hesitant retreat, feeling momentarily relieved by it. But they did not return to the shadows. Instead, they lingered, maintaining their intimidating stare, to Kara's annoyance. She longed for the pleasure of dispatching the captive, should the opportunity arise. It had been a while, and she liked the look of him. Yes. She would willingly have him wait for her, in *Valhalla*.

A movement then caught L'Ordana's eye; Magia Nera had, again, lured closer as the scent of warm blood teased his senses, but she knew he was stronger than his underlings, allowing his willpower to repress his urge.

The *Guide* watched the Warlock's steady advance with unease; there was no sound in his movement. *Best start talking!* he told himself. 'I can take you there,' he blurted, in submission to their demands and defined threats. 'But … it is not an easy journey, nor as straightforward as you might think,' he added.

'Then … we are not too late?' L'Ordana enquired.

'There is enough time … now that the nights grow darker.'

Lifting her head, she smiled and nodded, pleased to hear this.

'But …'

She frowned. She hated *that* word; it was filled with nothing but obstacles.

'… without the moonlight,' he continued, 'it is unlikely we will see the loch.'

'He lies!' Kara snarled, toying with the Obsidian, her grip tightening, eager to use it.

The *Guide* regarded the intimidating weapon and swallowed, imagining its silver tip hurdling towards him. It was evident, by its owner's growing frustration, she was capable of anything. *Not one sinew of goodness exists inside her body,* he reminded himself.

'I swear it!' he begged. 'On my father's—'

'If it were not for the fact that you know the route, and are *human*,' L'Ordana interrupted, then cast a sinister glance into the shadows, 'I would gladly let *them* have their way with you. But it amuses me—the weakness of man—when he is faced with a dilemma. The desperation to protect his loved ones … makes me almost—' She stopped and looked at him, with a sense of recognition. But her mind was elsewhere, lost in time, searching for fragments of a past that were trying desperately to remind her of another life: *the loch; the ghost; shimmering waters, beneath the glittering black sky; the sorrowful cries for help* … L'Ordana's eyes found his. 'I believe you are right, in what you say,' she said, surprised by her admission.

Magia Nera shot a wary glance at her; she failed to see it.

'You are acquainted with the lochs' history?' the *Guide* quizzed, side-glancing her.

'A little, it seems,' she replied, musing over the images that had surfaced from her subconscious.

'What are you looking for—on the other side?' he then asked.

L'Ordana, overlooking his question, unexpectedly edged closer to him, with intrigue. Suspicious, Magia followed behind, discreetly. She tilted her head, taking the captive in, then lifted her chin and raised a brow at him. 'Where do you hail from?' she asked, suddenly curious about his slight accent; it was difficult to place, but foreign, no less.

He grunted, bemused. 'Why should it matter—with my life hanging in the balance?'

A contemptuous smile appeared on her mouth, amused by his reply. 'A valid point,' she stated, then dismissed it. 'So, remind me!' she went on, dropping her voice to a whisper. 'The moonlight?'

'Without it'—he swallowed, feeling compelled to lower his voice, too—'the journey is pointless. But …'

She closed her eyes, frustrated, trying to obliterate *that* word from her mind.

'… should you brave it, then you will be faced with unspeakable danger.'

'Indeed,' she returned, raising her head to explore the ugliness of the forbidding sky. There was not a single shred of evidence to show that a moon existed beyond the black, heavy clouds. But it was there—and she knew it.

'A mere inconvenience!'

All eyes turned, on hearing Magia Nera's remark, his presence alone, commanding their attention. The dark Warlock then took "centre stage," like a great actor about to deliver his lines from a scene, specially written for him, by a famous Playwright.

The dark figures, still lingering in the shadows by the edge of the woods, grew restless when he moved towards them, his single *look* warning them to step away; they promptly retreated. L'Ordana grit her teeth as Magia's audience looked on, curious. She had no idea what he was going to do and resented him for it.

Smug and commanding, the dark Warlock stepped out onto his "stage" and spread his arms wide, in a theatrical manner. He tilted his head back, ready to embrace the night. Lifting his right arm, he pointed towards the heavens and, reaching higher, snatched something, clenching his hand so tightly it shook as his power accumulated. Closing his eyes, he silently uttered words, summoning the energy from inside him. It swelled rapidly, propelling itself upwards through his body until he grasped it inside his fist. Slowly and steadily, he opened his hand. There, in the hollow of his palm, a spherical crystal made of pure quartz shone brilliantly, its array of vivid colours swirling in unison with his increasing power. Magia extended his hand for all to see. L'Ordana glared at him; he sensed her annoyance and smirked. The small, perfectly formed object grew brighter as its energy accelerated. He then released it. All eyes watched, following the crystal as it gradually soared skywards, letting the clouds envelop it.

They waited.

When nothing happened, L'Ordana grinned to herself. But her smugness was brief when flashes of white light darted through the clouds, lighting up the dark as they penetrated their thickness. Magia stretched his hand wide, like a flower being woken by the morning light of the sun. The clouds followed suit, parting on his silent command. Through the gap it created, it seemed as though another world beckoned. Wider they parted, searching for the waning moon. They did not have long to wait; a stream of brilliant moonlight reached down, lighting up everything below it.

The *Guide* forced his eyes to look down. *I must see them properly!* he thought, his panic escalating. *I have to be sure!* His eyes widened with heightened fear as the truth revealed itself: a small army of creatures surrounded him—too many to count—and intent on having their way, should they be let.

Their pallid skin now glowed beneath the moonlight, revealing their finer features. No two were alike, save for the paleness of their hungry, red eyes, and the blackness of their clothing. Some, he surmised, were from the far reaches of the world, judging by their unusual features— one, in particular, standing out, his long, snow-white hair gleaming like silver against his darkened skin, in the moonlight. But their origins were of no consequence, for each *creature* was armed with a sword and staring right at him; however, it was the one with the white hair whose penetrating stare carried the most intense and intimidating look, forcing him to look away.

*What hope do I have?* He closed his eyes, willing them to disappear as panic set in.

'Something else you neglected to teach me,' L'Ordana sniped, glaring at Magia.

The dark Warlock promptly snatched his hand closed, concealing the moon from view. The crystal faded before falling to earth, back to the hand of its waiting master. He admired its beauty while displaying a wry smile at her remark, intent on reminding her who truly had the upper hand, despite her claims of possessing control over him.

Inside, L'Ordana was seething with jealousy, thinking of the years he had dedicated to her. "I will teach you everything I know, *Bella*," he had promised. She now regretted not having completed the book before its untimely disappearance.

'Why did you do that?!' bellowed Kara, marching towards Magia to confront him.

Magia looked up at the Valkyrie and grunted, refusing to answer her demand; nor was he obliged to. Deciding to antagonise her further, he cast a playful glance at Wareeshta. Kara looked sharp, catching the curl appearing at the side of the Dhampir's mouth. Unruffled by her fury, Wareeshta eyed the Valkyrie with a smug look. Infuriated that she should be made fun of, Kara moved to confront her colleague.

'We cannot risk informing our "friends" of our location,' Magia blurted, stopping the Valkyrie in her tracks. 'As you and your "pet" failed to follow their tracks, we must assume they are in pursuit of us.' Kara ground her teeth as her eyes slid away from his mockery. 'After all,' he went on, 'they know we have the girl. Therefore, the moon shall remain concealed until the time of my choosing,' he added, then hurdled the sphere of quartz up into the clouds until he required it again.

Magia quickly turned, his eyes glaring at their captive, then lunged towards him. The *Guide* stumbled, almost falling against L'Ordana; she swiftly stepped aside, avoiding his contact.

Again, the dark Warlock gripped the *Guide's* head, applying more pressure than before. Now, there was no denying the anger displayed through his crimson eyes, and the merciless contempt on his lips as he glowered at his victim. The *Guide's* eyes bulged with fear as he felt his neck stretch, to the point where he feared it would be torn from his body. His pleading eyes darted towards the Sorceress; he was certain he saw a hint of pity in her look as Magia increased the pressure on his skull.

'We have wasted enough time here, Sorceress,' Magia growled. 'Which way, "guide"? And do not attempt to point us on the wrong path or, I swear, I will tear your head off!'

Struggling within death's tightening grip, the *Guide's* eyes blinked rapidly, silently pleading with the dark Warlock to let go.

'Release him!' L'Ordana insisted. 'He will tell us!'

Once again, the *Guide* felt the impact of the damp ground beneath him, staring at the same pair of delicate, leather boots that had marked the beginning of his nightmare. One of them tapped furiously, then stopped, before they turned away from him. Cradling his throbbing head, he attempted to rise when a strong hand snatched him, lifting him to his feet.

'It makes no difference to me whether you live or die, *human!*' the Valkyrie stated, her raspy voice low and hostile. 'But as you cherish your life, I suggest you speak, truthfully!'

Faced with no option, but to tell them what they wished to know, the *Guide* opened his mouth to speak, then hesitated, on an *instinct*. He turned to the Sorceress. 'Did you not wish me to … *show* you the way?'

'Your directions will be sufficient,' Magia intervened, his tone dismissive.

L'Ordana shot a guarded look at the Warlock.

An unsettling feeling came over the *Guide*, intensifying his dread. It was how the cloaked woman reacted to the dark Warlock's statement; her look had been filled with suspicion and doubt. It was clear neither one trusted the other. Suddenly, the sinister truth behind his words rang through: *"Your directions will be sufficient."* No, the dark Warlock had no intention of taking him with them.

*No!* he screamed inside, as the reality of his predicament struck its harrowing blow. Death was closing in, and he could feel and smell its pallid approach. His mind began to clog with images of his demise. *Why me?* Still, he could not utter the words, stunned by disbelief.

The cloaked woman turned and stared at him with menace and a look of deceit in her eyes. He panicked, calling on his instincts of survival. *What to do?* If he told them the wrong way—he would most likely die; then again, should he set them on the right path …? Where was the choice? None had been given. One thing was clear, though: regardless of his decision … it would make no difference, whatsoever.

Now he was certain. He would never see another sunrise.

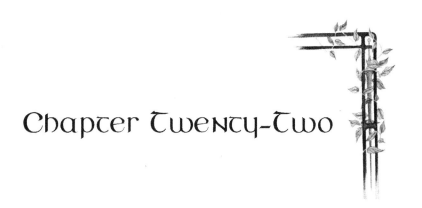

# Chapter Twenty-Two

'Choose well,' she whispered to him.

"Should you choose to lie," his father once told him, as a boy, "then do it well, for there are those who can see deception, through the clarity of innocence. Always look them in the eye, son."

Despite his comfortable upbringing, he felt his temptations, back then, had been typical of a curious young boy, spurred by his equally curious friends. He could still see their small, eager faces and hear their excitable voices, urging him to steal the ripe fruit from the farmer's profitable vines. He recalled looking up at the landowner's face, it red with anger as he was dragged to his father, in shame, kicking and writhing under the firm grip of his captor's grubby, calloused hands. Try as he did, though, he could not look his father in the eye—denying all blame.

*"Look them in the eye!"* His father's words continued to resonate. But he knew he could not lie; the individuals that scrutinised him now would see right through it. The truth, he hoped, may buy him some time—perhaps—even save his life. It was worth a try …

Finally, he proceeded to point them in the right direction. They listened intently as he relayed aspects of their journey—*The Twin Mountains; The Loch of Loyne; The Two Lovers*—with occasional looks of doubt being passed from one to the next. He grew concerned, thinking they did not believe him, while keeping a fixed eye on the agitated movements of the *creatures*, who waited anxiously for their orders, their eyes darting between him and whoever commanded them. Trying to avoid their stare, he pressed on …

'A lake with no water?!' Kara sneered.

'You may mock me,' he retorted. 'But that's the truth of it.'

'You have failed to notice something,' Kara boasted, taking a step back.

His eyes widened, startled at the unexpected sight as she proudly displayed her huge wings before him.

'I can fly over your *haunted* lake,' she sniped, slowly fanning him with their breath.

With a show of bravado, the *Guide* then smirked at her arrogance. 'I urge you to try,' he replied, to her smug face. '*Síofra* dominates the loch, and everything around it. Those,' he then added, pointing to her wings, 'will not guarantee your safety. So, do not presume you can outdo the one who presides over the loch.'

'Can we go around it?'

The soft voice made him look twice. Somehow it did not belong among the hostility of those in her company. Wareeshta stepped forward into view. He detected a kindness in her soft, round face—perhaps an assumption on his part. And yet, her deep-brown eyes exuded warmth, almost inviting him into her unknown world. As she drew closer, he noticed she shared a similarity to the dark *creatures* but could not place it.

'Can we?' she prompted, tilting her head with an edge of innocence.

'You may try,' he returned, with a faint smile. 'However, it will take … four days—'

'Over the escarpments!' L'Ordana blurted, retrieving another image from her mind.

He looked sharply at her. 'Indeed. Although, they are—'

'We do not have four days,' Magia cut in. 'Therefore, we are taking the *Pass*.' He turned abruptly to the *Guide*. 'You say, the *Hour* is not yet upon us—no?'

The *Guide* nodded.

'*Bene!*' Magia exclaimed. 'Good! It is all we need to know. *Grazie!* You have been … most helpful.'

In a sweeping theatrical bow, Magia Nera bid his final farewell, smirking at the *Guide*. But as the dark Warlock stepped away, their eyes met, locking in a moment; it was enough for him to know. *No!* Magia thought. The smirk fell from his face. *How did I not—* He leaned in, then whispered in the *Guide's* ear; 'I contemplated letting you live but—now that I—' Magia drew back, slowly shaking his head, holding the captive's confused gaze, then turned abruptly on his heel—the woods echoing his command as he made to leave.

'Destroy him!'

L'Ordana took a sharp breath. Despite all their threats, she did not expect Magia to carry one out, without her consent. 'How dare you!' she hissed after the Warlock. She had preferred to take the prisoner with them. Her lips parted, to protest further, when Magia stopped, turned and looked at her. She flinched when he moved rapidly to her side, for his *Encore!*

'What a fool you are, *Kristene!*' he murmured, emphasising the name from her past.

*"Kristene! Kristene!"*

She gasped at his impudence as the name churned in her mind. Swiftly composing herself, she moved to challenge him but was too late; he had gone, disappearing into the night—and with *her* warriors following suit … or so she thought.

Desperate, she turned to her servants. Kara and Wareeshta stared back at their mistress, waiting for her instructions when a voice called out:

'Look!' the *Guide* yelled.

Two figures emerged from the blackness, their eyes flaring with the excitement of indulging in their "sport." Their movements were steady and menacing, with the scent of the prisoner's blood hanging on their nostrils. They were young and brimming with unimaginable strength. Wareeshta glanced at the *Guide*, who appeared to be rooted to the place where he stood. She knew the *creatures* would despatch him in seconds, should the Sorceress not intervene.

'My Lady?' she urged her mistress—the subtle panic in her voice noticeable.

Kara raised the Obsidian and her sword, preparing to enter the battle. L'Ordana glanced at the two advancing *creatures*. Her eyes darted towards Wareeshta, who was staring at her, silently pleading to take pity on the prisoner. The two *creatures* continued in their slow advance, occasionally pausing to eye Kara and Wareeshta's positions. The Sorceress turned, contemplating the direction Magia Nera had gone. But before deciding to pursue the dark Warlock, she looked at the *Guide*; it was then, in that defining moment when he saw something in her as she moved to leave—something in that one look, it almost apologetic, throwing him a lifeline. Whether or not it had been intentional, his instincts told him to act on it.

'My Lady!' he echoed, playing on Wareeshta's words, glancing between the Sorceress and his impending demise. L'Ordana, determined to follow Magia, tried to ignore the captive's plea. 'I can give you the advantage over him!' he stated, keeping focused on the two *creatures*.

She looked sharply at him, then raised her hand.

'Leave him!' she demanded.

The *creatures* stalled, regarding one other; they seemed confused and undecided. Motioning Kara and Wareeshta to wait, L'Ordana approached the *Guide*, with new interest. Turning her head, a little to the side, she lifted her chin.

He had her attention.

'A desperate plea, to lengthen your short life?' she teased, aware of the urgency in his fearful tone. It was evident he wanted her to listen to him.

He shook his head, his eyes dancing back and forth, from one threat to the other, his chest heaving. He would do whatever it took to sustain his life—even if it meant "bending the truth" a little.

'I—I don't lie,' he stammered, then swallowed. 'You have the advantage ...'

She hesitated, raising a brow, expecting him to say *that* word again. When met with silence, she keenly asked; 'How?'

He inhaled deeply, relieved for his reprieve, however, knew he was not out-of-the-woods, yet. As he turned his eyes to the heavens, searching for guidance, he felt the first drop of rain spit down on his face, then looked directly at her. Her eyes sparked with resolve.

'Am I to assume you are … a true woman, in form?' he asked, glancing at her two servants, making comparisons; there were plenty.

L'Ordana drew her head back, reluctant to reply.

'I beg of you!' he pleaded. 'It's important.'

'I am,' she returned. 'However, do not presume—'

'Then, you have *Right of Way*,' he hastily revealed.

'Right of—I fail to understand what—' She stopped, momentarily distracted by a slight—yet noticeable—movement from the corner of her eye; the *creatures* were growing restless again. She was uncertain of her control over them now and inwardly cursed Magia Nera.

L'Ordana leaned towards the prisoner. He was her captive now. Her pleasant scent wafted over him as she whispered her warning; 'I do not know how long I can obstruct them, for they are unpredictable. Therefore, I suggest you tell me.'

'No man has right of way—over the loch,' he persisted. 'Only a *woman* has that privilege.'

'This is true?' she asked, with a scathing smile.

He looked her straight in the eye. No. He was not ready to die. 'The loch's spirit, Síofra, will allow a woman to cross, without harm.' He maintained his gaze. 'As long as you can see its waters you will have safe passage,' he added, purposely omitting one piece of vital information.

L'Ordana then heard the agitated rustling of leaves behind her. She looked back. Kara and Wareeshta were now feeling unsettled by the *creatures'* volatile behaviour; it seemed their uneasiness was aggravating their mounting aggression. It was only a matter of time before it would be unleashed. She promptly turned her attention back to the *Guide*, her eyes penetrating his.

Held by her intimidating stare, he struggled to sustain it. *"Do not look away!"* his instincts warned, while she searched for the truth behind his words. He then saw a flicker of doubt in her eyes and felt a dry tightness in his throat; he needed a drink. *"Do not look away!"*

Still, she persisted.

Feeling the strain of his omission, he desperately wanted to recoil from her look when his instincts intervened again, prompting him to speak.

'Remember—timing is crucial,' he blurted. 'You must consider the *Hour!*'

L'Ordana suddenly blinked, as if woken from a dream. 'The *Hour!*' she echoed, giving him the impression, she was acquainted with it.

He swallowed his relief, nodding.

'The deathly hour,' he stated, encouraging her.

'Ah!' she exclaimed, drawing back, with sudden insight. 'But of course! The "Witching Hour."'

*Who is the fool now, Magia?*

L'Ordana stepped back, grinning at the *Guide*. He knew his life now rested in her hands and questioned her expression. *What are your intentions?* he silently asked. The feeling of dread returned, clouding his thoughts. Inside, his whole body shook. He screamed at it, telling it to run, but it would not let him. An uncontrollable force of energy had somehow grounded him, completely; he felt utterly helpless and at her mercy. His eyes flickered at the two *creatures*—the sinister look in their eyes telling his instincts all he needed to know. Their intentions were clear: with or without the cloaked woman's help, they were going to strike.

Death was calling him.

Sensing their imminent attack, L'Ordana swiftly stepped aside.

'Dispatch them!' she ordered, addressing Kara and Wareeshta.

Kara smirked at her mistress' usage of her term; it was the only encouragement she needed.

The Valkyrie grinned from ear to ear as the anticipation of the fight took over her senses. She threw her head back and gave a sharp whistle. Nakia, her great, black hawk, swooped down from above; the *Guide* cowered away as she came within inches of his head. Kara intended to use her, to disorientate the *creatures*. She caressed the hilt of her sword before drawing it over her shoulder, then stabbed the earth with the Obsidian, leaving it there to wait for her, should she need it.

The *creatures* crouched, staring at the Valkyrie's double-edged longsword: the weapon had been fired from the finest steel with a fabricated iron inlay, on the blade. A copper and silver herringbone inlay adorned the hilt. Seeing it now, in all its glory, the *Guide* knew it was of the finest quality, and was aware of its capabilities. Even in the shadows of the dismal night, its polished metal radiated, boasting of its past glories.

The Sorceress regarded Wareeshta, narrowing her eyes; the Dhampir appeared reluctant to take part. The *Guide* noticed it, too.

'Trust me, Wareeshta,' L'Ordana exhorted. 'Magia Nera will not even notice their absence. Do it!'

The sound of L'Ordana's raised voice gave commencement to the fight. Wareeshta reached down, quickly removing a stiletto dagger from inside one of her knee-length, leather boots: the long, slender blade had been made to fit comfortably, to stay concealed from the enemy.

The four opponents circled one another, while L'Ordana kept her distance, knowing it would be short and swift.

Devoid of emotion, the *creatures* lunged towards their contenders. Kara embraced the attack with a skill far surpassing their intended victims.

Wareeshta, the smallest of the four, was sharp and slick. She gracefully stepped away, avoiding the lethal blade being thrust at her; it brushed by her into the void. She knew the poison, applied to their blades, had been a popular—and ancient—method: extracted from the venomous *Ursini* viper, it had been commonly used by her descendants, and followed on in "tradition" by many from her homeland. She also knew Magia Nera was no stranger to the technique. She caught Kara's smug grin—the Valkyrie pleased when *her* opponent's deadly blade almost struck, narrowly missing her. For an instant, Wareeshta was tempted to warn her of its fatal strike ... but kept her secret.

Wareeshta's assailant rushed her again, but her movement was too quick and powerful for him. One sideward step was all she required before he met with her dagger; the *Guide's* mouth gaped, in disbelief, appalled by the shrieking sound her victim made when it was struck by the lethal blade.

The *creature's* pitch heightened as Wareeshta made sure the dagger had been forced right through its heart—leaving it there. She then threw herself behind it and took hold of its head. Seizing a second dagger, from her other boot, she worked with the skill of a master butcher, driving it deep, twisting and worrying it, searching for the carotid artery. For an instant, she stopped. She had found it—and with little effort. One last thrust brought with it the spray of dark, rancid blood. Then, in her final act, she swiftly withdrew the dagger before drawing it across its blood-soaked throat, slicing it clean.

The *Guide* heaved as he witnessed the deep-crimson blood pouring from the *creature's* jugular. Its red eyes spasmed and bulged before the final twist of the blade; a moment is all it took for its body and head to become separated, forever. The heavy thud of its decapitated head made the *Guide* jump as it rolled away from its victor.

A temporary silence followed in the aftermath of the *creature's* demise. But it was short-lived.

'Now, it is *your* turn,' Kara spat at her opponent, wielding her sword at him. Nakia dived at the impending victim, but the *creature* seemed oblivious to the hawk's presence. The Valkyrie cautioned her "pet" to retreat, for fear of the hawk being killed. Kara now stood calm and collected as she toyed with the weapon in her right hand. Her eyes slid towards the Obsidian, embedded in the ground. Tempted to retrieve it, she changed her mind, knowing her sword would be sufficient. *One opponent—one weapon*, she mused, deciding to up the challenge, by giving her contender a fatal chance. She grunted to herself, amused by the thought.

She slowly tilted her head, pre-empting the *creature's* next move. His eyes darted at his fallen comrade; however, he seemed undisturbed by their gruesome demise. He then looked back at Kara, mirroring her actions. She smiled boldly at him, luring him, enticing him into the battle. He edged closer, within inches of her—the two regarding one another intensely.

The seconds rushed by, to the annoyance of the Sorceress. It was typical of Kara—stalling to see who would deliver the first strike, or at least try to. There was no more time for games. She was adamant the Valkyrie would finish her opponent so they could pursue the Warlock.

Armed with a single-edged backsword, in his left hand, the *creature* stretched the fingers of his right. Had it not been for her swiftness, Kara would have missed his movement. With both hands now swiftly grasping the hilt, he raised it on the attack; he intended to drive it through, with one clean thrust. But Kara locked her sword, raising it high against the clash of his blade as he forced it down on her.

Their eyes met.

She grinned, recognising him; he had been trained by the *Strange One*, Asai. It made no difference to her now; in fact, it made it all the more intriguing and challenging. She parted her sensual lips and narrowed her icy-grey eyes, seducing him. He felt her breath on his face. But little did he know, the one tiny human weakness still lurking deep inside, would ultimately betray him …

*Lust!* And Kara knew how to use it.

Still locked in battle, by their weapons, she unexpectedly looked up, his pale red eyes following hers. He blinked as heavy drops of rain momentarily impaired his sight, signalling her to strike.

Kara swiftly thrust her left hand up, forcing the threat of his single-edged sword away before plunging her blade into the side of his throat. As the *creature* fell to the ground, blood cascading down his neck, his weapon caught her arm as she dropped it to her side. She neglected to notice the small flesh wound her silver wristlet had failed to protect.

Standing tall, smug and victorious, the Valkyrie loomed over her victim, languishing in her triumph as the rain took momentum, it lashing down on the *creature*.

'Finish it, Kara!' L'Ordana snapped. She had had enough by now.

The Valkyrie grunted, having been denied her right to relish in her glory. But, despite it, Kara knew she had to be brief; the *creature* would soon recover, should he be spared the final *cut*, allowing his strength to replenish and increase. It was not an option.

He suddenly flinched.

'It's still alive!' The *Guide* could not believe his eyes, questioning how the *creature* could have survived the blow inflicted on it.

Kara, continuing to hover over her victim, playfully rolled her eyes as he reached for his sword. She smirked at his valiant effort.

'Die well!' she told him. 'I bid you a safe journey to *Valhalla*, where we will meet again.'

Retrieving her sword, from where she had left it—embedded in his throat—Kara raised it high, for all to see; it gleamed wet, from the stain of his blood.

Feeling his strength return, the *creature* snatched his sword, but as he lifted his hand to strike her, she stomped her foot, restraining him. He felt no pain. She let the seconds roll by, dangerously, feeling his energy as it began to restore itself; it would not take long. She heard her mistress's words echo behind her.

'Finish him! Now!'

As she smirked down at the *creature*, Kara felt a sting in her arm, telling her she had been injured. She glared at him. 'You should not have done that!' she growled, before plunging her sword clean through his heart, pinning him to the wet ground. The *creature's* failing body spasmed while she held the weapon in place, for a few seconds more. Then, for her final act, Kara drew the sword from his chest, raising it to examine the blade; his blood was still warm as it trickled down the cold steel. She could not resist closing her eyes, to inhale its sweetness. *Another victory,* she told herself.

Suddenly, her eyes flickered wide, alert to the unexpected movement beneath her feet. She glanced down. Had it not been for Wareeshta's timely intervention, the *creature* would have struck her. As its severed head rolled away, in the opposite direction of its dead counterpart, Kara leapt back, frowning at Wareeshta.

'He was *mine* to kill!' she snarled, glaring down at the headless corpse, beneath her feet. Wareeshta opened her mouth to challenge the ungrateful Valkyrie, then stalled when she noticed the cut on Kara's arm, just above her wristlet.

Kara followed her gaze.

'A scratch!' she snapped, pushing by Wareeshta, to retrieve the Obsidian. The lance sparked inside, its lustrous dark-green glass, recognising her touch. Kara, disgruntled, knew the Dhampir had saved her life, however, her arrogant pride would not admit it outwardly—let alone thank her; to thank someone for something they willingly choose to do was their choice, not hers. And to be grateful for another's actions was considered a weakness.

Wareeshta grit her teeth and held her tongue as she observed Kara licking her wound. *She will know, soon enough*, she assured herself, having witnessed the after-effects many times, deciding—in return for the Valkyrie's ungratefulness—she would now keep her silence.

'Losing your touch, Kara?' L'Ordana taunted.

Vexed by her mistress's snide comment, Kara approached L'Ordana, both weapons in hand. She noticed the Sorceress had remained by the *Guide*, throughout, and it played on her suspicions.

'I will live,' she retorted, raising her bloody sword. She pointed it at the captive, her stance threatening.

'Shall I finish this one?'

He threw a worrying glance at L'Ordana, who appeared unperturbed by the Valkyrie's words. Aware of Kara's intentions, Wareeshta followed behind, still clutching her daggers.

'You said you would spare me,' he promptly reminded the Sorceress, trying to hide his inner fear. Kara toyed with him, by slowly waving the stained blade across his face. He watched it, with care. Still wet from its kill, the Valkyrie continued to manipulate him. Having witnessed the hostility between the three women, he soon came to realise, there was no love lost between them. As for trust? It simply did not exist, regardless of their unusual alliance.

And yet, he questioned why the cloaked one allowed her servant to goad him. Perhaps, to test her loyalty? He sensed none.

'Ah, yes,' the Sorceress recalled. 'I had almost forgotten. But I wonder … what difference would it make now, whether I spare you— or not?'

Kara paused, hovering around the captive. Perhaps she *would* have her way, after all.

Feeling betrayed by her false promise, the *Guide's* inner torment quickly changed to raw anger, spurred by his need to survive. He would defend himself to the end—if that were the way of it. His mind urged him to reach for his precious sword—his only weapon—but still, the unknown force would not allow it. Once again, he could feel death resume its untimely approach.

L'Ordana, forcing the depraved Valkyrie away, pondered over her captive. Wareeshta looked on with an element of pity towards him, then turned away, distracted by the scent of blood. It was Kara's. The Dhampir's nostrils twitched, detecting the sharp tang of the venom coming from the graze as the blood trickled down the Valkyrie's arm; already, it was doing its work. Discreetly regarding the wound, she then noticed something different about it; it had an underlying subtle smell— one she could not quite detect—the snake's venom masking its origin. She was unsure.

The Valkyrie paused, paying close attention to the cut she had received, licking the red droplets; it was red raw and increasingly irritating. She grunted, turning away. A discreet smirk crept across Wareeshta's face as she relished in Kara's frustration. The Dhampir was more than aware of the wound's progression, knowing where it would eventually lead.

*Enjoy the time you have left, Kara,* Wareeshta silently told her, holding her thoughts.

The *Guide* paid no heed, staying focused on the cloaked one's eyes as she stared back at him, deciding his fate.

The Sorceress suddenly leaned forward.

'Perhaps … another time,' she whispered to him.

Before he could question her meaning, he felt the searing pressure of her touch shoot across his eyes. His vision became blurred. The three distorted figures seemed to dance and sway while watching him. Unable to speak, he desperately tried to focus, but dizziness soon followed, taking hold of him. His mind spun, out of control, with a myriad of warped images taunting and confusing him; it was nauseating. The invisible force now weighed heavily on him, taking complete control.

*What has she done to—*

His weary body slumped. As he dropped to his knees, he looked down; the rain was now beating hard against the ground, spattering wet mud up at him. Then, feeling the weight of his head drop to his chest, he toppled forward … into darkness.

# Chapter Twenty-Three

*The Ardgore Inn*

The shadowy figure standing in the stepwell paused, with uncertainty, before ducking his head, on entry. He breezed in on the wind and rain then forced the door closed, shutting them out. Silent faces stared at him. Although his weapon remained concealed inside its long, black leather sheath, protecting it from the elements, it was clear he was armed. He turned again, stretching to his full height as he regarded the Inn's residents, then threw back the hood of his muddy, oilskin coat, revealing his strong features. Despite the remnants of dirt on his face, his looks were imposing. Though in his mid-thirties, he was still regarded as a "fine catch" for any woman of child-bearing years—should she be brave enough to enter the uninviting establishment. His skin was sallow, complimenting his thick, dark locks, which he kept tied back. His dusky, grey eyes were unusual, adding to his appeal. The shadow of a beard was visible on his lean jawline, suggesting he regularly maintained his appearance; he scratched it subconsciously, his brows then knitting together in thought as his eyes darted about the Inn, as though he were looking for someone. He seemed agitated and disoriented. Suddenly, he was conscious of the many faces staring up at him, their looks of apprehension evident by their heavy silence, making them reluctant to move or shift slightly in their seats.

He stepped forward, defiant.

'Who stole my horse?!' he demanded, eyeing everyone with suspicion as he searched for the perpetrator.

'She returned—some hours ago,' the small familiar voice informed him. 'I think she was spooked by something but seems to have calmed now.'

He looked down at the boy and stared at him, his expression vacant as though he did not recognise the child, and yet—somehow—knew he did.

'I—I wondered where you were,' the boy then prompted, casting him a peculiar eye.

'What are you looking at …?' His words trailed, struggling to remember the child's name. He frowned, irked that the boy continued to stare at him, his youthful brows pinched in confusion as he looked him up and down. Curious, he followed the boy's look, drawing back when he saw his own sorry state; his coat was completely covered in mud. 'How on earth did that—' He stopped, at a loss, then held his hands out, staring at the dirt embedded in the lines of his palms. Also, his head throbbed; he blamed that on the cold and the tiredness of his aching limbs. But what disturbed him most was, he had no recollection of what had happened to him—when something clearly had.

When the boy handed him a cloth, he accepted it, smiling awkwardly, still confused that he should forget his name.

The boy watched with interest as the *Guide* methodically wiped his hands and face clean, his eyes now distracted in thought, paying no heed to those watching him. It was obvious to the child that something was wrong; when he returned from his outings, the *Guide* usually sought him out, by calling his name, to bring him food and whisky.

'Nahla is all right,' the boy said, nodding.

The *Guide* paused and looked sharp, on hearing his horse's name.

'She is … *here*, you say?' he enquired, conscious of his surroundings again, then was bewildered by his mare's ability to find her way back. She had never left him before, and he thought it strange; in fact, he thought the whole evening inexplicable.

The boy nodded.

'Aye, sir. I fed and watered her.'

'The weather must have caused her to bolt,' he muttered. 'My clever girl—finding her way back,' he added, returning the cloth to the boy. He forced a smile. 'Thank you … *James!*'

The boy smiled back before promptly resuming his duties. As he watched him walk away, the *Guide* questioned his failure to remember the lad's name, when he returned, even though he knew him. Although the momentary lapse had come and gone, it was enough to concern him. His head ached again. *I need a drink,* he thought, drawing a hand through his hair as he eyed the bar.

As he made his way towards it, he caught the slow shifting movements of two elderly brothers rising from their seats, their eyes firmly fixed on him. They had a look of desperation on their concerned faces; it was obvious they were eager to speak with him. He sighed, remembering why. In no mood for questions—or company—he attempted to avoid their constant stare. But they intervened, willing him to tell them what they needed to know.

'There will be no journey through the *Pass*, this night,' he abruptly announced, his voice clear and well-spoken.

The two old men shuffled forward—one bravely asking; 'And what of the—'

'I will tell you the same thing I told you—two days ago,' he snapped. 'The caves are impenetrable!'

'*The caves!*' Gill quickly looked at Reece but was promptly hushed by his grandfather; the Dhampir was keen to hear what the newcomer had to say, his statement suggesting he was a messenger, of sorts.

'I went there, again, and have seen it for myself,' the *Guide* went on. 'There is no other way to avoid the *Pass*, now. And, because of it,' he added, raising his voice, for all intended, 'I regret to inform you … I must increase my price.' A muttering of disgruntled voices could be heard, displaying their disapproval. But, despite their private objection, he knew they would still pay up, such was their desperation. 'However,' he continued, returning his attention to the two old men, 'the weather has taken a turn, and we will not be venturing near it tonight. We will try tomorrow. So—do not concern yourselves, for now. There is still time.'

A heated discussion then ensued between the elderly brothers, at the announcement. 'But I must go, Malcome!' the shorter of the two insisted, against the pleas of his taller, younger brother.

'Can we try again—tomorrow—Robe?' he begged.

The elder's lip quivered as the tears lodged in his eyes. He slowly shook his head.

'I cannot wait that long,' he stated, with regret. 'She is dying! If I delay, it may be too late. You know I am right.'

The brothers approached the *Guide*, who was now blocking the door, reluctant to let them venture out into the night, knowing the dangers. He was not *that* heartless, regardless of what some thought of him.

'Don't be a fool, old man!' he blurted, maintaining his stance. 'The sky is black with rain. There is no moonlight to guide you through. Take my advice and return to your seat.'

'Please, Robe! I implore you to listen to him. Despite his reputation and … I think—perhaps—he is right.'

'You would be wise to listen to your brother, old man,' the *Guide* warned. 'If you take the journey, you will be guaranteed a place in that cursed loch, among the spirits that haunt it.'

The small old man, crooked from years of working the land, was forced to raise his head, to make his address. There was a vacant look in his expression. His pale blue eyes—one glazed over, almost white from blindness—refused to divert their stare. Sensing his determination, the *Guide* knew his argument was in vain; the old man's mind was made up.

'Sir,' he began, his voice slow and hoarse. 'I have not seen my wife since the spring. Word came to me, some days passed, that she is gravely ill. If you have ever loved—truly loved—you would understand the want and need to be with them, in their final hours. And should I meet with death, in trying to reach her, then I know 'tis only a matter of time before we are together again.'

The elderly man's words stabbed Reece, filling him with regret. He felt a sense of shame as they seeped in, reaching the core of his heart.

*I should have been with Onóir,* he silently admitted.

'Then you should not have left her, in the first place,' the *Guide* threw back, in the most uncaring manner. Racked by guilt, the old man hung his head.

The callous remark infuriated Reece; it had been uncalled for. Without thought, he lunged forward, finding himself face to face with the dark figure. The *Guide* jumped back, startled by the stranger's unexpected assault.

'Let – Them – Pass,' Reece quietly snarled, gritting his teeth, unaware he had attracted his own audience.

Fearing a conflict, the brothers cowered away while the Landlord discreetly slid behind his counter, to hide his takings. To witness a confrontation in his establishment was rare indeed, as most travellers had more pressing matters on their minds—namely, the risk of having to face the ominous *Pass*.

He and the *Guide* had an agreement: for each soul led safely through the *Pass*, he insisted on a "share" of the takings—for the use of his Inn, as a temporary haven before their treacherous journey. And there were plenty who were willing to take the risk. At first, the *Guide* had been reluctant to do "business" with him, however, despite his dislike for the Landlord, he soon saw the potential in their casual contract, quickly shaking hands to seal it.

With the possibility of an awkward situation arising, Tam and Gill slowly rose from their seats, only to be discouraged by Asai; he would be the one to intervene, to avoid any trouble. No. The Inn's residents did not want to witness the provocation of a Dhampir.

The *Guide* smirked as he leaned towards Reece, antagonising him into a challenge. He contemplated using his sword, then suddenly snapped his head back—startled by the pale-red eyes glaring at him, their intensity jolting a memory. Then it was gone. He stepped back, quickly persuaded to discard any notion of using his weapon.

Reece tilted his head slowly, trying to control his aggravation. But the temptation to inflict pain on this individual was overwhelming; he should not have taunted the old man.

'Do not torture yourself, Reece-san.'

Reece flinched at the touch of Asai's hand, on his shoulder; he knew he would have gladly punished this stranger, had he not realised the infliction should have been his own—for the guilt he felt over Onóir. But the Samurai was his voice of reasoning in situations of conflict, Asai's calming words drawing him away from his potential victim.

Reece's eyes darted across the audience they had attracted. They were now staring at Asai; it was apparent the onlookers had now noticed the *Strange One,* with his peculiar look and attire, not to mention the unusual weapons clinging to his side.

'I think it wise,' Asai began, addressing the *Guide* in his soft voice, 'that you listen to my friend, and let the two gentlemen pass.' They held one another's stare, Asai's then shifting to a warm smile, urging him to take the advice.

'As you please.' He grunted, then turned to face the two brothers. 'You have been warned. Now you're on your own.' He snorted at them, then turned away, shaking his head before returning to the bar.

'Thank you,' a small, frail voice said.

Asai and Reece looked down at the two old men.

'That has been a long time coming, sir.'

Asai bowed.

'He has controlled the comings and goings of those who seek safe passage through the *Pass.* They come here in the hope they will make the journey—for a price, no less. True to say, he can lead us there, but he cannot protect us from what lies beneath the surface.'

'Auch! 'Tis a matter of luck and chance,' the younger brother added. 'And great wit.'

'Aye, that too, Robe,' came the reply. 'But most important: 'tis all about the timing.'

'In what way?' Reece asked.

The old men looked at one another, anxious and eager to press on, regardless of the weather—and the warnings. 'Ask *him!*' said the younger, throwing a nod over at the *Guide*, who was now nestling his head in his hands, staring into a large whisky.

'Perhaps, we will,' said Asai, noting their reluctance to speak of their journey. Despite their intervention, it was obvious the brothers still wished to mind their own business. The Samurai could not help but feel pity and concern for them. 'Are you still certain you wish to take your journey?' he enquired, troubled by their nervousness.

The brothers shared a look of mutual understanding, then nodded in silent agreement with their decision.

'Again, I thank ye,' the eldest said. 'But 'tis of great urgency that we go tonight.' He turned to his younger sibling, lifting his shoulders. 'Maybe the wind will carry the clouds away, Malcome,' he remarked, half-heartedly.

'Aye, Robe. Maybe,' his brother replied, grasping onto any flicker of hope that may come their way. ''Tis a chance we have to take.'

'Who knows?' the other returned. 'Luck may be on our side. And, besides, he is right … We still have time.'

Asai stepped aside and bowed gracefully, respecting their decision. The two elderly men returned smiles of gratitude to the strangers who had tried to help them. But as they shuffled by, under the Samurai's attentive look, their smiles faded—now replaced by inner fear and dread.

Asai watched as they disappeared into the darkness until he could no longer see them. He lifted his head, his nose twitching; there was a heavy smell of dampness in the air, carrying with it a foulness that preyed on his senses. It came from the direction the two men were heading. He wondered did they also sense its malignant breath. He prayed they did not.

'May good fortune travel with you,' he whispered after them. Asai then noticed the rain had begun to ease its burden from the Inn, and hoped it was a good sign.

For the duration, while preoccupied with the two old travellers, Asai's attention had temporarily drifted from his friend. He cast an uneasy glance around and found Reece seated again—eyes shut tight, battling against his inner emotions. As the Samurai returned to his colleagues, he tried to ignore the obvious stares and muttered comments; he could hear the curious whispers of the Inn's residents as they quietly questioned his strange origins, before eventually dragging themselves back to their own concerns.

Gill sat opposite Reece, scrutinising his grandfather with added interest, waiting for his eyes to open again; he was relieved when they smiled back at him.

'For a moment …' he began, 'I thought—'

'That I was going to kill him?' said Reece, sliding his eyes to where the *Guide* stood, with his back to them, propping up the bar. 'The thought had crossed my mind'—he bent his head slightly towards his grandson, to reassure him—'but only for a moment.'

'But was it necessary—to threaten him like that?' Gill pressed. 'Did your actions justify the situation?'

Reece lifted his head and stared at his grandson. Gill was right in what he had said; his actions had not been justified. Perhaps the *Guide* was being *cruel to be kind*—his way of trying to prevent the old men from leaving. But his efforts had been in vain, and it was clear he could not force them to stay.

Just as Reece was ready to make a speech on, "The Principals of Duty," as a pathetic excuse to cover the truth behind his actions, the sound of four more tankards being dropped on the table distracted him. He looked up into the boy's pale face. The child was staring at him.

Reece frowned. 'We did not order these!'

Speechless, James chewed on his lip and diverted his demure eyes, catching the Landlord's; he was watching his every movement. The boy swallowed, then nervously glanced back at Reece.

'A—a peace offering,' he stuttered, forcing a smile. Anything to avoid trouble.

'From whom?' Tam asked, in a calm voice, eagerly eyeing the tankards.

The boy turned his head in the direction of the bar, revealing their identity.

Reece glanced at the offering, unsure, when a large hand reached forward, helping itself. Tam, licking his lips, drew the sweet-honeyed drink to his mouth. Reece scowled at his colleague with his look of deception. Tam raised his thick brows and shrugged before taking a cautious sip.

'Perhaps—you should accept it, sir,' the boy anxiously suggested. 'He is not a bad person. Aye, 'tis true some do not like him, but he knows these lands, and beyond. Also, he is good to me ... despite what *they* think,' he added, casting a glance back, referring to the Inn's watchful eyes.

'But he hardly recognised you—when he came through the door,' Reece remarked.

The boy shrugged.

'But he did ... eventually.'

'Thank you,' Gill interrupted. James nodded, cleared the table, and then walked away. Gill looked over at the figure, standing at the bar watching them, then raised his tankard as a gesture of goodwill.

'Traitor!' Reece muttered under his breath, his mood lightening, to their relief. He leaned towards his three travelling companions, watching Gill as he supped his drink. 'So—what do you know of the *Pass*?' he then asked his grandson.

Gill paused, staring into the vessel in his hand. He had heard the tales of the *Whispering Waters,* and what lurked beneath. He could still hear Heckie Grant's voice in his head, relaying the story. Only now, it suddenly dawned on him: it no longer was one; the myth of the Cordhu Pass was chillingly real, confirming the niggling instinct he had always kept to himself.

'They say the loch is ... *haunted!'* he began, 'by the spirit of a young woman. I thought it was just another ghost story told to myself and

Eleanor when—' He stopped as his sister's name casually slipped from his mouth. It was as though he had forgotten. He then felt the immense cloud of guilt leaning on him and shook his head. 'This is wrong!' he confessed, pushing his drink away; it had suddenly lost its appeal. 'Here we are, drinking, while my sister is—'

'Do not think it, Gill-chan,' Asai insisted. 'She has not been harmed.'

'How do you know?' he retorted, clenching his jaw. 'You have not uttered her name for a while. Why Asai? Why is that?' The growing anger and frustration in his voice were evident, by his raised tone, drawing the hum of private conversations to slowly subside, as curious eyes fell on the angry, young man.

'I feel your sister's heartbeat … *here!*' Asai discreetly admitted, pointing to his heart. 'She is inside me, but yet I cannot reach her, at this time. There are moments when I feel her near, and yet distant. I cannot explain it. But, believe me when I tell you … I know Eleanor is alive. Trust my instincts, Gill.'

'You have no choice, but to,' Reece advised his grandson. 'If not, we lose heart and turn against one another—and you do not want that. We will get her back. I promise. But, at this moment in time, we need to know about the *Pass*, especially now, with no access to the caves.'

'Aye, lad,' said Tam. 'So, start talkin'.'

Gill released a long-winded sigh. 'I have always had my suspicions about the "myth." I once expressed my thoughts to Oran. He dismissed them as nonsensical yarns, made up to scare us young folk—a way to keep us in check, you could say.'

Reece raised a brow at Gill's off-hand usage of his father's name. *There!* he had just said it again, as he rambled on about how "They say this" and "They say that," or "It is said."

*He now calls his father, Oran, yet fails to notice,* he thought. His mother would have scolded him for his disrespect. But it was just another sign of Gill's increasing maturity and not his place to correct the boy. *Boy?* Gill was no "boy." He had noticed, on the day they had left Balloch, how the young man's physical appearance had already altered. It was also noticeable in the strength of his physique. Yes, his grandson was marked to be a great leader, but still had much to learn—and in a short space of time, too. And those who would teach him were now waiting anxiously for his arrival.

'Reece?'

The Dhampir looked sharp, on hearing his name. Gill threw him a look of annoyance. But his grandfather seemed distracted by something—something he was reluctant to share with them. Catching Gill's irritable look, Reece tilted his head, in apology.

'Forgive me.'

Gill continued. 'They say …' Reece rolled his eyes. '… centuries ago, the barbarians from the far northern lands travelled to our shores, with conquest on their minds. With no regard for life, they destroyed anything—and anyone—who stood in their path.' Gill drew images from his mind of the atrocities his home must have endured, through the passage of time. The three Dhampir listened attentively, but with little show of emotion; they were well acquainted with the devastation associated with war. 'People's lives were destroyed. Women and young girls were raped as a form of entertainment for the savage invaders. And, when they had had their fill, some of their innocent victims were murdered senselessly. Men and young boys, of relative strength, were taken as prisoners back to the barbarians' homelands.'

'For what purpose?' asked Asai.

'To sell as slaves, or force them into battles,' Gill surmised.

'Or were offered as a sacrifice to their god, Loki.'

The four looked up to find the *Guide* standing over their table, his whisky glass almost tipped to the brim.

Gill's eyes darted towards Reece, fearing more confrontation from his grandfather; Reece's eyes, though fixed on the *Guide*, looked relatively normal—or as normal as could be—with no sign of them changing from green to red. Reece, sensing his grandson's concern, acknowledged Gill with a subtle smile and nod. The *Guide* was safe. For now.

In an amiable show of respite, the *Guide* had removed his coat and weapon, leaving them behind the bar before bravely approaching the four strangers. Any soul that entered the Ardgore Inn was treated as such—a *stranger*—and nothing more. But there was something different about this diverting group of travellers, especially the individual who had intervened between him and the one with the red eyes. He was curious.

'Who is Loki?' said Gill, eyeing the *Guide*, then flashing another glance at Reece; good, still no sign of further confrontation. The three Dhampir looked at Gill. The young man's appetite for ghost-like tales had gotten the better of him.

'He was one of the more … unpleasant Gods, from Norse mythology,' he revealed, removing a chair from a nearby table. He sat, inviting himself into their company, with a wary eye fixed on Reece.

Silence reigned over the Inn as the onlookers watched and waited, to see what would happen. But Reece paid no heed to their prying, equally inquisitive as to what this individual had to say.

'According to our young friend …' Reece began, acknowledging the boy, who kept a keen eye on them. 'It seems we should listen to *you!*' The composure in his voice gradually eased the tension until it melted away. Any potential conflict had, thankfully, been avoided, to the Landlord's relief. He wanted no part of it. Nevertheless, for some, it would have come as a welcome distraction, from the prolonged wait of the unsettling journey that awaited them.

'What is it you know?' asked Gill, his enquiry filled with anticipation.

The *Guide* looked at the young man, through his eagerness; there was an aura about his presence, telling him he was not of common folk. He smiled warmly at his attentiveness.

'You began your story well—and I think it only right that you should finish it,' he insisted. 'That way, we can—' He stopped. 'My apologies,' he said, extending his hand.

Gill shared glances with his colleagues as they regarded the second peace offering from the stranger. Reece, admiring his bravery for taking his place among the unknown company, tilted his head, by way of approval.

'My name is …' He leaned in, lowering his voice. 'Daine.' Anyone who wanted to risk the *Pass* referred to him as the *Guide*. That was how he wanted to do business; allowing them to call him by his name was being too "personal." He wanted to avoid any form of attachment. However, these particular individuals … No, they were different.

'Gillis Shaw,' came the prompt reply—the gesture returned, by offering his hand, too.

Having been officially accepted into the strangers' company, Daine smiled and nodded, before continuing; 'As I said … that way, we can draw on our conclusions.'

After a prompt in his ear, from Tam, Gill proceeded. 'It was during this time of upheaval, many desperately tried to flee, by any means possible. A young couple—betrothed to one another—attempted the treacherous Highlands and lochs, as their means of escape, to the south. But, to their misfortune—and horror—they were found out, by a small group of barbarians. They were chased like wild animals, to the point of exhaustion. Both were tied and taken to a place between the lochs of Aber and Nessa. The young man was bound to a tree, where he was forced to watch his woman brutally tortured and raped.' Gill paused. Suddenly the childhood tale had come to *life!* through his description. He felt deep sympathy for the doomed lovers—two innocent lives severed by a cruel act of depravity—and it all for the self-gratification of others.

Meghan, the girl he was forced to leave behind, entered his thoughts. He felt an ache in his scarred heart from their separation. But there was nothing he could have done to prevent the cruel twist of fate that had torn them apart. He was thankful for one thing: at least she was alive.

'When the barbarians had finished their sport,' Daine added, thinking Gill was reluctant to continue, 'they took the young man away. He was never seen again.'

'And his woman?' Asai enquired, perceiving her fate.

'They tied a rope around her throat and attached it to a boulder. Then, in another senseless act of pure evil, they simply cast her into the loch, while she screamed for her young lover to save her. But, by then, it was too late. They left her to sink to the bottom of its unknown depths. And ever since, the loch has been controlled by nature's wrath.'

'Mmmph! And there lies the myth!' Tam sneered, with disdain, one eye on Gill and his story, the other on the Landlord; there was something sinister and austere in the way he peered at his young employee, and Tam could not help but notice how James cowered from his employer's manipulative stare.

Feeling patronised and rejected, by Tam's remark, Daine slammed his hand firmly on the table, waking Gill from his thoughts—the loud noise bringing attention to their corner, yet again. Tam scowled at him in return, for disrupting his suspicions of the Landlord. Daine leaned forward, lowering his voice. 'I do not know where you have come from or …' He paused, sliding his eyes towards Reece. 'Or *what* you are—nor do I care—but one thing is certain … this "story" is no myth or bedtime tale, conjured to keep children in check with their parents. No. It is not. And shall I tell you how I know?'

Daine glanced at the four faces peering at him, waiting for their response; the three Dhampir appeared unperturbed by his statement. He thought it unnatural. But, when Gill edged a little closer, intrigued, he chose to proceed.

'I've seen what happens there—with my own eyes!' He hesitated. 'And what is more … I have seen *her*.'

# Chapter Twenty-four

'The young woman?' said Gill, his enthusiasm soaring.

Daine nodded. As he opened his mouth to speak, Tam sniggered, igniting his fury. He quickly rose from his seat, pushing his chair back, prepared to challenge the offence made towards him, by the Highlander. Tam's expression suddenly changed; his face hardened, and his eyes slowly narrowed, penetrating Daine with a fixed, menacing stare. As the smirk fell from the Dhampir's face, Reece noticed the familiar red glow in his colleague's eyes. The Highlander was preparing to attack.

'Leave us!' Reece snapped, under his breath. 'See to the horses!'

Tam inhaled deeply before promptly leaving, followed by inquisitive eyes as he made his swift exit, disappearing into the solace of darkness.

'You must pardon our friend,' said Asai, lowering his head, by way of apology.

'He is young and sometimes reckless,' Reece added. 'His life has been somewhat … difficult. He is flighty, with a tendency to lose sight of who he is. At times, he forgets the company he keeps.'

Daine looked to the door; it remained ajar. He tilted his head, peering out, thankful there was no sign of the Highlander now. It was at this point he noticed the rain had eased. The two elderly brothers entered his mind. *Perhaps, I should have gone with them …*, he thought, then dismissed it. *They know the way.* The choice had been theirs. Still and all, he admired their bravery and hoped they would make it.

Daine propped his seat and joined the company once more, keeping his wits about him. He turned to Reece, observing him closely; the Dhampir knew he was being scrutinised.

'What is it you see?' said Reece, raising his chin as though inviting him to inspect his features, in more detail.

Daine, narrowing his dark eyes, ran his hand over his stubbled face, in contemplation.

'I am sure I have heard of your *kind* before …' His voice trailed with uncertainty.

Reece leaned forward. 'Then you will know how defenceless you are against us,' he whispered.

Daine recoiled. His weapon came to mind, and he cursed his negligence for leaving it behind the counter, then realised how pointless it would be to even attempt to use it against the intimidating strangers. He toiled over the sudden awkwardness of his position and contemplated leaving.

Sensing the guide's inner turmoil—as well as catching the obvious glare from his grandson—Reece, to assure Daine of his safety, drew back, removing the hint of hostility.

'We are not here to cause you harm … Daine,' he explained, using his name to be "civil." 'The purpose of our journey is a … "personal" one. It is vital we reach our destination, within two days. It is all we have. We had hoped to pass through the caves of Aber, but it is now apparent that we must change our plans.'

'How did *you* know about the caves?' Gill asked the guide. 'They are relatively unknown to man.'

'And yet, you are aware of them,' Daine retorted, feeling relieved his life was no longer under threat.

'A fair point,' said Asai, slowly nodding. 'Then, let us change our enquiry. How did you come by them?'

'By mere chance,' said Daine. 'I was returning from …' He stalled, unwilling to share *his* business with them. 'I was … visiting family. On my return, I found myself in a precarious situation: I was caught in the height of an unusual storm, deep in the valley, between the twin mountains. Unfortunately, I did not have my horse with me, at the time—she was sick and being nursed by James—so I had to look for cover. I climbed the rock-face, to take shelter among the trees. It is a difficult ascent, as the woods lining the mountainside are steep and dense. Had it not been for the lightning I never would have seen the caves; while nature marks their outline they blend in with their wild surroundings. I pushed through the thick moss and foliage that had concealed their entrance, eventually making my way inside, to escape the harsh elements. With nothing to light my way, inside, there was little I could do but stand alone in the blackness and wait for the storm to pass.

'It was when my eyes adjusted, I noticed a faint hue of green light, coming from the far reaches of the cave. At first, I thought it was a spectre—as its light was eerie and haunting. But I have a curious nature and decided to follow it. It gave sufficient light, enabling me to walk the cave's route until I found myself at its inner core.

'When I looked about, I noticed two other passages, each going in a different direction, away from the centre. Had I looked away for a moment, I would have lost my "guiding light", which would have left me in the dark, not knowing which way to go. And so, I followed it into the left passage. I had to know where it would lead—where its secrets would take me. The passage took a steep decline and eventually levelled. I followed it, for what seemed like an age until it rose again. It was high and damp and, when I finally emerged from its exit, I realised where I was …'

'The far side of the *Pass*,' Asai deduced.

Daine nodded.

'It ran in line beneath the loch. From then on, the caves provided a safer means to travel, avoiding what was above … for a time, that is. You see, mother nature had other plans … She took back its secret.'

'What happened?' asked Gill.

'A landslide—caused by flooding?' Daine shrugged. 'Who can say? Since then, my attempts to find an alternate route have, unfortunately, been in vain and, because of it, we have no choice now but to battle against the Cordhu Pass.'

'Which is where you saw an opportunity to improve your finances,' Reece remarked.

Daine held the Dhampir with a fixed look. 'If it means saving lives,' Daine reminded him, as his way of justifying the "Traveller's Toll." 'Think what you like, but I do not steal from these people,' he added, lifting his chin towards the Inn's anxious travellers, who kept their eyes on him, wondering if—or when—their journeys would resume. 'Though treacherous, the caves were a safe passage, and I charged little. Their safety, at the time, was guaranteed. Whereas now … it is not. Those who are desperate to get to the other side offer me all they possess. But I am no *Thief!* The caves were destroyed, and the journey is perilous, therefore, I had to increase my price. Lives are at stake now, and besides'—he slid his eyes towards the Landlord, who eyed him suspiciously, when not watching the boy—'there are certain … "fees" to be paid.'

'Surely, there's an easier way to make a living,' said Gill.

'I am a mason, by trade,' said Daine. 'The work is indefinite and, when offered, I take it, but with much reluctance, due to its nature. The labour is harsh—and the pay a pittance. But *this!*' he added, acknowledging the Inn and its "pilgrims". 'This pays. I know the terrain and how to cross the Cordhu Pass when time allows it. So, when there is no other option for them—'

'You referred to "nature's wrath",' Asai interrupted. 'That the lake is controlled by it?'

Daine nodded.

'By the light of the moon.'

Gill, Reece and Asai looked from one to the other, confused. 'A coincidence, perhaps?' Gill queried Reece, curious at the irony of it— coinciding with his coming of age.

'A coincidence?' Daine echoed.

'We must reach our destination before the moon has ended its cycle,' Reece informed him.

'May I ask, why?'

'You may not!'

Daine, now more suspicious, raised a brow at Reece's blunt reply, but the defined deadpan look of secrecy etched on the Dhampir's face told the guide, he had no intention of divulging their plans to him. And if that were the case …

'Then, why should I tell you?' Daine returned, with equal sarcasm in his tone.

'Because … we insist!'

Their attention now turned to the one person they had least expected to make threats; Gill was now sitting back in his chair, head tilted low, and arms folded, displaying his guard.

'Why the light of the moon?' he persisted, intimidating Daine with his hostile stare. An indistinct smirk of pride appeared on Reece's mouth. His grandson was learning fast.

Daine, inwardly admitting defeat to the strangers, sighed as they waited patiently.

'Centuries ago, the lochs of Aber and Nessa were regarded as one great loch—the Abberness. It was only in recent times it was decided to divide it—by name only—because of its vastness. The Aber marks the west, while the Nessa, the east—merely to mark the geography of the land. But while its width divides the north and south—as a border—it is still *one* loch. There was a time when all travellers could sail safely across its waters. However, that all changed when the young woman was thrown to her death. She cursed the great loch—and any man who attempted to cross it. Her spirit took charge of the waters, damning them. Since then, they have been treacherous and unpredictable, claiming countless lives. It is those lost souls—her *wraiths*—that haunt it, alongside her.

'The loch's waters are stabbing cold, through all seasons, and there are times it fools the eye into believing it is *dry*. Those who are ignorant of the curse have attempted to cross it, by foot.'

'Thinking it land?' said Gill.

Daine nodded.

'If they are foolish enough to cross the *mirage*—for that's what it is—they will be hurled into the loch's unknown depths and dragged beneath the surface, by her *wraiths*.'

'In revenge for her lost love,' Gill surmised, attempting to romanticise the horror of the loch's curse.

'There are many theories associated with it,' Daine went on. 'Some say …' Reece rolled his eyes. '… she still waits for the return of her lover. Whatever romantic notions some choose to believe, the reality is entirely different.'

'You mean—the lake is invisible?' Reece cut in, dismissing the absurdity of the idealists.

'I have seen it, in its two forms—land *and* water,' said Daine. 'When the eye is fooled—believing it to be dry land—no stone, no blade of grass, nor a single breath of wind betrays its true nature—day or night. Believe me, I have searched for signs of the water's edge when she disguises it as land, to no avail. No—Síofra controls it all!'

'Síofra?' said Asai.

'Síofra Cordhu,' Daine revealed. 'Of the Cordhu Clan, in the north of Scotland. The *Pass* was named after her.

'Despite her manipulation, I was determined to find some form of marker to indicate its border, to find a way across. There *had* to be one. And, when one's "needs" become a necessity … persistence becomes the driving force—and eventually pays off. That is when I discovered the *Two Lovers*.'

'*Two Lovers?*' Gill voiced, dropping his guard, sensing there *was* some romantic attachment to it, after all.

'The woods surrounding it are extremely dense, and their trees loom heavily over the loch,' said Daine. 'To the eye, they look as though they will fall into its depths, at any given moment,' he added. 'There is no "water's edge" … as such. But, provided you know which route to take, it is marked by the presence of two unusual trees, which are perfectly aligned with each other—*The Two Lovers*.'

'What makes them unusual?' Reece asked.

'You will know them by their strange shape; their deformed trunks twist as they rise before becoming entwined, as one. They are like no other. From a distance, you can see the arch they create, in their unity. But they are only "visible" if you know what you are looking for. Should a traveller step through their natural arch, unaware of its damnation, the loch will be waiting.'

'If the lake is as treacherous as you say …' Reece pressed. '… how can we hope to attempt the crossing—if we cannot see it?' He stopped when it suddenly dawned on him. 'Ah! But of course! The moon.'

'As long as the clouds do not blanket its light,' said Daine, 'the moon will reveal the loch's true, sinister nature—its waters—where Síofra dominates.'

'Then there is still time,' Asai murmured to Reece.

'We are in the third quarter of the moon's cycle,' Daine continued. 'In fact, the light is unusually vivid. I have never seen it so vibrant. Even as it wanes, it continues to illuminate almost everything beneath it.'

When the three strangers remained silent, Daine perceived, by their calm demeanour, that they had—perhaps—been informed, by another source. And yet, they maintained their reticence, adding to his curiosity.

'If you are fortunate enough to see the loch, be prepared for what you are up against—its tempestuous waters, as well as having Síofra and her *wraiths* to contend with.'

'Then, we simply find ourselves a boat,' Gill assumed.

When Daine threw his head back in laughter, the Inn fell silent for his mockery of the strangers.

'Trust me, my *friends!*' he sneered. 'If it were possible to cross the loch by boat, I assure you, I would not be sitting here. And this Inn would be a more welcoming place to enter, over the misery that seeps through its beams. There is only one way you can pass through the loch.'

'Through?' said Reece, leaning forward again.

Daine's eyes slid towards Reece; he now realised he had the Dhampir's undivided attention.

'By foot.'

'Impossible!' cried Gill. 'By foot?! Now you do mock us.'

'I speak the truth,' Daine proclaimed, raising his hands in defence. 'The moonlight can reveal a hidden path. You have my word on it.'

'How?' Asai calmly asked, intrigued.

Daine regarded the Samurai, for a moment. He was the only one in the company who kept his composure, with his peaceful manner. His willingness to intervene, in trying situations, encouraged Daine to give him his respect; also, the soothing tone in his unfamiliar accent brought about a stillness inside him, allowing him to speak with honesty.

'While the *Two Lovers* may mark the threshold between this world and the next,' said Daine, 'they also mark the only possible route across the loch. There is a window of opportunity, which allows the traveller a period of time to pass through, safely. You see, at the moment of her death, Síofra's residual energy lingered on, in the place where she drowned: at the narrowest point, between the lochs. From there, you can see the other side and would think it easy to cross. This is not so. Its unearthly influence continues to take effect at the same time each night—during the cycle of the moon when it is visible. An eerie calm sweeps over the loch, reflecting a mirror image of everything above and around it. It is strangely mesmerising. But it is the silence that follows which gives the loch its sinister atmosphere … to say the least.' He shuddered. 'You can sense its spirits watching you. When the moon throws its rays on the surface, it is at this point when the sinister waters part, unveiling a path, letting travellers through. But timing is crucial—and dangerously short.'

'Have you taken it?' asked Gill.

Daine shook his head.

'I have no reason to. Because of my knowledge of the *Pass,* I only guide those who are desperate to get to the other side. I take them as far as the *Two Lovers,* where I inform them of the dangers and, after giving my advice, I take my leave. I never stay. From there, they are placed into the hands of fate.'

'Were you ever tempted to *try*?' asked Asai.

'Once—nor have I any desire to take such a risk again. No, I had seen enough to deter me for a lifetime. The curse, alone, should have kept me away.

'No one had dared to venture near the loch for decades until rumours began to spread—rumours of travellers, who had left their trail and were never seen again. Because of that, my curiosity took me there, for the first time. After careful planning, I decided to brave the journey—to see for myself. I waited until the moon was full, before travelling to the place. My timing was perfect. That was when I saw the loch and the *Two Lovers* in all their splendour as the moon shone through the arch of their twisted branches. To see the loch illuminated by nature's light makes you almost dismiss the evil attached to it.'

'Almost?' said Reece, casting him a sideward glance.

Daine nodded.

'While its beauty is alluring to the eye, a foreboding atmosphere lingers there. You can feel it. It lures and wills you to take that fatal step. I did not know, then, of its ability to allow the traveller to pass through it, at a given time, therefore, through my ignorance, I could not help but loiter at its edge. I could feel its potent effect as it tried to tempt me into *her* domain. I stood there, staring down at its ghostly surface as it gleamed up at me. I must admit, I almost succumbed to it … But something held me back. Thankfully!'

'Your intuition?' said Asai.

Daine, influenced by Asai's calm and reassuring demeanour, smiled warmly at the Samurai, then nodded.

'My father always told me to listen to what it tells me. And I have lived by his words.' He hesitated, losing himself, for an instant, in their last moments together, then continued: 'As I forced myself from its lure, an unusual calm glided over the loch, as though it were resting from the turmoil most commonly associated with it.

'Though nothing stirred on its flat surface, I cautiously kept my distance, watching and waiting. Then it happened: the waters parted, creating a path—making no sound as they divided the great loch. I was stunned yet enamoured by it. And, for once, I ignored my father's guiding words.'

'You walked it?!' said Gill, his eyes wide with excitement.

'Almost to my death!' said Daine. 'I had taken no more than two paces onto the "path" when the moon's light was temporarily blocked out, by passing clouds. An inner voice told me to *Run!* It was then I felt the waters cave in around my feet. I turned and leapt for dry land. Had I delayed a second more, the hands of death would have surely dragged me to a watery grave. As I fell to the ground, I looked behind me …' He shuddered again, reminded of it.

'What did you see?' Gill, his arms still folded, slid them across the table.

'A white hand—disappear beneath the surface.'

'You think it was *her*?' said Gill.

'If not Síofra, then one of her *wraiths*, for sure. I swore never to return. But I did—for the next few nights—until the moon's light had completed its cycle. By studying it, as closely as I dared to, I quickly learned its pattern.'

'And kept it to yourself, for your personal gain,' Reece suggested.

'I did no such thing!' Daine retorted, insulted by the notion. 'I shared it with those who would listen. However, the few who believed me were not brave enough to see for themselves. Therefore, I offered to guide them, knowing when it was safe. They willingly accepted my offer. As for those who wish to brave it alone …?' He paused, questioning his principles. 'Well … that is their decision. Regardless of it, I will not risk my life for their stubbornness or stupidity.'

'And the two old men?' asked Reece. 'I saw your underlying pity.'

Daine sighed and slowly nodded.

'I regret their choice,' he said, lowering his eyes. 'Truthfully!' He then looked up. 'But it was theirs to make, as with any other. Those who choose to take the risk are well-informed and told to return, should the weather fail them. Some, unfortunately, do not come back.' He shrugged. 'One can only assume …'

Daine glanced at the door, trying to shake the images of Malcome and Robe from his mind when a large, dark shadow crossed the small opening. He presumed it to be the group's other travelling companion and hoped he had calmed, by now.

'What have you seen?' Asai asked, noting the look of regret in Daine's eyes.

'Men—who ignored my warnings—their lives taken before my very eyes, despite my pleas. Some are so desperate to cross the loch ...' He paused again, feeling the burden of his guilt. *I should have tried harder to stop them,* he told himself. 'Even when it is visible, the fools still insist on crossing it. Sometimes ... it is difficult to comprehend when there is nothing you can do to dissuade them—and I have tried, by urging them to travel by way of the Highlands. But the mountains are too sharp and steep for a horse, making the journey long and perilous, by foot. They would rather risk the loch, than waste five days' trek, over the Highlands.'

'The stubbornness and arrogance of man are often difficult to sway,' Asai remarked, to ease Daine's guilt. 'Once they have made up their mind, we are defenceless against their wrong judgements. Do not feel guilty for their senseless decisions.'

Asai's words had truth attached to them, but the guilt Daine felt for those who had failed the time-given passage had never left him, despite his efforts to detach his feelings from them. He had only begun to accept it. But when these four strangers crossed the Inn's threshold, little did he know their presence would change everything.

The night's revelations had now swayed his conscience, causing a sudden dull ache inside his head, and a heaviness behind his weary eyes. He was feeling drained from the long night.

'Do you think they all made it?' Gill asked, unable to hide his eagerness. '—the ones who took the path?'

'Some—but not all,' he returned, trying to fight his tiredness. 'I have seen them, within reach of the other side, while being watched by Síofra and her *wraiths* as they wait in the icy waters, willing away the moonlight.

But nature rules all things. And when it pushes the clouds together, blocking out the moon's iridescence, the loch closes in on itself, consuming everything again, giving little warning to those desperate—' He sighed and shook his head. 'The fools! I have heard their pathetic cries as the ghouls snatch them to their watery graves. It is not a pleasant sight.'

'You are not to blame,' said Asai, trying to reassure him. 'Their fates were sealed by their choices.'

'Then let us hope the light is with us when *we* challenge it,' Reece stated, unperturbed by the risk.

Daine stared at him, perplexed. 'You're going to take the *Pass?!* After what I have just told you?!'

'We do not have five days,' Reece admitted, without any show of emotion.

'While I understand, that everyone has their reasons for taking the *Pass* …' said Daine, eyeing Gill with suspicion. 'I sense yours is of great significance.'

'You said, "men."'

They stopped and looked at Asai. The Samurai's comment was significant and timely.

'Men?' Daine returned, half-heartedly.

'"*Men*, their lives taken before my very eyes,"' Asai reminded him. 'Were these not *your* words?' Daine stared at him with a blank expression. 'A metaphor, perhaps?' the Samurai prompted. 'Or do you speak *only* of men?'

Daine's brows shot up, grasping Asai's meaning.

'Aye, he's right!' said Gill, shuffling in his seat.

'It seems you have taken, from my subconscious, something that must have become an oversight, with time,' Daine confessed, after hearing his own words echoed back to him. 'I had forgotten! How observant of you!'

'It is part of my friend's nature,' said Reece. 'He notices the little— but significant—things.'

'And, it seems, it is no metaphor,' Daine revealed, sliding his joined hands across the table. 'I have been told, Síofra allows the safe passage of *women* across her loch—unlike their male counterparts.'

'Is this true?' asked Reece, narrowing his eyes.

'I ... I'm not sure ...,' said Daine, shaking his head wearily. 'I ... I heard stories.' He lingered on his thoughts, confused, struggling to recall what he may have heard, his mind feeling the effects of the day catching up on him. Rubbing the strain from his eyes, he then blinked continuously, trying to fight his growing tiredness.

'Then again ...' he said, shrugging it off, his voice slowing, 'it is most likely ... hearsay—a "myth" that has been handed down, through time—altered by wagging tongues. However, if there is any truth to it ... I have never witnessed it. The few women who dwell in these parts are superstitious, and refuse to go near the loch, believing their lives are in peril!'

'And what is your belief?' Gill enquired.

'I—' Daine suddenly jolted in his seat. Then, as if his body had been possessed by an entity, was wrenched back. The two Dhampir and Gill flinched at the unexpected motion. Daine looked down over the table's wooden surface, his eyes dancing, as though he was scrutinising the grain, polished by the oily hands of times past. Unable to control himself, he fell into his thoughts, losing himself to the will of another.

As a woman's face entered those thoughts, he became oblivious to his present company and the Inn's residents, who were now looking on, bewildered, distracted by his sudden—and obscure—behaviour. Threatened by his invader's presence of mind, Daine feared for his sanity as he tried desperately to fight against her, but the throbbing in his head was hampering his ability to do so.

Gill shared a worrying glance with his colleagues before leaning towards the guide, concerned.

'Are you all right?' he asked.

Daine failed to hear the young man's voice, overcome by inner fear. Unable to move, he felt it rise to the surface, for all to see, it manifesting in his features as his chest heaved with the want to breathe in the musty air. He then stopped, momentarily devoid of life.

As Gill reached out to jolt Daine from his inner torment, the guide suddenly exhaled, slowly releasing his demons. His eyes flashed open, meeting Reece's intense stare.

'There *was* a woman!' he blurted, his eyes wide and fixed; it was clear, by the distressed look on his face, he was taken aback by his admission.

'Who?!' Gill snapped.

Daine flinched from the young man's demand, seeing the flickering in his eager eyes. Mouth gaping, he shook his head, silently apologising to Gill for his ignorance; he was struggling to remember. He then began to mumble in a confused state.

'I must have—' He stopped. 'No! I—I couldn't have …'

The others shared wary looks as Daine strived to join the pieces together, uttering words that made no sense to them.

'But—I was there … I saw her …' He nodded. 'I saw them!'

'What did you see?!' Gill persisted, growing visibly agitated, half-rising from his seat.

'Think!' Asai urged, in his calm tone, certain it was connected to Eleanor. He was also aware of Gill's growing frustration, it marked by his clenched fists, ready to pound the table at any moment. The Samurai knew what would happen, should the guide fail to answer.

'This woman. What does she look like?' Reece, also aware of the guide's inner conflict, unexpectedly became the voice of reason, to Asai's surprise.

Daine slowly raised his head as pieces of what had happened that same evening toyed with his memory. He stared at their faces, doubting his mind—doubting everything—then dropped his head into his hands; it ached again, compelling him to nurse its throbbing pain.

'How could I forget something like that?' he mumbled.

Irritated, Gill pressed on him. 'Forget what?!'

Daine slowly looked up. 'An absence of time,' he revealed.

Gill, Reece and Asai drew back, raising their brows.

'I see her face clearly, and yet scarcely recall what happened.'

'You must remember!' Reece patiently insisted, trying not to deter him.

'When I told you, I had heard of your *kind* ...' Daine hesitated. 'I was wrong.' He shook his head. 'I have not *heard* of them ...'

They leaned closer.

'I have *seen* them—this very night!'

Gill's eyes widened. *Eleanor!*

Reece, driven by thoughts of his granddaughter, now pushed Daine further.

'This "woman" ... did she pass through the loch?'

'I—I don't know!' he replied, lifting his hands, in a gesture of helplessness.

'Think!'

Daine closed his eyes tightly, fighting to reclaim his thoughts. Then, they flickered open—the glint of recognition shining from the darkness of their greyness, as fragments of the evening began to emerge. As they pieced together, finally making sense, he regarded the three faces, their penetrating eyes watching him, with ardour.

'I remember!'

# Chapter Twenty-five

Daine slumped in his chair, exhaustion taking over as the barrage of questions was hurled at him:

'What was her name?'

'Did you see my sister?'

'Where were they going?'

'How many were there?'

The interrogations continued to come thick and fast after he had relayed the bizarre—not to mention alarming—events of his evening. His head now pounded from their persistence—'How many were there? Tell us! The woman?'—they eventually merging into a strain of nonsense.

At first, his memory had struggled to retrieve the entire incident. But, as their features gradually returned to haunt him—*the cloaked woman; her two servants; the devilish one; and the creatures*—it became apparent the ordeal had been all too real, creeping back like an unwanted scourge, refusing to release its hold on him.

'Why me?' he mumbled, trying to come to terms with it all. He recalled the threats made on his life—threats made in a manner he had never experienced before; nor would he ever forget. And the way the *devilish one* had looked at him, and what he had said before his departure. "Destroy him!" He thought his end had come, but *she* had spared him. 'Why did she do that?' he muttered to himself, trying to ignore Gill's voice as he continued to hound him.

'What did she say—the woman? Did she speak of the *Pass*?'

Worn out, Daine rested his head in his hands, and let his fingers massage his temples, wishing Gill would stop. *Enough!* he whined inside, gritting his teeth, his inner torment getting the better of him; it was too much. He groaned. 'What has she done to me?'

'Shall I tell you?'

Daine stopped and slowly looked up, his mouth gaping, and stared at Reece through the heaviness of his eyes.

'She did to you …' the Dhampir continued, his tone calm and defined, 'what she once did to me.'

Daine shook his head.

'What—what do you mean?'

'It was a long time ago,' Reece added.

'Did What?!' Daine snarled, his face contorting in anger.

Reece leaned forward. 'She wanted you to *forget!*'

'Forget?'

Reece nodded.

'Your timely "meeting" with her. She did not want you to remember it. It was also a precaution—to stop you from relaying what happened tonight—should *our* paths cross.'

Daine, his mind still a muddle of confusion, threw back a large mouthful of his whisky, coughed, feeling its fiery warmth hit the back of his throat, and slumped back, trying to make sense of Reece's statement.

'But … there is a difference here,' said Asai, adding his piece.

Daine looked from one to the other, frowning. 'Well?!'

'You have already remembered,' the Samurai then stated.

'Whereas, it was years before *I* did,' said Reece. 'She—the woman you speak of—has unspeakable—' He stopped and turned to Asai; they were both thinking the same thing: her attempt to overcome the guide had failed, making them question her powers. 'Do you think they could be …?'

Asai nodded; without her precious book and dagger, it was possible and, most likely, she was weakening. The events of the night had now taken an unexpected turn. They would have to act fast if they were to catch up with the Sorceress and her force.

Frustrated, Daine slammed his glass on the table, splashing Gill with some of the contents, in the process; the young man flinched, taken aback by the guide's sudden action, then brushed off what had been a waste of a good dram.

'Is someone going to tell me—'

Daine jolted when his further enquiry was disrupted, by the sound of heavy coins being tossed onto the table. He watched, momentarily riveted as they spun, revolving like a ticking timepiece, their glint of silver holding his attention until they stopped dead, falling flat on the table's surface. When he looked up, Reece was gone.

Daine, then feeling two strong hands on him, gulped the last of his whisky before being ushered out in pursuit of Reece, while, also, aware the Inn's eager eyes were closely watching them.

'Go back to your tedious conversations!' he snapped, glaring at them as he was being hauled away from their prying; they cowered from his anger before speculating on his return as the Samurai swiftly led him through the doorway, with Gill eventually following behind.

Outside, Reece and Tam were engrossed in conversation, while keeping their wits about them; there was an urgency in the brevity of their heightened tone. With a quick nod, Tam left their company, once more, to retrieve their horses—and also relieved to be finally moving on.

'Which one is yours?' Reece promptly asked.

Daine shook his head.

'I want nothing to do with this,' he returned, shrugging off Asai's grip. 'I don't know what connects you to those …' He paused as the image of the *devilish one's* words returned, burning into his memory: *"Destroy him!"* He shook it away. 'Nor do I care,' he stressed. 'I don't want to—'

'You are going to take us to the lake,' Reece, insisted. 'We have wasted too much time here, as it is.'

Still defiant, Daine stepped back, in retaliation. 'I refuse to—'

'We insist!' Gill unexpectedly whispered in his ear.

Daine spun, to see the young man he had likened from the moment of their first meeting now grinning at him. He had come across as more "human" than his three colleagues, and yet when he whispered those two words—*"We insist!"*—he had suddenly taken on a superiority of his own. Now aware of the underlying threat, he heeded caution. Reluctant, he pointed to the Friesian with the unusual markings, her distinguished white tail and mane standing out among the rest.

Tam, eager to get moving, wasted no time, and quickly returned with five horses, in tow.

'I presume she is yours,' he remarked, having observed Daine point to the Friesian. He handed the horse back to her owner. In her eagerness to go to him, it was evident Nahla was happy to see her master, and he, equally, relieved to be reunited with his one true companion. She nudged him, sensing his agitation, while he caressed her flank, calming her.

'As far as the lake,' Reece continued, mounting his horse. 'And then you are free to go.' The guide's eyes met the Dhampir's. 'A fair exchange, I would think?' added Reece.

Daine hesitated; he did not want to imagine the consequences, should he persist in his refusal to accompany them, at their insistence. There was no choice to be had as he cautiously eyed the four strangers surrounding him now. Releasing a long-winded sigh, he unwillingly nodded.

'To the loch—and then you are on your own,' he retorted.

'Agreed,' said Asai, intervening, wanting to avoid further aggravation.

As they prepared to leave, the sound of quickening footsteps could be heard running from the Inn—along with a small voice, calling out;

'Wait!'

The young boy stopped dead, panting heavily, then glanced back at the Inn, his eyes wide with a fixed stare as he wrung his trembling hands. Seeing his distress, Tam jumped from his horse and leaned down towards him. He then felt his anger surge when he saw the notable deep-red-and-purple markings on the side of the child's pale face; they were not there earlier. His cheeks were also stained from the flow of tears, where he had been crying.

'Did *he* do this to you?' he asked the boy, pre-empting his reply—the answer etched on James's face. The child swallowed and blinked as the five faces peered down at him.

'*Who* has done what?' Daine asked, with growing concern. He stopped short, seeing the bruising on James's cheek. 'He beats you?!' he demanded to know, leaning to meet the boy's saddened eyes. It was evident, from the swell of tears, that had been the case. 'You should have told me, James,' he insisted.

The boy hung his head, feeling shame. He had wanted to tell someone. But who would have listened? And besides, he had been warned: "Tell another soul of this, and I will drag you to the loch and gladly toss you in. I hear Síofra favours them young."

'I knew there was something about him,' Tam snarled, rising to his feet. He regarded the Inn before deciding to teach the boy's callous employer a lesson he would not forget; in fact, he intended to make sure the Landlord would never remember—from the coldness of his final resting place.

'Please, take me with you!' the child begged.

It was an impossible request. Daine then stood behind James and placed his protective hands on his slight shoulders. He would plead the boy's case to the four travellers. It was the least he could do.

Reece, having anticipated the appeal, shook his head, determined.

'The child is not our concern,' he stated.

Daine frowned, in disbelief. How could they desert a vulnerable child, and leave him to the mistreatment of his attacker? The notion of it was abysmal, to say the least. He then turned his supplications to Tam, sensing he had softened to the boy. But the larger-than-life Dhampir shook his head grimly; the child would only hamper their journey, endangering their lives, and his. No. It was out of the question, and yet the guilt of having to reject his pleas plagued the Highlander's conscience. Still, he had no choice.

''Tis impossible,' Tam informed Daine, with regret. 'But you have my word: he will never lay another hand on the wee lad.' With that, the Dhampir turned abruptly; nothing would please him more, at that moment, than to put an end to the boy's abuse, for the last time. With vengeance on his mind, Tam made for the Inn.

'If we cannot take him with us,' Gill mediated, 'then we must help him.'

Tam halted, hearing Gill's suggestion, then lingered, to see what he proposed to do.

Reece stared at his grandson as the young man stretched out his hand towards him, pointing to his cloak.

'I know what treasures you hide in that leather pouch,' said Gill. 'How else would you have paid for these fine horses?'

Reece rolled his eyes at the mere mention of the wealth he kept on his person. Asai looked sharp at his colleague, aware Gill was referring to their "spoils of war." The Samurai had wanted nothing to do with them, from the onset. "Those jewels you carry, Reece-san, are stained with blood. Do not forget it." But Reece had ignored his friends' morals, casting them aside, knowing those very "spoils" would be needed, at some point in time. But, conscious of the Samurai's persistent stare, he knew he could no longer avoid it.

'Let some good be associated with them, my friend,' Asai urged, eyeing the boy.

Reece looked down into the child's wounded eyes; they were filled with fear. He then saw the obvious swelling, where the marks now displayed the severity of the blows he had to endure. He, too, would happily teach the Landlord a lesson, should time allow it. However, the last thing he wanted was to be hunted down for the murder of a *mortal*; besides, the inconvenience would only disrupt their task.

*"Do some good with them."*

Reece quietly groaned. Asai was right. He was always right, and it irked him at times. But as the Samurai's words played on his conscience, he knew they could not leave the child to the humiliation of his abuser.

Convinced, he gladly handed over some gold coins and two precious gems to his grandson. Gill dismounted and approached the boy.

'Take these!' he urged the child. 'Keep them safe and take yourself from this place of evil before it draws you further into its grip. Make a good life for yourself, James. Promise me?' he added, throwing him a sidelong glance.

Astonished, James stared down at his sudden wealth, sniffling and wiping away the tears, unable to find the words to express his gratitude.

'And do not go back in there!' Tam warned him. The Dhampir glanced at the stable where the horses were tied and anxiously waiting for their masters to return, their fears marked by their uneasiness of the perverse atmosphere surrounding the Inn.

'*His*—is the sable mare,' Daine informed the Dhampir, pointing to the Landlord's prized horse. He then looked down at James. When their eyes met, he felt immense guilt for failing to see the cruelty that had been inflicted on the child—and right under his nose, too. *How did I not notice?* He had no reason to suspect his "business partner" was beating the boy, despite his uncaring personality. He had no right; after all, he was not his father. He shared in Gill's advice: the boy needed to get away if he were to pursue his dreams—whatever they may be. He deeply regretted not knowing, but most of all regretted being blinded to his plight. He then grinned at James and nodded towards the mare.

'Take her!'

The child's eyes widened, mixed with apprehension and excitement. He looked over at his employer's horse, terrified at the suggestion that he should *steal* her. On the rare occasion, when the Landlord had been away on business, he had taken it upon himself to ride the mare, unbeknownst to anyone. And, in doing so, he had developed a bond with her, taking great care to avoid any contact when the Landlord was about, so as not to arouse his suspicions. And now, the idea of owning his abuser's horse thrilled yet frightened him, knowing he would be beaten within an inch of his life for even looking at her, should he be caught out.

'Aye, lad, take her!' Gill urged, adding to Daine's encouragement. 'Go! Everything you want and need is there in your hands.' The boy held the coins and gems tightly to his chest. 'There is a wonderful world out there, waiting for you. Do not be afraid to face it, James. Now, go! We will wait until you are gone.'

*We will?* Reece thought, lifting his brows, growing increasingly anxious, on hearing Gill's words. *I do not think so!* He moved to protest. Time was pressing on them, more than ever. But when he saw his colleagues unite, urging the child on, he thought of the objections he would have to endure, should he disagree.

'Do it, boy!' he then snapped.

James leapt at Reece's abruptness and ran towards the sable mare, aided by Tam. The Dhampir helped the boy mount his abuser's fine horse. He looked so small, nestled on her broad back, but Tam knew he was capable. James looked down into the "giant's" eyes, now seeing the peculiarity of their warm amber glow, but notably their honesty. They smiled at each other, in a moment of understanding. Then, with a simple nod of gratitude, James stole himself away into the dead of night, leaving behind the life he had almost surrendered to, comforted by the clinking of his newfound wealth now safely tucked away in his pocket.

'Let us hope there will still be a world for him to embrace,' Reece stated, looking at his grandson.

Gill regarded his grandfather, conscious of the harsh truth in what he had said, making him feel the added weight of his burden. 'Then I am determined he will see it,' Gill staunchly replied.

Daine turned his back on the boy's departure when he faded from view, then made for the Inn.

'Leave him!' Reece called out. 'The matter has been dealt with. You have nothing to gain by punishing him, except for the noose they will place around your neck.'

'As tempted as I am,' Daine replied, through gritted teeth, 'it is not my "business partner" I return for.'

'Is *this* what you want?'

Daine turned to see Gill holding out his weapon, it still intact within its leather sheath. He snatched it from the hand that had "thieved" it from the Inn and then took his coat when it was offered from Gill's other hand. Gill released a short grunt at his abruptness. But it was evident the guide cherished the item, by his brief sigh of relief when it was returned to him.

Daine narrowed his eyes and looked at Gill. 'How did you …?'

'Oh, what the eye does not see,' said Gill, with a mischievous grin. 'They were too preoccupied with your "abduction" to notice the "theft" of your weapon.'

Daine was stumped; he had failed to notice it, too. 'And the Landlord?'

'I did not see him. But I'm sure 'tis only a matter of time before he notices our absence.'

Daine, shaking his head, suddenly realised he knew nothing, whatsoever, about the four individuals he was about to travel with— then thought it best not to ask; perhaps he was better off not knowing. Still, despite their strange animosity, he felt unusually safe in their company. But for how long? They would be outnumbered if their paths were to cross with those he had encountered, earlier that evening. And yet, they seemed impervious to the potential threat. *That remains to be seen,* he thought.

He wondered where *their* journey, beyond the *Pass*, would take them—and why the urgency … Regardless of it, he had no intention of finding out. *To the loch—no farther,* he quietly vowed, knowing his services would be well-rewarded, having seen the riches given to the boy. *No matter what!* It was then a thought occurred to him, prompting him to speak out;

'They may have already passed through the loch,' he admitted, looking to the sky; the rain had stopped and the wind was rising, trying its best to push the clouds away. Intermittent specks of tiny lights winked down, suggesting the sky might clear. The possibility was great.

Reece looked up, nodding in agreement.

'We will know, soon enough,' he replied, spurring his horse on, towards the unknown.

Daine stalled and looked back towards the Inn, his brows drawn together. The temptation …

'No more time for contemplation,' Reece added, riding away.

Disinclined, the guide immediately followed the four curious individuals, their fate yet undetermined.

Stumbling out from the staleness of his establishment, the Landlord squinted his beady eyes, searching the small courtyard. He saw no one and heard nothing, save for the eeriness of the damp night. He hated it. It made him feel uneasy. He hoped it would rain again; the sound of its constant pour would drown out the dour stillness. Why he stayed, he did not know. Had it not been for the lucrative arrangement he had with the guide, he would sell up. But who would purchase a run-down establishment like The Ardgore Inn? And, if an offer were made, it would only be a pittance.

He glanced up. The sky was clearing. He looked around again. There was no sign of the guide, and a thought entered his mind: he hoped he was not being duped by him; besides, he would never leave without his precious sword. He glanced back at the Inn. Perhaps he had taken the weapon. He then dismissed the notion; he would have seen him retrieve it. As for the boy … He, too, was nowhere to be seen.

The horses stirred in the open stable. He looked across at them; some were missing, including Nahla. His growing suspicions hinted that the guide had been in cahoots with the strangers, all along; they had looked cosy, in their huddled conversation. He then noticed the absence of another horse. He limped towards the stable, dragging his right foot behind—the wet mud slippery beneath his feet. He winced in pain when he almost lost his balance; his lame foot had twisted over itself. Pain shot through the limb, rising sharply. He cursed his affliction, blaming the incompetent physician who had set it wrong when he had broken it as a child, leaving him maimed for life and at the mercy of the other children, who used to mock him.

He stopped short of the stable, staring wildly into it, speechless, at first. *They've stolen her!* 'You'll pay for this—thieving bastards!' he snarled, through his teeth. He called out the boy's name; there was no reply. He called again, his voice now raised in anger. It reverberated through the woods. He contemplated looking for him, then changed his mind. *I am not going in there!* 'Runt!' he sneered, imagining what he was going to do to the child with his foul hands when he returned. It excited him to see the look of terror in his eyes as his pathetic pleas implored him to stop. He would wait until no one was around so he could be alone, to have his way with him. The thought of it roused him into drawing another breath.

He prepared to shout out when a sound, approaching from behind, compelled him to stop. It grew louder—*Thump! Thump!*—drawing closer, its pace quickening, almost deafening to his ears.

It suddenly halted.

He froze, afraid to look around.

It was right behind him.

# Chapter Twenty-Six

*Elboru*

His determined footsteps screamed his unspoken arrival as the great doors of the Hall of Eminence were thrust wide open, against their will. Each step echoed loudly, heightening in pace as he pushed himself forward, determined. He ignored the growing sense of being watched by the spirits of its past, their voices forever silent. Former Warlocks, who had participated in long—but not forgotten—wars, came here to die when their time had come. Here, their ashes were interred inside one of the many great pylons lining its vast gallery, while others rested peacefully beneath the stone floor, their tombs marked by their cartouche—carved into the limestone, in sunken reliefs. He, however, had no intention of becoming another of the Hall's permanent residents. No. Not just yet.

His eyes darted towards one of the pylons: that of his close friend, Tekkian—now long gone. He paused for a moment in front of it, then bowed, out of respect for his colleague. He regretted not knowing of his death, placing some of the blame on the Elliyan … But mostly, on himself. He sighed, and as he made to move away, a voice rang in his mind:

*"What's done is done!"*

Oran hesitated and stared back at the pylon, thinking he had heard his friend's voice.

He regarded it, then shook his head.

'Impossible!' he mumbled, accusing his mind of playing tricks on him. He turned and pressed on.

The dimly lit Hall seemed to spy on him as he stomped through— the flames from its torches swaying, altering his movements as they followed him, throwing his giant shadow to the walls, overemphasising his presence. He neglected to notice, his mind a blizzard of thoughts and suspicions.

Oran, frustrated by his peer's questionable behaviour, suspected the Elliyan had been lying to him. No. He was sure of it; Kai was not the one who had delivered the message to them. He had sensed it in his council's demeanour when he quizzed them about his son. *Something is wrong*, he thought. *And they are making a point of keeping it from me. Not for long, though.* Therefore, in alliance with his instincts, he had made his decision: he would take back the book and go. *I'll find out for myself!*

Gradually his steps slowed as he approached the end of the Great Hall, his eyes searching the stones beneath his feet. He knew it would be there, concealed in the only tomb without a resident. It was kept empty for one purpose: to safeguard items of value from thieving hands. *Except for mine*, he thought, grinning to himself.

He stopped, pausing to look around. Good, he was alone. Wasting no time, he reached his hand out over the sealed tomb and, as if pushed down by an invisible weight, the great slab obeyed his silent command and lowered, taking the form of steps.

Falling steeply before him, they disappeared into a cauldron of darkness. He stalled again, and glanced around, before turning to face them. His eyes followed their descent into what seemed like an abyss, to the chamber where it was kept. *As close to hell as possible*, he thought, sneering to himself. *A fitting place, indeed, for an item of damnation.*

Locked away—not that he needed a key—deep beneath the foundations, it was thought the book should reside there until *they*— namely Greer—could decipher its full meaning. Aware his fellow High Warlock could—and would—eventually translate its ancient text, he took it upon himself to relieve them of the task, by removing it entirely for his own purpose. In doing so, he would then find a way to decipher it properly, and, after using it for his sole purpose, would then destroy it.

He stared down into the blackness. 'It's now or never!' he muttered, taking his first step.

'It is not there,' came the soft voice from behind.

Oran spun to find Lothian, his thin hands clasped behind his back, looking calmly at him. He had failed to hear the Great Warlock's approach.

Lothian, the oldest of all living Warlocks had left his Realm, Ockram, in the hands of another to come to Elboru, to live out his final years. Slight in frame, the cruel signs of centuries of battle were etched on his oval face. Though lined with age, when he smiled, his amethyst eyes sparkled with life, lifting his features. No one knew his true age, though some believed him to be almost a *Millenia*, and when he had once questioned his senior, Oran recalled the Great Warlock's response: a wink of the eye. Even now, he was still none-the-wiser.

'Where is it?!' he demanded.

'They are trying to unravel the rest of its secrets,' said Lothian. 'It is a long and complex process. Tepés was no fool when he created it. Quite the genius, I must admit.'

'Despite his madness.'

'Despite it,' said Lothian, lifting his narrow shoulders. 'The text stems back centuries, through his family line, using the language of his ancestors—one that is almost lost. But we are fortunate in that Greer is familiar with the script. If luck favours us, we shall soon have the means to destroy Magia Nera … and the Sorceress.'

Oran met the Great Warlock with a startled look. 'Soon?!' he echoed.

'The sooner, the better,' said Lothian, adamant.

The certainty of the Great Warlock's words fell on Oran like a great strain. But he had also sensed an urgency in his tone. Tilting his head forward, Oran held Lothian's gaze. 'You fear them!' he stated.

'You must understand, Lord Oran, we are quite vulnerable at this challenging time. Without a Supreme Warlock to rule us, we are in no position to take risks. This has turned into a race against time, while we wait for him. As confident as we are, that your son is in safe hands and, en route, the threat out there is real, and shall remain so until he is safely here. We do not know the whereabouts of the Sorceress and Magia Nera—nor are we prepared to venture out, to search for them. Elboru must be guarded at all times.' Lothian paused in a moment of thought. 'Can you imagine the extent of their powers, combined? Unspeakable! We cannot even begin to.'

Oran, his mind racing, turned away, mumbling to himself. 'You can't kill them!'

'And why not?'

'I see your hearing is still as sharp as your mind, Lord Lothian,' he remarked, turning to confront the Great Warlock.

'Why not destroy them?!' Lothian retorted. 'Is it not *their* intention—to destroy us?'

'You know it is against our ruling to kill another Warlock.'

'I need no reminding,' said Lothian. 'But Magia is no ordinary Warlock—as you well know.'

'Aye! True to say, Magia lost his way when he crossed paths with Tepés,' said Oran. 'But I believe he is not in partnership with L'Ordana—not while she still possesses his amulet and the—'

'You know how important it is—that Magia's is returned to us.'

'I know!' snapped Oran. 'Tuan has done nothing but constantly remind me—and my "failure" to do so, since my return.'

'Then I shall also remind you, Lord Oran. Without all five, the *Sixth*—the Shenn—will not be bonded with its rightful owner—your son!'

'Do you not think I'm aware of that?!' Oran hit back, stepping closer to his elder, his face hardening, marking his frustration. He then stopped—took a deep breath—and calmed himself. 'Please, hear me out!'

Lothian tilted his head, intrigued, then extended his hand towards the High Warlock, silently motioning him to proceed.

'I believe Magia is biding his time,' he maintained, 'until he can take back what is his.'

'For what purpose?' said Lothian. 'To purloin what he cannot have? Even *he* knows the Shenn is beyond his reach.'

Oran shook his head.

'I do not refer to his amulet; he cares nothing for that. There can only be one reason he stays with her.'

Lothian raised a brow. It then dawned on him. 'Ah, yes! He thinks she still has the book.'

Oran nodded in agreement.

'And, as he is so desperate to reclaim it, it makes me question his agenda.'

'He must never have access to it again!' Lothian stated, resolute. 'Magia Nera has done much wrong in the past ...' He hesitated, momentarily lost in a memory, then cast it away. 'And he has turned his back on our ways. For that, alone, *they* want him destroyed.'

'And the Sorceress?'

'She is the greater risk. Can you imagine the destruction if she were to covet the Shenn? Magia would be the least of our worries. We would be exposed and forced to live in a world of darkness and despair—ruled by her tyranny—should we survive. If so, then mankind would simply not endure—' He stopped, and looked directly at Oran. 'But you already know that.'

'I know I can stop her, and retrieve Magia's amulet,' Oran blurted, trying to obliterate the image of her potential death from his mind. He did not want that.

Lothian, drawing back his head in surprise, lifted his brows. 'I believe you do have a place in your heart for her, Lord Oran. I saw it—just there'—he pointed—'in your eyes. Lord Greer had sensed it, too, when you returned to us. He shared his concerns with me. I had no reason to believe him, and yet should have; his perceptions are seldom—if ever— wrong.'

Shaking his head in denial, Oran approached Lothian.

'No—not like a lover!' he stated, raising his hands in an act of defence. 'Like a ...'

'I know,' said Lothian. 'The woman you spoke of—*Kristene!*'

Lowering his eyes, Oran reluctantly nodded.

Staring at the High Warlock, Lothian could not help but feel sympathy for him, sensing his inner turmoil. He smiled. 'While I am trying to understand, Lord Oran,' he began, 'I am at a loss as to why you—'

'*He* influenced her,' Oran cut in, his eyes wide and intense as he stared back at the Great Warlock. 'Magia lured her away from me when we lived in—'

'Triora.'

Oran's mouth gaped. 'How—how did you …?' He shook his head, stumped.

'Because I followed you.'

'You?!'

Lothian nodded.

'The Servitor—Kai—was not alone. I made it my business to accompany him—to … keep an eye on you … in a manner of speaking.'

'How long?'

'Oh … years!' Lothian casually replied. 'You were quite ostentatious in how you lived which, I must admit, made it quite easy to find you, at first; your opulent lifestyle made no secret of your wealth. Rather flamboyant, I would say.'

'I feel no shame for my past indiscretions,' said Oran, standing his ground, determined to defend himself. 'Tell me, Lord Lothian, would you not have done the same?'

The Great Warlock returned his answer with a knowing smile. 'Yes, I envied you, while I watched from afar but—I also saw the harm it was doing.'

'Then, why not intervene?' said Oran, with an air of sarcasm in his tone.

'It was not my place to interfere. Your chosen life was your own. *You* wanted it, which is why we allowed you to pursue it.'

Oran shook his head.

'So, you gladly stood by—in the wings—watching,' he sneered, 'as I dragged myself down, almost destroying myself?'

'And, for a time, I thought you had.'

Oran frowned, bemused.

'You see, your trail was suddenly severed, after your time in Triora,' Lothian continued. 'It was as if you ... no longer existed. Gone! Just like that!' he added, clicking his fingers.

'I—I decided to ... "leave" there,' he replied, diverting his eyes from Lothian's constant, curious stare.

'Or ... perhaps ... you had no other option,' the Great Warlock stated.

Oran shook his head.

'I—I don't know what you mean.'

'We saw them—the mob—as they made their assault on your home. Even *I* could sense the evil attached to it.'

'I did not kill the girl!' Oran declared, stepping closer to his elder. 'On all that is sacred to me, I did not take her life. I treated her, and the boy—' He stopped dead. *Petrio!* It was the first time the child's name had entered his head, in years. He could still clearly see his little face, terrified by the angry mob as they battered down the door of their home.

'You will be pleased to know he escaped—unharmed—with a woman.'

'Sofia!' Oran blurted, overwhelmed and smiling as he spoke his old cook's name. 'Good. I had hoped they survived.' But the smile quickly faded when he was reminded of the brutal reality of time, and its ability to wait for no one. He hoped, at least, the boy had made something of his life. *What does it matter now?* he thought, aware that time, no doubt, had caught up with them. He hoped their last moments were peaceful ones when death finally came knocking.

'But why did you not pursue them?' asked Lothian, breaking his train of thought. 'Magia, and—'

'Krist—' Oran stopped, to correct his *faux-pas*. 'It was *she* who murdered the girl—my young servant, Lucia. However, I refused to accuse her of her guilt,' he insisted. '*He* was to blame for everything. While under Magia's influence, she was out of my reach; she barely recognised me. I had no option but to let her go to him. But she duped us both with her new powers and disappeared with his amulet. It was the last thing I—*we*—expected.'

'You cannot place all the blame on your counterpart, Lord Oran; you were partially to blame. You chose to run away, after letting her escape when, by right, you should have—'

'Why not?!' snapped Oran, irritated by the accusation. 'She was *his* problem. Besides, I had more pressing matters to contend with, at the time. As the villagers tore down my door, I was forced to make some hasty decisions; I was not prepared to reveal who I was, through my anger. No. The wrath of a Warlock should not be played out upon the innocent, despite the mob's cruel intentions.'

'So, you fled—to save them,' Lothian stated.

Oran nodded.

'Ah! Now I understand,' said Lothian.

'From there, I took to travelling alone. I kept to myself, living a life opposite that which I had been accustomed to. I rid myself of all my luxuries, while keeping enough to live on, for as long as I needed.'

'Hence the reason we could not find you. We travelled to all five Realms—even revisiting your old battleground, where Tepés once ruled—and still, we could not locate you. Once more, it was as if you vanished from the face of the earth. And, because of that, we feared the worst, and reluctantly returned to the Elliyan.'

Oran sighed. 'Until my son was born.'

'Suggesting you were still alive. But even then, it was difficult to locate you, as the Shenn had only been reborn. We knew it would be years before then.' Lothian grunted, a little amused. 'And to think …'

Oran met the Great Warlock's eyes; they were smiling with a look of pride.

'… all the while, you were right under our noses.'

'Sometimes, the most obvious is the least noticed,' said Oran.

'How true,' Lothian returned, slowly nodding. 'But what brought you back to Urquille, in the first place—before your new life, and your new family?'

'A longing, perhaps?' said Oran, shrugging. 'Urquille is my Realm—my home—and I wanted to return, to do some good. So, I went to Eddin, where I took up duty as a soldier, at the castle.'

'Like a *mortal?*'

'Aye, it was a refreshing change …' He paused. 'Though frustrating at times.'

'I do not doubt it,' said Lothian, amused by the thought of a Warlock locked in battle, alongside a mortal. 'Their methods of combat are quite … minimal, to say the least.' He then looked sharp at him. 'I hope you did not—'

'No!' Oran quickly returned. 'They never knew. However, they came to recognise my … "unique" skills.'

'Or, perhaps, you *let* them?' said Lothian, turning his head sideways, casting his fellow Warlock a mischievous look.

'Oh, perhaps, a little.' A shameless curl appeared at the corner of Oran's mouth. 'I was quickly promoted as personal guard to the King, allowing me to live at the castle. It was there I met my wife-to-be.'

'Rosalyn.'

'Aye!' he said, grinning, recalling the first moment their eyes met, the uniqueness of hers—one blue, one green—attracting him to her, instantly. She had not worked there long and was unaccustomed to the labour. She had been given the task of carrying her weight in food for the guardsmen when she lost her balance, her foot catching in her long skirt. She had dropped some of her load on top of him. He would never forget her embarrassment as she showered him with apologies … until he mocked her. It was then, through the sharpness of her tongue, he truly admired her, her self-defence driven by strength, and a passion he could not resist. 'She was a young widow, trying to raise a bairn,' he continued. 'They lived just outside Eddin, with her mother, Onóir …' Lothian's eyes darted towards Oran at the mention of Onóir's name, almost betraying himself. '… and she looked after the child—Eleanor—while Rosalyn worked as a cook at the castle. I knew instantly she was the "one" for me. I pursued her until she accepted my marriage offer, with some encouragement from her mother. It was the first time since—' He shook his head. 'I cannot say how long … But I was overwhelmed by her. I wanted to protect her—to protect them all. And so, I decided to …' He paused and smiled. '*Retire!*'

'I find that difficult to believe,' said Lothian, throwing him a knowing look.

'Oh, the *powers of persuasion* are a wonderous thing.' Oran smirked. 'When you know how!'

'And how *bold* of you, Lord Oran! By using them on their King!'

'He did not suspect a thing,' said Oran, casually waving away the alleged indiscretion with the flick of a hand. 'He released me from my duties, willingly.'

'And from there you went to Balloch?'

Oran nodded.

'Away from prying eyes. We were safe, there—concealed in our little world … or so I thought. Naturally, everything changed after Gill was born.'

'It was only a matter of knowing *when* you would eventually be betrayed.'

'Betrayed?!'

Lothian nodded.

'Indeed, Lord Oran. By the one thing we have no control over.'

Oran sighed. '*Time!*'

'Precisely! The Shenn and your son would grow stronger together—find their way—draw us to him … and you. But you always knew that.'

'I know,' he said, closing his eyes, feeling shame. 'I just chose to *forget!*'

Lothian regarded the High Warlock in his moment of self-guilt. Then, through his pity for him, said, 'I have always favoured you … Oran,' he admitted, dismissing the rules of protocol when one Warlock addressed the other.

Oran's eyes sprung open, and he stared at his elder, taken aback by this familiarity. It had been another of the Elliyan's criteria: no Warlock could favour another—the rule enforced, to create an air of detachment between them.

"Tis true!' Lothian admitted, noting Oran's expression. 'When I look at you, I see a mirror image of how *I* once was,' he continued. He hesitated, musing over his next revelation. 'I, too, have truly loved … more than once. I had a wife, you know.'

Oran's mouth gaped.

'It was before your time. She gave me two daughters—one of whom was blind. Despite her affliction, I treated them equally, loving one no less than the other. They were my most precious jewels.' He glanced down. 'More precious than the one that hangs around my neck. *This!*—he pointed to his amulet—'is a "duty" I am bound to. Whereas *they* were my life. So, you see, I, too, craved a *mortal* life—and found it … as brief as it was.'

'Your family—did they know who you were?'

'We had no secrets.'

'And the Elliyan? Did they know of them?'

Lothian nodded.

'But they were unstable times, then—full of turmoil, and on the constant brink of war. There seemed no end to it. I tried to escape it but … death found us out, no matter where our journey took us. The Elliyan were not so forgiven and, like you, I was forced to leave my family. Because of their mortality, they were vulnerable and unaware, and without my protection, their fate was sealed.' Lothian paused, lingering on the harrowing memory of having to part from them. He could still hear their mourning cries.

'What happened?'

'They soon fell victim to conflict,' he said, his voice sombre in tone. 'I had nothing left. My resentment towards the Elliyan almost got the better of me; however, I was fortunate in that the Magus set me on the right path until I found my place again.'

Oran watched and listened patiently as Lothian spoke of his past. And, as he did, he was reminded of his own before Rosalyn: his wife, Sahraya, and their child, Raya—the two losing their lives to the cruel sea. He, too, had lost his mind for a time, his suspicions around their deaths heightening his unbearable pain. Deep down, he still refused to believe their deaths had been "accidental!"

It was now clear, as the Great Warlock relayed his story to him, Oran saw traces of grief still ingrained on his face; Lothian's resentment, although buried deep inside, was still present.

'I am deeply sorry for your loss,' he said, unable to hide his sympathy.

'It was a long time ago,' Lothian replied, returning the memory to the back of his mind.

'However, *I* have no intention of losing my family,' stated Oran.

Lothian raised his eyes to meet the High Warlock's, then slowly nodded.

'Then, we must make certain you do not. Time is short,' he added, placing his hand on his amulet. 'See how brightly the precious stones shine? The Shenn is almost complete!'

Oran needed no reminding when he looked down at the Great Warlock's amulet. The stone was now vibrant—a deep yellow—like a setting sun, pulsating, almost breathing as though it were alive. *But it is!* he realised.

'I see you continue to conceal yours,' said Lothian.

'For what I am bound to wear around my neck, hangs like a great burden,' Oran replied, without acknowledging it. 'It is a grim reminder of what lies ahead for my son.'

Lothian smirked, turning his eyes away from him.

'You find it amusing?' Oran sneered, feeling mocked.

'I can still see their faces,' said Lothian, unable to wipe away the smile of self-gratification.

'Whose?'

'None more so than Tuan's,' he maintained, 'when he discovered *who* had fathered our new Magus. Apart from knowing you were still alive, it was the pleasure of seeing his humiliation—and displayed so publicly, too—which provided me with real contentment. I am glad you had those precious years with your son, Oran—and that you refused to give him up before his time. It was only right he stayed with you, to learn what it was to be … *human,* without the Elliyan's stoic influence.' He paused, considering the High Warlock, then nodded. 'Yes. You have tutored your son well. Even after your "departure" Kai took him under his wing, to continue what you had begun: his training.'

Oran frowned, irked by the notion of one of those *creatures* looking after his son.

'Do not judge Kai,' said Lothian. 'He is the most trustworthy of all the Servitor. You should be thankful for his guidance—and thankful to the *one* he sought out to help him; they have done you great justice and, because of it, your son is prepared for his task. Yes. He and the Shenn will bond perfectly.'

Oran, prompted by the mention of the Servitor's name again, hesitated. *They?* he thought, narrowing his eyes. 'But of course!' he exclaimed. 'The other one you spoke of—when I returned here,' he stated, tilting his head.

'The other?'

'Aye! *She,* whose name you failed—*refused*—to mention?'

The Great Warlock stared at him, his expression now blank.

'Do not play me for a fool, Lothian!' he provoked. 'Kai's collaborator! The so-called *Watcher?*'

Lothian, holding his gaze, was taken aback; he hoped the High Warlock had forgotten. Then again … this was Oran Shaw they were dealing with …

'I cannot—nor shall I reveal their name to you. We pledged to protect their identity.'

'*Her* identity, you mean,' Oran lashed back.

Lothian paused, lowering his eyes, then nodded.

'Even in death.'

'And by that,' Oran perceived, 'I assume *it* has found her.'

'To our great misfortune,' Lothian returned, lifting his eyes. 'But it is comforting to know, your son is still in capable hands, despite the threat hovering over us. Kai has assured me of your friends' capabilities.'

'Then, tell me this, Lothian. While my son is being protected, who watches over my family, now?'

# Chapter Twenty-Seven

L othian's face slowly fell. It was only a matter of time before they would be forced to tell Oran of his daughter's plight, the passing of Onóir, and as for his wife, Rosalyn … If he discovered she had left Balloch, to search for the others, to join them on their journey …

'Well, Lothian?' Oran urged. 'Can you not tell me, or … maybe you do not wish to?'

Inside, Lothian's head was battling against his heart, deciding whether to tell the High Warlock what he had a right to know. *Now is the time*, he decided. *He deserves to know.* As he took a deep breath, Oran moved closer, with expectation.

'They are waiting for you,' came an unexpected voice from the shadows.

Lothian and Oran spun, searching for the source when Lorne stepped out into their presence, composed and tranquil. The Servitor's radiance brought with it a calming influence, dousing the mounting tension he had felt upon entering the Great Hall. He bowed slightly when Lothian greeted him—the Great Warlock thankful for the Servitor's timely intrusion.

'Has there been much progress?' asked Lothian.

'Lord Greer has been successful!' Lorne answered, his large black eyes subtly lowering, observing the opened tomb.

Lothian, having noticed this, stepped away, summoning the Servitor to follow him. 'And the others?' he asked, drawing Lorne's attention away from the crypt. It was at this point Oran sealed it again, then promptly joined them.

'They are almost gathered, and the Bullwark are in place,' said Lorne, glancing back at Oran—the High Warlock tilting his head, while displaying a false smile.

Lothian slowly nodded as Lorne relayed the preparations for the imminent arrival of their Magus, known as the *Assembly*: the gradual gathering of other Warlocks from the five Realms, and the preparations for the ceremony in the Sanctuary of Armistice.

'Good! This is very good!' exclaimed Lothian, attempting to brighten his tone. He turned to Oran, smiling. 'Victory is imminent, Lord Oran!' he added, returning to formalities in the Servitor's presence. 'All will be well.'

Confused, Oran narrowed his eyes, then forced another smile.

'Thank you, Lorne,' said Lothian, turning to acknowledge the Servitor, once more. 'We will be there, presently!'

For a brief moment, the Servitor held their gaze, his eyes sliding from one to the other as if trying to read their thoughts; he suspected something was afoot.

The Warlocks, aware of his scrutiny of them, remained poised and calm, maintaining their pleasantries.

*How dare he!* Oran thought, through his forced smile, tempted to scold Lorne for his suspicions of them. *Oh, to have the pleasure …*

Unable to sense anything, the Servitor bowed gracefully towards the Warlocks before his silent exit.

Angered by this, Oran moved to follow him. 'The nerve of that—' He stopped, prompted by Lothian's raised hand, signalling him to hold his tongue until the Servitor had left, Lorne's perpetual glow fading as he departed the Hall of Eminence.

'Wait!' whispered Lothian, keeping his hand suspended.

Once again, silence resumed.

'Why did you just stand there and let him question our thoughts?' said Oran.

'Because …' Lothian then turned to him. 'I do not trust Lorne.'

Oran drew back, raising his brows. 'But I thought …'

'That I pitied him?'

Oran nodded.

'Once, perhaps,' said Lothian, lifting his shoulders. 'But now ... I have sensed a change in Lorne, and, for that, I am keeping a watchful eye.'

They looked to where the Servitor had left, and listened; he was gone. Satisfied they were alone, once again, Lothian turned to Oran, apprehensive.

'The *book!*' he quickly prompted. 'While it was in your possession, did you decipher any of it?'

'Only scattered words, I'm afraid—but enough to release the three Dhampir,' said Oran. 'Time did not allow me to try to translate more, due to the peril of our situation. Also, the daggers' influence did not help matters, its presence making it difficult; together, both items are dangerous.'

'Which is why we separated them.'

'Where is it now—the dagger?' asked Oran, glancing back at the unmarked tomb.

'Somewhere safe, where it cannot influence its collaborator,' said Lothian. Oran raised a brow and slowly lowered his head at the Great Warlock, waiting for him to elaborate. 'It is hidden in a wall, in my chamber,' he revealed. 'In a silver box, laid out on a bed of salt. A simple yet effective precaution, to contain its evil.'

Oran smiled, then nodded his approval.

'Good. She will never have them again.'

'Let us hope so,' said Lothian.

Oran shot him a glance, sparked by yet another reminder of something he had almost omitted.

Lothian leaned closer. 'What is it?'

'When Magia took her under his wing, he taught her the *Black Arts.*'

'We are aware of it.'

'That was when—through the power of the book—he placed the spirit of an ancient Witch inside her. This *entity* is the cause of her evil.'

Lothian, on hearing this, slowly lifted his head, his eyes attentive, listening.

'But, to me, she is still *Kristene*,' Oran maintained. 'However, while she is controlled by this *spirit* ...' He sighed.

Lothian nodded and looked away, his mind exploring.

'And the name "L'Ordana" ... Is this the ... *entity's* true name?' he then asked, intrigued.

'No!'

Lothian's eyes flashed to the High Warlock, alert.

'It was given to her,' said Oran. 'By Magia.'

For a few moments, a dense silence separated them. Oran stared, frowning at his elder; the Great Warlock appeared lost. 'My Lord?' he prompted.

Lothian flinched, as though caught off-guard, then smiled. 'Forgive me, Oran,' he said. 'Just the wandering thoughts of an old man. Please, continue.'

As Oran revealed the more intimate details of his life with *Kristene*, Lothian nodded, absorbing everything he was being told, with new insight.

'Therefore, I believe that is why she kept me alive, while I was her captive,' Oran perceived, shrugging. 'She had no reason to spare me; I refused to talk.'

'It seems—subconsciously—she could not bring herself to kill her "saviour",' Lothian concluded. 'Something deep within would not *let* her.'

'Now you understand why I can't destroy her,' Oran confessed. 'As long as there is still an ember of *Kristene* inside, I will not do it!' Oran shook his head, defiant. 'So, please—do not judge me!'

Lothian smiled warmly at Oran's gallantry. 'It is not my intention to do so.'

'I know the spell to release the *spirit* from her is there, deep inside those pages,' Oran implored.

'Hence the reason you came here,' said Lothian.

'If only I could …'

'The Elliyan will not let you have free reign of the book, Oran. They doubt you. They wish to destroy L'Ordana, whatever the cost. And, if what you say is true, I cannot support you. This—this *spirit* inside her risks being released—perhaps, even into another victim,' he added, shaking his head at the notion of it.

Oran suddenly realised the Great Warlock's meaning. 'No! No, my friend,' he insisted. 'It was placed inside the well-tutored Kristene, by the power of the book, and can only be removed by the same means. It has no bearing on its movements.'

'Ah! Therefore, it cannot choose to enter another *host*—of its own free will.'

'We must tell the Elliyan!' Oran suggested.

Lothian shook his head.

'Why not?!' said Oran.

'They will not jeopardise the life of your son, no matter how much we prevail on them. Nor can we rule out Magia Nera knowing the spell, without the help of the book; it is possible he already knows.'

'Then that'—Oran released a heavy sigh—'is a risk we must take.'

Lothian regarded Oran for several moments, then turned, taking a deep breath. 'This puts me in a difficult position,' he admitted, joining his hands together. Oran watched as the Great Warlock lifted them, flexing his long, stem-like fingers methodically, as though to aid his concentration. Staring at him, it suddenly dawned on Oran how small and frail this once-great Warlock had become. He had heard tales of Lothian's epic battles. Once regarded as the strongest of the Elliyan, he had been admired and respected for his ability to overthrow the enemy, effortlessly. But what he lacked in his fading years was now made up by his wisdom—his greatest, personal treasure.

Lifting his head, Lothian looked up into the dark reaches, above the Halls' high rafters, searching for a solution. Although he could not see them, he could hear the distant, constant flapping of little wings as they fluttered wildly in and out between the beams. Every now and then, their tiny black forms flew close to the huge ornate lanterns—the light throwing their enlarged silhouettes on the dimly lit walls. And then they would disappear again, into their world of darkness.

'I will find a way,' he then stated when his gaze met the disheartened look on Oran's face. And, as he smiled at the High Warlock, Lothian saw the flicker of hope return in his eyes. Placing his hand over his heart, Lothian bowed. 'And I give you my word of honour, Oran,' he added. 'I will find the spell you require.' He then looked him straight in the eye. 'But I should warn you …'

Oran waited, his look now intense.

'Once the book is in your possession, I urge you to do the right thing—if all else fails.'

'Fail?' Oran returned. 'Why should it? She knows nothing about—'

'Are you certain of that?' said Lothian, tilting his head forward; there was a risk the girl—Eleanor—had "talked," or had been forced to. He then immediately regretted asking.

'If L'Ordana has an inkling, or even *knows*'—Oran approached him, his face hardening—'she did not hear it from me!' Struck by a notion, he drew away from the Great Warlock, side-glancing him. 'What else do you know—that I do not?'

Lothian, holding his poise, stared back at Oran; if there was a time to tell him, it was now. But instead, before his conscience could win him over, he decided to take his leave.

'Do nothing rash, Oran,' he advised, turning away, wanting to avoid further questioning. 'Leave it with me.'

Thrown by his hastiness to go, Oran stood speechless and frustrated as he watched his superior shuffle away, Lothian's baffling behaviour charging his suspicions. *No, you don't!*

'Well, Lothian?' he called after him, persistent.

The Great Warlock, still battling with his thoughts, paused, keeping his back to him.

'What of my son?'

Lothian inhaled, reluctant to speak.

'Tell me!' Oran persisted. 'Have they passed through it yet—the loch?'

'No,' Lothian stated firmly, without looking back. 'They have not!'

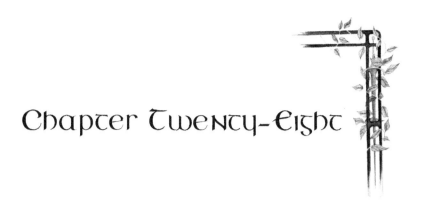

# Chapter Twenty-Eight

*"She awakens beneath the inky depths, stirred by the moon's ghostly hue as it slowly moves, spreading her curse across the water; it shimmers and reaches down to her, through the gloom. Her eyes open, touched by it. Like a black split in wood, her mouth moves to a smile, and she rises—the call of death seducing her as she breaks the surface ..."*

Eilidh Stiùbhar
*Seanchaidh à Peairt.*

*The Cordhu Pass*

The *Two Lovers* rose high above them, their thick branches entwined in perpetual unity, leaning towards each other, forming the arch of their embrace. Grandiose in stature, they waited—as they had done for centuries—for those who were unfortunate enough to find them, and for those who were desperate enough to cross their threshold.

The travellers slowed on their approach, drawing to a halt, then stared out over the dark, barren wasteland, its strangeness challenging their imagination.

'What do you see?' came the adamant voice.

'*Niente!*'

'Surely, with your sight, Magia,' L'Ordana argued, 'you can see *something!*'

The dark Warlock turned and, noting how she cautiously kept her distance behind him, smirked.

'Even with my vision … *Bella!*' he returned, emphasising his pet name for her, to grind on her annoyance, 'I see only dry land stretched out before us, under our blanket of night. I know nothing of what is to come.' He stepped aside, motioning her forward. 'Come—see for yourself!'

She stared at him, unsure.

'Are you not curious about their tales and myths?' he mocked, holding his grin. 'Also, to see if he was telling the truth? May his soul rest for eternity,' he added, tempted to make the sign of the Cross for the *Guide's* demise. He grunted at the irony of it.

She frowned at his evasiveness, then stared back at him, an equally smug grin appearing on her lips, pleased she had let the *Guide* live.

Intrigued, she stepped forward close to the dividing line, beneath the *Lovers'* arch. Nothing stirred. She glanced up; the clouds were low, with no sign of them parting.

*Have I missed the Witching Hour?* she wondered. There was no way of knowing, beneath a cloud-covered sky. *If only they would part …* Then she would have the advantage; however, at this moment in time … *Damn it!*

'I know you are curious, *Bella*,' Magia teased, disturbing her thoughts. He lifted his head, looking over her shoulder and beyond her two servants, then pointed to the small legion of Dhampir warriors.

'You!' he called out, beckoning one towards him.

L'Ordana, Kara and Wareeshta turned, following his line.

'Come here!'

Obediently, the Dhampir warrior stepped forward, his immediate response aggravating the Sorceress. *He did not even hesitate*, she thought as he brushed by her, eager to please and serve his new master. *Who does he think he is?!*

The Dhampir stopped and faced the Warlock. Smiling, with contempt, Magia stepped aside, unblocking the gap between the trees, revealing what lay beyond.

'Go through it!' he ordered, stretching his long, slim arm, pointing out over the expanse. 'Then tell me what you see.'

Suddenly aware of Magia's intentions, L'Ordana stepped forward to intervene; she could not afford to lose more warriors. Although it had been necessary to dispatch the two, who had been a threat to the *Guide*, she did not want to repeat it, despite feeling compelled to save him. But as she moved closer, Magia stepped in her way before ordering the warrior to proceed.

'Do not think for one moment,' he snarled in her ear, his tone low and sinister, 'that it has gone unnoticed—*their* absence.'

She lifted her head slightly and looked at him, pan-faced. 'I have no idea what you mean!' she retorted, challenging him. 'And may I remind you … they are not *your* warriors.'

'The two I ordered to kill the *Guide*,' he said, ignoring her remark, 'they have failed to re-group.'

L'Ordana, maintaining her hardened stare, refused to let him intimidate her further. 'It was on *your* orders they obeyed,' she flatly replied. 'Not mine! As to what became of them, after …?' She shrugged. 'Well, you can see how disloyal they can be. They are no longer of any consequence to me.'

Vexed by her reply, he turned to the lone Dhampir, signalling him to proceed over the threshold. *I will show you who is in command, now*, he thought.

The warrior took two long strides forward, then paused. Intrigued, Kara and Wareeshta inched forward to watch.

'I did not tell you to stop!' Magia snapped at him.

Keeping his gaze fixed directly ahead, the lone Dhampir looked out before him, then down at his feet. Though invisible to the mortal eye, he could see it—the faint line—marking the fatal threshold between *life!* and *death!* For the first time, since he had been enslaved into the depraved world of the Dhampir, he sensed inner tension; it was foreboding, making him uneasy.

'Do not make me repeat myself!' Magia growled from behind.

Unexpectedly, the Dhampir found himself taking a deep breath—one of the many human traits he had already forgotten—as he grasped the hilt of his sword.

Magia tilted his head, fascinated by this startling reaction, then grew wary. He stepped closer to him.

'Do it!'

Again, the warrior hesitated, his eyes sliding sidewards, knowing the dark Warlock was right behind him, his foul breath creeping over his shoulder. It troubled him; nor was he alone in his thinking. Having witnessed his menace towards the reluctant warrior, L'Ordana secretly shared in the Dhampir's discomfort. However, bound to obey, the lone warrior took another step closer, then raised his foot, letting it hover over the boundary. Already, he could feel the force of an unknown energy, pulling him, enticing him forward. Balancing on one foot, he unexpectedly felt a need to draw his sword. But nothing prepared him, or his spectators, for what was about to happen …

The moment his foot touched the ground, he felt the sudden sharpness of icy water seep into his boot. He looked down, sharply. The ground had come to *life!* It had transformed into water, as black as ink, and its surface was now chomping at his foot. Suddenly, a ghostly white hand emerged, plunging up from the icy depths with such velocity it made him jolt, causing him to lose his balance. As the lone Dhampir fell back, the claw-like hand grabbed hold of its victim. Feeling the hard tug of its ice-cold grip, he struggled as it dragged him away from the safety of the water's edge, then down …

No one moved to save him.

No one dared.

Magia, amazed by the swiftness of it all, edged closer, then smirked with amusement, hearing the sudden release of a gasp from behind. *Too late, Bella!* he sneered inside.

L'Ordana, in anticipation, rushed forward, then stopped dead, catching the last glimpse of the lone Dhampir before he was wrenched to his murky grave. And then he was gone—in an instant—lost to the haunted waters before they returned to their deceitful state again.

He never made a sound.

At first, L'Ordana thought she had imagined it, then realised it was all too real. Speechless, she stared in disbelief, seeing nothing now but barren wasteland again.

For a short while, a stale, heavy silence breathed over them as they waited with expectation for something else to happen. Nothing did. Except for the wind, when it suddenly picked up, rustling the dead leaves still clinging to the *Lovers'* entwined branches.

Unperturbed, Magia casually turned, displaying a look of contentment. 'It would appear their "myth" is true,' he stated, breaking the momentum. 'Most intriguing!'

Enraged by his arrogance, L'Ordana clenched her fists; what she would give to wipe the condescending grin off his pale face, right now. 'You may have the upper hand, here, Warlock,' she seethed, 'but remember—it is *I* who has your precious amulet and book. If you dare use another of my warriors to do your bidding, I cannot—and will not—guarantee the safe return of your items.'

Magia pulled a face. 'And I thought they were of "no consequence" to you!' he mocked.

Bemused, she turned on her heel and approached her two servants. 'Wake the girl!' she instructed Kara. 'Then bring her to me.'

Warreshta looked sharp, hearing this.

'Is that wise?' asked Kara. 'By doing so, she may lead the others to us.'

'I am well aware that her rescuers are in pursuit of her, but there is a possibility the girl may know—' She stopped and drew back from the Valkyrie, observing the eerie strand of light crossing Kara's strong features, it emphasising her icy-grey eyes. Wareeshta, having noticed it, too, turned to see Magia Nera's hand stretched towards the heavens.

'My Lady!' she whispered. 'Look!'

L'Ordana turned and lifted her head, seeing the moon in its crescent, glowing spectacularly down on the loch. Quietly, she motioned to Kara to fetch the girl. Then she and Wareeshta approached the gap between the *Two Lovers*, leaving the Dhampir warriors behind. Having just observed the demise of one of their colleagues, she had become conscious of their growing restlessness, their volatile behaviour gnawing on her concerns.

Although in its late phase, the moon radiated its iridescent light, unveiling the glistening waters of the infamous loch and its surroundings. It had a mesmerising beauty, stretching its evocative aura out as if trying to reach the far ends of the earth. And yet, there was no disputing the evil attached to it. L'Ordana stepped forward, daring herself to move nearer. There was something about it that seemed familiar yet she struggled to recall what it was.

Now, devoid of all movement, the loch's polished, flat surface reflected the mirror image of the black-velvet sky, its tiny speckles of light blinking down at them, from within the cloud's central eye— forced open again by the Warlocks' might. It was at that moment she felt the sudden heat of his amulet press against her, reminding her of its presence—and Magia's dominance.

L'Ordana looked up and down its banks, regarding the endless wall of ghostly trees towering over the loch, in a protective manner, as though concealing its secret. And in the distance, where the eye could see, the opposite side waited—for those who were lucky to make it across.

*So, the Guide was right!* It would take too long to go around it. Had they done so, they still would have had to face the treacherous mountains; they, too, were almost impassable. And to cross the loch, without its time of intervention, was simply out of the question. *The Witching Hour,* she thought, hoping it had yet to come.

The *Guide's* words came back to her:

*"Only a woman has the privilege."*

They—*she*—could do nothing now but hope they were not too late.

'How peaceful and alluring it is,' said Magia, addressing her. 'I can almost feel it tempting us to cross. What do you say? Shall we?'

As he spoke, a biting wind crept up from behind, its invisible presence making itself known as it travelled through the arch. As it pushed the trees forward, their branches finally let go of the last of their dead leaves, carrying them out over the loch, bringing its whispering waters to life, and distorting its images into a wild frenzy before quietening again.

'Did you hear it?!' said Magia, lifting his head, thrilled by its unpredictable nature. He gasped. 'It is as though it wants to … speak to us.'

'Perhaps the *Hour* is upon us!' Wareeshta muttered beneath her cold breath.

'Let me go!' the young voice protested, from behind.

All eyes turned to see Kara forcing Eleanor into their company—the girl tripping over herself, only to be caught by the Valkyrie. Eleanor cast off Kara's grip, repulsed by her presence, not to mention the new, unpleasant smell wafting from her; it was different from her usual, heavy scent of lemon oil.

Eleanor reluctantly stepped into the intimidating company, finding her stance, and letting them believe she was not afraid. Her eyes told a different story, though; still heavy from induced sleep, they darted frantically while, inside, she feared for her life. Weary and dishevelled, she shivered from the dampness of the night as it crept into her lungs; she pulled the cloak they had given her across her shoulders, in a bid to keep it out.

Thinking the girl might be familiar with the loch, L'Ordana motioned her to approach. As Eleanor dragged herself to where the Sorceress stood—near the water's edge—she hesitated when a movement caught her eye. L'Ordana followed the girl's look, returning her gaze to the loch, its waters still visible beneath the moonlight.

The loch began to heave and swell of its own accord. Seeing this, they promptly moved back, fearing the same fate as the lone Dhampir. But still, the waters crept towards them like a pool of blood, blackened by evil, spreading its unavoidable threat nearer. A thought then entered L'Ordana's mind, prompting her to observe the girl. Curious, she glanced back at the loch, then at Eleanor again. *Could it be her?* she thought, reminding herself of the *Guide's* words, questioning why the loch had not reacted to her presence.

*"Only a woman has the privilege."*

Suddenly the water shrunk back, then separated, like a piece of silk being slowly torn apart. Longer and wider it stretched itself out before them, laying bare a path no more than four feet in width.

*How interesting!* thought Magia, eyeing Eleanor, with suspicion. It prompted him to step forward.

With the moon shining fiercely down on the loch, its luminescence made the path look like a silver snake, slithering through the inky waters as it made its way to the other side.

Magia moved closer, his curiosity heightened by Eleanor's enigmatic presence.

Catching his roving eye, Kara reached out, gripping Eleanor again. She drew her near, her threatening words reminding the young woman: 'If I hear you conversing with your "lover" again, I will rip your heart out,' she quietly warned. 'Do you hear me?'

Listening to the Valkyrie's silent threats towards the girl, Magia could not help but be amused by it and grinned to himself. But his smirk quickly slipped from his face, distracted by something: a familiar scent caught on a subtle breeze. He lifted his head slightly, his eyes sweeping across to where Kara continued her taunts—and oblivious to the fact he was observing her. His eyes then dropped, seeing the swelling above the silver wristlet, on her arm, instantly recognising the smell. He shot a glance at Wareeshta; she had seen and sensed it, too.

Wareeshta had been keeping a fixed eye when she noticed Kara subconsciously dropping her arm to her side—the Valkyrie stretching her thick fingers, then clenching them into a fist repeatedly, displaying the whites of her knuckles. Wareeshta regarded the cut Kara had received from the Dhampir's poisonous blade: it was red raw and weeping, and she could see beneath the layers of her skin—the venom sneaking its way through her veins, like a silent predator. Wareeshta discreetly eyed her counterpart; had Kara been *human*, she would be dead by now. Secretly, she mused over the venom, assuming it was doing its work; by now, it would be polluting her veins, and then it would begin to burn—the heat gradually taking control of her insides until they disintegrated. It would be a slow and painful death for the Valkyrie—one that would take time. *I can wait,* she thought. To avoid suspicion, Wareeshta drew her eyes up, then flinched when they unexpectedly met with Eleanor's.

'What are you looking at, girl?!' sneered Kara. Wareeshta subtly shook her head, signalling to Eleanor to stay quiet, then swiftly diverted her eyes, to avoid the Valkyrie's distrust.

'Bring her to me!' Magia ordered.

'No!' cried L'Ordana, stepping between them. 'I will not let you—' She stopped dead when Magia, disregarding her protest, wrenched Eleanor from the Valkyrie's grip, and dragged her to the water's edge. Eleanor gasped, trying to catch her breath as she was forced to face the menacing path. Marked clearly by the moonlight, it stretched out, luring them towards it. 'I warn you, Magia, if—'

'Or you will do what?' sneered Magia, cutting L'Ordana off as he gripped Eleanor's wrist tighter. Feeling his sharp nails dig into her skin, the young woman winced, then put up a fight, trying to break free. But with each struggle, he tightened his hold, digging deeper. 'I am certain no harm will come to *her*,' he teased L'Ordana, as he eyed the loch, his deep-rooted laugh, mocking her.

'Let me go!' cried Eleanor, using all her force to fight him off.

'*Silenzioso!*' he snapped, grinding his teeth. But the girl—desperate to detach herself from his grip—continued to thrash out, her determination antagonising him more. Magia's eyes flared.

His anger now visible, L'Ordana moved closer, anxious to stop him. She glared at the Warlock as he held on to *her* prisoner with deadly malice, then stopped abruptly. 'What do you mean—no harm will come to—'

With no warning, Magia wrenched Eleanor off her feet, then hurdled her out onto the waiting path.

# Chapter Twenty-Nine

'No!' cried L'Ordana.

The Sorceress rushed forward but was stopped by the Warlock who, now grinning at her, was revelling in his own pleasure. Unamused, she pushed by him, then froze, holding her breath, watching … waiting …

As Eleanor crashed to her knees, the waters on each side of her came alive, dancing wildly, reacting to her presence. Struck by fear, she scrambled to her feet, ignoring the pain in her joints, overcome by what she was seeing. She hesitated, her cold, erratic breath exhaling, like small puffs of smoke, dissolving into the dead of night. She opened her hand, imagining her father's in hers, protecting her. *Be strong!* she repeated in her mind until something made her stop. She tilted her head and leaned forward; a pale, white glow appeared beneath the surface, growing larger as it slowly made its way upwards. Eleanor glanced back at her captors. She was farther away from them—more than she realised.

Eleanor's audience watched in anticipation, from beneath the *Lovers'* arch, their eyes then drawing away from her out onto the loch, to her right. She slowly turned her head, following their gaze, then jolted with fright, seeing the apparition as it broke the loch's inky surface.

Eleanor stood rigid as the ghostly figure, its form like that of a young woman, glided through the waters, leaving its surface rippling behind her.

Curious, the spectre sashayed through the water, its gaunt, waif-like body illuminated beneath the surface as it drew dangerously close; Eleanor swallowed, her mouth gaping when it came within inches of her. She gasped, then froze.

As the waters held her naturally, the female's long black hair swirled about her, enveloping her naked body. Despite her haunting appearance, her features were striking: her skin was polished like the finest, whitest porcelain; her lips were full, displaying an unlikely taint of pink; and her almond-shaped eyes were small, their pewter colour, cold and hardened.

The evocative figure levitated with habitual ease in her watery domain, her hair continuing to caress her in an unruly fashion. For a long-drawn-out moment, the two looked at one another, with interest. Eleanor imagined they shared the same age, at that moment in time. Then, the unexpected happened: the spirit smiled warmly at her—the black split of death across her lips momentarily disappearing.

Unsure, Eleanor swallowed, then smiled back, awkwardly. As the woman in the water held her gaze, she felt compelled to inch closer; the ghostly figure slowly nodded, urging her to.

Eleanor then stopped.

An ethereal silence fell over the loch as they continued to stare at one other. From the water's edge, Eleanor could hear voices calling out to her; despite their persistence, she ignored them, mesmerised by the haunting figure.

*Speak to her*, she told herself, chewing on her lip. She took a nervous breath. Then, releasing it, knelt, ignoring her aching limbs.

'Are—are you the spirit of the loch?' she quietly asked, reminded of the tales she and her brother had been told when they were younger.

She waited.

'I am Síofra,' the spectre replied, her voice surprisingly soft and inviting.

Eleanor gasped, taken aback by her, then swallowed. 'I—I wish to cross the loch,' she stated, her voice timid with nerves.

'I see you are a woman of good heart,' replied Síofra, '… which gives you *Right of Way*. For that, you may cross—and without harm.'

Looking into the spirit's eyes, Eleanor saw they were filled with deep sadness, from the burden she had carried with her through the centuries, waiting for the return of a love so cruelly snatched from her—a love long gone.

*Asai!* In her mind, she desperately spoke his name.

The spirit smiled at her again, as though she had heard her thoughts.

Reawakened by the Samurai's name, Eleanor rediscovered something inside her—a determination to fight, to remain strong and, no matter what, not to succumb to the same fate as the retched soul before her. No. She was too young to die. There was too much to live for, and so much yet to experience, like that of the beauty of love in its true, physical state.

Eleanor threw a glance back at her captors before returning her attention to the spirit. She opened her mouth to speak, but drew back, wary. As though she had read her mind, Síofra slowly turned her head and stared at them. Then Eleanor saw it—the sinister, distorting change appear in the spectre's features; it was an enviable look of hunger married with hate as Síofra now focused her eyes on Eleanor's abductors. There and then, she threw out her icy breath over the loch towards the enemy, drowning their ears in a myriad of deafening whispers, confusing their thoughts and minds. But when she looked back at Eleanor, her features had changed again, giving the girl a comforting smile, and making her feel safe in her company again.

'They cannot hear you, for now,' she revealed. 'But time is short. Therefore, I urge you to speak, or your moment will be lost.'

'Please, help me!' Eleanor quietly begged, still ignoring the rising voices behind her. 'I am their prisoner. And others are pursuing us; *those* who want to rescue me.'

'Do you love him?' asked Síofra.

Eleanor gasped, struck by the question. *How did she*— But her thoughts were abruptly disrupted when Síofra smiled, knowingly.

'With all my heart,' she replied, her eyes filling with tears.

Seeing the honesty in the girl's steely-blue eyes, Síofra felt bound to help her. She nodded. 'Only the pure of heart keeps the path visible outside the *Hour*,' she revealed. 'You are one of the lucky ones ... unlike some,' she added, glancing back at L'Ordana. 'For that, I will allow it to stay open until you reach the other side. The waters shall then close in, from behind, concealing the path, once more. The only time I have no control over it is during the *Hour*. But, be warned: when your feet touch the dry land—on the far side—the water will rise swiftly, consuming everything in its path as it takes back control.'

Eleanor's eyes widened. 'But—what of my friends and family, who will surely follow?'

Síofra looked sharp, to her left, alerted by the approach of a horse and its rider. Magia Nera was looming closer; she had sensed his anger and frustration. Promptly, she turned to meet Eleanor's pleading gaze—the girl waiting anxiously for her reply.

'Only you can help them,' she whispered, smiling. And before sinking below the unholy waters, she momentarily held Eleanor's stare, then said, '*Run!*'

Eleanor's eyes widened. She drew back and looked up, glancing towards the opposite side of the loch.

*"Run!"*

Wasting no more precious time, and casting her cloak away, she rose and made a dash towards her freedom.

Conscious of the uneven and unhallowed ground beneath her feet, Eleanor focused hard on her escape, eyes fixed on the other side, knowing her life depended on it. On each side of her, the black waters erupted, dancing eagerly again, aware of her; she thought she had seen countless, ghostly white hands reaching above the surface, clutching at the night. Were they real? She diverted her eyes, keeping them level, not wanting to know. Inside, her heart swelled and beat loudly as she pushed herself, her cold, visible breath panting wildly ahead of her as she pursued it. In her mind, she then thought she heard a sinister voice laughing, from behind. But as she tried to block it out, she suddenly felt her body being wrenched back, against her will, by an invisible force.

Once again, Eleanor found herself face to face with the dark Warlock, his eyes flamed with anger, his sharp teeth exposed.

'I know you spoke to her!' he growled, frustrated he had been unable to hear their conversation. 'What did she say?!'

Eleanor shook her head, lips pressed together, refusing to speak as he peered back at her through his enraged eyes. She would stand her ground. Her eyes widened when he drew his tongue across his exposed teeth, their sharpness threatening and fatal. But still, she remained resolute, holding his stare in a brave show of determination.

*No fear,* she told herself.

'Tell me!' he seethed through gritted teeth. Placing the tips of his fingers on her brow, he began to apply pressure, to inflict pain on the girl. He would force it out of her.

'Enough!' yelled L'Ordana, catching up. 'The path is now clear. But we have no way of knowing for how long, so I suggest we mount our horses and cross—while we still have time!'

Swiftly, L'Ordana turned on her heel and, throwing out her orders, signalled to those who were waiting until it was safe to cross.

As she made her way back, her eyes looked down at the water, its surface choppy and angry, objecting to their presence. Alert to its hostility, she paused and stared into its depths; there was much activity beneath the surface. An image then flashed in her mind; it made her uneasy—the familiarity of it. She glanced around. *I know this place,'* she thought, but was then distracted by the approach of heavy footfall and horse's hooves; the Dhampir warriors and her two servants had made their way onto the path. Then, hearing Magia's voice, she promptly looked back; he was still holding on to the girl. She frowned. *What is he doing?!*

'I know she spoke to you,' Magia sneered. 'So, if you think I am going to let you out of my sight, you are mistaken. Think of yourself as my … *guarantee!'*

In one sweep, Eleanor found herself thrown upon the Warlock's horse, unable to dismount, as he gripped her tightly. Magia drove his horse on, followed by the others, in their desperate bid to reach the other side, unaware of the valuable time given to them, through Eleanor.

The rhythmic sound of hooves, galloping over the rocky surface, echoed across the loch as they made their way—Eleanor enduring the pain of the dark Warlock's firm grip as he threatened her with every step. In return, he sensed her fearlessness, it vented through her silence. He glanced up at the sky; the moon was now dipping in and out from behind the sluggish clouds, its light quenching and occasionally escaping his hold, and yet when he looked, the path remained visible. *Why is that?* he mused, but his thoughts were severed by his horse—the black stallion growing restless and difficult to control; something was making him nervous. He pushed the horse harder, driving it on. In the distance, the shadowy line of the trees beckoned, marking the place where the path merged with dry land.

*"When your feet touch dry land, the waters will rise swiftly."*

Síofra's words entered Eleanor's thoughts as the other side loomed. Behind her, the sound of L'Ordana, Kara and Wareeshta grew dangerously near, along with the small legion of Dhampir.

As the end of the path narrowed, the stallion made one giant leap as if its life hinged on it, and finally touched dry land. But it was clear—by its escalating speed—it wanted to keep going, to escape the ungodly terrain.

As Magia tried to control his horse, Eleanor grabbed her opportunity and threw herself from the stallion when it was forced to stop, and planted her two feet firmly on the ground, with Síofra's words still ringing in her ears:

*"When your feet touch dry land, the waters will rise swiftly."*

She spun round to face the loch, stepping as close as she'd dare … then held her breath.

Magia, his anger fuelled by this, leapt off his stallion, ready to interrogate the young woman again when a sudden and obvious calm swept over them. Drawn back to the loch, he turned; in the distance, from where they came, an underlying murmur could be heard, it slowly rising in volume, grinding and rumbling under their feet. Eleanor looked down, feeling the ground tremble beneath her.

Gradually they could see the water rise and advance; its force was such, they knew nothing could withstand its merciless assault. Eleanor's eyes widened with hope, praying the others would not make it. Inside, she felt exhilarated at the thought of the Sorceress and her servants—not to mention the small army of Dhampir—being wiped out. She closed her eyes briefly—*Thank you, Síofra!*—then jolted, wincing, when Magia grasped her arm and dragged her dangerously close to the edge.

*'Più veloce!'* he yelled out. 'Faster, you fools!'

But no sooner had Eleanor silently thanked her ghost, L'Ordana and Wareeshta touched land. She then looked up, seeing Kara; the Valkyrie appeared to be lagging. However, the smirk on Kara's face told Eleanor a different tale; she had purposely slowed, to indulge in the thrill of the race, while refusing to look behind her.

But as the waters advanced harder on the foot soldiers—and despite their speed—it quickly became clear they were unable to outrun it.

One by one it consumed them, tearing them from the path, then wrenching them into the waters, where the hands of death took over, snatching and clawing at their victims. There was no stopping it. Panic ensued on Eleanor as she watched the remaining Dhampir on horseback heighten their pace. Behind them, Kara was the last to be pursued by the waters as their crests reached up and out, trying to grip her; and just as she felt her horse being wrenched from under her, she spread her great wings and lifted herself skywards, her high-pitched laughter echoing across the loch, mocking its failure to mark her demise.

Horrified, Eleanor held her breath, her chest rising and falling rapidly, anticipating the impact. Then, as if recognising its defeat, the wall of water stopped dead, within feet of the lucky ones who had made it.

A heavy stillness held the survivors as they reassembled, waiting, staring at the black wall of water in front of them. Gone was the thunderous noise of its attack, along with the maddening sound of its haunting voices that had whispered fearlessly after them. Then, on Síofra's command, the wall disintegrated before their eyes, followed by an unearthly quietude sweeping over the glassy loch.

No one spoke for several moments, their eyes fixed firmly on the surface, waiting and wondering if the Dhampir that had been pulled to the depths would resurface. All remained strangely serene.

One of the surviving warriors, Dakkus, stepped forward, his ashen-black skin shining like midnight blue, under the moonlight. He regarded the loch, searching for his comrades.

'They cannot be lost, forever!' he said, unable to comprehend their disappearance. His pale-brown eyes darted towards Wareeshta, searching for answers. She stayed silent. 'Are we not Dhampir?' he asked, questioning their status. 'Are we not *immortal?!*'

Wareeshta felt everyone's eyes on her. She looked down into the water; she, too, had expected them to surface at any moment. Still, nothing happened. She was at a loss. Her eyes slid towards Dakkus, whose head was now tilted low, his eyes flaring at her, wanting answers.

'Do not look at me that way!' she retorted. 'They should have—'

'Look!' growled Kara, pointing to the loch.

There, out of the depths, the ghostly figure of Síofra re-emerged—the smirk creeping across her pale lips, pleased by her victory. She then turned her attention to Eleanor—the smirk now fading to a warm smile—and nodded, before disappearing again beneath the surface.

Having just witnessed the unexpected loss of most of her warriors, L'Ordana flew into a rage; she had spent years travelling, creating her army from the strongest and most capable young men, moulding them to her requirements for the great task ahead: the siege of Elboru, where she would possess the Shenn and overthrow the new Overlord. But she knew she could never replace them. Not now. Not with time pressing on them. Incensed, she spun round, her eyes filled with revenge, pointing the finger of blame at the one person who would pay for it.

Terrified, Eleanor's first impulse was to run but, instead, found herself sheltering behind Wareeshta. The Sorceress marched towards them, making the Dhampir wary; she could do without the attention. But, as she signalled to her servant to step aside, L'Ordana realised she was too late; Magia had snatched the girl, yet again, dragging her to the water's edge. This time, Eleanor knew she was on her own, without Síofra's help.

Without hesitation, the Warlock threw the helpless young woman out over the water, suspending her in mid-air.

'Let us see if your new "friend" saves you now!' he cried in anger.

Unsure, L'Ordana rushed to his side and stared at the water; there was no movement in it. Her eyes darted up to where Eleanor was hovering and trying to keep her balance; the girl's arms were spread out like a bird, gliding over its surface, but frozen, unable to move. Another image assaulted L'Ordana's mind: that of a girl—a prisoner to her fate—just like the young woman before her now. In a flickering moment—reminded of a vague past—L'Ordana suddenly recognised Eleanor's terror, knowing what waited for her beneath the inky surface—*Death!*

*"Drown her! Drown the witch!"*

'No, Magia!' she blurted, spurred and haunted by the voices in her head.

He pushed her away. 'This is all *her* doing!' he said. 'She deserves to die!'

Eleanor looked down and saw an image staring back at her, its reflection gripped by trauma and fear and realised … it was her own. She saw her eyes fill with tears. One by one they fell on the surface, distorting her features and creating ripples, they silently widening, leaving her behind with nothing but evil to contend with.

A sudden, pre-emptive movement caught Magia's attention. He looked sharp, seeing Wareeshta; she was about to intervene. He glared at her, his determined stare warning her not to. Reluctantly, the Dhampir recoiled.

'Say good night, sweet *Bambino!*' he scorned, stretching his hand towards Eleanor. 'Death beckons you!'

Eleanor's scream filled the night as the waters rose to greet her, and, as they did, she imagined her name being echoed back to her, in a familiar voice—a voice that was not her own.

# Chapter Thirty

The five riders came to a sudden halt, lifting their heads to the mass of dark, grey clouds pressing their gloom down on everything below. It was a depressing sight—enough to almost convince the ignorant their world was coming to its end.

A desolate place—some would say, forsaken by *God* himself—a place where the brave wagered with death. Most stayed away … but not all.

'Why have we stopped?' asked Gill, eager to keep moving.

'Wait!' said Reece, his eyes fixed on the sky. 'There!' he said, pointing.

In the distance, above the trees, they saw flashing light, its spectacular array of colours shooting through the clouds like lightning, forcing them apart.

'Look!' said Tam.

There, pushing its way through the gap, they watched the moon's dazzling beam stretch itself downwards, its fluorescence guiding them.

'It seems luck is on our side,' said Daine, smiling.

'This has nothing to do with *luck!*' said Reece, dampening his spirits. 'Luck does not exist in our world. Things happen by chance, and in this case … it is Magia Nera's doing.'

Daine's eyes widened with fear, hearing the name—the brutal reminder of the evil that had terrorised him, earlier that night.

'He is the one controlling it,' Reece continued.

'How?' said Daine.

'Who knows? But while we can see the light, I suggest we follow it before it disappears. No doubt, that is where we will find our fabled lake.'

Spurred by their riders' command, the horses leapt forward.

'How much farther?' shouted Gill to Daine, above the noise of the hooves as they heightened in pace.

'No more than two leagues!' he calculated.

Onwards they rode, full of strength and resolution, each buried in their thoughts. Gill, his mind preoccupied with finding his sister, had momentarily forgotten the true nature of their journey. He checked for Eleanor's dirk; the dagger was still in its sheath, resting on his thigh. Inside, he cursed himself for taking her weapon, vowing to return it.

In the few days since his true identity had been revealed to him, he had felt the profound change from within—and the uncontrollable dominance intensifying with the coming of each new day, bringing him closer to the time in question. And how dangerously near it was, too. His strenuous efforts to fight against it had finally been defeated—the reality overwhelming him when he ultimately accepted his forthcoming responsibilities. Together, mind and body gave him the strength to his weaknesses, which were slowly fading. Whatever task awaited, he would embrace it. He had to; there was too much at stake now.

*One thing at a time*, he told himself, his mind on rescuing his sister.

Reece glanced at his two colleagues: Tam's eyes were dancing, exhilarated, longing for a battle—the Highlander, no doubt, finding the whole adventure invigorating. He then looked at Asai: the Samurai was keeping his silence; he had been in deep thought, searching for Eleanor. At least they knew she was still alive … for now.

His attention turned to their guide, Daine. He, too, had suddenly grown quiet, since hearing the dark Warlock's name. He could only imagine the physical and psychological impact that meeting had had on the mortal; nevertheless, he kept it well hidden—a reflection of his bravery. But there was something about the newcomer that preyed on his suspicions—something familiar—something he could not quite put his finger on.

Daine, temporarily trapped in his thoughts, felt restless, despite being in the company he now kept. He wondered what awaited them as they made their way to the *Two Lovers*. On rare occasions, he had witnessed the loch's sinister secret yet only caught a brief glimpse of Síofra, once. Once was enough. He would never forget it, his instinct—the ever-constant reminder—warning him to venture only as far as he was required to go.

He had removed his guilt a long time ago from those who had chosen to cross—those who had paid him handsomely. And, had any succeeded—he doubted it—he had also chosen not to care; their lives had been theirs to do as they please. After all, he was not *God*—if there was such a thing. Besides, who would have spared *him* a thought, had he crossed the loch and failed? No—he had no intention of doing that.

He wondered when, or if, he would get paid; no coinage had yet exchanged hands from his conspicuous travelling "companions." They seemed confident of success. Regardless of it, he told himself he would treat them no differently from those gone before them. He would show them the *Lover's* arch, demand his payment, and then leave.

*"To the loch—then you are on your own."*

That had been the agreement, and he was sticking to it. *No matter what!* he decided, cautiously eyeing the four colleagues. Yes. That was what he was going to do. Then he could continue what he had started; he had his own agenda.

Suddenly one of the horses halted, on the command of its rider. The others followed suit, seeing Asai staring in the direction of the moonbeam, his face now alive with hope. He had heard her in his head.

*"Asai!"*

'Is it Eleanor?!' an eager voice asked.

'Hai!' the Samurai replied, with a sharp nod. 'I feel her! Her strength has increased … and the beat of her heart is strong. It is as if she is standing alongside us.' He nodded, relieved. 'She is well, Gill-san. I assure you.'

'Then we are close,' said Reece.

'Which means, we must take care,' Daine warned.

'We are aware of the dangers, lad,' Tam informed him. 'And are ready to fight!'

Motivated by Asai's revelation, they drove their horses on. Ahead, in the distance, the dark outline of an impressive arch gradually appeared. Rising above them, its thick, ancient branches converged, intertwined in their everlasting embrace.

Asai grew uneasy, now sensing Eleanor's fear as his heart pounded in unison with hers. A feeling of doom gripped him, urging him to increase his speed.

A faint, thunder-like sound came from the direction they were heading. Reece glanced at Daine, unsure.

'Impossible!' Daine cried, shaking his head.

'What do ye mean, lad?' said Tam.

'They could not have crossed it, already; it's not the *Hour* yet.'

They stalled briefly, listening to the sound as it grew louder before subsiding, thus sending a warning to Daine that the path was closing in again.

'Quick!' he shouted.

Spurred by the urgency in Daine's voice, they pounded onward until they finally reached the *Lover's* arch—Gill, the first to arrive. But in his desperate need to save his sister, there was no sign of him stopping.

'No, Gill!' yelled Daine. 'Do not pass through it!'

Hearing the guide's warning cry, Gill pulled hard on the reigns of his horse, causing it great alarm and confusion by the sudden wrench. Instantly, it yielded to his authority, stopping within a breath of the *Lover's* threshold.

Speaking words of reassurance to the nervous horse, Gill waited until the others joined him. Together, they quickly dismounted and approached the narrow margin between them and the loch, alert to its peril. Their eyes widened at the spectacle before them: the dark waters had risen and pushed forward, blocking their view of the events already taking place, on the far side.

The faint distant sound of heightened voices, mixed with horses' hooves, echoed back across the loch.

'Faster, you fools!'

The dark Warlock's voice, though faint, was clear, its domination ringing through to their ears. It was then quickly followed by the deathly sound of doom when they saw the wall of water rise higher and then stall, it followed by a dense silence.

'What's happening?' said Gill, inching towards the water's edge.

Daine shook his head, stunned by the sight; he had seen nothing like it before.

'I—I don't know,' he replied, then snatched at Gill's cloak, drawing him back. 'Be careful!'

'Look!' said Asai, pointing, when the wall of water collapsed back into the loch.

What little moonlight remained was sufficient to reveal what was now transpiring on the other side. Gill's mouth gaped as his eyes focused on the scene unfolding before them: his sister was levitating over the volatile waters, held by a destructive force—and it was right behind her.

'There he is!' said Tam, pointing. 'Magia Nera!'

The dark Warlock, his arms stretched out, was the force keeping Gill's sister right where he wanted her—out of their reach. Gill's heart sank in despair. With no regard for himself, and desperate to reach his sister, he let go of his horse.

'Do not even think it!'

Gill jolted, feeling his grandfather's firm grip. He looked up, staring into Reece's concerned face, realising he had been stopped from making a grave mistake. Inside, his heart pounded.

'Are you mad?!' cried Daine, stepping forward. 'Look at it!'

Gill, following his aim, looked down; he was standing within inches of the water's edge again. He flinched when the water leapt up, alive and ferocious, ready to wrench another victim to its depths.

As the surface danced erratically, drawing the groups' attention, they caught sight of the ghostly apparitions of tortured faces breaking the surface, their heads bobbing up and down, their dead, unblinking eyes, watching them.

'What are they?' asked Gill, his face scrunched in revulsion.

'Oh, my—' Daine stopped when one of the ghouls waded closer and stared up at him with lifeless eyes. Drawing his hand over his mouth, he shook his head as he regarded the ghastly face peering back at him. It was the eye—white from blindness—that had caught his attention. He now recognised the poor soul wading in the waters, lost to the spirit of the loch; it was one of the old men—the brothers—from the Ardgore Inn.

'He never made it!' he mumbled, horrified, unable to take his eyes off him. 'Oh, the fool!' he added, overcome with deep regret, his eyes then searching, looking for his brother; he was nowhere to be seen. Had he survived? It was doubtful.

'Remember—it was their choice,' said Reece.

'Why didn't they stay? They should have listened. I could have prevented this!'

'They knew the risks,' Reece added flatly, detaching himself from the guide's emotions. He had more important matters to contend with; namely Eleanor and getting across the loch.

Daine glared at him. 'And for that, he will never be reunited with the woman he longed to be with—the one he risked his life for, to say goodbye. Even in *death*'—he shook his head—'she will never know. He is cursed ... Forever!'

Reece lowered his head, his eyes sliding towards Daine in a moment of resentment, as though the guide had stabbed him in the heart.

'We must do something,' Asai intervened, sensing his colleague's inner torment. 'There must be—' He stopped dead, his expression changing to one of dismay.

'Asai?' said Reece, disregarding the guide.

The Samurai stepped forward between Gill and Daine, staring directly ahead—the waters reacting to his closeness by dancing feverishly and snatching at his feet with fervent hunger.

'He plans to—' Asai's sentence was abruptly broken by the terrifying scream, reaching out to them for help.

'Eleanor!' cried Gill. But as his voice replied to his sisters' plea, the group drew back in horror when she suddenly fell towards the loch.

Eleanor closed her eyes tight and, reaching out, prepared to enter her watery grave. When the impact came, she groaned, having collided, instead, with a hard surface. Her eyes flashed open. She was on the path, once more. Still on her hands and knees, she stared down at it, bewildered.

'How is this possible?' she muttered.

'What type of sorcery is this?!' L'Ordana seethed, as she witnessed the unthinkable.

'A potent one I am not acquainted with,' Magia remarked. 'But it is not without its influence,' he added, eyeing Eleanor.

'She is the key!' he growled, pointing.

'Never!' L'Ordana retorted.

He grabbed hold of her, still pointing. 'Look at the girl! *She* is the one who opened the passage.'

'How dare you!' L'Ordana snapped, wrenching her arm away.

'Did you see how the waters reacted to her?'

The Sorceress stared out in silence, keeping her thoughts. She had seen it, all right, and was furious. She now regretted letting the *Guide* go. *He lied to me!* she thought, fuming inside.

'She spoke to her—the *spirit*,' Magia continued.

''Tis absurd!'

'You think?!' he said, sneering at her. 'I know what I saw. Is the proof not there'—he pointed towards Eleanor as she picked herself up—'in front of our eyes?!'

'What does it matter?' L'Ordana lashed out. 'The path was ours to cross. Have we not made it to the other side?' She threw her hand out, pointing. 'Unlike *them!* We have the advantage now—and the upper hand—whereas, they have no option but to take the long route. And by then, it will be too late.'

Eleanor dragged herself to her feet, then moved on a little, away from her captors—they too caught up in their dispute. She hesitated, her eyes now focusing on where she was. She looked out to the other side—her path to freedom—then caught her breath.

'Gill!' she quietly sobbed, then hesitated, hearing a worrying silence behind her. She looked back. Her captors were now staring at her, uncertain; while the path remained open, with only a few paces dividing them, each had no idea what the other was going to do. In her mind, she heard Síofra again, urging her to run. She then looked to where Gill and the others were waiting. *Yes!* She had to run—run to them. With another glance back at her enemy, her mind was made up. *I can make it!*

At that final glance, her captors read the warning sign, telling them her plan. L'Ordana rushed forward but was stopped by Wareeshta's sudden grip on her arm; she glared at her servant for touching her.

'It is not safe, Mistress.'

Confused, L'Ordana followed Wareeshta's gaze. Rising from the deep, Síofra had resurfaced and was now gliding through the water behind Eleanor, following her as she began her escape.

Shrugging off Wareeshta, L'Ordana moved forward. But as her foot touched the path the waters heaved, lashing out at her. She stepped back, glaring out at Eleanor, her rage burning inside, her frustration now visible to those in her company.

'Think you can stop, me?!' she yelled, stretching her hands out. She closed her eyes, conjuring words familiar to Magia. He moved to her side, keeping his eyes on Eleanor—the girl gradually backing away from the oncoming waters.

'She is now doomed!' he said, thinking the Sorceress was behind its control.

L'Ordana's eyes flew open. She shook her head.

'I—I am not the one controlling it,' she admitted, stumped.

*What magic is this?* he thought, fascinated.

'I feel powerless against it,' L'Ordana said, staring down into her empty hands and then up again.

Seeing the advancing waters weave their way towards her, Eleanor's fear heightened.

'Oh, no!' she sobbed, 'What is happening?'

She backed away, terrified, her heart pounding inside her chest as the waters persisted; they were catching up on her. And even if she tried to flee, she knew she could never outrun them. Then, unexpectedly, they stopped at her feet, going no further. Holding her breath, she took a step back; they followed her, halting again when she did. She looked around. As she did so, Síofra surfaced beside her, her ghostly features calm.

'The waters will protect you until you reach your friends,' she said. 'Now, go!' She turned her head towards Eleanor's captors. 'They cannot follow you, for now.'

Eleanor, now alert to the advantage she had over her abductors, looked at them for a brief moment, then smirked.

'Go!' Síofra urged.

On the spirits' command, she turned and made a desperate dash towards freedom, with the waters following from behind, shielding her.

'She is protecting her!' cried Magia, watching the waters cave in around the girl, like a loyal dog, preventing them from pursuing her, while concealing the path.

'No!'

L'Ordana's outraged voice reached out across the loch, in its pursuit of Eleanor, it driving the girl on in her escape. Helpless, the Sorceress spun round and glared at Magia, as if passing the blame to him.

'Do something!' she commanded through gritted teeth, her voice firm and controlling.

Magia shrugged. 'I can do … *niente!*'

'We cannot let her escape! If she can get to the other side,' she argued, 'then she will be able to return … with *them!* With most of my warriors gone, they will follow us. I do not think you realise, Magia, their true worth; Reece and Asai were my best. It was *they* who taught these soldiers,' she added, pointing to the Dhampir on horseback—what remained of them. Driven by the gravity of her own words, L'Ordana quickly looked to her only chance, and threw out her command:

'Bring her back!'

)

'Run, Eleanor!'

The girl's heart skipped a beat, hearing the voice that had willed her on, while held captive at the castle. Only now, it was not through their thoughts. He—Asai—was there, just a short distance ahead, spurring her on, towards him. The mere sound of his voice pulled her closer as she continued to run for her life. She could now see him—she could see them all, their familiar features as their voices rose, calling her. In front, the waters spread wide, clearing the path for her. She threw a glance over her shoulder.

'Don't look back—or up—Nori!' Gill yelled, reaching for his longbow. 'Keep going!'

Eleanor suddenly stopped and clutched her chest, trying to catch her breath. She then gasped, realising she should have done what her brother had told her *not* to do …

Her eyes widened in disbelief when she looked up, seeing the advance of a familiar—and threatening—shape in the sky, their great wings spread-eagled, heading straight for her.

Cries of encouragement now grew frantically louder. There was one she did not recognise—nor did she care, at that moment.

'Run!' shouted Daine, joining in, encouraging her.

Eleanor spun and pushed herself like never before, her heart racing; on the other side, another beat rapidly in time with hers, anxious. Onwards she ran, the stretch of water narrowing between them, while, above her, the beating of the Valkyrie's powerful wings grew louder and closer. Panic gripped her; she could not bear the thought of the creature's vile grip, again.

She then heard the whistle of an arrow flying over her head. She glanced up to see another following in its path, then another; Gill was trying to stop the Valkyrie. Motivated by this, Eleanor pushed herself on, her chest swelling, trying to refill her lungs. In her battle to keep up with her breath, she failed to notice the bobbing heads in the water, eyeing her every movement. But they kept their distance.

'Do not look back!'

She could now hear her grandfather's voice bellowing at her as the arrows continued to soar towards their target, unsuccessfully—Kara darting from side to side with ease, avoiding them. But Eleanor—swayed by her instincts—looked up again. As she did so, she lost sight of her footing. Down she fell—hard—feeling the impact of the uneven ground once more.

'Now, Kara!' the Sorceress, cried out. 'Take her! Now!'

On her orders, Kara grinned, revelling in the chase, her black hawk, Nakia, concealed behind her as she stretched her great wings, preparing to dive. Kara then paused in mid-flight; the assault of arrows had stopped. Peering down at the five figures, still urging her victim on, the Valkyrie saw the young man with the longbow looking defeated. He had no arrows left.

'Try stopping me now, *mortal!*' she screeched down at him.

Extending her great wings, Kara turned her attention back to Eleanor, to see the young woman scrambling to her feet. Releasing a war-like cry, the Valkyrie prepared to dive, then jolted, when something tugged on her foot: a funnel of water had shot up from the depths and wrapped itself around her ankle. Then, feeling an ice-cold grip, she looked down sharply and drew back, seeing the long, white sinewy hands holding onto her. She lurched when they began to drag her towards the loch, then thrashed out, eventually breaking free.

The ghostly hands recoiled into the funnel before dropping back beneath the surface. Kara laughed out loud, amused by their failure to catch her. She rose higher, but when another shot up, touching the tip of her wing, she felt one of the wraith's hands as it tugged hard. She glared furiously at it when she saw one of her white feathers float to the surface of the water, before being snatched beneath it. Again, another funnel rose, then another, and another, catching her off-guard. She spun, struggling to avoid them. It was no longer a game. Quicker they came—the hands of death—grabbing at her from every angle. Below, Eleanor could only watch in anticipation—the deadly attack on her enemy—as the Valkyrie fought hard to avoid it. She then saw Síofra and her *wraiths* rising to the surface, lifting themselves above the loch, and taking control.

'She cannot harm you,' Síofra called out. 'Quickly! You are almost there.'

In one last desperate push, Eleanor, ignoring the pain inflicted on her by her fall, ploughed on.

Loud high-pitched squawks could now be heard across the loch as Nakia darted in and out between the spouts of water, trying to protect her mistress. From both sides, the spectators watched the Valkyrie battle against the onslaught. Higher she soared away from their fatal grasp. And just as she thought she had escaped it, another funnel rose above her; this time, carrying Síofra with it, her long black mane hugging her ghostly white body. Slowly the spectre shook her head, her deathlike stare warning the Valkyrie not to proceed. Suddenly, Síofra's hand darted towards her. Startled, Kara flinched, then recoiled.

It was too late.

It had been the slightest of touches; the ice-cold pain had shot through the Valkyrie's body the moment the spirit's hand touched her wounded arm, making her aware of the injury she had received from the slain Dhampir's blade. Kara, sensing she was losing control over her actions, drew back further—the spirit's pewter eyes, mocking her. Inside, she felt her strength wane. She was at a loss. She would have to retreat—get back to her company—before the spectre had her way. Then, unexpectedly, Nakia dived down between her mistress and Síofra, disrupting the spirit's presence. Síofra reached out, trying to snatch the hawk, but Nakia was too quick, giving the Valkyrie mere seconds to turn and make her retreat. In the moments given to her, Kara took flight, leaving behind her failure and wounded pride.

Finally, Eleanor could see her loved ones clearly, her eyes then brightening when Asai stepped closer to the threshold, his hand stretched out over the water, reaching for her.

*I've made it!* she told herself, but then began to feel the weight of another struggle, her body being dragged by exhaustion. She felt her pace slowing, her form weakening, and yet still felt the will to run. She so desperately wanted to, but somehow could not. It took seconds for her to realise why …

Struggling against the power dragging her back, Eleanor tried to push herself, while being forced to listen to the voices of her loved ones as they gradually grew faint, only for them to be drowned out by a piercing, deafening cry, filling the night. She followed its haunting sound, her eyes widening with shock as she discovered the source: there, in the water, her ally, Síofra, thrashed out wildly, wailing like a *Banshee*. Thrown by the spirit's sudden show of madness, Eleanor felt disheartened, her dismay then deepening, unable to hear her loved ones now. She drew her hands over her ears, trying to block out Síofra's agony—to no avail—while the force behind her grew stronger, determined to take back control.

'No!' she whimpered, feeling the ache in her heart. Sooner or later, she knew her body would give up the fight; the force was too much for her to endure. She stretched her hands out, imagining she could reach the others, but with each passing second, they shrank away, their features now distorted and unclear, through her tears. Ultimately, she surrendered.

Once again, Eleanor found herself in the grip of her enemy.

But it was not whom she expected.

L'Ordana smirked down at her captive, then tilted her head.

'There is nothing they can do for you, now,' she said, her tone defined and victorious as her eyes regarded the five faces peering out across the water, helpless. 'So near and yet so—' She stopped, recognising the new addition to the young woman's band of "heroes" in the distance; it was the *Guide*.

*I should have*— Discarding the thought, she hastily reached out, prompting Eleanor to take her hand. 'They cannot save you,' she snapped.

Eleanor, consumed by the ceaseless sobbing coming from the water, looked to Síofra, her *wraiths* circling the overseer of the loch, sympathetic to her temporary plight.

'*She* cannot help you, either.'

'What do you mean?'

'Take my hand!' L'Ordana yelled.

Defeated and heartbroken, Eleanor had no option now but to do so. She lifted her hand. When L'Ordana grabbed it, she caught her breath, Eleanor's cold touch making her flinch. For an instant, their eyes locked and, as Eleanor stared into the Sorceress's pale turquoise eyes, she met with the face of another—a face she did not know. She blinked—and then it was gone.

Dragging Eleanor with her, L'Ordana glanced back, at intervals, making sure the waters followed, preventing the girl's rescuers from pursuing them. All the while, in her forced retreat, Eleanor did not look back, leaving the sound of misery behind her.

As they reached the far side, L'Ordana finally released her grip on Eleanor. The girl stalled, holding back, watching the Sorceress as she stepped over the line of "death" to join her company.

L'Ordana turned, observing her. 'Why do you stall, child?' she asked, narrowing her eyes.

Eleanor lifted her head and slowly shook it. Baffled and broken, her weary eyes filled with tears.

'How?' It was all she could say.

'Why—the *Hour*—of course,' L'Ordana replied, smugly. 'How fortunate for me,' she bragged, then pulled a solemn face. 'Though, unfortunate for you.'

Eleanor looked down to where her feet stood firmly on the visible path, feeling a dark heaviness upon her sinking heart.

'This way, child!' said the Sorceress, her tone hard and defined.

Paying no heed, the young woman looked sideways into the water. Beneath the surface, the lost souls grew restless, unable to help her at that time—the *Hour* preventing their interference. Her eyes scanned the loch, searching for Síofra; she was nowhere to be seen. The spectre's words then came back to haunt her:

*"I have no control over it, during the Hour."*

Now, also feeling lost and abandoned, Eleanor's heart sank deeper, slipping into depression as she stared into the blackness. It was a tempting thought.

L'Ordana, wary of the girl's state of mind, inclined her head, then extended a hand towards her. 'Come with me!' she encouraged, her voice softening.

Eleanor slowly lifted her eyes; they were now devoid of life and hope as they met with L'Ordana's. She looked down at the waiting hand and contemplated it, for a moment … then took a step back.

As she moved to step from the path, the sadness in the girl's blue eyes alerted the Sorceress; it was clear what she intended to do: give herself to the *wraiths*. Now overcome by a sudden need to fight for her own life, L'Ordana rushed forward and grabbed hold of Eleanor.

*"I'll not let you drown!"* the voice inside her cried.

The moment Eleanor's feet reunited with dry land, Magia promptly stepped forward. In the distance, he could make out the silhouettes of the five travellers, on the opposite side of the loch. Triumphant and arrogant, he stared across at Reece and his companions, now also aware of the new addition to their company; she had let the *Guide* live. His eyes slid towards L'Ordana. She avoided his glare. *No matter*, he thought; *they are no longer a threat.*

'A valiant effort!' he called out to them, his irritating voice carrying its smugness to their ears. They hesitated, on hearing him. He could sense their aggravation. He grinned. 'However, not valiant enough!' he boasted, grasping Eleanor's arm, his nails puncturing her skin, deeply. She winced. He smirked, then inhaled as he felt the warmth of her blood flowing into his palm. On that thought, he turned to the remaining Dhampir warriors, then lifted her arm, teasing them. Their nostrils flared and their eyes burned, driving them to a near frenzy. But their pleasure was short-lived when L'Ordana quickly intervened, by standing between them and the girl.

'Stop it!' she growled, taking hold of Eleanor. 'I warn you, Magia. Should any more harm come to her, I will personally destroy them!' she falsely threatened, pointing to her warriors.

Magia held her gaze. She did not flinch.

'As you wish, *Bella!*' he casually stated, turning away. And, as he did, he subtly drew his hand across his mouth, relishing in the girl's taste. L'Ordana dragged her eyes from him, repulsed by his sadistic action.

The dark Warlock sauntered towards the loch, its behaviour unstable and angered by his closeness. He grunted, bemused, and then looked to the night sky. Lifting a hand, he opened it—the sphere now visible, its array of colours glowing in his palm. For a moment, he regarded its beauty, then smirked to himself.

'*Grazie!*' he purred, then sent it back to the heavens, it taking the moonlight with it.

Gone was the crescent.

Gone was the loch.

Gone—the rival.

# Chapter Thirty-One

An abnormal stillness crept over the divide, following the heavy veil of darkness that had been cast upon them. An unearthly white mist crept across it, temporarily smothering their view before lifting, to reveal what remained of the horror they had witnessed.

Gill peered out through the *Lover's* arch, to where he had last seen Eleanor.

*Here I am,* he thought, *destined to be a great ruler, with great powers, and yet could do nothing to save her.*

*"I am sorry."*

A voice swept through his mind, disrupting his thoughts. He ignored it, holding on to the distressing image of his sister as the Sorceress dragged her away from him. *So near and—*

Heartbroken, he closed his eyes, listening to the *Two Lovers* as they moaned—the wind whistling between the gaps in their branches as though lamenting his loss. *She's gone!* he thought, unable, at first, to speak a word, choked up by dismay.

'How …?' he mumbled, trying to digest their failure to save her. He heard the voice again.

*"I am sorry."*

This time it was clearer, its tone comforting, almost reassuring. His eyes shot open, feeling the presence of a hand on his shoulder.

'I'm sorry.'

Gill spun, catching Daine off-guard. He glared at the guide.

'Sorry?!' he yelled, wrenching him off his feet. 'This is all your—' He stopped when their eyes met. An intense moment passed between them as fear collided with anger. However, in that instant, the three Dhampir promptly intervened, prizing them apart.

'Leave him, Gill!' Reece growled as the two were separated. 'Do not lose sight of who you are,' he then whispered in his grandson's ear.

Daine, certain he had overheard Reece, looked at the Dhampir, his suspicions sharpening. Reece averted his eyes.

Infuriated, Gill shrugged off his grandfather and marched towards the guide to confront him, scowling at Asai and Tam as they stood by Daine's side, as a precaution.

'How could this have happened?!' he demanded. 'You said we could cross it—during the *Hour!*'

Daine could feel the young man's angry breath bearing down on him. He struggled for an explanation as Gill clenched his fists—the skin stretching over his knuckles. Right now, he wanted to avoid any further physical confrontation—the strength of Gill's hold, stunning him; it had been effortless. And, as they faced one another, Daine was forced to lift his head to meet Gill's determined stare; he had grown in both stature and physique since their paths had crossed.

*How is that even possible?* 'Who *are* you?' he then boldly asked.

Reece looked sharp on Daine's enquiry.

'You lied!' Gill persisted, dismissing it.

At the accusation, Daine's eyes widened as he shook his head in defiance.

'No! I never—'

'But you told us!'

'Enough, Gill!' said Reece, intervening, observing the stark and worried look in the guide's eyes. 'He is not lying.'

Gill's mouth fell as he turned to his grandfather, then scowled at him. 'Are you siding with *him*, now?!' he argued, shoving Daine away.

'This is not about taking sides, Gill-san,' said Asai—the voice of reason.

'Then what is it?' he persisted, turning to Asai. 'Because—*I* don't know.'

'Please, hear me out!' cried Daine, with both hands outstretched and looking from one to the other, in a bid to plead his case.

'Why should we listen to you?' snapped Gill, throwing a menacing look at the guide.

'Give him a chance, lad. Aye?'

Gill now turned his attention to Tam. 'You, also?!' He was beginning to feel outnumbered.

'In answer to your question, Gill-san,' said Asai. 'It is about understanding, trying to find a solution to this obstacle.'

'It is more than that, Asai,' Gill retorted.

'It is one, I believe, we can overcome, but we will not succeed if we find ourselves in conflict with each other.'

Frustrated, Gill shook his head.

'How can you be so calm, when—'

'He's right!'

The three Dhampir and Gill paused, turned, and stared at the guide.

'I knew it!' said Gill, through gritted teeth.

'No!' Daine retaliated, waving his hands in defence. 'It's not what you think …'

'Go on, lad,' said Tam.

The Highlander suddenly wavered as the guide began his explanation, his eyes veering, on an instinct. Tam, his hearing sharper than his two colleagues, turned his attention towards the thicket of trees. He tilted his head a little, thinking he had heard an unusual noise—a sound inconsistent with their surroundings. He checked the horses; they appeared nervous. *No surprise, in a place like this,* he thought. He then strolled, un-noticed, to where the horses had teamed together, in a bid to calm them.

'True—we should have been able to cross,' Daine went on. Reece and Asai, unaware Tam had moved away from them, nodded, listening intently to what the guide had to say. 'The *Hour* is the *Witching Hour*— the time when the path is revealed by moonlight. But no one knows how long the traveller is given to reach the other side, despite its reference.' He shrugged. 'Regardless of it, you saw Síofra's reaction; she was powerless against it, during that time.'

'Then she must have known,' said Reece, '—the Sorceress.'

Daine shook his head.

'She was only aware of the *Hour.*'

Gill grunted. 'I wonder who told her?'

His snide remark grated on Daine's nerves. 'That is all *I* told her!' he hit back. 'I purposely neglected to mention Síofra being unable to use her powers, during the *Hour*. But she must have worked it out for herself.'

'Therefore, seizing her opportunity to …' Reece added, his voice trailing, distracted, as his eyes glided towards Tam. His colleague seemed preoccupied while tending to their horses. Reece shared a glance with Asai, concerned; the Samurai had noticed it, too. It was likely the Highlander needed to "feed."

Oblivious, Gill groaned as he approached them. His mood had not lifted. 'Well? What do we do now?' he snarled, addressing Reece.

Daine looked up. 'Perhaps … the clouds will part for us. Perhaps … it is still the *Hour*. If so, it could give us another—'

'I somehow doubt it,' snapped Gill, lifting his eyes; the thick, heavy roof of black clouds seemed to loom closer—with little sign of retreat. And, although he could feel the dampness on his skin, Gill was unaware of the cold. However, Daine was more susceptible, feeling the tightness in his chest as the dank air found its way to his lungs. The events of the night were taking their toll; he was cold and tired. And the longer he spent in their company, the more he struggled to contain the sense of inadequacy he was feeling, even though he was armed. He wanted to run—to get away from them—to get away from this place, and if that meant abandoning his journey, so be it. He had had enough. He would happily walk away without his fee if it meant staying alive. His mind raced, contemplating how he could part ways with them. Taking a deep breath, he stepped forward.

'I have taken you to where you wanted to go,' he bravely stated.

They turned and stared at him.

Daine swallowed, intimidated by their blank expressions. This was not going to be easy. 'That was the agreement,' he promptly reminded them, his chest heaving with uneasiness.

Asai—the constant peacemaker—nodded.

'He is right.'

'What?!' cried Gill. 'You're going to let him go?! We still have to get to the other side.'

'I must agree with Asai,' said Reece. 'We gave Daine our word.'

Inside, Daine sighed with relief. If there was a time to go, it was *now!* 'I know nothing of what lies beyond it,' he said. 'That is the truth. I have done all I can to help.'

Gill rolled his eyes, shaking his head, refusing to believe him.

'I wish you luck,' said Daine, trying to ease the tension between himself and the young man. 'And … I hope you find her—your sister,' he added.

A brief, uncomfortable silence passed between them. *Leave. Now!* his instincts warned him. Diverting his eyes, Daine nodded awkwardly, turned and strolled towards his horse, fully aware his every movement was being scrutinised. He prayed they would not stop him. *Keep going,* he urged himself.

Gill scowled at Reece and Asai in disbelief, then looked back through the *Lover's* arch. Even now—from where he stood, staring at it, in its current lifeless state—he could feel its sinister influence taking charge and knew the loch was there, waiting … waiting for its next victim. *And you shall have it,* he silently told it.

When Gill unexpectedly launched himself at Daine, chaos swiftly followed as his intentions came to the fore: he was going to sacrifice the guide to Síofra and her *wraiths*, out of spite.

At first, Reece and Asai could not move, stunned by Gill's abnormal behaviour. Then, alert to the reality of the guides' plight, they glanced around, their eyes darting, searching for Tam; the Highlander was nowhere to be seen. Distracted by Gill's protests, they had failed to notice his sudden absence. 'We will deal with Tam, later,' said Reece, fearing for Daine's life; Gill had already hauled the target of his anger to the edge of death's divide, prepared to hurl him in, ignoring his desperate pleas.

Just then, a shard of moonlight escaped through the clouds, revealing the loch. Its waters were wild with expectation, dancing recklessly—the lurid hands of death breaking the surface, ready to snatch Gill's "offering."

'Take him!' cried Gill, his voice echoing across the loch as he prepared to offer up his struggling victim, like a sacrificial lamb.

But as Reece and Asai leapt to the guide's rescue, in those vital seconds, a voice cried out:

'Stop, Gill!'

# Chapter Thirty-Two

Gill spun on the command, his grip still firmly on the guide. He looked down at Daine, horrified, shaking his head in disbelief as Reece and Asai rushed in, hauling his potential victim away from him. Trembling, Gill stared down into his empty hands, then recoiled, seeing the blackness of his deed, it crawling along the lines of his palms, like a disease, making its mark. He shook them, throwing off the uncontrollable scourge he had felt when he attacked the guide. He checked them again, turning them over repeatedly.

It had now gone.

*I must be going mad!* he thought. However, the feeling was profound, as though he had felt the guide's blood on his hands. It disturbed him.

He glanced at Daine, out of the corner of his eye, reluctant to face him, shocked by what he had done.

'What are ye doing, lad?' Tam bellowed.

Gill jumped, startled by the Highlander's unexpected outburst, drawing back as Tam marched towards him—the sound of his heavy stride, prominent.

Reece threw his colleague a steely glance. 'Where were you?!' he snarled, his eyes following him.

'Auch! It seems I arrived just in time,' Tam remarked, glancing over at Daine—the guide dazed and shaken by the unexpected incident.

'I—I don't know what came over me,' Gill blurted, shaking his head and discreetly stealing another glance at his hands. He stopped and looked at his grandfather. 'Do you think it is—'

'Perhaps,' Reece interrupted, not wanting the guide to know any more than he already did.

Remorseful of his actions, Gill turned to Daine, extending his hand—the look of guilt etched on his face. 'Please—forgive me?'

The guide stepped away, raising his defence as if expecting a repeat attack. Now he knew it was time to leave.

Again, Gill approached him. 'Please—I—'

'Keep your distance!' Daine cried, declining the hand of peace, while subconsciously reaching for his sword.

Catching the guide's movement, Asai promptly intervened. 'Do not use it, Daine-san,' he warned, stepping in. The Samurai stared at him, his enigmatic eyes cautioning against any retaliation.

Daine, taking heed, left his weapon alone, realising it would be useless against the strength of his allies. He grunted. *Allies?* he thought. *The irony of it!* Then, in a daring move, he stood up to the Samurai, staring into his dark, almond-shaped eyes, challenging him.

'Then, tell me!' he demanded, pointing at Gill. 'Who is he?!'

'We need to get to the other side,' Reece jumped in, evading the enquiry.

The Samurai's eyes slid towards Reece, conscious of the guide's penetrating stare as he waited for an answer. Avoiding it, Asai inclined his head to Reece in agreement, but his colleague's attention had been diverted to where Tam had reappeared from his temporary absence. Reece glanced at Asai; the Samurai discreetly sniffed the air, having heard it, too, and looked at Tam. The Highlander shrugged, throwing off their air of suspicion with it.

Gill moved closer to them, apprehensive. 'What is it?' he asked, lowering his voice. They remained silent. He followed their line to the edge of the woods. Although he saw and heard nothing, he trusted their capabilities.

Behind them, Daine was growing restless again—the ongoing sense of danger refusing to leave his thoughts and imagination. He looked at the Dhampir and Gill as they regarded the woods; something had distracted them away from him. Had he just been handed an opportunity? *Just go!* he thought, his mind racing. *While they are distracted.*

As he inched away, a damp wisp of wind suddenly cut across him. He shuddered, feeling its harsh effect, and coughed.

'Quiet!' Gill snapped, throwing him back a scathing look.

Daine paused, holding his breath, feeling the agitation in his lungs return, and waited for it to pass. But as he watched Gill resume his mounting curiosity, he sensed a further threat and continued to back away, discreetly. He looked to where Nahla was tied; the Friesian was stomping the damp ground, agitated. *Just a few more feet*, he thought. *Then I'll make a break for it.* His eyes darted back to the four figures; they failed to notice him—too preoccupied with the impending threat.

*Go! Now!* he thought, prompted by his instincts.

'Wait!' said Reece, lifting his hand, signalling to them.

Daine froze and closed his eyes.

Silence.

Afraid to look around, Daine waited, listening, then jolted, hearing a blade being drawn from its sheath, it then promptly followed by another. His heart raced.

'I can hear it now!' Gill voiced, raising his head, alert.

Daine spun, his mouth gaping when he saw the Dhampir armed and ready, to defend themselves.

'What—what is it?' he stuttered, joining them again; if they were going to be attacked, he would be safer in their company.

They remained still.

As Gill slowly reached for his sister's dirk, he felt the firm hand of another, preventing him. He looked up to see Tam grinning and shaking his head. Gill frowned at him, confused, then recoiled when he heard the oncoming threat getting louder. His mouth gaped subconsciously as he craned his head, observing the thick foliage being disturbed by the unknown danger as it advanced towards them. His eyes rushed from Asai to Reece for reassurance; still, they remained motionless and alert, their weapons held firm.

*Why are they just standing there?* Daine thought, his dread mounting; *it* was almost upon them. Inside, it was difficult for him to comprehend that only a few moments before the Highlander's return, he had hovered at death's door. And now it seemed they had completely disregarded the incident, turning their sights on something else.

Despite the Samurai's warning, Daine's instinct told him to arm himself. Abandoning his plan to escape, he moved to draw his sword.

'You will not be needing that,' said Asai, motioning to the guide to refrain from using his weapon as he swiftly returned the katana and wakizashi to their place. Daine stared at him, puzzled, then looked at Reece, his broadsword now casually resting on his shoulder.

'I think it is safe to say …' Reece began, 'we should not underestimate my—'

'Maw?!' Gill exclaimed, his eyes widening, like a child who had been handed a magic toy.

Tam, amused by his little secret, let out a bellowing laugh as he joined Gill, nodding with enthusiasm.

'Nor is she alone, lad,' he hinted.

The familiar—and welcoming—sound echoed through the woods, searching for him. Gill could now hear it clearly—the excitement as they pounded their way towards them.

'Rave!'

For an instant, the hound stopped, hearing her master's voice, then came crashing through the undergrowth. Daine gawped as he watched Gill fall to his knees, his broad arms stretched wide, waiting to embrace his dog. Rave bounced willingly towards him, her tongue hanging from the side of her mouth. Overcome with enthusiasm, she danced around her owner, elated by their reunion, barking and howling at him as though telling him about her travels. Overwhelmed, Gill beamed with joy as he tried to hold her, while she continued to leap about, her tail wagging so hard, it occasionally whipping him. He barely noticed.

In their reunion, Daine could not help but smile faintly when an image momentarily jumped into his mind, reminding him of when *he* was a boy, his family having reared dogs throughout their lives. He felt a pang in his heart, missing those days.

Gill suddenly lifted his head, then rose to his feet, now hearing the oncoming sound of horses' hooves. He looked up at Tam. The Dhampir was still grinning from ear to ear; he had heard her approach in the distance, well before his two colleagues, taking it upon himself to investigate, to Rosalyn's surprise. Despite their hostile start, in their first meeting, the two were genuinely pleased to see one another, Rosalyn relieved she had reached them on time.

The sight of his mother stunned Gill, having believed he would never see her again.

Reece, the first to greet his daughter, smiled. 'So, you found us!' he mocked, helping her dismount. As her feet touched the ground, father and daughter held each other's looks until the glint of metal caught his eye. His gaze shifted, falling on the silver, interlaced brooch she had fastened to the front of her tartan shawl, to keep it in place. He lifted his hand, his fore-finger delicately touching the pale-blue sapphire, sensing Onóir's residual energy, where she had kissed it before handing the piece of jewellery down to their daughter. Rosalyn blinked away the tears at the subtle and rare tender moment her father displayed as he reflected on the piece of jewellery he had gifted his wife, on their wedding day.

''Tis almost as if you expected me,' she said, purposely distracting him.

Reece opened his mouth to reply but was interrupted, by someone eager to speak to his mother.

'How—' Gill swallowed, trying to find the words. 'How did you find us, Maw?'

Rosalyn, pleased to be reunited with her son, fell into his embrace. Reece, Asai and Tam lingered, allowing mother and son their private moment. Gill, forgetting his strength, enveloped her. She tensed, trying to endure his powerful hold. He quickly released her and drew back, staring at her; she looked drawn and tired, for the want of sleep. He lowered his eyes, regarding her unladylike attire and gave her a sidelong look, his brows knitting together, seeing the buckskin trousers she had on; they were tucked inside her leather boots and matched her dark-tanned buckskin jacket. His eyes then narrowed, noting the familiar piece of clothing that was once his—the black shirt having been altered to suit her slender frame. His eyes widened, alerted to her intentions. He shot her a warning glance, his face stiffening; he intended to prevent her from accompanying them, on what was evidently a dangerous journey. He shook his head, about to object when he felt a sharpness pinching his legs and looked down; Rave was pawing at him, craving his attention, and foiling his attempt to scold his mother. Rosalyn rolled her eyes, knowing his protests would have been useless, and so did he.

She scrutinised her son with a curious eye as he leaned down to pet his dog again. There were things she needed to say—things she needed to tell him … She pursed her lips and frowned, contemplating it.

'Gill?'

He paused, his hand resting on Rave's back, and looked up at her, his face full of youth and enquiry, waiting for her to speak. She released a short gasp, suddenly aware of him, then decided against telling him; where was the point in it now?

'What is it?' he asked.

'Even in the short time I have not seen you'—she paused, narrowing her eyes, then slowly shook her head as he rose—'you've changed … again!' she stated. He straightened as she looked up at him, meeting his keen eyes. When he blinked, they glinted—the tiny flecks of gold standing out in the gloom. 'The *boy* I knew, a few days ago, has grown into this fine young man.' Rosalyn would have doubted the rapid change in her son, had she not seen it for herself. His hair had grown and was now falling beyond his broad shoulders. And the beard, he had desired for so long, now added to his strong features, even though he had not yet come of age. It was then she was reminded of it: his birth date. She gasped. *It's tomorrow! How will he look when—* Her thoughts were then disrupted by Rave—the hound's ongoing display of excitement, disturbing them.

'Hush!' she commanded.

Rave obediently cowered away, her tail, though, still flicking with joy. Gill raised a sharp brow; it was the first time he had seen the dog take orders from his mother.

'We have become well-acquainted, on our journey,' said Rosalyn. 'I must admit, she has been a great comfort to me,' she added, recalling a minor incident with a wild boar—Rave protecting her from its hungry attack—both hound and wild pig eventually parting ways, amicably, without drawing blood. 'As to how I found you …?' she continued, her eyes travelling from one to the next until they fell on the stranger, who was keeping his silent distance. She hesitated. His mouth twitched in an awkward smile; when it was not returned, he felt foolish and looked away. 'The landlord of that God-forsaken Inn'—she shook her head—'eventually put me on the right path.'

'Eventually?' said Reece, moving to her side, scowling, reminded of the owner's sinister reputation.

She nodded as the corner of her mouth slowly lifted into a captious grin.

'He did his best to persuade me to stay,' she continued, still cringing from his limp, clammy hand when he touched hers. Holding her smirk, she eyed the sword attached to Farrow's saddle. 'But I managed to convince him, otherwise.'

'Your husband taught you well, Rosalyn-san,' Asai remarked, bowing. 'Perhaps, you will be our *Hōgo-sha!*'

She frowned, unsure.

'Our *Protector!*' he stated, noting her enquiring look.

Rosalyn lowered her eyes, hiding her modesty, and the elusive curl at the side of her mouth. But it quickly fell from her face when she caught sight of her daughter's dagger still clinging to her son. She looked up, her eyes assertive and filled with dread.

'Eleanor!' she blurted, turning to Asai, anxious and fearful. 'What of my—'

'She is still alive,' he stated, nodding, to assure her. 'And we are hopeful.'

Accepting the Samurai's word, she released a long-winded sigh of relief.

'Your daughter—' Daine stopped abruptly when they all turned and stared at him in silence. It was clear who the outsider was. He hesitated, swallowed, then bravely strode forward, extending his hand, holding it out in mid-air, all the while keeping his eyes forward, aware of the Dhampirs' inquisitive looks.

Rosalyn lifted her head to the stranger, her eyes inspecting him briefly; his approach had been bold and confident yet uncertain.

He tilted his head towards her.

'My apologies,' he said, his hand still out-stretched. 'My name is Daine.' His accent was slight yet unfamiliar to her, hinting he was not native to their land. The seconds passed before she raised her hand.

'And had it not been for his guidance …' Reece promptly interrupted, placing a protective arm around his daughter—also, wanting to discard the incident where her son had almost killed the guide, '… we might have perished.'

*Would have,* thought Daine, sensing the strong bond between the two and recalling the way Reece had touched her when she dismounted. He rolled his eyes and shook his head.

'Your husband is too modest,' he was forced to respond, taking a step back.

On his remark, the rest of the group shared amusing glances. Despite being caught up in a trying situation, it provided them with some humour, though brief. Daine narrowed his eyes, bemused, feeling slightly wounded by their mockery. He glanced at Rosalyn, noting she had refused to take part in it, her expression appearing almost sympathetic towards him.

With that, Tam, scratching his deformed ear, approached the guide and patted him hard on the shoulder. 'Ah, forgive us, lad!' he said, feigning his guilt, looking down his broad nose at him. Daine stretched himself up and broadened his chest, trying to match the Highlander's towering height, but failed miserably.

'Rosalyn is not my wife,' Reece informed him, feeling the ache in his heart, thinking of Onóir.

*Rosalyn*, thought Daine, staring at her. *"Beautiful!"* He quoted its meaning in his mind, tempted to speak it, then thought better of it.

'I'm Reece's daughter,' she stated.

Gill snorted. 'This will be interesting,' he mumbled to Asai, from the side of his mouth.

'His—' Daine stopped, confused, his dark eyes moving back and forth, between father and daughter, scrutinising them. 'No. You could not be his …' He shook his head.

'It is a long story,' said Reece, avoiding further questioning. 'Perhaps, for another time.'

'What of Onóir, Maw?' asked Gill, eyeing his grandmother's brooch.

Rosalyn contained herself as her son looked down at it; his expression was one of concern, and yet she sensed an underlying meaning to his question. She moved towards him, her smile forced, catching a look from Reece before she spoke.

'Onóir is in good hands,' she replied, using her words carefully—the image of her mother under Kai's devoted care, before she died, coming back to her. Reece felt relieved. It had been the right thing for her to say, at this time; the news of his grandmother's passing would only occupy Gill's mind, distracting him from the importance of their journey. They still had some way to go with the little time they had left, and, without knowing what was beyond the loch … Its complex crossing was going to be a challenge, from what they had seen. But Gill had already detected the grief behind his mother's eyes. He knew Onóir was dead, despite asking after her. He had also seen it in Reece's demeanour, during the early part of their journey, his grandfather choosing to keep his silence and bury his grief, in order to pursue his duty. But he had sensed his grandmother's presence the instant Reece had felt her passing. He now pitied his grandfather, aware of the torment and heartbreak placed upon him; it was a loss that would endure for the rest of his days—a loss they had no time to mourn.

*'Do not mourn me.'* The voice in his head was clear and defined. He held his mother's gaze and nodded in understanding, then was distracted when she reached inside her waistcoat, drawing out something. He frowned when she held it up for him to see.

"'Tis yours now,' she said, then raised herself onto her toes, to attach the silver brooch to the damask cloak he still wore. Gill pulled his face, looking down as she fixed it. She then brushed over the soft, luxurious material before stepping back with a sharp nod of approval, and a feeling of inner pride. She glanced at Tam—the Highlander also nodding his approval. Her eyes slowly returned to Gill.

'Never forget who you are, son,' she said, giving the heirloom a quick polish, to remove any smudges. Now he remembered; his father had shown it to him, once. And although the motto was upside down and worn with age, he knew it: *Fide et Fortitudine.* He took a deep breath.

'Never!'

'I know,' Rosalyn replied. 'Now, we must concentrate on getting your sister back,' she went on, her tone firm and resolute. 'Do you know where she is?'

A brief account of what had happened, before her unexpected—and timely—arrival was swiftly relayed, Daine pointing out any details they failed to omit, to Reece's annoyance. Rosalyn nodded, taking everything in, with mixed emotions. It enraged her—the image of the dark Warlock, his hands, stained with death, on her daughter. She turned her head, staring at the void beyond the *Lover's* arch, in disbelief. She grew anxious, fearing Eleanor's state of mind, after her ordeal, only to be eased by Asai's reassurance and Gill's vivid description of his sister's attempt to escape.

'My brave girl!' she said proudly, regarding the empty quiver on her son's back, where he had used up all his arrows in his valiant effort to kill the Valkyrie. A faint grin appeared on her mouth; she was now glad she had brought the Albrecht sword with her. What once belonged to Oran would soon be handed to their son. She knew Gill had always yearned for the ancient weapon, and soon he would have it; it was only right. But she knew it must pass from father to son, first. She hoped it would. If not … She refused to think otherwise.

As details of the night's events were conveyed, she became conscious of the guide's presence each time he moved closer, to correct any misplaced aspect of the story, it occasionally imposing on her concentration.

'The wee lass tried her best to keep the path open,' said Tam, '—for us to help her.'

'So that we could cross it,' added Reece. 'But—as you can see …' He pointed with his chin, to where they had last seen Eleanor.

Rosalyn followed her father's line. It seemed almost impossible to think—to believe—the malevolence that lay in wait out there, for the ignorant souls willing to take such a horrendous risk, to get to the other side. And now, here they were—faced with the same intolerable task.

'It is not impossible, now.'

Again, they all turned and stared at the guide.

Daine's eyes slid towards their one—and *only*—chance.

'No—you don't!' cried Gill, stepping in front of his mother and folding his muscular arms, as if shielding her from a sinister accusation. 'She will not be our—'

'Please—let me explain!'

Protected from all potential threats, Rosalyn tried stepping around her son, only to be denied, Gill insisting on keeping his mother safe. She protested. 'Do you not think I—'

'Your mother is a woman of noble heart, Gill,' Asai commented.

'Aye, tell her,' said Tam, addressing the guide.

Daine nodded and moved towards them, hesitating, as he faced her protector; Gill was staring him down with his challenging look. Rosalyn, sensing an air of tension between her son and the guide, placed a gentle hand on her son's shoulder, comforted by the softness of his father's damask cloak. Its luxurious material, still soft and vibrant, had not deteriorated in all the years she had known Oran. Feeling his mother's touch, Gill reluctantly moved aside, releasing her from her confinement.

'A woman has right of way,' Daine revealed. He turned to Rosalyn. 'And what is more …' he went on, his eyes engaging with hers, '… you are *mortal!*'

Rosalyn's eyes travelled from one to the next while they watched and waited for her reaction, and as the guide's meaning finally registered, instilling her with hope, they widened with clarity.

'I'll do it!'

# Chapter Thirty-Three

'Are you sure?'

When Rosalyn hesitated, in a moment of contemplation, Daine tilted his head forward.

'Are you?' he asked again softly, under his breath.

She nodded, determined, drawing her brow and pressing her lips together, her valour suddenly stirring his senses.

'I am certain,' she returned.

'However,' stressed Reece, joining them. '*I* am not.'

Rosalyn, turning away from Daine, looked at her father.

'I am willing to risk it, Reece,' she argued.

'What?!' cried Gill, shaking his head with disapproval. It had taken all but an instant for the reality to hit him. He moved to intervene. 'We cannot know if the loch will part for you. No, Maw, you—' He stopped, observing her stern look, then abandoned his protest, knowing it would be a losing battle to contend with a woman like Rosalyn Shaw.

She was determined now, more than ever. 'No—I am going to *try*.' She approached her father. 'I'm confident I can do it,' she stated. 'I—I can feel it.'

'Then, it is settled,' said Reece, proud of his daughter's bravery. He looked to his colleagues, acknowledging them, Asai and Tam nodding with esteem.

She smiled at Gill, her son still frowning his displeasure, and slowly lifted her shoulders. 'It's not like we have a choice, is it?'

He sighed, defeated.

'We will make certain you are well protected,' said Asai, bowing, openly displaying his respect for her.

Rosalyn—with her protective force now close behind—edged towards the arch, her eyes fixed in concentration. As she approached the unusual trees—they united by their tragic past—she stalled and peered up at them, following the exceptional curvature of their branches. She found herself drawn to them as the *myth* came to mind, then realised, with a hidden sense of fear ... *This is no myth!*

But then a wave of compassion for the doomed couple swept over her. 'So, they *do* exist!' she muttered. 'The *Lovers!*'

Captivated by their unique and haunting beauty, she felt compelled to move nearer, her companions close at her heel. But as she stepped closer, an underlying root—camouflaged by fallen leaves—went unnoticed, and Rosalyn was propelled forward when she caught her foot beneath it; had it not been for the intervention of one of her protectors, she would have been hurdled through the arch, unprepared.

Their eyes found each other with mutual interest. Daine's heart leapt when a moment passed between them; their eyes locked together, mere inches apart, and yet ... He stared at them, awed into silence when he noticed the uniqueness of their colour: one blue, one green—the green standing out in the gloomy night—hardly noticeable from a distance yet distinctive, up close. They were simply ... *captivating!*

For a few moments, they were fully conscious of one another, as if they were alone, shutting the world out from their awareness. Daine could not deny the feeling. And, although they had just met, he imagined he had known her, for an age. He was unable to comprehend it—the feeling it evoked—it awakening him.

Asai glanced at Reece; he, too, had witnessed the brief exchange. However, the Samurai had sensed something deeper the moment the guide's eyes found Rosalyn's—a connection—something he knew all about:

*Kama!*

What seemed like hours for Daine and Rosalyn, passed in seconds for those around them, until they were disturbed.

'Are you hurt, Maw?' cried Gill, shoving between them.

Rosalyn quickly diverted her eyes from Daine as she straightened, fixing herself, attempting to spare her blushes, having felt the judgemental stare from her father.

'No, Gill,' she said, ignoring Reece. 'And … thank you,' she added, tilting her head towards the guide, reluctant to look him in the eye.

Shrugging off her clumsiness, she composed herself, then went to the threshold, hiding her guilt. Inside, she was shaking, still feeling the warmth of his hands on her. She had never allowed another man—let alone a stranger—to touch her in that way. Not since Oran. It roused a feeling in her—one she had not felt in a long time. *Damn you, Oran Shaw!*

Standing beneath the arch, she tried discarding shameful thoughts from her mind but was unable, his lingering touch still stimulating her senses, making her quiver.

'We are right behind you, Maw.'

A sharp intake of breath, on hearing her son's voice, snapped her back to reality. *Thank you, Gill,* she thought, closing her eyes briefly, then nodded.

Rosalyn looked down, assessing the emptiness before her, and listened intently to her surroundings. She could now feel the ominous presence, so much so nature itself had chosen to stay away; no animal or bird stirred. And if God did exist, it seemed he had chosen to look the other way. *This is an evil place*, she realised.

Nonetheless, she knew what she had to do …

Inhaling deeply, she then trembled inside as she released her breath, watching it fade from her into nothing. Behind her, her protectors inched closer, all except Daine—the guide keeping his distance when he caught a threatening glance from Reece, reminding him of the company he kept. He needed none.

He looked over at Nahla, his mare anxious for her master's company, and motioned the Friesian forward. She strode towards him, neighing.

'You sense it, too,' he muttered to her, her ears flicking back in response to his voice. Again, he contemplated going while the others were distracted. He desperately wanted to. He wanted to put it all behind him, to forget what happened this night, to forget … But as he toiled over his decision, Rosalyn threw a hasty glance over her shoulder, catching his eye … and his breath. He knew, there and then, he could not leave.

With the three Dhampir and her son standing behind, waiting to snatch her, should something go wrong, Rosalyn was finally ready. Poised and ready, she blocked all thoughts of the newcomer from her mind and focused hard on what she was about to do.

Rosalyn gasped, drawing in her amazement as the barren wasteland transformed itself on her first contact, parting again in honour of a good heart. At first, the loch swelled, aware of another disturbance. A second step took her beyond the arch, urging her on as the secret path was unveiled, allowing her to pass freely. With each step, she felt exhilarated, while on each side of her the water lapped calmly at her presence. She lingered in its wonderment, smiling to herself, then looked back at the adamant faces peering out at her, nodding at her achievement. Even Rave, sensing their relief, howled; she, too, was eager to join her mistress.

Hearing the hound, Rosalyn turned and reached out her hand, coaxing them towards her.

'Shall we?'

Quickly they gathered their horses, letting Farrow go first to join Rosalyn. Gill went next, with Rave cowering at his heel—the hound having sensed the evil lurking beneath. They were then promptly followed by Tam and Asai.

As Daine made to follow, clutching Nahla's reins, Reece blocked his path. 'You have been of great service to us, Daine.'

The guide, sensing an underlying threat, held the Dhampir's hostile gaze, seeing the intensity in his green eyes. He dared not look at Rosalyn while her father regarded him with a wary eye.

*Quite the brave one*, thought Reece. 'You are free to go … if you wish.'

As Daine's heart raced, Reece smirked; he could hear its anxious beat, like a battle drum, marking something imminent.

*Do not look at her. Do not look at her*, the voice inside his mind warned. 'And, if I choose to go with you …?' he said, almost goading the Dhampir.

Reece lifted a brow and tilted his head. 'Only you can decide your fate, Daine.'

'Hurry, you two!'

Hearing her voice, Daine twitched, nearly diverting his eyes.

'You are welcome to travel with us, but'—Reece leaned forward within an inch of the guide's face, Daine feeling his cold breath—'be mindful of who you are with, and the uncertainty of your future.'

'I am well aware of it,' he said, staunch in his reply.

Reece slowly nodded, then turned abruptly to join his daughter and colleagues, smiling to himself, hearing the guide's sigh of relief behind him.

Rosalyn had already reached halfway when she paused and stared out over the loch.

'Can you hear it?' said Gill, observing the bewildered look on her face.

She strained to listen, then drew back, alarmed, as the wind lifted, carrying with it the faint, relentless sound of whispering voices.

'What are they saying?' she asked. 'And—*who* are they?'

'No one knows,' Daine replied, bobbing his head forward, urging her to keep moving; the last thing he wanted was to fall victim to what they had seen, earlier. He felt nervous as it was, and quickened his pace, his eyes skimming the loch.

Beneath the surface, the waters swirled wildly, with the occasional glimpse of pale silhouettes, their human-like forms twisting and gliding, reminding the onlookers of Síofra's curse.

Quietly and steadily, they moved in single file—the waters gradually falling silent as they made their way across. The only sound now was the slow rhythmic movement of their horses' hooves; even Rave crouched low, her tail between her legs as she treaded carefully beside her master, her sixth sense connecting with the loch's lost souls.

As the opposite side loomed, Rosalyn felt her excitement heighten with the hope of finding her daughter. Guiding Farrow behind her, she quickened her step, eager to reach the far side.

'Take your time!' said Daine, his voice almost a whisper as he nervously glanced over his shoulder.

Failing to hear the guide, she mounted Farrow and spurred the horse on, ready to pursue their enemy. But as soon as the steed's hooves passed over the threshold, touching "safe" ground, Rosalyn felt the sudden vibration of the earth beneath them. She drew Farrow to a sudden halt. Forced to dismount, she rushed to the water's edge, hearing the thunderous noise.

Rosalyn's mouth gaped, her eyes widening then slowly lifting when she saw the unyielding wall of black water rise and rush towards them. She glanced down; the others were almost there.

'Hurry!' she yelled out—the panic in her voice present.

In a matter of seconds, they finally joined her. She looked up, lifting her head as the waters rose higher, picking up pace. She stepped back in horror—the horses growing unsteady behind her, seeing the great mass hurdling closer, its roaring sound drowning out their fear.

'It won't touch us, Maw,' said Gill, moving to her side.

Unsure, she stared up at her son, bewildered, as he smiled down at her. 'What do you—'

'Watch,' he said, pointing.

Fearful, she crouched behind Gill, gasping when the waters abruptly stopped, a few feet in front of them.

'See?' he said, reassuring her. She looked to the others, who were nodding in agreement.

Nervous, she crept out from behind Gill, briefly stalling before taking a brave step forward, her eyes fixed, staring up at the great wall of water before them, its height overbearing and menacing. She inched closer, slowly lifting her hand, then cautiously reached out. As the tips of her fingers touched its freezing edge, wetting them, she jumped back, almost colliding with the guide. But this time she failed to notice him, her attention now stolen by the face of the ghostly image peering back at her, from within its gloomy depths.

Rosalyn leaned her head to the side, regarding the young woman staring back at her, her long black hair swirling about her pale, thin naked body.

Resolute, she moved closer.

'No, Rosalyn!' Reece grabbed hold of his daughter's arm, unsure.

'I must look at her,' she said, fascinated.

He stayed with her. They all did.

For a few moments, the current took hold of Síofra's hair, dragging it back away from her face. Rosalyn drew her hand over her mouth, seeing the thick, deep-purple scar around the entity's throat. To her astonishment, the spirit smiled and then looked beyond her. Rosalyn turned to see what she was looking at; she was staring directly at Asai, as though she knew him. Closing his eyes, the Samurai bowed, silently thanking her. Satisfied her work was done, Síofra glided away from them, her ghostly form diminishing from view as she returned to the cavern of her bleak domain.

Together, they lingered in silence, then jolted when the wall of water collapsed and receded before surrendering again to its damnation.

Gill embraced his mother, relieved—and grateful—for her presence.

'Without you,' he began, then pulled away from her, 'we never would have crossed it.'

'We still have some way to go,' Reece stated. 'Time is against us, and we have yet to face the most arduous part of our journey.'

Gill knew he was right; he could now feel the Shenn's influence pulsating through his blood, like iron. It sparked with exuberance. Unavoidable, yet strangely enticing, he was aware of its powerful effect the closer they drew to their destination, its growing presence heightening his concerns. The unacceptable attack on the guide had thrown him; he had no memory of it until the Dhampir's intervention. He lifted his eyes to meet Daine's. It was clear, by the guide's steely look, he had not been forgiven. And, like a child, afraid of being caught out for his wrongdoing, he swore never to tell his mother. But Rosalyn had sensed something was amiss between the two and was itching to know.

'Time to press on,' said Reece, observing the curious look in his daughter's eye as she regarded Gill and Daine—the two eyeing each other gingerly.

'Now there's a sight I thought I would never be glad to see,' said Tam, distracting them. He looked up, then lifted himself in his saddle, pointing high to the gaps between the trees; the sky was brightening in the far distance—the faint, yellow haze of dawn, trying to push away the bleak remnants of a long—and eventful—night. 'The day is awakening,' he added, grinning.

Reece and Asai smiled at each other.

'What is so amusing?' asked Daine, feeling slightly put out by their sudden complacency.

'How inconvenient!' said Reece.

Daine frowned, confused.

'It is, to his misfortune,' Tam replied, 'and, by *him*, we mean, Magia Nera; he can only travel by night, under the protection of darkness.'

At first, Daine could not fathom his meaning. Then it struck. 'You mean—he is a—' He stopped dead, unable to utter the word.

'Aye,' said Tam, nodding. 'Which gives us an advantage.'

'His weakness is sunlight,' said Reece. 'Although, while the days are short, during these cold months, the sun is less visible.'

'He can still travel by day?'

'A little, under a mask of clouds, which, thankfully, limit his powers.'

'This will be a great "inconvenience" to the Sorceress,' Asai added. 'It will slow them down.'

'Then let's not delay any longer,' said Rosalyn, guiding Farrow away.

Reece watched his daughter with pride as she mounted her husband's horse, taking control. He then looked up, his eyes regarding the brightening, morning sky.

'Well …' he said, turning to the guide. 'It seems *luck* is on our side, after all.'

# Chapter Thirty-four

*Elboru*

'They have taken the *Pass*, my lord.'

'And the lake?'

Kai nodded as Tuan rose to meet the Servitor, his long, thin fingers straightening the black, silk belt displaying his *nomen* for all to see, reminding those, who needed it, of his status within the Elliyan. The Great Warlock, his long, pale face, lacking emotion, approached the Servitor, meeting his wide onyx eyes.

'And Síofra permitted them?'

Kai hesitated. 'They had the help of another, Lord Tuan.'

The Great Warlock's face hardened. 'You interfered? You know it is for—'

'No—I did not,' he jumped in, defending himself.

Tuan lowered his head and glowered at Kai for interrupting him; had he not been the most loyal of the Servitor, he would have punished him, by returning him to Purgatory, for a spell.

'Forgive me, my lord.'

'Then … who did?' Tuan queried. 'Indulge me.'

Kai paused before continuing—having sensed the presence of another, lurking within the vastness of the Great Hall. Aware of the eavesdropper, he prayed the dim light would not betray their shadow— or their identity. Reluctant to elaborate to his peer, the Servitor knew he would have to be vague in his replies but was finding it increasingly difficult; it was expected of him to speak the truth. It had always been that way.

'Do not make me wait, Kai,' Tuan pressed on him, slowly lifting his chin, his listless eyes staring at the Servitor in a sanctimonious way—a look he so often displayed as another indication of his status.

'A woman has joined their company.'

The Great Warlock now tilted his head, intrigued, then extended his hand, prompting the Servitor to proceed.

'His wife.'

Tuan frowned. 'Whose?'

Kai resisted diverting his eyes from his superior, so as not to deceive the *eavesdropper.*

'She is the wife of Lord Oran.'

Tuan's brows shot up. 'Quite the family affair, it is becoming,' he mocked.

'It transpires they never would have crossed the lake, had it not been for her timely arrival,' said Kai.

'Then we must be grateful to her—for saving our Magus. I assume he is unharmed?'

Kai bowed.

'And, he has flourished greatly,' he added, with pride. 'I sense the Shenn has chosen well. He is well protected; Oran's choice of companions has been flawless—the perfect replacement for—' Kai stopped himself from saying *her* name, aware Oran was still listening from his hiding place. He hoped Tuan was ignorant of the High Warlock's lingering presence.

'Ah! Yes,' said Tuan, nodding. 'The *Watcher!* He mused over her. 'An unlikely candidate—for such an immense undertaking. Nonetheless, she proved her worth, in the end.'

'A worthy one, indeed—and due the great honour she so rightly deserves.'

'Do I detect a resilience in your tone, Kai?' the Warlock challenged, taken aback by the Servitor's defensiveness; it was shunned upon to question the authority of their superiors. Both were now aware of the tension between them intensifying.

Conscious of it, Kai refused to be deterred. 'After everything she has done for you, you have barely acknowledged her existence, simply discarding it since I passed her on into the universe.'

Tuan pressed down on his thin lips, lowering his head. The light, emanating from the huge lanterns high above them, cast grotesque shadows beneath his hard features, displaying the callousness that lurked inside him. The Servitor needed no visible reminder of it; it had always existed beneath Tuan's cold exterior. Still, Kai persisted: 'Your Magus would not be the man he is today had it not been for her loyalty—not to mention her influence over him.'

Tuan slowly lifted his head from out of its shadowy façade and stared at the Servitor.

*Well, well—you are the bold one*, he thought. *I will deal with you when all is done.*

'I assure you, Kai.' He smiled wryly at the Servitor. 'We shall, in time, honour the one you call'—he hesitated as if he had forgotten her name—'*Onóir.*'

The Servitor's black eyes widened as the name echoed, travelling down the Great Hall of Eminence, reaching out to the hidden shape in the shadows. Kai hoped it would not drive Oran from his hiding place. The Servitor regarded Tuan with suspicion, detecting a hint of arrogance in his stare as though he knew Oran was listening.

'But, for now, it is of no consequence to us,' he went on. 'Our priority is our Magus. They must reach us by the waning light of the moon's final crescent, which gives them little time.'

'They still have a full day, and the advantage of a long night,' Kai retorted.

Tuan nodded.

'We are prepared for his arrival.'

'And the Sorceress?' said Kai. 'Are you prepared for the onslaught of the unknown if—'

'If?!' snapped Tuan. 'We are more than confident that the Overlord shall take his rightful place on the Throne of Council, in the Sanctuary of Armistice, where he—and *only* he—belongs. You forget, Kai ... we still possess the book, and are grateful to Lord Greer that he has finally been able to unlock its secrets.'

'It appears you have neglected to mention something vital ... Lord Tuan.'

Tuan was now seething inside. *Make the best of the time you have left in this world,* he silently threatened, *for you shall be returning to where we dragged you from ... for good.* On this vow, the Great Warlock restored his composure. 'Neglected to mention something?' he replied, throwing the Servitor a sideward glance. 'Oh, I think not.'

'The girl?' Kai reminded him.

'She is of no importance to us,' said Tuan, dismissing Eleanor with a single sweep of his hand as though she were standing beside him.

Inside, Kai felt betrayed by his superior—Tuan's lack of loyalty clearly portrayed by his arrogance. It was now evident the Servitor were nothing more than a commodity to this hard-hearted Warlock, threatening their existence. Already, Kai knew he was under threat, for speaking out.

Unless called upon, Kai knew it was forbidden for them to interfere in the Elliyan's business. But things were about to change as his gaze fell thoughtfully on the Great Warlock. *No more,* he decided. Oran's family had welcomed him into their lives as one of their own, cherishing their true friendship; nor could he have imagined—or experienced— the bond he had shared with Onóir—a bond that continued to consume him. They had made him re-discover what it was like to be almost "human" again. He owed them much, and what was more ... he had given Onóir his word.

Kai was now resolved to make that change—beginning with the realisation of his true loyalty, and where it lay. Then, in a bold move— and aware of the consequences—he matched another revelation, to that of the Great Warlock.

*Onóir is dead?!*

Oran's eyes widened, hearing her name—the mere mention of it swirling in his mind, and the shock of discovering she was gone … It played on his conscience, swamping him in guilt. There had been no warning, no hint of her demise, and how Tuan had casually said it … It enraged him. *All this time*, he thought. *Onóir was the one watching over Gill?*

It had been a revelation, shocking him to the core, and yet it filled him with pride, knowing his son would inherit good morals, from the person he had looked up to as a child, without even knowing his fate. *So*, he realised, *the Servitor was with her in the end*. Having discovered this, Oran felt his heart warm a little to Kai. *But when?* he wondered. *When did*— He stopped dead when he heard Kai mention the Sorceress, tilting his head against the pylon concealing him, listening intently. He then frowned.

*Girl?*

He strained to listen to their voices, Tuan muttering on about something or other, then followed by the Servitor, who, unexpectedly uttered a name—a name he did not expect to hear.

Oran bolted up as the name echoed clearly through the Hall of Eminence as if it had been revealed for his benefit. But when Tuan repeated it, he clenched his fists against the pylon he was hiding behind, his knuckles grinding on the solid surface, fighting the temptation to show himself and confront the Great Warlock, once and for all. It sickened him—the mere idea of Tuan speaking her name … *their* names. Knowing Onóir was dead had been a great blow, but then to discover his daughter was now in the hands of the woman he thought he could not destroy, was too much to bear. For an instant, he regretted the birth of his son. *None of this would have happened if Gill …*

Oran shook his head, trying to block out the disturbing images conjured in his head: his daughter's imprisonment; his life had Gill not been born. *How could I think such a thing? Forgive me, Gill.* It was no good. He could stand it no longer. He had to know. Even if …

He straightened up, still hearing their voices.

*I am going to end this!*

But as he moved to make his confrontation, an unexpected voice in his head stopped him.

*"It will achieve nothing, my old friend."*

Oran stopped dead, his eyes darting, searching.

*"Tuan's death will only seal yours."*

His mouth gaped as he slowly looked up, staring at the pylon, its cartouche bearing the name of his one-time great friend.

*Tekkian!*

Oran lifted his hand and placed his palm gently on the cold, precious metal, then traced his name with his finger. *I hear you, friend*, he returned. *What can I do?*

*"Go to the Naoi."*

*The Sacred Shrine?*

*"You must trust me."*

That was all he heard. But it was enough, for he had never doubted his old colleague, having always trusted his word.

The sudden silence then called for his attention. It was evident, by the absence of their voices, Tuan and Kai had left. He had failed to notice. Swiftly—and quietly—he made his way out of the Great Hall, leaving it behind in its serenity.

As he marched the long passages, his mind raced with every step. *Why there?* he wondered. *Why the Naoi?*

Regarded as *their* most revered vestige, the *Naoi* was a sacred shrine housed inside a simple chamber—the stone walls free of all writings, so as not to distract the worshipper while in deep thought.

Encased in pure gold, two constant flames adorned each side of the *Naoi*, illuminating the exquisite workmanship, where the story of the birth of the first Over Lord, *Lumeri*, was depicted, in sunken reliefs. And, inside, waiting for its new master, lay the most precious item—the Shenn amulet—placed there by its protector: the *Ushabti*.

One Warlock was permitted entry at a time, where he could give devotions to, or ask forgiveness of, their Magus, in absolute privacy.

Only once had he entered its sanctity since his return: to beg forgiveness for denying his son to the Elliyan. Despite the cleansing of his conscience, the guilt of that denial had stuck, and he would have to live with it for the rest of his life—whatever the outcome. Another thought struck him: *How could I have forgotten her?*

'Rosalyn!'

He stopped abruptly, his heart sinking. With all the revelations that had seeped from the Great Hall, he had neglected to think of his wife. There had been no more mention of her, no utterance of her name as if she did not matter in all this. And yet, she was the one who guided the others across the loch. He groaned, shaking and lowering his head.

'Oh, Rosalyn! I have failed you.'

'Your wife is quite safe.'

Oran spun, hearing the voice behind him. Suspicious, he stared at the stranger who was smiling at him with his warm, brown eyes. Oran stepped back, taking him in. His pale skin complimented his dark hair— neatly tied back—matching his well-groomed beard. And when the stranger smiled again, it was a smile befitting that of a lifelong friend. Oran's eyes then dropped, observing the fine, red scar lining his throat.

'Who the hell are—' He stopped when the stranger lifted his hand, commanding his silence.

'Be calm, my friend,' he begged in a soft voice.

'Who are you?'

'We do not want their attention,' he advised, tipping his head slightly.

'*Their* attention? I—I don't understand.'

'Then ... allow me.'

Oran's eyes widened as the "stranger" transformed himself, their luminescence momentarily blinding him until it faded to the ghostly form, he was more than familiar with.

They stared at him through their onyx eyes—their most prominent feature. Their hair, its colour like that of the blackest night, was drawn back in a long tail, highlighting the beauty and perfection of their oval face.

'Kai?'

The Servitor bowed.

'I still don't …' Oran shrugged.

'Your family do,' said Kai. 'That is how they knew me, at first. The Elliyan allowed me to return to my earthly form, to avoid suspicion. However, I was eventually found out, and forced to reveal my true identity.'

An unsettling thought occurred to the High Warlock, his eyes narrowing as he stared into the depths of the Servitor's eyes. 'Are you here to stop me?'

'I would not dare,' said Kai, smiling.

Calmed by the Servitor's profound aura, Oran gathered himself, relieved.

'No doubt you have many questions, Lord Oran,' Kai began. 'I knew you were listening,' he then added, his eyes travelling to Tekkian's burial place, then back to Oran.

'Why keep those secrets from me? The years you spent with my family—and all the while you and Onóir …' He paused. 'Onóir. How did she—'

'Peacefully,' Kai broke in. Oran dismissed the Servitor's lack of respect, for interrupting him; he had no more time for rules. 'I give you my word, Lord Oran, no other hand was involved in her death. It was simply … *her* time.'

Oran lowered his head in a moment of quietude, out of respect for the woman he owed so much to. *Thank you, Onóir*, he silently told her.

'I share your pain, and shall assist you in your task, my friend.'

*"My friend."*

Oran lifted his head sharply at the statement. The Servitor had called him "friend," and to think how much he had detested their kind, forgetting they were once mortal, referring to them as nothing more than "creatures." It then occurred to him:

'Are you not forbidden to interfere in our doings?' he prompted the Servitor.

'For too long we have endured the Elliyan's ruling,' Kai confessed. 'The true meaning of loyalty came to light when I watched over your family, after your departure. It was through Onóir, I discovered that loyalty and sincerity. It was most deeply felt after her loss. I made a vow to her before she left this world.'

'A vow?'

'A personal one—one I am honoured to see through.'

Warlock and Servitor looked at one another with mutual understanding. Then Oran begged the question:

'And Eleanor? What about my daughter?'

'Come with me,' Kai urged. 'We can talk along the way.'

As they rushed through the corridors of the castle, Kai promptly relayed what had happened, in precise detail—the *Cordhu Pass*; *the Whispering Waters*; the loss of a large number of L'Ordana's warriors; Síofra and her *wraiths*; and Eleanor's brave attempt to escape—revealing how he watched the events unfold but was unable to intervene, while Oran listened attentively. Soon, they reached the five steps leading up to the lofty doors of the sacred chamber.

Unyielding, Oran threw out his hands, disregarding the laborious rituals before gaining entry: the measured approach; the supplications; and the sacrificial offer of a most personal object. *No time for that,* he thought.

Despite his command, the doors remained closed to him, refusing to open. Oran and Kai looked at one another.

'They will not shut me out!' he told the Servitor, approaching the door again—this time with caution. He regarded its smooth, ebony wood, covered in ancient hieroglyphics—carved by the hands of past devoted subjects—each relaying stories from a bygone era, of every Magus who had ruled, from inception to their present.

'Gill's name will soon grace this piece of art,' he muttered, letting his hand guide over each name. He could feel their lingering presence— even at that moment. 'No time to lament,' he said, stepping back.

He would force the doors open.

Again, he raised his hands. But as he did so, a force hindered his second attempt, momentarily paralyzing him. Through no intervention of his own, the doors slowly parted, silently stretching out before them, inviting them into the company of those who were standing, waiting for their arrival.

'Lothian!' whispered Oran, his hands suddenly dropping—the feeling of movement now given back to him. 'How did you know I would—' He halted, then drew back, in awe of the majestic figure standing behind the Great Warlock. Now he understood why he was unable to open the doors.

Protector of the Shenn, the *Ushabti* stood calm and peaceful, his hands open and shielding his perfect round features as he prayed, while presiding over the hallowed shrine. Head tilted low, his hairless crown glowed in the candlelight, like burnished copper, highlighting his flawless skin. And though he kept his silence, his captivating aura was felt by those in his presence.

Aware he was no longer alone, the *Ushabti* lifted his head and slowly lowered his hands. As he did so, the two pure gold rings, worn on each index finger, bearing the *nomen* "Lumeri"—the name Gill would take upon gaining his title—glinted when caught by the flickering flames.

As he regarded Oran, flecks of gold glinted from the *Ushabti's* almond-shaped eyes, through their deep shade of lapiz lazuli, their colour matching that of his sleeveless, full-length linen robe. For a moment, he held the High Warlock's gaze, then returned to his duty, watching over the *Naoi*.

'Does it matter how I know?' said Lothian, smiling shrewdly, drawing Oran's attention away from the *Ushabti*. 'You are here now, and that is what *truly* matters.'

'But I ...' Oran stalled when his eyes dropped to the item being held out to him—the weight of its devilish past a notable strain on Lothian's aged hands—the blue veins beneath his pale, translucent-like skin, bulging.

'Take it!' Lothian urged him.

The High Warlock then turned to look at Kai, but the Servitor had remained where he was, hovering at the entrance, reluctant to cross over the threshold.

Oran turned back and stared down at the book—the presence of the unorthodox cross and dragon seared into its oxblood, leather-bound ancient cover, reminding him of its malevolence. His eyes darted between Lothian and the *Ushabti* before reaching out. But, within an inch of its touch, he snatched his hand back—the dragon's tail unexpectedly writhing, in the company of another who would have it again. It was as though it remembered him.

'As much as it protests against our control over its powers,' said Lothian, 'it cannot harm us—not while in *our* possession.' The ancient Warlock extended his hands, prompting Oran to accept it. 'As strangely captivating as it is, its pages have absorbed nothing but the blood-stained hands of those who corrupted it, over the ages.'

'If you do this, Lothian,' said Oran, hesitant, 'you are betraying the Elliyan.'

'Oran of Urquille,' Lothian began. 'There is nothing the Elliyan can do to me, that they have not already done. I simply ... *exist* in their world, now. True, I have my uses ... when required, which is little, even in these times.' He lowered his head, insisting on Oran's attention. 'You recall our discussion, recently?'

Oran nodded, throwing a cautious eye on the sinister item being held out to him, while occasionally casting the other towards the *Ushabti*; the Shenn's Protector appeared detached from their conversation, and yet Oran was under no illusion that he was absorbing their discussion, with invested interest.

'While time has long since deserted me, it is still on your side, Oran,' Lothian went on. 'There is hope for you—a chance to have your life back.' He shuffled forward. 'Now—take it!'

The instant he touched the cold, hard surface, a chill ran down Oran's spine, sensing its malice, remembering the struggle against its might when he tried to release the three Dhampir from the citadel.

Relieved of its burden, Lothian promptly stepped back, clasping his hands together—the book's ice-cold touch still lingering on his fingertips.

'And remember,' he added, 'use it for the sole purpose for which you require it, then destroy it. And find Magia Nera's amulet; we must have all *five* to complete the process. The bond our amulets share is what keeps the Realms of *our* world united. Without them—without the Shenn—that unique bond will be broken and will lead to our destruction.'

Lifting his eyes from the book, Oran held the Great Warlock's reserved gaze.

'And the dagger?'

Again, the dragon's tail twisted, protesting.

'It stays where it is,' said Lothian. '... away from *that!*' he added, sliding his eyes towards the book.

Oran nodded in complete understanding of what he had to do now. What little sentiment he may have held for L'Ordana—regardless of the woman he had once known as *Kristene*—was now gone.

'Good,' said Lothian. 'I have carefully marked the page you seek. You will know when you see it. But—be warned: do not let it fall under another's influence, or let it consume you when the time comes.'

'I do not know what lies ahead of us, this day,' Oran admitted, his eyes filled with uncertainty. 'Who knows what challenges we face, against L'Ordana's followers? And, as long as Magia Nera believes she still has the book ...'

'We can assume it is the only reason he stays with her,' added Lothian.

'.... she will keep him under pretence,' continued Oran, 'in the hope she will unravel the secret of his amulet.'

Lothian nodded.

'Also, to be certain she finds her way to Elboru, avoiding any obstacles.' He frowned, in thought. 'I wonder ... Does she realise it is *guiding* her?'

'Regardless of it, her time is limited.'

Oran and Lothian looked around when the Servitor spoke, watching him as he disregarded the Elliyan's law, by gliding over the threshold and entering the sanctum, for the first time.

Kai cast a wary glance at the *Ushabti*, but the Shenn's Protector overlooked the "offence", knowing this Servitor was *worthy*.

'Remember—her legion of warriors has diminished in size.'

Oran gasped as Kai's words resonated, his hopes now rising. 'But of course!'

'And with the precious time there is left,' Kai went on, 'L'Ordana simply has no time to spare, to replenish her numbers.'

Oran's thoughts raced as he nodded eagerly, his mind ticking away at his plan.

'This is good,' he said. 'This is—' He halted. 'Eleanor!'

They stared at him, hearing the girl's name.

'Why does L'Ordana keep her alive?' When Kai and Lothian shared a knowing look, he drew back. 'She knows who Eleanor is!' he stated, his eyes looking from one to the other, his concern mounting. 'Well? Am I right?' he pressed, glowering at Kai.

'Partially,' the Servitor replied.

Oran cast him a sidelong glance. 'Do not keep me in the dark, Kai,' he warned. ''Tis your duty to tell the truth, when asked. This is one rule I will not let you break.'

'I must concede … it is true; the Sorceress *is* aware of Eleanor's identity.'

Oran stared at the Servitor, shaking his head, his mind an arena of insufferable thoughts, fearing for his daughter's life.

'*This* is not good.'

'However, at this point in time,' Kai continued. Oran narrowed his eyes. 'It is of no relevance to you *or* your son, for that matter.'

'Then … *whom* is it relevant to?'

Kai hesitated. Oran tilted his head, his face hardening, waiting.

'Her grandfather.'

Oran spun, hearing the soft, melodic voice, and stared at the *Ushabti*, shocked by yet another revelation.

'Her what?!'

Lothian stepped forward.

'Her grandfather … Reece.'

# Chapter Thirty-five

*North-West – Beyond the Cordhu Pass*

The Ardmanoth mountains rose high in the distance, their monstrous, ragged peaks daring and unwelcoming in the early morning mist as it struggled to lift itself from the dawn. But with each passing second of the new morning, the sun was gradually making its ascent from behind their immense size, its translucent pale-yellow light pushing away the gloom, revealing Ardmanoth's true magnificence, to the awakening world below.

The riders drove their horses on, leaving behind the stretch of miles taking them farther from the horror of the Cordhu Pass. Closer they drew to the vast mountainous range, its crests gradually emerging from the mist.

As lazy signs of wildlife began to make their appearance, the group caught the occasional glimpse of mortals, travelling with their own agenda. It prompted them to keep their distance, avoiding small villages and their occupants, so as not to bring attention to themselves; it was best to detach the mortals from the threatening evil hanging in the air. But, despite its menace, they seemed oblivious to its lingering presence. Gill hoped it would stay that way.

*God help them, should I fail,* he told himself, now more aware of the added weight of his burden. So much—so many—relied on him. In that same moment, those he had loved and left behind visited his thoughts: Heckie and Blair Grant; Meghan Downy; and his grandmother. He missed them all, though sensed Onóir's presence. If that feeling stayed with him, it gave him the added courage to persist. And when the face of his sister entered his mind, he considered her absence as only "temporary." *We'll get you back, Nori,* he inwardly vowed, his own words reassuring him.

He felt it.

He *knew* it.

But there were still other concerns—one in particular: after almost killing the guide, he feared it would happen again; only next time, to someone close to him. He would never forgive himself should … He discarded the thought. No—he had to take control; to lose *that* would be catastrophic. He would put the unfortunate incident down to the pressures of his new responsibilities. *It will not happen again*, he determined, glancing over at his mother as they galloped on. It was then he noticed something striking about her; she looked stronger, like an unsung warrior among men. *Men!* He grunted at the notion.

'Look!' said Reece, slowing. He pointed to the great wave of trees now blocking their distant view.

'That must be the forest of Garve,' said Gill.

Slowing, they approached the wall of trees, falling into their long shadows before entering the forest's unknown domain. Nature seemed quiet, save for the occasional hurried rustling in nearby foliage—the trespassers' presence, disturbing the forest's inhabitants.

Silently they pressed on, in single file, carefully guiding their horses through the dense forest—known for its giant *sequoia* trees. The conifers, with their unusual, twisted bark, stretched so high one could imagine their crests almost tipping the heavens above. Crowded together, they cloaked the brightness, temporarily casting the travellers into their dizzying, gloomy world; and yet, when it found its way, filtering through their branches, the sun's rays would occasionally sprinkle the forest floor with speckles of glittering light.

After a while, the forest gradually grew sparse, widening out, inviting them to indulge in the spectacular view presented to them.

High and majestic, the mighty Ardmanoth mountains dominated the skyline, as they had done since the birth of their creation. Grandiose in scale, they still blocked out the sun as it continued to rise, its wide fingers of pale-gold light, stretching up through the wispy clouds above. As it glimpsed from behind the snow-capped peaks, rising steadily, it dropped its powerful watery rays over the summit, temporarily shrouding their magnificence.

The travellers looked up in awe at their vastness, squinting when the sun crept over their peaks, then lowered their gaze from the intense light. Temporarily silhouetted by the dazzling sun, the great mountain range loomed over its realm. Tam, the youngest of the Dhampir, cupped his shovel-sized hand over his sensitive eyes—the light irritating them.

Daine, provoked by curiosity, found himself staring at the three Dhampir, their true features now prominent under the light of the new day. Gone was the pale, waxen hue, visible through the eye of night. There was now a hint of colour in their tone, making them appear a little … *human*. However, when he looked into their inscrutable eyes, he saw a different story: they were lacking life, failing to see through the sight of "mortals"—and it was clear to Daine they were not so.

'How different the world looks now … after the events of last night,' said Gill. "Tis almost as if … it never happened.'

'Make no mistake,' said Reece. 'It happened.'

How could they forget?

Enticed by the smell of fresh water, they crossed the open terrain, to a tributary that had strayed from loch Nessa—the loch once married to the Aber—the two now divided by the Cordhu Pass. They followed its course, stopping a short while to rest and water their horses. To Gill's relief, his mother had packed food for them—the cured meat and dried biscuits a welcome sight to her son and the guide, while *Mother Nature* provided them with water—the purity of its sweetness, quenching their thirst.

From there, parting ways with the tributary, they rode on into a narrow valley, its length no more than a league. Hemmed in on both sides, by layers of folding mountains, the valley remained unusually quiet; the only sound was the heavy thud of their horses, galloping over the moss-covered surface. From behind, the long arm of the sun's light followed them, creeping along the valley floor, awakening nature's morning glory, while highlighting its splashes of colour.

Finally, the six riders emerged from the valley, bringing them out onto a sprawling landscape, cocooned inside a crescent-shaped dome of mountains.

Rosalyn slowly lifted her eyes, her lips parting as she caught her breath, watching the sky in full view of its awakening beauty. Daine, unable to resist, stole a glance: her cheeks were flushed and radiant from the cool air, and her long hair, its strands of gold highlighted by the sun, curled in the early morning dampness. He quickly diverted his eyes when she turned her head.

Rosalyn looked over at Gill; in the honest light of day, she was taken aback by his physical change, it now obvious.

Daine had noticed it, too. *Who are you?* he thought. It was clear the young man was someone of immense importance; it was apparent by his whole demeanour and poise—if he was *human* at all. Also, he had noticed it in his eyes—the flecks of gold glinting when caught by the light. He needed to know, his curiosity slowly turning into an obsession. But as long as the underlying threat from Reece was still prevalent, his enquiry would remain unanswered, for the time being.

Frustrated, Daine quietly sighed—the events from the night before, taking their toll again; his head ached and he was cold, the lack of nature's remedy—a good night's sleep—being the culprit. He glanced down at his clothes, relieved he still wore his oil-skin coat. He would need it; the weather would deteriorate the farther north they went. The last thing he needed was to run the risk of another infection to his lungs—the northern climate being disagreeable to his health. And, despite the food Rosalyn gave him—he saw her blush when their fingers lightly touched—he craved a hot meal and a glass of whisky. But when she caught his eye, before turning away, he knew he had no intention of going back. He was involved now and determined to know the true purpose of their journey—and *where* they were going.

Now and then, Gill smiled over at him with the same look of apology—still feeling the guilt of his attack—and he decided the young man had no control over what had happened. He could sympathise, through his own lack of it; he was finding it increasingly difficult to keep his eyes from Rosalyn. But when another rider drew alongside him, he quickly took back his look of enquiry, aware of her father's penetrating stare.

Averting his eyes, he peered up at the colossal mountain range, its relentless border stretching beyond their limits, giving the illusion they were impassable.

*We'll never cross them*, he thought, then voiced; 'How are we meant to—'

'We will—' Reece suddenly stopped, pulling hard on the reins, his horse instantly stalling, bowing to its master's strong command. He dismounted, with Asai and Tam at his heel. Reece, shading his eyes from the morning sun, surveyed the sweeping landscape.

'Well?!' said Daine, desperately trying to keep a lid on his frustrations.

Ignoring the guide, Reece maintained his stare.

'What is it?' asked Tam—the Highlander squinting, his eyes still irritated by the severity of the sun's watery glare.

'We need to go back!' Reece stated. He had sensed something was wrong when they emerged from the forest of Garve; the dizzying effect of the over-bearing trees had thrown them, mistakenly leading them west.

Asai nodded, in agreement.

Taken aback by this unexpected turn, Rosalyn and Daine jumped from their horses and rushed to their sides.

'Go back?!' cried Daine.

Rosalyn shook her head, defiant.

'We—we can't go back!'

'East!' said Reece. He was calm and collected, despite their aggravation.

They glared at the Dhampir.

'He is right,' said Asai. 'We must keep east of these mountains; Oran-san was adamant we stick to that route.'

Daine, now on the brink of losing his temper, challenged the Dhampir. 'If we go back that way,' he argued, pointing back towards the valley. 'Who is to say—'

'Where's Gill?!' Rosalyn cried out, gripped by sudden panic.

Gill had stepped away from their company, to take in their location. In the early light of the late autumn morning, the mist was burning away, revealing the true exquisiteness of the land he felt they were trespassing on. Even in its desolation, it was clear its beauty had been untouched by man.

As the mist evaporated, hints of colour began to appear—cross-leaved heather, its purple flowers still clinging to the tops of their stems and prickly deep-yellow gorse, its exotic scent wafting through the cool air—while in the distance, up on the higher bare tops, exposure kept the heather away, leaving the peaks grey, or white with early snow.

Gill inhaled his surroundings as though he knew them. They seemed … *familiar*—with or without Kai's directions.

> *"They who lie down at night, faint and weary,*
> *Rise in the morning, active and lively."*

The old folklore song Heckie Grant would quote, after inhaling the dawn, came back to him. Gill, following his friend's habit, did the same—the freshness of the crisp air filling his lungs while renewing his soul.

He then sensed the others behind him, conscious of their enquiring eyes. As he turned to look back at them, he stalled, catching sight of five wild stags appearing on the peak of a crag—the unusual precipice shaped like a great pedestal.

The forefront of the group—the leader—with its thick rust-coloured coat, was regarded as the *Ancient Power Symbol of Scotland*. It stood staunch and majestic, staring down at him, bearing the weight of its branches, solid and proud; part of his left one was missing—perhaps lost during a rutting duel with another male, fighting for the dominance of a doe. Gill was more than aware of its governance over its territory, just as its bloodlines had done, for thousands of years. He recalled Heckie telling him how the stag personified the power of the *Other World*: the realms of the *Dead* and the *Gods*.

The leader began lightly stomping his hooves, alerting the bucks of possible danger. It then lowered its head and snorted, lifting its tail. Gill knew it was angry. But then it shot up, grunting, stretching its great torso as it raised its massive head, stating its supremacy. Gill moved closer, keeping his eyes fixed on the five magnificent mammals. Strangely, they did not move. As he neared the crag, the dominant male peered down at him; Gill stopped when his eyes met with its unflinching glare. His eyes then lifted, seeing it—in the distance—just above the stag's half-missing antler: there, in the dawn light, the moon's waning crescent shone like pale gold, visible and powerful. His mouth gaped when he recognised the symbolism of both—the stag in all its majestic poise standing for greatness, a true symbol of authority and leadership, while the moon reminded him of the scarcity of time.

As his eyes lowered, meeting the stag's once more, Gill tilted his head in recognition of his—of *their*—sovereignty, and the importance of the immense task facing him.

Nearby, his colleagues—distracted from their mounting argument—watched, in disbelief, at the profound exchange between man and beast.

'He is no *man*,' muttered Daine.

'No,' said the voice beside him. 'He is not.'

# Chapter Thirty-Six

*Elboru*

'Reece?!' cried Oran. '*He* is Eleanor's grandfather?!' He stopped short. 'But—how?!'

'Onóir, of course.'

Oran spun, staring wildly at Kai, then shook his head, bewildered, mumbling to himself. 'How could—I find it a little—no—how—' He halted—the deep lines of confusion etched between his drawn brow as he tried to grasp the impossibility of it.

'You have no reason to doubt us, my friend,' said Kai, attempting to reassure the Warlock.

Then the answer arrived, as clear as day.

Oran slowly looked up at them. 'That means—Reece is—' He could hardly say it, let alone think it.

'Rosalyn's father,' the Servitor prompted.

Oran's startled eyes glided over the ancient stone floor as if searching for answers, trying desperately to work it out as Kai provided him with a brief yet profound analysis, adding how Reece now played a dominant role within his family.

'It seems, subconsciously,' said Lothian, 'you chose the right guardian to protect all that is dear to you.'

''Tis hard to believe,' continued Oran, overwhelmed by yet another disclosure. 'Then again …' His voice trailed as he tried to unravel it in his mind. *Reece had also been L'Ordana's captive*, he thought. *She made him what he is: a prisoner to time.* Elements of their conversation, during their incarceration in the citadel, returned to him. 'But—he told me he had no children, and that his wife was dead.'

Kai nodded.

'That is what he was led to believe.'

Oran grunted and shook his head.

'The cruelty of it,' he muttered. 'Aye … it's beginning to make sense.' He then jolted and shot an enquiring look at the Servitor. 'Onóir! Did they—before she …?'

'Yes,' said Kai. 'They *found* one another again.' He smiled, recalling their reunion. 'It was most humbling, to say the least.'

'She always believed he was still alive,' Oran maintained, '… despite the odds. And then to be torn apart … a second time!' A niggling feeling of guilt disturbed him.

'How were you to know, Oran?' said Lothian, sensing the Warlock's self-doubt.

'Lord Lothian is right,' said Kai. 'Onóir was determined Reece completed his task; after all, he had made a vow—a vow with a deeper meaning.'

Lothian nodded, adding; 'It appears you are more than allies now—bonded by *blood*. There is nothing more honourable.'

Another thought gripped Oran. 'Rosalyn!' he exclaimed, then shook his head. 'For my wife to have met her father, after all that time, thinking he was—' He drew back. 'And my children! He is their …. *grandfather!*'

'For them, it was a strained reunion,' Kai admitted. 'However, it was eventually accepted by one and all. There was too much at stake—to waste time questioning the past. They knew—and still know—what is important. It has given them all a purpose, especially Reece and his two colleagues.'

'Tam and Asai are still with him?'

Kai nodded.

'Indeed.'

'Good. My confidence has just been revived.'

'And they have grown quite attached to your family,' Kai added.

Oran narrowed his eyes at the Servitor, his inquisitive look sensing an underlying meaning to Kai's statement. 'What do you—'

'Keep it safe, and out of sight,' Lothian interrupted, acknowledging the book. The last thing Oran needed, was to know about the blossoming romance between his daughter and a Dhampir; he had more to contend with than having to deal with a relationship between Eleanor and the Samurai. 'Now you *both* must take your leave,' he urged. 'Finish this.'

'What about the Elliyan?' said Oran, disregarding what Kai had said; right now, he was more concerned about his peers and their sometimes over-bearing influence.

Lothian smirked. 'For now, they are too preoccupied with the *Assembly*.' He then cast a glance over his shoulder. 'The *Ushabti* has seen to that.'

Oran's eyes darted to the figure guarding the *Naoi*, his brows then lifting, convinced he had caught a faint smile on the corner of their mouth.

'Let's just say …' Lothian continued, 'we have bought you time.' Though he frowned at this, Oran asked no questions. 'The Shenn waits for its new master,' Lothian went on, raising his amulet—the centre stone now dominant in all its wonderous glory. 'It is only a matter of time, and you know the consequences, should we fail …'

Seeing Lothian's amulet, Oran promptly removed his own. And there it was—in its centre—the *Key*: The *Egress*—the portal which would take Gill to the sanctuary, where the Elliyan would be waiting for him. It was perceived, by all Warlocks, at the last light of the waning moon, before being shrouded by the darkness, on that given day, the amulets would guide them to the *Egress*, giving them a window of time to reach it. Then—and only then—were they allowed to enter through this portal. But should they fail … All their defences would then weaken, leaving Elboru vulnerable, and giving free rein to those who would take the Shenn for themselves.

It would mean the end of all that is good.

'You must take him there, guide him through, but not without the missing amulet.'

Oran sighed, hoping *she* still had Magia Nera's. And yet, attached to that hope, there was a growing fear she could be privy to its secret.

'You must leave—now!' Lothian implored. 'Take pride in your honour, Oran of Urquille. But be warned ...' he added, his eyes lowering, staring at the book. 'The *Devil* still lurks within its detail.'

With nothing else to say—and with countless thoughts churning in his mind—Oran left the sacred chamber with Kai proudly by his side.

Lothian watched and waited as they disappeared down the long corridor. Satisfied they were out of sight, he re-entered the chamber. Turning to close its doors, he hesitated, sharing a look with the *Ushabti*.

'Remove yourself from the shadows,' he said, his tone now superior and commanding.

Knowing they had been found out, the *spy* momentarily contemplated fleeing from their hiding place.

'Do not even think it,' warned Lothian.

Lorne glided towards the dimly lit chamber, then paused at its entrance, lingering in a moment of thought before having to face his inquisition. Lothian motioned the Servitor to enter, to where he had never been permitted ... until now. Keeping his eyes diverted from the *Ushabti*, Lorne nervously stepped over the sacred threshold.

Secure in the knowledge they were alone, Lothian sealed the great doors, their coming together silent and hushed. The serenity of its enclosure pleased the Great Warlock, and he turned to face the gold shrine for a moment, musing over its spellbinding aura and what lay protected inside.

'How did you know I was—'

'I have grown accustomed to your movements, Lorne,' Lothian interrupted, turning to face him. 'As difficult as they are to detect, your silence, however, is ...' He paused. '... *unique!*'

The Servitor stared at him without blinking, his large, black eyes fixed on the ancient Warlock, unsure.

'Why do you lurk in the shadows—like a thief—stealing our words for the Elliyan?'

'They asked—commanded—me to watch over Lord Oran,' Lorne replied, his eyes moving nervously between the Great Warlock and the *Ushabti.*

Lothian sneered down at him. '*Spy*, I would think is the more appropriate term.'

'No, my lord!' he begged. 'I swear it! They asked me to … *watch* him.'

'How clever they are in their usage of words—should you be found out,' he remarked, turning away from the Servitor's uneasiness.

'I was merely obeying my orders. They expect a full account of Lord Oran's movements.'

'And *that* is precisely what you shall do,' returned Lothian.

Confused, Lorne tilted his head sideways, inwardly questioning the Great Warlock's loyalties. Had Lothian secretly planned to betray Oran and Kai? *Surely not!* he thought. *Not in the presence of—*

'Only …' Lothian turned, clasping his thin hands together. 'You shall use *your* words carefully … as you do so well.'

'But …' Lorne's unspoken words drifted from his mind as he failed to explain himself, and the predicament that had been placed upon him.

'If you inform the Elliyan of Lord Oran's true plans,' Lothian persisted, ignoring the Servitor's pleas, his voice low, steady and threatening, 'then heed *my* words: I shall cast you from this life—the one you have known for so long—and return you to where you came from, back to your prison of Purgatory, where I will see to it that you shall have the company of no other but your own.

Lorne's mouth gaped, instantly reminded of his time in Purgatory; even when he had shared its intolerable seclusion with other sufferers, it had been enduring——but to be threatened with never-ending isolation … It was unspeakable imprisonment no restless soul could bear.

'My Lord! I beg of you. What will become of me if they discover the truth?'

'Then, my young Servitor, there is only one thing you *can* do.'

'My Lord?'

Lothian moved towards him, his soft features now hardened and filled with malice. But it was not the Great Warlock who answered him.

'*Lie!*'

# Chapter Thirty-Seven

*The Ruins of Moyne: East of the Ardmanoth Mountains.*

Magia Nera stared out at the threatening daylight from inside his haven yet glowered at his confinement. If only he could leave, to summons the clouds ... A few moments were all he needed. But while the sun jeopardised his every movement, a mere step beyond the threshold would surely bring about his demise. No—the risk was too great; his skin would melt—disintegrate—until his body burned, turning to ash. It would be an agonising death. For now, he was a prisoner to nature's dominance. Irritated, he cursed his "creator" while envying Wareeshta's ability to move freely—during daylight—she having the added advantage of being half-human.

His one consolation, though, was L'Ordana's reliance on him to get her to Elboru. As long as he kept her in the dark, he knew she would not abandon him. They needed one another ... for the time being.

He grinned at the irony of it; his amulet was guiding her, and yet she was unaware it would lead them to the *Egress*, anyway. He grunted. 'Oh, little do you realise, *Bella!*' Naturally, he had no intention of telling her ... At least, not yet. *Time enough,* he thought. Besides, she was welcome to his amulet. And while he no longer required it, he was fully aware of those who did; *they* would need the missing item, for when the new Magus reached Elboru before the last light of the moon. He laughed to himself. 'When? *If* he makes it.'

He mused over the poor unfortunate soul—chosen from the moment of his conception—and the burdens he would have to bear.

He almost pitied him—having to contend with the Elliyan and rule over a world, unknown to mortals, while protecting them from a growing evil they had no concept of, as they potter about, living their pathetic little lives, beneath the weight of its mass. He was well out of it.

*Well, not quite*, he thought, glancing at the sunlit entrance. All he needed was his book, and once he had that … Yes, his plans were set.

He paced up and down his cave-like holding, hands clasped tightly behind his back, his steady eyes darting back and forth to the wide entrance, narrowing them from the sunlight as it teased him with its fatal threat.

It was through his misjudgement he had imprisoned himself in the confined space: he had needed some "nourishment" and ventured out before dawn to find some, but was caught unawares by the sun's sudden appearance, above the ruins, its rays slicing through the dawn, in pursuit of him. Another second and … He cast the sickening image aside. Despite its unappealing "ambience" he was thankful for the cave's shelter.

For now, there was nothing he could do … but wait.

Bored, he stopped to consider the ancient walls adorned with their unusual writings—too old and faded for him to read. The skeletal ruins of Moyne had lain desolate for centuries. Echoes of its past sporadically manifested themselves, as a warning to the unfortunate traveller who happened upon them. Fore-warnings of the unknown would wail through their decaying shells, urging them to *"Go back!"* He sneered at the absurdity of it all; it was another of the Servitor's many uses: occasionally made to walk the ruins, their ghostly forms would frighten away those who strayed from their path. It was a deterrent, to protect the mortals, preventing them from knowing what was truly hidden beyond where they had dared to tread. A harmless yet effective method. But he knew no Servitor was haunting the place, now. No. *They* would be in Elboru, along with the *Assembly*, waiting for the arrival of the new Overlord.

The sound of cautious footsteps approaching distracted him from his reverie. He listened while they lingered outside his temporary abode. Their silhouette cast a shadow on the ground, revealing their outline before being blanketed by a passing cloud; he made a start, moving towards the entrance, then recoiled when it passed over—the sunlight almost blinding him. Almost.

Magia grew optimistic as her indecisive shadow came and went, alerting him to the possibility that he would be able to leave the confines of his holding—sooner than anticipated. Hopeful, he watched while she still hovered, contemplating her next move.

Grinning, he stepped back, smoothing his long, sable hair while indulging in its softness, and then waited …

)

L'Ordana looked up, searching the morning sky, letting her face bathe in the little warmth the sun emanated. Then, aware of its ageing effect, she swiftly pulled her hood over her head and turned away. She touched her face—the tightness of her skin irritating her. The rich oil she had made for herself was no longer working its "magic". She had surprised herself by collecting the Rosehip, then crushing the red berries to extract the precious oil—renowned for its beautifying effect on the skin. She never knew she could do that until her subconscious told her; or had it been a memory? She could not say. She just … *knew*.

In the distance, she regarded the darkening sky; it was laden with thick, grey menacing clouds, which were slowly making their way down from the Highlands, towards them. *Good*, she thought, nodding, though knew it would be a while before they made their descent, detaining the dark Warlock a little longer. This frustrated her. Her thoughts then briefly fell on *those* who had been following them. She grinned, knowing they could never cross the loch now.

As she turned and faced the entrance to his private domain, she hesitated, her eyes dropping to the item concealed on her person; it was pressing against her, throbbing, like the beating of an anxious heart, urgent and alive. Her constant awareness of its presence was beginning to prey on her desperation. She sensed its pull, and yet it seemed to drag her as if draining her energy and her looks. She missed her precious mirror and regretted having the Valkyrie destroy it. She could have lived with the flaw the Samurai had etched upon its workmanship, in his bid to reclaim a piece of his history. But, then again, the constant reminder of seeing his name engraved—and so crudely, too—on the mirror, would have left a lingering sense of intimidation.

Lifting her hand, she touched the scar below her left ear—the one Asai had inflicted on her, on their first meeting. It felt unusually thick. Curious, she pressed on it, then winced, as if he were there, delivering the same blow with his sword. Where the act had gone unpunished, she would now make him pay for his other *crime*: for stealing her dagger. She wondered where it was, and if he still had it. He most likely gave it to the Warlock. A dreadful image assaulted her mind: *What if—what if Oran has both the book and the dagger?* No. She could not bear the thought of that, or him wielding them in front of her while she faded into obscurity. She needed them back if she were to gain total dominance. Yes—and she would go to any lengths to have them. *I've come this far,* she told herself, then felt the amulet again, tugging on her fears as though it were trying to tell her something.

But what?

She sighed, feeling the strain of keeping up the pretence—of making Magia believe she had his book.

*Not for much longer,* she hoped.

Checking her hood, to conceal her emerging flaws, L'Ordana hovered as she prepared herself for the dark Warlock, her mind a flurry of thoughts. *I must know what—*

'Come to visit, *Bella*?' he teased, smirking as he watched the entrance, sensing her reluctance and hearing the anguish in her breathing; it was fast and hollow.

She looked sharp and paused, momentarily tempted to walk away.

'Don't be shy. You are always—' He stopped short when she finally entered—the sun briefly catching her face as she crossed over into his black world.

He leered at her through the dim, candlelight, trying to take her in. Still, she kept her hood up and her head tilted slightly low.

L'Ordana lifted her eyes and glared at him. 'What are you looking at?' she hissed. When he grinned back at her, she knew why and looked away.

It amused him to know she was aware of her diminishing looks. It was also clear her moods were changing, making her unpredictable— and making him doubt her character. This concerned and frustrated him; while a part of him believed she still had his precious book, the other—his gut instinct—told him differently. But, until he was sure, he would have to humour her … to a degree.

'The girl?' he asked, changing the subject.

'She is well,' L'Ordana replied, feigning her confidence as she lifted her head, looking down her nose at him. 'She is strong and is—'

'Like her grandfather,' he interrupted. He had only seen Reece's unusual eyes up close on one occasion: when the Dhampir and his colleague accosted him in her chamber before imprisoning him, beneath it. Their unique green colour—like peridot—was unmistakable … and unforgettable.

L'Ordana blinked, startled by his remark.

'I saw it,' he said. 'In her eyes; though dissimilar in colour, I detected the unique taint of *his*. Plain to see, when close enough. Now I understand why they were pursuing us. It was to rescue her. But'—he lifted his finger, leaving it suspended for a moment, then wagged it as if scolding a child—'there *is* something else—something in her demeanour and her look when she so bravely confronted me at the lake. I have seen it before … But where …?' He tutted, frustrated, unable to recall, then dismissed it with a flick of his hand. 'No matter. I am sure it will eventually come to me …' He paused and looked at L'Ordana, then drew closer, silently demanding her attention with his profound stare;

she pulled back, checking her hood again, not wanting him to see her, up close.

'Why did you not let me destroy her?' he said. 'The girl is nothing but a burden and distraction from our task.'

L'Ordana released a frustrated sigh. 'Surely *now* you can see my reason for keeping her alive.'

'Ah, but of course!' he exclaimed, lifting his hands in a moment of *Eureka!* as it registered.

'Precisely! I can use her—to *barter* with.'

'*We* can barter her, *Bella*,' he insinuated.

She smiled wryly at him, slowly tilting her head. '*We.*'

'Then we must do our utmost to protect our "goods",' he insisted. 'Who watches over her?'

'Wareeshta. I have made certain the correct amount of potion is given, just enough to keep her in *Utopia*; after all, we cannot have her communicating with her *lover* again. Even though there is no hope of the others catching up with us, I am taking no risks.'

Magia slid his eyes towards her—the pale, flickering light from the candle mirrored in his dilated pupils. 'Wareeshta?' he casually asked. 'Is it not the Valkyrie who guards her?'

L'Ordana lowered her eyes. Kara had returned to the loch—on her orders—to make sure the girl's friends had not found a way across. However, the Valkyrie had been gone a while. No doubt Kara was looking for her "pet" as it usually stayed close to its mistress. There had been no sign of the black hawk, either—not that she minded; she hated the vile creature. Despite Kara's untimely absence, she had no intention of sharing her misgivings with the dark Warlock. But Magia had also noticed the hawk was missing and could see the anxious look in L'Ordana's paling eyes before she diverted them from his scrutiny. He forced himself from smirking at her, while, inside, revelling in the knowledge that her "loyal and trusted" servant had most likely deserted her, with her own devious plan.

'Kara is scouting,' she lied, turning her back on him, staring blankly at the faded reliefs on the moss-ridden stone walls. 'The last thing we want is the inconvenience of having to deal with mortals.'

She could still feel his eyes staring at her from behind, trying to read her thoughts. Avoiding further inquisition, she slipped a white silk glove on her hand and reached inside her robe. Carefully, she removed the black-satin pouch, containing his amulet, and then turned to face him. She held it out.

Magia drew back, his lips parting in awe; it had changed. He craned his head forward, his eyes narrowing, full of intrigue as the amulet dropped from her gloved hand—the thick, gold chain securely wound on her middle finger.

Emanating the brightest light from its centred stone, its shade of deep-ochre intensifying, it began to swing like a time-piece, commanding the shadows it cast on the walls to mimic its movement. Then slowing, it eventually stopped. Lifting it to the level of his alluring eyes, she watched his reaction.

'See how it shines?' she taunted. 'I sense its increasing power, as though it is ...' She was unsure. 'Am I to presume we are nearing its conclusion?'

'Almost,' he muttered, now taunting *her*; he, too, could play that game.

Frowning at his insinuation, she turned her gaze back to the precious jewel, her eyes then narrowing when she noticed something— something she had failed to see—deep inside its core. Leaning her head sideways, mouth partially open, she scrutinised it, unaware Magia was watching *her*, fascinated.

'What is it?' she asked, her eyes widening, enthralled.

He paused before relaying his own request, seeing the reflection of the jewel in her enlarged pupils.

'Return my book to me, *Bella*,' he stated, his tone smug and collective. '*Then* I shall tell you.'

# Chapter Thirty-Eight

*The Forest of Garve: North of the Cordhu Pass.*

K ara raised her hand, shielding her icy-grey eyes from the blinding sun; it was unusually hot and burning against her sensitive skin. Despite being on the doorstep of winter, its feverish heat was intensifying—the droplets of sweat crawling down her forehead and into her eyes, stinging them. Wiping them clear, she looked up, searching the sky for Nakia; the black hawk was nowhere to be seen, considering it rarely left her side. She assumed it was hunting for food.

Kara drew her arm across her forehead, wiping away the sweat, then winced, dropping her lance, feeling the piercing pain tearing through her veins. It was then she took notice of it—the wound where the Dhampir's poisonous blade had cut her skin, just above her silver wristlet. She regarded it closely, drawing it to her senses, then flinched from the strong, almond-like smell of putrefying blood. Her face stiffened when the wound began to weep profusely—the watery-red liquid sliding down her arm as she lifted it. Curious, she touched it with her other hand, then quickly pulled it away—the pain shooting through her whole body as the blistering lesion continued to weep heavily. Again, she looked up, her eyes now blinking rapidly from the sun's irritating light.

Still feverish, she glanced around, seeing a small brook. She would clean the wound and return to the others. They could never see her like this; they would assume she was weak.

As she moved towards the water, her pace slow and heavy with each laboured step, she could feel the sun's blistering rays as they reached down, penetrating each layer of her skin.

Though mere few feet away, it seemed to take an age for her to reach the brook, and when she did, she dropped the Obsidian and fell into the water, welcoming its cool embrace as she immersed her arm beneath it. Catching her reflection, she jolted; her eyes were bulging and heavily bloodshot, and her skin was pallid, almost translucent. But the relief was short-lived; the swelling around her silver wristlet burned red as the skin tightened, antagonising her pain. If she did not remove it, it would soon cut into her. She then grew agitated when a numbness began to spread through the limb. Feeling its deadening effect, she tugged at it, gritting her teeth through her agony. It would not give. She pulled harder—the wound now oozing freely, while her infected blood stained the waters' purity.

In one last desperate attempt, she finally wrenched it away—the silver wristlet snapping in two, then slowly sinking, its metal still glinting beneath the clear water. She paid no heed to it, her concern now mounting as the sun began to scorch her skin; her crooked nose wrinkled from the smell of her burning flesh. Weakened by its effect, she dragged herself to her feet, lifting her hand to her head, feeling nauseous.

'What is happening to me?!' Frantic, her instincts told her to search for shelter—somewhere shaded. She had to find it—and quick!

She looked to the ground for the Obsidian and reached for it. But as she lifted the spear, for support, the sun reflected off its dark-green glass, catching her eyes, and momentarily blinding her. She staggered around, scrambling for cover—the heat of the sun now almost unbearable. As her eyes adjusted, the shadowy outline of woodland slowly emerged. She stumbled towards it, reaching out …

Propped against—and shaded beneath—a large tree, she leaned on the Obsidian, her breathing now deep and uncontrolled. Kara, searching for some sense of calm, closed her eyes and listened to the unsteady beating of her black heart as it throbbed inside her head. A breeze rushed by and she felt its soothing effect, giving her temporary relief. But as it carried with it some of autumn's dying leaves, they fell, touching her over-sensitive skin. Her first instinct was to cry out, their sharp, dry edges stabbing her like thorns; instead, she cast her hand over her mouth, muffling the sound of her agony. If the others heard her cries, they would surely come looking for her and revel in her pain. *They will finish me!* she thought, letting paranoia creep in. *I cannot let them do—*

Her eyes darted, hearing a noise.

The little wild hare stood close by, watching the *creature* who had trespassed on its territory. Terrified, it remained motionless until she caught its eye. She hissed at it, then watched its retreat before it disappeared, beneath a hedgerow. She wondered where it had gone. With the need to survive, urging her on, she staggered after it—the Obsidian bearing her weight.

Through her surging pain, Kara fell to her knees. Then, removing the sword—attached to the back of her bodice of armour—she hacked away at the wild bushes, in pursuit of the hare.

With strenuous effort, she crawled through the hedgerow, on all fours, dragging her weapons with her, and the leaded weight of her body as she followed the little mammal—the prickly branches tugging and scratching her skin as she scrambled on.

It was not long before she found it—the entrance to a large burrow. 'So, that is where you went!' she mumbled, her chest now aching and wheezing from the growing infection; it had made its way to her lungs.

Exhausted, Kara dragged herself into the cave-like burrow, away from the light. Casting aside her sword and the Obsidian, she collapsed to the damp ground, its rotting stench clinging to her failing lungs and senses. She drew her hand over her mouth and nose, its smell nauseating and overbearing.

Sheltered from the sun—and her skin no longer burning—Kara was then overcome by a new suffering: her stiffening muscles now throbbed as though she was being stretched on a rack, like a common prisoner.

And, with her wristlet now gone, she could feel and smell the blood dripping down her arm, its poison foul to her senses.

As the venom burned and coursed through her veins, like liquid fire, she arched her back in agonising pain. Unable to withstand its domination, she finally cried out:

'Is this to be my end?!'

Kara stretched out her body, tensing, as the pain deepened, forcing her to submit to that which was claiming her.

Faded images entered her mind, full of anger and mockery. She saw her parents displaying the same agony she had left on their faces—after murdering them—and their disapproval of her disturbing ways. They were looking down on her, scorning her for all her wrong-doings. Then more faces emerged, other victims of her sadistic crimes. They, too, scoffed and ridiculed her.

*"Who will believe you?"* one of them sneered, while the other ogled her. Gritting her teeth, she reached up to seize his throat. But the image melted away, his curdling laugh still echoing in her head.

'You deserved to die—for the crime you committed upon *me!*' she snarled through her suffering. 'I was just a child. *I* was the victim. I trusted—' She jolted, her body then seizing, no longer able to bear the excruciating pain. As her body raged with fever, a single tear dropped to her face; she felt it trickle down the side of her cheek, then glide onto her throat, its soothing warmth momentarily taking her mind from her pain.

But then it returned—ten-fold.

'Take me there … Now!' she sobbed, tormented as it reached its climax.

Then, for a few moments, she was transferred to a state of *high,* and smiled, seeing the majestic tree of *Glasir,* its shimmering gold leaves— the most beautiful among the Gods—welcoming her to the gates of *Valhalla.* As her torture momentarily subsided again, she fell into a false ecstasy, making her believe she had entered the *Halls of the Kingdom,* to live an eternal life of debauchery.

The final image to meet her was that of the one who had saved her—the old woman, Pökk—urging, enticing her forward. Kara raised her hand, wanting the aged woman to take it, to guide her safely to *Valhalla*. But the moment was torn from her when the face became distorted, their features twisting and writhing with the return of her intolerable suffering, it worsening as the seconds raced by.

*No! No!* she cried out in her mind, unable to speak, such was the endurance.

Gradually, the featureless face took on a form she knew. Her eyes, now bulging and red, with blood seeping from their lids, recognised it.

'*Loki!*'

It was her last spoken word as she reached out to him—ready to enter her darkening world.

# Chapter Thirty-Nine

*The Ruins of Moyne*

eleanor soaked her mind with thoughts of Asai, occasionally sensing his presence inside her—as faint as it was. Nonetheless, she knew he was there. She tightened her eyes, hoping to grasp the feeling for as long as she could, savouring each precious moment.

*"They have made it—they have crossed the loch."*

The soft voice inside her head gave her hope. As she mumbled their words, repeatedly, a faint smile graced her weary face, grateful for their safety.

All was not lost.

'Dreaming of your *lover?*'

Eleanor's eyes flashed open, to see Wareeshta standing over her. She sat up, feeling strangely invigorated. She had no idea how long she had slept, or how long they had kept her that way.

'How—how long have you …?'

'Long enough,' said Wareeshta, smiling down at her. 'So, your friends have reached the other side of the loch, then?'

Eleanor gasped; it was clear the Dhampir had been watching her as she slept.

Wareeshta nodded in a moment of captivated thought.

'Impressive!' she then added. 'I wonder how they managed to accomplish that?' She shrugged. 'No matter; it will all be decided, soon enough.'

Eleanor frowned. 'What do you mean?' she asked, slowly rising to her feet, her head surprisingly clear, considering the drowsiness she had been experiencing from being kept in constant slumber.

'Feeling better?' Wareeshta enquired, now toying with a small item in her hand.

Eleanor drew back, wary.

'What—what is that?'

Wareeshta stepped closer and held a little grey vial in front of her eyes, then shook its contents—the thick, dark liquid coating the inside of its baroque glass. It was half empty.

'One drop too many … and it will *kill* you,' she revealed, eyeing their captive.

Eleanor's innocent eyes widened with fear as she peered at the vial and the way it was being flaunted in front of her, as though it were mocking her. She swallowed, trying to release the tightness in her throat. She would challenge the Dhampir, should her life depend on it.

'Is this where I'm to meet my end—*here*—in this miserable place?'

She watched as Wareeshta slowly unlocked its tiny lid, while selfishly taunting her with her profound eyes.

'Stop!' cried Eleanor, through gritted teeth. She clenched her fists, ignoring the sharpness of her nails digging into her palms. 'Stop it, I say! Do what you have been ordered to do and be done with it!' She winced, now feeling the sting of her self-inflicted pain, it alerting her. No—she would fight the Dhampir—*Regardless!*—though aware of the outcome.

When a feeling of guilt came over Wareeshta, she stopped toying with the vial. She never meant to harm the girl; in fact, she had grown quite fond of her, after discovering they had much in common. With that, she casually turned the vial upside down, smirking as the contents poured out.

Stunned, Eleanor drew a sharp breath as the remaining fluid was emptied onto the stone floor of the sepulchre. Shaped like a dome, the crumbling ruin, cut from a single rock formation, clung to the remnants of what may have once been a chapel, its only entrance a small arch.

Eleanor drew back, speechless, when the poison came into contact with the ground, melting into the stone like boiling tar, spitting and simmering as it created a hole before sliding down into the consecrated ground below. They lifted their nose away from its sulphur-like stench, its potency stinging their nostrils. Raising the hem of her skirt, Eleanor covered her nose and mouth from its potential harm and stepped back, as far as she could.

As she observed the smug grin lining the Dhampir's mouth, Eleanor was briefly reminded of their first meeting; she had sensed goodness in Wareeshta, then—no doubt passed down from her mother. And now, here she was, proving the human qualities she inherited still existed inside her.

Cautiously, she removed her skirt. 'Why did you do that?' she asked, relieved to see the last drop disappear from the emptied vial.

'Until now,' Wareeshta began, 'Kara has been the one administering the potion, adding it to your water, to keep you sedated, so you could not communicate with your … with Asai.'

Eleanor's mouth gaped. *So that's why!* She had no idea. And the fact she was still alive, beggared belief! Her life had hung in the balance—by a single droplet. Her eyes slid to the dark-grey stone floor, where the toxic liquid had left its black smear, marking the rim of the deep hole it had formed. She shot a glance at Wareeshta.

'Where is she?'

Wareeshta's mouth curled into a mischievous grin. 'I am sure, by now, Kara has gone to join her victims in the glorious *Halls of Valhalla.*'

Shocked yet overwhelmed by relief, Eleanor moved towards the Dhampir.

'You mean—she's dead?!'

Wareeshta suddenly reached for the girl, clasping her hand over her mouth. Caught off-guard, Eleanor froze, feeling the cold palm against her silence, her eyes wide with uncertainty.

'Quiet!' Wareeshta hissed, staring into her steel-blue eyes. She could feel Eleanor's warm, rapid breath in her cupped hand as they remained still, while her heightened senses listened intently for oncoming footsteps.

Nothing.

There was no sign of the Sorceress; she assumed her mistress would be paying *him* another anxious visit while he was still detained by the sunlight. In the distance, she could hear the remaining twelve Dhampir soldiers—she had made a point of counting how many were left, after the Cordhu Pass—going about their restless business, waiting for orders.

'A warning to you, child …' Wareeshta paused at the irony of calling Eleanor "child" when there was little more than a year between them—in age, perhaps, but not time. Slowly, she removed her hand, closing it, to savour the girl's warmth, then motioned to her to keep her voice low; Eleanor nodded. 'Be sure to avoid the Dhampir's blade,' she then stated.

Eleanor scrunched her face, shaking her head, baffled by the statement.

'Their blades—they are coated with deadly venom. If you—a *mortal*—should come into contact with it, death will find you swiftly. You would be lucky to survive an hour.' She glanced at the entrance in a moment of thought, muttering, 'I did not think it would take so long to finish her …' She grunted and turned her attention back to Eleanor. 'However,' she continued, 'Kara, as you know, is no mortal. Nevertheless, I am confident the poison has done its work.'

'That was how she met her end?'

Wareeshta smiled, then nodded.

'What will you do now?' asked Eleanor.

The Dhampir, avoiding her question, moved to the sepulchre's entrance. Standing on the step, in its doorless arch, she contemplated her next move and looked skywards.

'The sun is toying with the clouds, preventing him from leaving,' she said, her voice low and calculating. 'It will give us time—and your friends the advantage—while Magia is restricted. But the clouds *will* come, releasing him. Then finally I can—' Wareeshta stopped, looked up, then glanced back at the girl—the startled look on Eleanor's face telling her, she had heard it, too: the chilling high-pitched sound—the wind carrying it from the west.

Eleanor rushed to Wareeshta's side and peered out, her voice small and anxious.

'What was that?'

# Chapter Forty

**B**ack and forth it swung before his haughty eyes. He now knew what the centre of the precious stone was revealing: The *Egress*. Little does she know the portal is her only way to enter Elboru, Magia thought.

She had to find it first, though.

But, for now, he would persist with the games, grinding on her frustrations, each biding their time in a bid to see who would weaken, first. Neither had any intention of doing so.

'One thing I am sure of,' L'Ordana maintained, 'is that we are on the right path.'

He looked sharp.

*"Path."* Something struck him: *The Paths! Of course!* He could lead them back and go west—it was not far from where they were—then head north, to Affin Shire, luring them to the *Gap of Lome*. It was a challenging place … and risky; although he had never been there, he had heard certain "things" about it—enough to convince him.

The Gap of Lome, though shorter, was a dangerous route to the Egress—for reasons known to him—compared to the one they were currently taking. She was oblivious to its existence. Yes—he could have Wareeshta steal the book and, by the time they reached the *Paths*, could take it for himself and vanish, leaving L'Ordana to fend for herself. She would never get through them; only a Warlock—if faced with the task—had the insight to do that. And, with her mind in turmoil, he could play on her weaknesses. *It just might work!* he thought.

He grinned at her, smug-like. 'Are you sure of that …?' He hesitated, tempted to call her, *Kristene*, then changed his mind. '… *Bella*?'

Prompted by a seed of doubt, her eyes dropped to the amulet. A subtle frown appeared between her brows, second-guessing it. 'But I—feel it—*guiding* me,' she claimed.

Detecting the delicate tone of uncertainty in her voice, he raised a mischievous brow. 'But you are not its mistress. How could you possibly know *that?*'

Offended by his patronising remark, L'Ordana pressed down hard on her lips, grinding her teeth.

'Your *book!*' she hit back, snatching the amulet away, then concealing it again, inside her cloak.

He shrugged, casually. 'I have no use for it.'

She second-glanced him.

'My amulet,' he prompted, pointing with his chin to where she had put it, then smirked.

Her face hardened. 'Why do you always refer to it as *your* book—when we are both fully aware of its *true* origins?'

'What possible use could Tepés have had for it when his corpse lay rotting and sealed from the world?' he retorted, dismissing the notion that the book belonged to anyone else, but *him*.

Still, the games continued …

'Can *you* be certain of that?' she replied, teasing his thoughts.

Magia lowered his head—the taint of red slowly appearing in his eyes. He frowned.

'You were not there,' he snarled, fighting the urge to lunge at her. '*I* was present when they removed his head; *I* watched how his servants adorned their master in a red and purple robe, to signify his "Royalty," as *they* put it. It was *I* who carried that book, and *I* who held it in my hands, agonising over the decision—whether to bury it with him or destroy it. Despite their loyalty, his servants agreed it should not rest with him.' He nodded, recalling their reluctance to even touch it. 'They were more than aware of its evil influence. Therefore, *I* accepted the task, to rid the world of its wickedness.'

L'Ordana smirked. 'But it got the better of you.'

When the light outside faded behind her, Magia's eyes slipped from hers. She followed his steady gaze. But when the sun reared its head again, he grunted. *The book! The book!* he quietly reminded himself, then drew back, controlling his frustration.

'Even his own daughter could not bear to say goodbye,' he continued. 'Such was Tepés' immortality, they feared his return. But—his death was assured.' He hesitated. 'I tried to destroy it, you know—the book—several times, in fact.'

She raised a brow and lowered her head, unconvinced.

'Oh, it is quite true, but—' He stopped. 'Well, you have seen it for yourself, *Bella*. You cannot deny its beauty. *Magnifico!* Centuries of war and chaos have surrounded it, and yet it endures—even outliving its master. As time lingered on, I pondered less over its demise, allowing it to become my guardian to the underworld where, ultimately, I became its servant.'

'While denying *me!*' she said—the tone of disdain in her voice, marking her envy.

'I was protecting you,' he protested. 'You have no comprehension of the stain upon its pages; it has inhaled a lifetime of wickedness and is only too willing to exhale its influence. You, L'Ordana, even with the powers you cling to, have no concept of—'

'Believe me, Warlock,' she hissed, persisting in her deceit as she looked into his narrowing eyes. 'It is safe—more than you know. And as for *this* …' she added, tapping the place where she kept his amulet, tucked away from prying eyes and twitching fingers.

'Keep it!' he insisted. 'As a keepsake of our'—he tilted his head from side to side, undecided—'how shall I say? *Amoré?* Although, it is not quite the expression I would use for our … *acquaintance*, as curious and interesting as it has been.'

She cast him a mournful look, pouting. 'You speak as if it is over, Magia,' she said, feigning her sorrow. She then approached him, her face warming, her eyes inviting until they met with his. Then, unexpectedly, she raised her hand to his pale face. He inclined his head, giving her a suspicious, sideward look. Keeping her paling eyes on his, she touched his ice-cold cheek, drawing, tempting him in.

'I see it in your wanting eyes, Magia,' she purred. 'How you regard this world with envy. You crave it. And, besides, you would miss me.'

He turned to face her directly and leaned closer. She smiled as he lifted his chin, taking in her fading scent—the sweet, amber oil now losing its allure. 'If you value your life, *Bella!*' he whispered. She frowned. 'Then do not tempt me with your failing seduction.'

L'Ordana recoiled from his foul breath, glaring at him as he sneered back at her.

'As much as I admire your tenacity, Sorceress, I am certain we are destined to part, through whatever means is decided. If it were not for my book, I would have had you long before now.'

Magia watched his rejection of her gradually appear on her hardening face. Her chest heaved as her anger seethed through her nose, her lips pursing, trying to contain it.

*So unappealing,* he thought. Now, up close, there was something else he could see clearly, even though she had tried to shroud it with her hood. But the sunlight had betrayed her, on her entrance. How quickly her beauty was dying—the lines of age now visible on her face. He had suspected it. But now, there it was, plain to see. And behind those eyes, which once exuded life and lust, they, too, had now lost their appeal; in them, he could see nothing but desperation, married with determination. Not only was she in a race against time to take the Shenn, but she also had another motive—a desperate one: to gain immortality and the endless possibilities that would come with it.

'Think of it, Warlock!' she exclaimed, hiding her inner fear. 'You and me! Together, we can overthrow the Elliyan, take the Shenn for ourselves, and rule the five Realms of their world. Then we could have it all, even that of the mortals.' She turned away from him, nodding her head, her eyes widening as her plan evolved—the boundaries of her determination expanding. 'Yes! We will divide them—share them, evenly!'

As Magia continued to stare at her while she dictated their future together, his eyes darted—the distant high-pitched screech abruptly distracting him. He grinned. He knew what had made that agonising sound.

L'Ordana stopped and spun, staring wildly at him, noting the smirk on his face.

'I think I have convinced you, Magia,' she said. It was clear she had failed to hear the distant sound—too caught up in her narcissism.

'Perhaps!' he replied casually, slowly tilting his head as he lifted his shoulders.

'How could you *not* be tempted?' she returned.

Magia's thoughts raced, now sure of the Valkyrie's demise. He thought of Wareeshta, then regarded the Sorceress as she continued to indulge in her plans a while longer, unaware her hood had slipped from her head. He raised his brows, fascinated by her waning beauty. Her long hair—once vibrant, its titian colour like that of a deep setting sun—now lacked its lustre as strands of silver marked the reality of her struggle to stay young. Without the dagger, she would continue to lose her fight. It tempted his inquiring mind, so much so that he failed to hear the intense silence that had captured them.

They were now staring at one another.

As his voiceless curiosity screamed at her, she slowly became aware of his compulsion, like he was studying an old work of art. She realised why:

Her face was now fully exposed.

Conscious of what had just taken place, L'Ordana turned away from him, promptly covering her weakness.

'Give it your final thought,' she said briskly, preparing to leave, her tone now firm and challenging. 'Or I will destroy it!'

Marked by her threat, Magia watched her storm out, his mind now made up.

# Chapter Forty-One

Wareeshta smirked to herself; she, too, knew what had made that paralysing sound.

'It seems ...' she began, unable to wipe the conceited look from her face—Eleanor noticed the smug curl; the Dhampir was clearly relishing in the moment of something significant—'Kara's "pet" has gone to join its mistress.'

Wareeshta, now turning to meet Eleanor's blank expression, maintained her grin with added confidence.

'The hawk,' she said, reminding her. 'The vile creature—may it rot in ... wherever it came from. This day has just improved.'

'Do you think L'Ordana knows?' asked Eleanor, her eyes brightening, Wareeshta's confidence now lifting her own. To be finally spared further interrogation by the Valkyrie was welcoming news, but most of all, encouraging.

'She would be calling for me, by now.' Wareeshta shook her head. '*Nu!* She is too preoccupied; however, when she hears of Kara's death, she will be more vulnerable.'

'But ... I thought *he* was on her side.'

'Magia would have abandoned her by now if it were not for—' She stopped and closed her eyes.

'For ...?' prompted Eleanor.

The smile that had adorned Wareeshta's youthful features slipped away as she was reminded of her own task—her duty. She had kept it to herself, never sharing it with another. Her eyes flashed open, to find herself staring into Eleanor's honest face, then warming to the connection they shared. She now realised she could trust the girl; after all, they both wanted the same thing: their freedom—and to be with the ones they loved.

Eleanor tilted her head forward in little nods, smiling, coaxing the Dhampir from her reluctance, urging her to speak.

'L'Ordana stole a particular item from Magia Nera—something that is rightfully mine—something that is part of my legacy, as evil as it was—and still is—in the wrong hands. Whereas, in mine, I can control it.'

Eleanor moved to speak but was then hushed by the Dhampir's raised hand, asking for her patience.

'Please?' Wareeshta insisted.

Eleanor nodded.

'The item I speak of was buried alongside the headless corpse of my father, in a place called Snagov. It is on the borders of the eastern Realm of Saó—Romania.'

'Your home,' Eleanor recalled.

'*Da!*' said Wareeshta, smiling, pleased the girl remembered. But then her face grew solemn, lingering on a memory. 'I watched them bury him—from a distance—but left before they sealed his tomb, only to later discover the item had been stolen by'—she paused and closed her eyes, torn between her head and her slow-beating heart—'by the *one* I love.'

'Magia Nera?'

Wareeshta's eyes shot open. 'How did you know?'

'I know the look of love,' said Eleanor—the victim of her own torment. 'I saw the way you regarded him when we were at the loch.' She then shook her head, disapproving. 'But … he is a—'

'There *is* goodness in him,' Wareeshta protested, '… beneath the cold exterior he portrays to those around him.'

When Eleanor pressed down on her lips and looked away, the Dhampir felt compelled to justify the dark Warlock's actions.

'For all that Magia Nera is—no thanks to my father'—she shook her head—'*he*, not Magia, is the one to blame.'

'Your father?'

Wareeshta nodded and held out her wrists—the thick, blue veins prominent beneath her porcelain skin.

'My father's blood runs through our veins—mine and Magia's—bonding us. Regardless of its influence, though, the *Warlock* inside Magia is still prevalent.' She grunted, then smiled, nodding.

'What is it?' Eleanor pressed.

'Despite their differences … I noted similarities, between him and the other one.'

'The *other* one?' said Eleanor, momentarily forgetting herself.

'*Da!* The other Warlock, who was L'Ordana's captive.' She paused. 'The one you claimed to know nothing about … at first.'

Eleanor felt the sudden rush of anticipation down her spine. *Elboru! Elboru!* The name would be etched on her mind for the rest of her life—the name she had been forced to reveal to the Dhampir.

'I must …' Wareeshta hesitated. '… apologise—for how I stole it from you.' She lifted her shoulders. 'But the Sorceress would have let Kara have her way, and Kara's *way* only led to one outcome.' Already, Wareeshta was referring to the Valkyrie in the past tense.

'I understand,' said Eleanor. 'And … thank you—for saving my life.'

'We all need an ally,' said Wareeshta. 'And I …' She was struggling to get the words out. 'Thank you—for trusting me.'

The new friends shared a smile of mutual understanding, giving Eleanor the confidence to ask; 'This item you speak of …?' Her eyes tapered, full of enquiry.

'It is a book. L'Ordana keeps it in a safe place. But I need time to find it. And now, with Kara out of the way, I have the freedom to do so. It is also the reason Magia remains her ally. He wants it, too. They are equally tenacious in their quest to possess it. From what I gather, they plan to overthrow *he* who would be Magus, before he is united with the item they call, *Shenn.*'

'Gill!' whispered Eleanor, under her breath. She looked sharp, then challenged the Dhampir. 'And what is *your* intention?'

'To destroy the book.'

They both searched one another's eyes, for a moment, each content with their honesty until Eleanor queried the Dhampir again.

'When did you last see it?'

'Before we left the citadel. Not since—' Wareeshta stopped and leaned her head to one side, curious. 'Why do you ask?'

'Because—I know who has it,' said Eleanor—the excitement mounting inside her. She could barely contain it.

Wareeshta lifted her brows, unsure.

'The other Warlock,' Eleanor revealed.

The Dhampir narrowed her deep-set brown eyes, confused. 'You mean—Oran?'

Eleanor nodded, brimming with enthusiasm.

'My father.'

Wareeshta's mouth fell, stunned. 'Your—do you mock me?!' she hissed—the veins in her throat standing out, her eyes glaring as the whites slowly changed colour.

Startled, Eleanor dropped her smile and swallowed. But she refused to recoil from the Dhampir's burning red eyes.

'Is this some attempt to—'

'No!' Eleanor snapped back, her fists clenched, standing her ground. 'I'm telling you the truth! Oran Shaw *is* my father. He is the *other* Warlock.'

Wareeshta drew back, trying to contain her anger. 'Why did you not tell me this?!'

'I think that was obvious. But now that things have changed, I feel the need to—'

'And where is your *Father* now?'

'In Elboru … I hope!' she replied, looking away, biting her lip. 'But I assure you, I had no knowledge of his whereabouts, or of his true identity—his being a Warlock—until a few days ago when Reece and his companions made themselves known to us. Before then, we had come to believe my father was …' Her words trailed.

'And how do you know about the book?'

'I heard them say how he used it to help them escape. So, I assumed it was the item in question.'

'And now, with the book in your father's—'

'He is my stepfather,' stated Eleanor. 'I was just a few months old when my mother met him. She was a widow.'

Wareeshta circled the young woman, letting her speak, listening to what she had to say.

'…. then my brother was born …'

'The name you whispered.'

Eleanor drew in a sharp breath.

'Am I to believe it is *he* who is about to come of age?' said Wareeshta.

Caught unawares, Eleanor searched inside for a lie to protect Gill, but Wareeshta had already worked it out, by her silence. It all made sense now.

'So, *he* is the chosen Magus.' It was not a question.

Eleanor's heart sank as she lowered her head, sensing everything was about to slip away from her. But inside, the fight was not over …

Not yet.

'I would—and *will*—die for my brother!' she stated, rearing her head, her face an effigy of bravery, love and resolve.

'There will be no need for that.' Wareeshta smiled. 'I admire your valour, and if the same courage lives inside him, your brother will make a great Magus.'

Eleanor, fighting back the tears, stared at Wareeshta, perplexed.

'After years of war, depravity and death,' she started, 'it is time for peace. The book and the Shenn cannot fall into L'Ordana's hands; it would be devastating for all of us.' She nodded. 'I am relieved to know the book—*my* book—is in safe hands.'

'For the time being,' said Eleanor, apprehensive.

Sensing her doubt, Wareeshta reassured her. 'This *does* change everything. Magia will no longer have to tie himself to L'Ordana, and with her weaknesses filtering through …' A look of excitement appeared on her face, her mind galloping. *I must tell him,* she thought, then shot a glance at Eleanor. *But first, I must help her.*

Wareeshta looked towards the sepulchre's entrance; it was still bright outside—the sun refusing to be overshadowed.

'Ah!' She beamed, peeping out. '*Bun!* Good. The sun has not lost its battle—just yet. This gives us time.'

'What about the book?' said Eleanor.

'As long as it remains where it is—and protected—we must make sure it prevails.' She approached Eleanor, one last time. Then, in a kind and—unexpected—comforting gesture, she tenderly placed her dainty hand on the young woman's shoulder. 'But now it is time …'

'Time?'

The Dhampir nodded.

'For you.'

'Me?' said Eleanor, drawing her head back.

'To escape!'

*Escape?!*

Eleanor recoiled, shaking her head.

'Have you lost your mind?! L'Ordana's warriors! Even if they fail to see me, they will sniff me out and then … Her words died as harrowing images entered her thoughts, but when she saw the mischievous curl appear at the side of Wareeshta's mouth, she narrowed her eyes.

The Dhampir leaned in and winked. '*I* "created" them, therefore, I know their weakness. I will distract them, lure them away until you are gone.'

'But—what about—' Eleanor stopped, reminded of Magia's threats when she was under his control, at the Cordhu Pass.

'He is too busy with *her*,' Wareeshta hissed, her jealousy briefly rising to the surface. 'While they continue to duel against each other's egos, it is unlikely they will even notice. Nevertheless, we cannot afford to be complacent.' Her eyes slid to the entrance again, then back to Eleanor. 'Time is crucial. When all is quiet, *then* you make your escape. Now, listen …'

Eleanor cupped her hands over her mouth, her eyes fixed in concentration as she listened to Wareeshta's instructions, nodding nervously while gnawing on her lip. She had to do it. She had to take the bold risk.

'And, when you do ...' Wareeshta continued, her tone adamant.

'*If!*' Eleanor mumbled.

'*When!*' Wareeshta firmly stated. 'Find your companions! Tell them what has happened. Warn them!' She then took hold of Eleanor's shoulders—the determined look in her eyes solid. 'Do you understand?'

Eleanor, pressing her lips together, nodded—the two fixed lines between her brows, branding her commitment to the task ahead of her.

'And now,' said Wareeshta, 'this is where I take my leave,' she then stated, stepping away.

'Will—will we see each other again?' said Eleanor, suddenly aware she would no longer have Wareeshta's company; she had become accustomed to it and—for what it was worth—her protection, too.

'Perhaps.' This restored a little of Eleanor's waning confidence. 'But, for now,' Wareeshta went on, 'this is where we part. Take some time, after I have gone. And remember, Magia's senses are temporarily weakened as long as sunlight persists. Be mindful of it—and of *time!*'

'Then what?'

'*Run!*'

Wareeshta hovered at the entrance, her cunning eyes darting, watching every movement as she prepared her plan. As she made to leave, she hesitated.

'There is one thing I ask of you, in return,' she said quietly, to the nervous but fervent young woman behind her.

'Ask it,' said Eleanor, her confidence beginning to soar.

'Should we meet again ... do not let them kill me.'

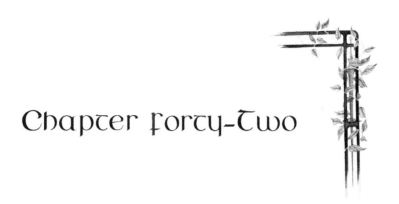

# Chapter Forty-Two

*Ardmanoth: North-West*

'Who *is* he?' insisted Daine, his voice rising as he turned to confront Reece, yet again. The Dhampir, however, was too preoccupied; he was watching his grandson, with enquiry.

'Tell me!' Daine demanded.

They all turned and stared at the guide, then looked at one another—Rosalyn inwardly questioning Daine's insistence.

'Well? I have a right to—'

'You have *no* right!' Reece retorted.

Daine drew back, raising his brows, then sneered at the Dhampir. 'After what I have done for you?! Had I not told you about the Cordhu Pass …'

'You are not committed to this journey,' snapped Reece, his eyes slowly turning pale red. At this point, Asai and Tam edged closer to their colleague, concerned, once again, for the guide. 'I gave you the chance to leave—to return to your … whatever little "arrangement" you had with that sadistic abuser you call *Landlord!*'

'Enough!' cried Rosalyn. 'We are here for one purpose only …'

'Which is?' Daine was still persistent.

They fell silent, exchanging looks of uncertainty, their underlying frustrations mounting.

Gill sighed. 'With time pressing on us,' he said, 'there is none to spare for disputes and demands. Daine is right, he should—'

'Wait!'

They all turned, hearing Asai's commanding voice. The Samurai was looking skyward, beyond the crag where the stags had presided, his hands hovering over his weapons.

'I see it,' said Tam, joining him.

'See what?' asked Rosalyn, her eyes following theirs, nervously searching, aware of the rising tension in the air.

The black, menacing shape grew larger as it soared under the pale, turquoise sky, knowing exactly what it was doing—what it was *sent* to do.

Reece slowly nodded.

'*Nakia!*'

'They must be near,' said Gill, catching sight of the huge black hawk, its wings rising and falling on the breath of the wind, expanding as it glided closer on its course. A low, deep-rooted snarl came from Gill's side; Rave had seen it, too. The hound, her hackles raised and protruding along her spine, like fine needles, crouched low, her sharp teeth now exposed. No one reprimanded the dog for her defence.

'So, Kara has sent her "pet",' snarled Tam.

'That's her *pet?!*' cried Rosalyn, stunned; she had never seen the like of it.

'Aye, lass! 'Tis hunting, to see where we are—if we made it across the loch.'

'But how would it know?'

The Highlander looked down into Rosalyn's inquisitive eyes. 'Kara is too cunning to risk finding out for herself. She has Nakia to do *that* for her.'

'And, if the hawk is successful in its hunt,' added Asai, 'it will bring her mistress back a *trophy*.'

Rosalyn gasped and threw her hand over her mouth when she realised their meaning. She lifted her eyes again to the approaching menace. Nakia was picking up speed, her immense size coming to the fore.

Before she knew what had happened, Rosalyn found herself staring through her human-like enclosure, protected by those who cared for her. She felt like a small field mouse, ensnared—and *she* the bait.

She looked up again, to see the larger-than-life raptor circling fearlessly, its feathers glistening like oil against the strong, low autumn sun. She could also see its menacing red eyes now, their onyx centre watching *her*—its prey.

'Nakia usually stays within view of her mistress, rarely leaving her side,' Tam remarked to her, glancing over his shoulder. 'We must assume Kara is near.'

'Is it going to attack?' said Rosalyn, keeping her voice low.

Silence.

*That says it all!* she thought. She glanced to where the horses had banded together; they were rearing and whinnying, alert to the impending attack. 'Damn!' She scolded herself for leaving the Albrecht tied to Farrow's saddle. Despite what Oran had said, she would use it, if necessary.

But it was out of reach and, at this moment in time, she had no intention of leaving her "protection." It was not worth the risk.

'No harm will come to you, Maw,' Gill assured her, throwing her back a smile and a wink.

The group, armed and ready, craned their necks, watching the hawk as it circled faster, its dizzying hypnotic movement making Rosalyn sway. She reached out to steady herself.

'Do not look at it!' warned Asai. She quickly diverted her eyes, regaining her balance. 'That is what it does until you lose consciousness,' he added.

'I would like to know where the Valkyrie is?' said Tam, suspicious. 'I don't see her.'

'My thoughts, too,' added Reece, stepping away from the group.

Just then, the hawk changed direction, distancing itself before temporarily fading from view. Wary, Asai followed his colleague, motioning to the others to stay with Rosalyn.

A sense of uneasiness came over her when the two Dhampir moved away, breaking her protective barrier. She reached down, searching for Rave, but felt the touch of another leaning softly against her. The sudden awareness of his presence, again, urged her to edge away; however, temptation prevailed, reawakening the sense of fervour she had felt at his first touch. She should have recoiled when he moved closer, but her body refused to ignore the rousing effect he had on it. From behind, she could feel the heat from his body.

*Do not look at him,* she told herself.

Reminded of Reece's warning, Daine kept his eyes fixed on the Dhampir, though was fully conscious of Rosalyn's enticing energy absorbing him, in her reluctance to move away. There was no denying the feeling of underlying passion. Rosalyn, momentarily distracted from the threat above, closed her eyes, feeling the adrenaline covet her body as he pressed against her. Her heart was pounding; she could barely control her breathing. But when an image of Oran entered her mind, she succumbed to her guilt. Her eyes flashed open. She gasped; Tam was looking over his shoulder and down at her. Guilt-ridden, Rosalyn promptly lowered her eyes, ashamed.

'Be careful, lass,' he warned.

She shot a glance up at him, but the Highlander was no longer looking at her, his attention now diverted.

'It's coming back!' Daine cautioned.

For all the unusual calmness in the guide's voice, it did nothing to ease Rosalyn's dread.

'Oh, God!' she whispered, fearing it would hear her.

'Brace yourselves!' Tam alerted them, removing his weapons. ''Tis going to attack!'

Reece and Asai marched farther away from the group, to meet the great hawk head-on, with Gill following close behind.

'No, Gill!' cried Rosalyn. 'Don't!'

He paused, calling back to her; 'Don't worry, Maw, Tam will protect you.' He then made after Reece and Asai. Daine lifted his eyes to the heavens and held his tongue, feeling the insult as though he did not matter.

Together, the three ran towards the great crag, keeping their sharp eyes on the black raptor. If they failed to take her down, they knew her attack would be brutal, quick and violent. They had seen it too often: the strength of its wings diving down, disorienting its victim; the lethal hook-like beak, its tip as sharp as a blade—and used like a weapon, to gouge the eyes of a man in one swoop, before swallowing them whole. This was Nakia's method. Then, as her blind victim staggered helpless and vulnerable, she would make her final attack, by hooking her talons into their throat, then driving them in, severing the jugular vein. It was an art form, one greatly admired by its mistress—the Valkyrie relishing in the *kill*, each time.

As Reece prepared to rush towards the bird of prey, he was swiftly ushered aside by the Samurai.

'She is mine, Reece-san!' he said, reminded of the hawks' intervention, when he and Eleanor discovered each other before her abduction.

Wakizashi—the twelve-inch auxiliary sword, specially forged for the Samurai to accompany his katana—was swiftly drawn by its master's skilled hand. Asai aimed it at the predator, pre-empting its next move, it proving difficult as the hawk picked up speed, cleverly gliding from left to right as it made its way towards them. Suddenly the hawk dropped, just beneath the sun's path, its bright, watery glare, momentarily obstructing their view. As they blinked away the strong sunlight, they glanced around, baffled.

'Where is it?' said Gill, straining his eyes through the glare.

'*That* is what I'd like to know,' answered Reece. He tilted his head sideways, listening, then shook his head.

There was no sight nor sound of it.

Gill stepped forward, looking above the crag's ragged peaks; the sky was still and clear—the morning mist long gone, along with the five stags. However, in the distance, a hue of grey loomed on the horizon.

'Perhaps, Nakia has returned to her mistress,' said Asai, his voice lowered in open thought.

Reece grunted, unconvinced.

'Do you think it has—' Gill stopped dead and spun, hearing his mother's scream. 'Oh, no!'

Reece, Asai and Gill ran as fast as their speed could take them as the black hawk dived towards Rosalyn, reaching down with its great talons, and aiming straight at her. Tam, wielding his claymore and axe, fought desperately to fight it off, but Nakia was too quick and agile. The guide, pulling Rosalyn away, for her safety, shoved her to the ground; he was willing to take the brunt of the attack. The raptor lunged down, closer, its scolding call deafening and masking the heavy beat of its huge wings. But as it reared its head, its sharp beak protruding, ready to strike, it changed direction again, evading the Samurai's clutches. Without her *trophy*, Nakia shot skywards, then turned.

'It is heading east!' said Reece, pointing. 'Now, Asai! Before it flees!'

The Samurai ran a short distance out into a clearing, marking his target, then abruptly stopped; behind him, the others stalled, sharing anxious looks, wondering why he had done so.

Asai had felt something stir inside him: the presence of another heart, awake and beating in unison with his. *Eleanor!* He had her back, feeling her warmth emanate through him. For a brief moment—too absorbed in his reverie of her—he forgot himself. But when Reece's voice called out his name, he jolted and looked up, sharp; Nakia had stopped in mid-air, her great black wings shining like graphite.

Asai nodded.

'You should not have done that,' he quietly said, his trained eyes calculating Nakia's next move.

Calm and collected, Asai pressed his lips to the hilt of the dagger. '*Subayaku!*' he whispered to its spirit, asking it to be *"swift."* With precision, he then threw the wakizashi. The lethal weapon sliced through the air—the glint of the sun catching its steel before quickly finding its target.

The others cupped their hands over their ears, muffling the chilling, deafening screeches released in the hawk's death throw. Rave yelped, cowering from the noise, her sensitive ears also pained by it. Together, they watched the lifeless, black mass as it fell beyond the crag before hearing the thud of its corpse as it collided with the ground.

In the silence that followed, the group broke away, joining Reece and Gill. By now, Asai had gone to retrieve his precious dagger. The wakizashi could never be parted from the katana; together, they were "one" in *Daisho!*

With the blade wiped clean of its victim, he promptly returned, replacing his prized weapon.

Taken aback by what they had witnessed, Rosalyn and Daine regarded the Samurai with awe, on his approach: the confidence in his stride, like that of a true warrior, married with the accuracy of his skilled mind as he had contemplated the hawks' movements before releasing the cause of its demise. But when he joined them, Asai's mind was already on more pressing matters. He turned to Rosalyn and looked her in the eye.

'What is it?' she said, now with Gill by her side. When the Samurai smiled at mother and son, nodding, they knew why: Eleanor was very much alive and alert. It was all they needed to know.

'You do realise what this means,' Tam remarked, pointing to where the hawk had once dominated the sky.

'They'll know we have crossed the loch,' Daine replied.

'We can be sure of it,' said Reece, taking in their surroundings; they were too exposed and vulnerable in the wide-open terrain, it prompting an imminent attack. The hawk had been heading east—no doubt returning to their enemy. *East*, he thought. That was the direction Oran had given him. But it was out of the question now; to go that way, would lead them right into the *Lion's Den.*

''Tis strange,' Tam remarked, frowning, and scratching his deformed ear. 'No Valkyrie. Kara would be quick to avenge the loss of her "pet".'

With no sign of attack, Reece nodded in agreement.

'Something is amiss, here.'

'Then while it is,' said Asai, eager to press on, 'we should use our time, wisely.' He looked up. '… while the sun is still our ally.'

'Let's keep going, then,' Gill urged, remounting.

Reece swiftly leapt in front of his grandson's horse, taking hold of the reins.

'We can no longer go east. They will be—'

'I know,' said Gill, smiling down at him.

*"Trust the power of your instincts; they, too, will guide you—more than you know."*

Kai's words came back as though the Servitor was there, guiding him. And yet, somehow, he already *knew*. It became apparent when he had looked into the great stag's eyes, a moment of mutual understanding had passed between them.

'There is another way,' he said—the confidence in his tone, clear and certain.

'There is?' said Tam, lifting his head and raising a curious brow.

Rosalyn guided Farrow alongside her son. 'How do you know, Gill?'

Gill shrugged. 'I just do.'

'And *I* would not dispute it,' said Asai.

'Nor would I,' added Reece.

*I hope, for all our sakes, he's right,* thought Daine. Then, choosing to forego his demands, he asked no more questions; besides, he was sure the answers would come, soon enough.

Guided by his instincts, Gill turned north, promptly followed by the others, riding closely behind.

On they rode towards Affin Shire, along the base of the great Ardmanoth mountains, occasionally peering up at their mass, hovering over them like a giant canopy. The farther north they rode, the light soon began to fade—the gathering grey clouds gradually blocking out the sun as its shards of stray light struggled to peep through their shrinking gaps.

As the day withered away, taking the travellers closer to Elboru, each lost in their thoughts, three images flashed through Gill's mind. He flinched, momentarily thrown by their unexpected appearance. Then they were gone, leaving him baffled—and unaware of their warning …

He had yet to face his greatest challenge.

# Chapter Forty-Three

*The Ruins of Moyne*

areeshta stalled for a moment, after leaving the sepulchre. The conversation she had had with Eleanor excited her now; it had been informative and satisfying. Not only that, but she was also relieved to know her father's precious book was safe—and yet, she was apprehensive. How would the Elliyan use it?

*Do they even know how?* she wondered.

She then remembered what Eleanor had told her—about Oran using it to free Reece and his companions, from the citadel. Therefore, she could not assume they were ignorant of its powers.

She now regarded Eleanor as her ally. She liked her, and the idea of her being a *friend* was equally intriguing. She could barely recall the last time she remotely "liked" someone, let alone a *mortal*. How long had it been? It was not important. The fact was the feeling was a pleasant and hopeful one. Also, she realised something else: they needed one other. But now she had a dilemma: what would she tell Magia Nera? Until now, she had secretly been keeping him "company" and allowing him to indulge her with his charm and dark wit.

She paused as she approached his holding, where he was still indisposed. Suddenly she was torn between her new friend and the *one* she had grown to "love". It troubled and confused her. She would have to decide before entering, otherwise he would know she was hiding something. Perhaps she *would* tell him … If so, then she would need to be cautious.

Rehearsing it in her mind—what she would relay to him—Wareeshta edged closer to Magia's holding, ready to enter when the sound of an angry voice made her stop in her tracks.

*The Sorceress is still with him!* She would now have to act quickly while L'Ordana and Magia Nera were in the throes of yet another "discussion"—and while sunlight still dominated, giving herself and Eleanor the precious time that was needed.

Wareeshta surveyed the grounds of the ruins; the remaining Dhampir soldiers were still hovering about, looking bored, as they waited impatiently for further instructions. She threw a glance over at the sepulchre, catching a glimpse of Eleanor peeping out, then looked across at the Dhampir. Luckily, they were too preoccupied with their weapons—constantly sharpening and checking them over—to notice her ... or the girl.

*Perfect*, she thought. Now, with Kara out of the way, she could easily distract them, by leading them from the ruins and urging them to *feed*, before their "final battle." At least, that's what she would tell them— the lie making it easier to manipulate them. With the warriors out of the way, the girl could then escape.

With time against her and an eye on the sky, Wareeshta sprang into action.

As planned, she coaxed the Dhampir away from the ruins, with the assurance the Sorceress would be "none-the-wiser" to their temporary absence, telling them she would watch over the girl until their return.

Satisfied they were out of sight, she leapt with nimble agility, pausing briefly, by the sepulchre.

All was quiet.

Quickly, she left there, then jumped behind a small crumbling wall, near Magia's holding, concealing herself from view. She closed her eyes, homing in on the ongoing heated conversation between the dark Warlock and the Sorceress, musing over their words with heightened interest.

'... or I will destroy it!'

Wareeshta's eyes flashed open, hearing L'Ordana's threat—it echoing in her mind.

*"Or I will destroy it!"*

She crouched lower in her hiding place, listening to L'Ordana's exasperated footsteps as she stomped away, leaving behind a vexed and frustrated Warlock.

Unsure of the direction her mistress was heading, Wareeshta peeped over the wall, watching her. But when the Sorceress suddenly made for the sepulchre, the Dhampir held her breath …

L'Ordana stopped and looked towards it, her head inclined as she lingered.

Inside, Wareeshta panicked; if her mistress were to visit the girl, she would have to intervene, *somehow!* She would do what was necessary, to give the girl a chance to escape. Wareeshta, her mind a maze of thoughts, counted the seconds, desperately deciding what to do. There was only one thing to do …

She would have to stop her.

It was now or never.

But, in that vital moment of wavering, the unexpected happened: the Sorceress turned abruptly on her heel and headed in the opposite direction—back to her tent—her mind too distracted, to waste time on the sleeping prisoner or to notice the absence of her warriors.

Reassured, Wareeshta jumped out, her eyes darting around at the emptiness. There was no sign of the Dhampir soldiers returning—not just yet.

Quietly, and swiftly, she slipped inside the dark Warlock's holding.

Magia looked sharp, his aggravation easing from her presence.

'Kara is no more,' she stated, her face eager as he turned to acknowledge her.

He studied her face for a moment, then frowned, sceptical.

She nodded.

'It took longer than we envisaged, but the poison has done its work. She is—'

'Can you be sure of that?' he pressed. 'Did you see her corpse?'

'*Nu*, my lord, but—'

'Then we cannot presume.'

'But her "pet" is dead!' she determined.

'I know… I heard its beautiful song of *la morte!*'

'There was no reprisal for its death—from its mistress. I should imagine *that* is proof enough of Kara's demise.'

'Perhaps,' he mumbled. 'But I am curious to know *who* "despatched" it.' He grunted at his casual usage of what was once Kara's term for "death."

Deep in thought, he tapped his foot on the ground, then paused, when a strong ray of light slipped in, slicing its way towards him. He stepped back, avoiding it, his impatient eyes watching and waiting. But the light still flickered outside between some passing clouds, antagonising him. He tutted, then mused over the girls' rescuers. *Could it have been one of them?* he thought. *Is it possible they crossed the lake?* He shook his head at the impossibility of it. *Then again …*

Aware of his frustration, Wareeshta felt pity for him and, in her moment of weakness, wished he could leave his menagerie with her, there and then. Her thoughts returned to the book, feeling an element of guilt. Her conscience began to niggle at her. It was at times like this she resented being half-human. She sighed, unable to fight it.

'My Lord, there is something I—' She stopped when he shook his head.

'Something is not quite right,' he blurted, ignoring her. He lifted his hand, wagging his finger against the air. 'I incline … that she is *lying* to me,' he muttered.

Wareeshta drew back, her guilt mounting. She swallowed. '*Who*, my lord?'

'Your mistress,' he stated, churning over his thoughts and suspicions. 'I think she has … *misplaced* it.'

Wareeshta raised her guard. 'Misplaced what?'

'A particular item, belonging to me.'

'If you mean your amulet, I assure you—'

'No!' he snapped, turning to her. 'I have no use for *that*—not now.' He grunted. 'The Sorceress has the ignorance to believe that I am nothing without my "precious" amulet.'

'But do you not need it—to find the Shenn?'

Magia leered at the young Dhampir then threw his head back in laughter, adding to her confusion.

'Oh, *Mi Piccolo*, how your naivety amuses me, at times. The Shenn?' He shook his head. 'Unlike the Sorceress, *I* am no fool. She has no comprehension of the true nature of its power.' He approached her with menace, his eyes deadening as he lowered his head. 'And ... it shall remain that way. *Sì!*'

Wareeshta slowly nodded, thrown by his underlying threat.

'I am no longer a *true* Warlock,' he stated. 'Should I even attempt to take the Shenn, it will consume and destroy me. I have no right to it. That privilege belongs to the *Chosen One*. From the moment of his conception, his fate was sealed. It belongs to *him*—the true Magus—and no other.'

'Then—why are you still here?' she quizzed. 'You have had many opportunities to leave. Why stay?'

'Oh, but I shall leave ... And soon. But not before I retrieve *that* which is mine.'

Wareeshta moved towards him, her face softening, her eyes almost pleading. 'When that time comes,' she said, leaning closer, 'will you take me with you?'

Feeling the touch of her body against his, Magia raised his hand and, gently stroking her flawless face with his fingertips, smiled down at her. Her lips parted slightly. He could feel the warmth of her breath on his, tempting him.

'How could I not, *little one?*' he purred, his thin lips barely touching hers. 'Are we not of the same blood? No. To leave you here as her slave would be madness, and besides, I—' He broke off, tearing his eyes from her wanting.

Wareeshta followed his gaze—the tension in his hand displaying his anticipation. He snatched it away, leaving the marks of his fingers on her cheek. Disregarding the Dhampir, he watched the stream of sunlight as it crawled its way from the entrance to his "prison," announcing its departure. The path it left in its shadow invited him to follow it. He lingered, transfixed, expecting the flickering light to return. Blocked out by a sombre-looking sky, it eventually diminished——the grey taking over, giving him a sense of freedom, enticing him from his menagerie.

As Wareeshta observed him, with curiosity, her eyes then briefly drifted, her thoughts returning to Eleanor; she hoped the girl was gone. If not—

Her eyes darted when Magia moved to the entrance, his hands tensing as they braced its surrounds. Still wary, he peered out, beyond the threshold. Head leaned to one side, he narrowed his eyes, then closed them, inhaling the dreariness—welcoming its return.

'The time has come, Wareeshta!' he exclaimed, staring out into the colourless world, it waiting to embrace him, once again. She beamed at him, spurred by his promise to take her with him. 'But first'—he turned to meet her fervid expectations—'tell me where she has hidden it.'

Wareeshta, her intuition sparking a warning, stared back at his impatience, her look of hope slipping from her face.

'The *book!*' he snarled, his face stiffening to a deadened glare.

Her eyes blinked, startled by the sudden change in his demeanour.

He bolted towards her, taking hold of her arm.

'You *have* seen it?!' he demanded.

As if woken from a dream, she started, unprepared. '*Da!* Yes—yes!' she stuttered, her mind now full of doubt and mixed emotions. She cursed her human side as she searched for a reply.

'Where is it, then?' he hissed, his impatience visible, by his reddening eyes and foul breath.

Inside, she feared losing her nerve. *Think, Wareeshta!* 'She moves it—from time to time,' she promptly replied. '… to conceal it from prying eyes.'

Now, devoid of passion, Magia slowly lifted his head, regarding her with his dead-pan stare. 'Do you lie to me, Wareeshta?' The tone in his voice was deliberate and hostile.

As she watched him slide his tongue across his teeth, their sharpness lethal, Wareeshta was under no illusion; his threat was unyielding, and she knew he was capable of destroying her.

'Why would I lie to you?' she hit back, her voice strengthening. 'After all … are we not of the "same blood"?'

Through survival instinct, Wareeshta found herself again and stood her ground against him. She now realised he had no intentions towards her. She had been nothing but his plaything, manipulating her through the bond they shared. *No more!* she decided, feeling a new strength brewing inside her, as though the spirit of her late mother was dominating and influencing her instincts; to have lived as a mortal among the undead, her mother must have been strong in mind and body.

Guided by this emerging strength, Wareeshta lifted her head with pride and stared back at the dark Warlock, eyes flooded with deceit.

'I assure you, Magia,' she lied, her voice now sturdy and convincing. 'L'Ordana has your book.'

# Chapter Forty-four

*Elboru*

'We were not alone in the sacred chamber.'

'I had my suspicions,' said Oran.

'Do not concern yourself with Lorne,' said Kai. 'He is a young and foolish Servitor, eager to please the Elliyan.'

Oran scowled. 'Are you sure of that?'

'What worries you?'

'I can't put my finger on it. But there is something in the way he looks at me … Whether it is pity, hate or …' Oran frowned, momentarily deep in thought, trying to decide, then shook his head, frustrated.

'You have my word,' said Kai. 'Lord Lothian will deal with Lorne.'

They hurried on through the long winding passages in silence—the Servitor musing over the Warlock's challenging task—until his curiosity finally got the better of him.

'Do you love her?'

'Who?' said Oran, throwing Kai a glance.

'The woman you call … *Kristene.*'

Oran halted and stared into Kai's solemn face; the question had thrown him off-guard. It was now clear to him that the time spent with his family had stimulated the Servitor's inquisitiveness. He clenched the book tighter, feeling its strength pulsating through his fingers, his mind consumed by it. He looked down at its worn cover, daring to let *her* into his thoughts.

'Is it possible to love two women, Kai?'

'I cannot say, my friend,' he replied, with honesty.

Oran glanced at the Servitor, aware of his meaning: as a mortal, Kai had been condemned, and hanged by his murderers, for simply loving another man. However, the Elliyan, conscious of the honesty and goodness he had shown—before his untimely death—disregarded Kai's sexuality, and chose to release him from the perpetual limbo, that was Purgatory. And, by doing this, they were giving the condemned soul a sense of "belonging."

'Forgive me,' said Oran. 'I had …' His voice trailed as his eyes returned to the item in his hands.

Kai's large, black eyes fell on the book, noting the constant attention the Warlock was showing it. 'Is it your intention to release the evil housed inside L'Ordana—to bring back the goodness of Kristene?'

It was a fair and honest question and deserved an honest reply. 'It is,' said Oran, nodding, despite his hatred towards L'Ordana, for abducting Eleanor. 'As long as there is hope …' He gripped it harder, fearing it would fall from his hold and into the clutches of another.

'Then you must follow it through,' Kai urged. 'However, you must— '

'I know.'

'—be prepared to accept the *other* consequences,' Kai persisted.

Oran lifted his head, unsure.

'—of having to choose between your wife … and the other woman.'

Oran stopped abruptly.

'Kristene is not the "other woman!",' he snapped. 'She was a part of my life, long before I met Rosalyn. I knew her … well.' He was then reminded of the promise he made to her, all those years ago, after saving her life:

*"They shall never harm you again. You have my word."*

'No!' he blurted. 'I cannot—and will not—abandon *kristene*. I made a vow, and besides … I have a good reason …' He hesitated, seeing the look on the Servitor's face; it was one of pity. 'I …' Oran sighed, shaking his head. "Tis nothing. My mind is a mix of confusion, tied up with loyalty and fear of failure.'

'I do not doubt your incertitude, Oran, but you must forgive me when I say that, for now, this is not about you. Everything that has happened, these past few days, has been for one reason.'

Oran lowered his head in shame, his eyes now coveting the cursed manuscript.

*Gill!*

'Also, you must abandon these thoughts of failure and doubt,' said Kai, breaking the guilt overshadowing the Warlock. 'Think of the task ahead of us, this very day, as it continues to stretch out before us.'

'Only a day left,' Oran muttered. He needed no reminding.

'We do have sufficient time, though—before the new moon takes its last light from us.'

Encouraged by the Servitor's words, Oran tore his eyes from the book and peered down the passage, undaunted.

'You are right! Let's get out of here!'

'No!'

Oran spun.

'What?!'

Kai smiled. 'Not that way.'

Oran stalled, casting the Servitor a long glance when Kai motioned him to step away; he then indicated to the solid wall behind him.

Cobwebs and centuries of accumulated dust—its only artefacts—concealed something known only to this lone Servitor. Closing his eyes, Kai let his hands hover over the uneven surface, manipulating it. Oran stood back in awe when the Servitor glowed—the intensity forcing him to shield his eyes. Kai guided his hands, creating the shape of a perfect oval, resembling that of a portal. Taking a deep breath, he slowly released it—the cloud of ether gradually disintegrating the stone, revealing an entrance, it leading to a tunnel.

'More secrets?' Oran remarked, pointing with his chin. It was bad enough he not knowing the history of the castles' attachment to the Magus—as cynically pointed out to him by Tuan—then, to discover the Servitor had been keeping their secrets, within its walls. *When this is all over*, he thought, *I will make it my business to explore every "crevice."* He grunted, reminded of the sneering remark Tuan aimed at his tempestuous past.

'The Elliyan know nothing of it,' said Kai. This brightened the Warlock's spirits. 'No one knows; this is *my* secret—and mine only. We cannot risk leaving through known exits; there is too much activity above, during the *Assembly*. Someone is bound to see us.'

'They will note our absence, soon enough, though.'

'True,' said Kai. 'But, for now, this will buy us time.'

Oran poked his head in and sniffed the air. 'Do I smell water? Where does this lead?'

'To an underground stream, which will guide us to Muir.'

Trusting the Servitor, Oran followed him.

United, they hurried on through the long, winding tunnel, it eventually leading them away from the castle, then out beyond the grounds, to the edge of Muir forest, its puzzling weald a force to contend with, to those who were ignorant of it.

Soon, they emerged into the light of day, Oran inhaling the morning air, its freshness invigorating.

'I have arranged your means of transport,' said Kai, smiling. He then whistled, so softly, the Warlock failed to hear it.

Oran looked around, hearing the snap of branches before the beautiful mare appeared from the thicket. She strode towards the Servitor, her chestnut-colour coat, shining like silk in the daylight.

'Is that …?'

'Nephtys.' Kai reached up and stroked the mare's flank; she leaned into him, responding to his gentle touch.

'I think Lord Greer would have something to say about this—for taking his horse.'

'We are merely … *borrowing* her,' said Kai.

Oran grinned; it seemed the Servitor had a sense of humour, after all. And, despite knowing his ability to transform into an animal, it seemed Kai knew he would need a horse.

'I think it is only right, as they did not allow Farrow to come with you when you were summoned back.'

The Warlock's face brightened, hearing the name of his horse.

'Farrow is safe,' Kai assured him. 'He returned to your family.'

Oran nodded, pleased, then jolted.

'And the—'

'It is making its way to you, as we speak.'

Assuming Gill was now carrying the Albrecht sword, Oran's heart swelled with pride. He could only imagine the look on his son's face. He hoped Rosalyn had given it to him, in his absence, disregarding tradition and protocol; Gill would need the weapon. And yet, at the same time, he felt the deep ache for not being the one to hand it down; it had always been that way—the father presenting his prized weapon to his son. He sighed. *What's done, is done!* he thought, approaching Nephtys. 'As long as they are together.'

Oran, expecting some protest from Greer's horse, mounted with caution, but the mare showed no objection, his calm voice soothing her. He glanced down at the saddle, seeing a leather satchel attached. Kai *had* thought of everything. Promptly, he slipped the book into it, out of sight, thankful it was separated from its sinister partner: the dagger.

'I hope they have reached the Glen of Muir,' said Kai, looking up at the sky, his tone now solemn, seeing the dullness creep over the tips of the trees.

'Anything to avoid the *Paths of Lome*,' said Oran.

Kai slowly nodded, his mind suddenly troubled by a niggling feeling—an uncomfortable one.

'But ...' He paused. 'If fate dictates otherwise ...'

Oran glared at the Servitor. '*But? If?*'

Those were two words he did not want to hear. No. He had instructed Reece and Asai to stay east of the Ardmanoth mountains. They were to continue north, following their base until they reached a narrow river—distinguishable by its uniqueness: its bed glinted of gold when touched by sunlight, and yet no hand could ever claim its treasure.

This unusual river would bring them to the hidden—and well-protected—Glen of Muir. Although the longer route, it was, by far, their only option. The Glen was known only to the Elliyan and the Servitor, and it was there, he and Kai would be waiting for them, to guide them through the complexity of Elboru's natural fortress—the Forest of Muir. And from there, they would take Gill to the *Egress*.

Oran shook his head in protest.

'But Gill does not know about the Paths, Kai. For obvious reasons!'

'Have faith in your son, Oran; I know he would choose the right one, should he—'

'But no one knows *which* Path to choose, which is why we—*they*—need to avoid them. You know that, Kai.'

'Then ... it is most likely they have done that,' said Kai, reassuring him. 'With Gill's chosen companions by his side, I am confident of it.'

'And as for our enemy?'

'Alas! I am not so confident,' said Kai. 'Because one thing is certain ...'

He hesitated, on a foreboding instinct.

'*They* are coming.'

The lone figure moved cautiously within the castle's hidden passageways, knowing precisely where they were going, their mind a storm of thoughts and spiteful deeds. Floating ahead, along the chosen route, a single flame guided them through the darkness, flickering and guttering with the passing of an occasional draught.

A distant noise made them stop, momentarily, its echo finding its way down the winding corridors before fading. When silence resumed, they proceeded, their footsteps picking up pace. As they pressed on, they felt they were not alone, sensing the presence of souls who had once walked the same path—as if they were eavesdropping on their thoughts. They could almost hear their disapproval, of what they were about to do. They disregarded it, their mind on more important matters.

The flame came to a standstill, hovering at their destination. They had familiarised themselves with the route before putting their plan into action. They had to be sure, evading any interruption; to be found out would mean instant punishment for their betrayal. But their confidence had been such, no one suspected a thing … except for *one*; however, after reaching an understanding, they were "persuaded" to keep their silence.

Hidden within each Warlock's chamber was a door—a secret one—leading out to the maze of passages that weaved their way between the castle walls, allowing the occupant to come and go, in secret.

Through the flame's warm glow, they waited for their eyes to adjust until the faint line appeared, marking the doors' entrance, its arch bricked up to fool the eye of a potential intruder.

A salacious grin crept across their face, and they rolled their eyes. *Easy, when you know how*, they thought, lifting their nose, catching the faint scent of what was concealed behind. They raised their hand, letting it follow the line until the stone slowly vanished, exposing a door—the smell of its Agarwood prominent on their nose. The dense, dark, resin-embedded wood was rare and priceless, due to its unique properties: the result of a mould, its infection producing the aromatic resin, while its strength made it impenetrable.

Almost.

With a flick of a finger, they diminished the flame, then quietly slipped through the door and into the chamber. A lantern still glowed, telling them its resident may return at any given time. They grunted, knowing they would sense them well in advance.

Their eyes darted about the chamber, gliding over the memories of a long-lost past: weapons from glorious battles, adorning the walls. They glanced at the bed; it was unkept. *Unusual*, they thought—*for a Warlock who takes pride in his neatness*. A wave of jealousy then swept over them; to have once shared their own with another. A memory of the unrequited love came back to haunt them: it had been a compelling and obsessive affair—one of the mind—and filled with resentment, driving them to the brink of madness, forcing them to do the unthinkable: destroy innocent lives. And yet, despite their actions, they still secretly mourned their loss.

The sound of falling candle grease hissed in its flame, taking them from their thoughts. Their eyes now searched the walls, looking for a flaw—one not so obvious to the roving eye. It frustrated them. Nonetheless, they knew they would find it.

Promptly they moved across the chamber, their senses on constant alert. They paused when their eyes fell on a plain, ebony table, its surface crowded with discoloured papers and scrolls filled with unknown words. Again, they noticed the unruly mess, rousing their curiosity. *I believe Lord Lothian may have something to hide,* they suspected, lingering over the parchments. They smirked, conjuring images in their mind, tempted to read them—more than tempted—but decided against it. *The old Warlock is no fool.*

Turning away, their thoughts a mix of curiosities, they stalled again when their eyes caught a peculiarity in the walls' stonework. They grinned, knowing the purpose behind it.

'There you are!' they whispered.

They approached the pale, buff-coloured sandstone wall—one block, on close inspection, standing out, with its variable dark, wispy markings. They let their hands caress its surface, its smoothness different to that of the rest. Satisfied, they nodded, knowing what was hidden behind it …

With some carefully-applied pressure, they pushed the block into the crevice of the wall, feeling along the sides as it slid away from them, their hand groping, searching for the *gap.*

The moment their fingers touched the item they sought, they flinched, feeling the ice-cold effect of what was inside. Mindful of time, they wrenched it from its hidden place and threw back the silver lid.

Lying on a bed of salt, inside the precious box, the small weapon looked blunt and rusted—the effects of its bed, hindering its influence.

'Not for long,' they muttered. They snatched it into their hand.

Suddenly the blade lit up, its crimson eerie glow spreading out over the metal and onto their hand, like blood flow, reawakening it. The dragon's tail flicked, then wrapped itself around the unorthodox cross, as if protecting it.

'Missing your counterpart?'

The tail unravelled itself, thrashing out, as though it understood.

They smirked, pleased.

'Well, then … let us reunite you!'

## To Be Continued …

Now read on, for a sneak preview of the third instalment of
The Sixth Amulet series.

# A
# Flutter on the
# Wind

## M. A. MADDOCK

Coming Soon ...

# Chapter One

*Scotland: North-West – 1630*
*The Forest of Garve – Near Armanoth*

Her body flinched, reawakened by the sound of something scurrying about her.

Oblivious, the small mammal continued to go about its business, scavenging for food. Listening intently, she followed the sound of its quick labour, her eyes dancing wildly beneath their tightly closed lids, fighting to unlock the newfound sight which would soon astound her. Then, through no control of her own, they flew open, vibrant with new life.

Reluctant to move, Kara remained motionless and unsure. She then had a vague recollection of intense pain. Fearing its return, she kept still, her new—and heightened—senses taking over. Beyond the cave's shelter, she became aware of the outside world: the babbling brook, where she had tried to ease the agony of the blistering sun on her skin; the trees, their branches clicking loudly as the wind pushed them together, it hissing and sighing as it passed by; and the animated sounds of natures' residents, enhanced—so loud, it almost crowded her thoughts.

Her newborn eyes travelled around the large cave-like burrow, its dank smell burning her nostrils. Despite the lack of daylight, she could make out its uneven dome-like shape, with its moss-covered roof—the flowerless, green plant, carpeting the surface. Within its *pile,* insects and spiders scattered frantically, disturbed by her presence. One thing was certain: she was not in *Valhalla.*

Although anxious, Kara felt an added resilience to her previous strength; her mind was clearer, sharper and tenacious. Her thoughts returned to the images that had tortured her mind before she had fallen into darkness, now aware they had been nothing but a figment of her torturous end. *But this is not my end*, she realised. No, she felt alive—more than ever—and yet still feared the pain. *What if it comes back?*

There was only one way to find out …

Carefully, she extended her long fingers, feeling the knuckles crack. She flexed them. It felt good. Her eyes suddenly darted, reminding her … She was not alone.

The little ground squirrel stopped abruptly and raised its head, its curious nose twitching, searching for the familiar scent of food to stockpile before the harsh winter set in. It then became aware of the stranger sharing the cave with it. It edged closer, stopping and starting, unsure.

Kara listened to its approach, hearing the tap of its tiny nails on the hard ground. In an unpredicted move, she snatched the little creature. It screeched in pain. She drew it closer, scrutinising it; it stared into her red eyes, frozen with fear, having sensed her malevolence. It felt soft between her thick fingers; she could feel its tiny heartbeat accelerate, pounding with distress as it wriggled in its pathetic attempt to escape from her clutch. Beneath its fur, she could feel its tiny bones—so fragile she knew she could crush them, without effort. *Just like that!* she thought.

As if reading her mind, the squirrel's survival instincts kicked in; it bit down, hard. She winced, letting it go, and then examined her hand, musing over her reaction; she had felt no pain, and yet the marks of its sharp teeth were visibly deep. She tilted her head, fascinated when the blood began to seep, its sweet, fresh metallic smell, enticing her rising senses; her nostrils flared as it continued to ooze from the puncture wounds. Watching it, she swallowed—the sudden dryness in her throat urging her to taste it. She let her tongue glide over the wounds, her taste buds heightening as the blood slid down her throat. As she closed her eyes to languish in its appeal, she remained alert; even after its hasty departure, she could still hear the squirrel's escape, in the distance, listening to the patter of its tiny paws as they faded away.

Reminded of its bite, and the sweet taste in her mouth, she turned her attention back to her hand, then paused; the bite had faded, leaving nothing behind, except two faint scars.

Kara was now aware of the influence of her mind and the rousing effect it was having on her new body; it made her detect an unfamiliar capability—one she no longer feared.

Free of pain and nightmares, she rose with a bearing grace, then looked down. Raising her arms, she examined herself: the muscles beneath her pale, porcelain-like skin were twitching, exuding strength, and the veins, still blackened by the venom, pulsated and brimmed with life. Gone were her battle scars, where arrowheads had once left their permanent dents—the marks of past victories. She inspected the wound on her arm, where the Dhampir's blade had sliced the skin; it was almost gone, save for a dark, brownish-red line—the reminder of her transformation. She reached up, stretching and bending her body like an accomplished athlete, conscious of every muscle and sinew reawakening as her strength increased.

Glancing down, she eyed some moss-ridden stones, scattered carelessly on the ground. She picked up two, recoiling from their strong, mouldy stench. Clenching her fists, she squeezed, grinding them into fine powder. She gasped at the minimal effort it took, then laughed out. A sudden rush of mixed emotions then overwhelmed her: she felt exhilarated, excited and aroused by her new body.

*Why not?* she thought, arms stretched out as she admired herself. *Am I not perfect? Desirable?*

It was at that point, she realised she was naked; it seemed she had pulled away her armour and tunic, during her painful transformation, and yet had no recollection of doing so. She examined her impeccable torso with her probing hands, guiding them over her body: her breasts were full and high, her abdomen hard a toned, and her thighs lean and shapely.

Alerted, once more, to the outside world, she promptly clothed herself—the tunic now clinging to her firm body, where it had once hung loosely.

Without inviting him in, Magia Nera intruded on her thoughts, as though he were inside her. It then occurred to her … It was all *his* doing. *The blade was smeared with venom*, she thought. She was now cursed, just like him.

She shot a glance at the entrance to the cave. Like a young child braving its first step, she took *one*—the thud of her foot, breaking ground. She wanted to run, run for miles, without stopping. She made to exit, then hesitated, when a stream of sunlight managed to find its way in, as though searching for her. Unsure, she stepped back. The threatening single ray, with its tiny particles of dust dancing through its shimmering light, crept towards her. However, as it made its advance, she sensed nothing—neither cold nor heat—yet still felt trapped within her confines. *It cannot be like this*, she thought, alerted to an unusual sense of fear seeping in. *Fear?* She shook her head, staring at the ray of sunlight, challenging it.

'I fear nothing!' she snarled, her new voice strident and emotionless.

Resilient to the core, Kara threw her hand out into the path of the sunbeam.

Nothing happened.

Relieved, she smiled and, keeping her hand there, bathed her fingers in the light, letting it penetrate her luminescent skin—the glow of her deep, carmine blood, visible. She then noticed the palm of her hand, where the skin had been burned and melted away when she attempted to take the dark Warlock's amulet. The unsightly scar was now gone.

She gasped, in awe. 'Just like Wareestha!' she muttered, visualising the things she could do, now. She paused for thought. 'It could all be mine!'

Her eyes then fell on the Obsidian—the spear lying lazily on the ground, dormant. She snatched it up; however, it failed to spark at her touch, as though it no longer recognised her, and yet it *felt* the same. She caressed it with both hands, reacquainting it with its mistress, bonding with it again. Within moments, it sparked to life! Flashes of light danced wildly, highlighting the beauty of its deep-emerald glass, while its serrated, silver tip gleamed like new.

Reunited, once again.

Kara eyed the silver armour which once graced her body. She contemplated leaving it behind in the cave, along with the spirit of her former self but then changed her mind. She had always worn it with pride—the symbol of who she was and where she came from. As she put it on, it still fitted, hugging her firm body like the return of a long-lost lover, never wanting to leave again. She squirmed with discomfort, feeling something press against her, then checked beneath its girth, feeling the small dagger she had overlooked.

'You will be useful,' she told it.

Strewn on the ground, lay her double-edged longsword—the other weapon she relied on—and returned it to its pride of place: attached to her bodice of armour, on her back.

Kara emerged from the cave, now fearless of all possible threats. She looked around, more alert to nature, its shades vibrant and new to her, and its distinctive sounds and movements now dominating her senses.

She jolted, reminded of the added weight on her back. Inhaling deeply, she arched her spine, feeling their release, then looked over her shoulder. Kara's great wings expanded larger and wider than before. Her eyes widened as she marvelled at their beauty—the sun enhancing their newness. Their colour—once white—now glistened like polished onyx, like that of the precious stone in her gold headband, matching her blackened heart.

Prompted by a sudden instinct, she looked sharp, distracted by a distant, high-pitched sound. She turned and looked up, quickly locating the source. Without thought, she ran, her speed swift and exhilarating.

Kara stopped when she saw Nakia in the distance; the hawk was in her final descent towards the earth, her death-like screech echoing before silently disappearing beyond the mountains.

Where once she may have felt pity—and avenged the killing of her "pet" after years of companionship and loyalty—Kara now felt empty inside. The hawk had served its purpose.

She no longer needed it … or *anyone*, for that matter.

Turning away from where it had disappeared, her attention was diverted, once again, by the amplified sounds of *life!* It was the here and now that interested her, and it all made sense: the Dhampir's poisonous blade; the venom; her near-death; and the transformation. She inhaled deeply, drawing in the smell of her new heightened senses, and grinned. She finally had what Wareeshta had always denied her—the gift of long life, with added strength.

With the possibility of greater power—now there for the taking—Kara was lured back in the direction from whence she came … hell-bent on destruction.

As she turned, leaving her past behind to rot away in the little cave, Kara paused on another instinct: apart from the hawk's death cry, she thought she had heard another sound. No—she was certain of it; it had been that of a woman's voice, screaming for help.

A disturbing, sinister curl crept across her face ….

# Acknowledgements

While writing a book can be a solitary—and in most cases enjoyable—process, it's what happens after the manuscript is complete, and what goes on behind the scenes. While getting a book published can be difficult, I've been fortunate to find a great team to help me do this, once my part has been done. So, it is, for this reason, I would like to thank the following people for all their help and support.

Diana Toledo Calcado – from Triumph Book Covers – for creating my beautiful covers. She is so talented and passionate about her craft. Website: www.triumphbookcovers.com

Becky Wright (author) – from Platform House Publishing – for her wonderful formatting skills on the interior.

Lewis Hickson – from Fantasy Maps – for creating another 𝕺𝖑𝖉𝖊 𝖂𝖔𝖗𝖑𝖉𝖊 map – the next leg of the journey for my poor suffering characters.

Tegan Sommers (artist) – for her beautiful artwork on the cover of *The Moon Chasers* (Bruce, the stag), and the butterfly (the page preceding chapter one of Book Three, *A Flutter on the Wind* – due for release in Spring 2024).

Jake Warren Black – my 'Wee Master of the Web' for the upkeep of my website.

Geraldine O'Malley (artist) – for her beautiful illustrations.

Alyson Gleeson – for her help with those tricky Japanese words.

Julie Embleton (author) – a good friend, who navigated me through the whole publishing and marketing process. I'm indebted to her for all her help, advice and support, as well as our chats over wine and cheese (but that's another story!).

J. Dallin Taylor (actor) – the voice behind all my characters (no easy task!) for the audiobooks.

Eileen Budd – a good friend, author and Bard, who is passionate about keeping Scotland's myths and legends alive. I want to thank her for contributing the foreword for *The Moon Chasers,* and helping me with her provocative piece for Síofra's story.

Paul Frederick Waite – my 'Wandering Wizard' – for his contribution, for creating Oran's spell, to help the three Dhampir escape.

Linda Ganzini (author) – a good friend whose wonderful support I'm grateful for, and for lending a 'third eye' during the creative process.

To the authors who were simply there for me with their moral support: Steve; Gavin (Gav!); Graeme (and Molly); Sarah; David; Alan; Julia; and all the other authors on social media who have been so supportive.

To my dear friends – Ciara, Billy and Megan Aitken, who continue to welcome me into their home whenever I visit Balloch. I also can't forget Brenda, Aileen (remembering her beloved Tara), Mary, Emma M, Mary B., Emma Ní B., and Anne.

And finally, a huge thank you to Ruth - the best sis in the world! - Ken, Naomi, Rachel, Adam, Jake and Belle (can't forget the pooches!) for their ongoing love and support.

If I have forgotten anyone, please forgive me and know that your support is hugely appreciated – more than you know X.

### Typos & Errors (It's a fact!)

Every writer will admit, even after their books are put through the rigorous editing process—and with many eyes having scanned through the words and pages—sometimes the human eye misses something. Even famous writers will admit this. And there's no shame in it. I get excited if/when I spot a typo in a famous author's work. It happens occasionally. Because, at the end of the day, we are all just human.

> *"Don't compare your Chapter 1 to someone else's Chapter 20."*
> Unknown.

# About the Author

Asking an Irish person to write a 'few' words about themselves is, putting it mildly, almost impossible! But, here goes … My name is Miriam and I was born and raised in Dublin, Ireland.

Having dabbled in other 'interests' over the years (I won't bore you), in the background, however, I was always an avid reader, with words constantly floating around in my mind yet doing nothing about them—in a literary sense. I used to always say, 'One day, I'll write that book!' But never seemed to get around to doing it. I think the mere thought of putting those words—along with my imagination—to literary use, was daunting, therefore, I was always putting it off. That is, until 2011 when I finally took the plunge and picked up that pen and notebook (still have them, too!). I began to string those words into sentences, then paragraphs, then pages, eventually joining them together to create my first novel—*The Sixth Amulet - Book One*. Then my imagination had other plans; it didn't want to stop at just one. Why would it? And so, one novel turned into two, then three, then ... Who knows where it will end?

I believe everyone has a story to tell, a potential book tucked away inside them, just dying to get out. And all that's needed to create it is a simple recipe: a pen and a notebook. So, open your mind and let your imagination roam through the endless possibilities it has to offer ... then simply write!

I hope you enjoyed *The Moon Chasers* and I promise to have part three of my epic adventure – *A Flutter on the Wind* - out by Spring 2024.

**An important note to you, the reader:** Reviews are important to authors. Unfortunately, not many are aware of how important. They don't have to be long; a word, a sentence or a short paragraph is all we seek—and it only takes a couple of minutes. It really does! A simple acknowledgement means a lot to us. So, please, make an author's day, and share your thoughts. Thank you so much. Happy reading! X

Feel free to check me out on the following:

http://www.mamaddockauthor.ie
Instagram: ma.maddock_author
Twitter: @mamaddock1_a
Facebook: M.A. Maddock @thesixthamuletseries
https://shepherd.com/best-books/blood-curdling-time-travelling-adventures

Printed in Great Britain
by Amazon